DESIRE'S POTION

In the shadows of the overhanging balcony, Drake pulled Selene into his arms and crushed her close. Drawing her head back, he jerked out the pins that held her hair then buried his hands in the wild fiery tresses cascading around her shoulders.

Selene knew she should get away from him, but instead she was drawn to his heat, his power, his passion.

"You might as well give in and admit you want me," he whispered.

"No, I—"

He didn't allow her to finish. Instead his hot, hard lips touched hers in a hungry kiss of desire. Her senses reeled, and she clung to him for support as her body grew surprisingly languid. She knew she should get away from him, but her senses seemed no longer hers to command . . .

Jane Archer

Bayou Passion

ZEBRA BOOKS
KENSINGTON PUBLISHING CORP.

For the Dennis Clan

ZEBRA BOOKS

are published by

Kensington Publishing Corp.
475 Park Avenue South
New York, NY 10016

First printing: August, 1991

Printed in the United States of America

A touch of rosemary,
a pinch of thyme,
a pull of the Moon
and love sublime.

—Granny Morgan

Part One

New Orleans, Louisiana
Spring 1886

Chapter 1

"There'd better be a damn good reason I found this under my pillow." Drake Dalton slammed the door behind him, and took off his cowboy hat as he crossed the room.

"Sir?" Selene Morgan glanced up from her desk, surprised at the noise, then further amazed at the sight of the man before her.

He was tall, muscled, good-looking, but that wasn't what most caught her attention. First, it was his clothes. Where had he gotten the denim trousers, the fringed leather shirt, the boots, the huge silver belt buckle, the enormous white hat? Then there was that feeling about him, as if he belonged in the wide-open spaces. Finally, she couldn't help but notice the sharp contrast between his deep tan and sun-bleached blond hair, worn long.

No doubt, he was a striking man in his late twenties. But there was one thing for certain. He wasn't from New Orleans. Dressed like that he had to be from some place out West or just off a Wild West show. And the other thing was that he made her shop feel tiny and unimportant. She hated the feeling and wanted him gone.

Dropping a small velvet bag on her desk, he locked eyes with her. "Who bought that and why?" But he was distracted by the shop's scent which was sweet, tart, and pungent. He felt caught between a sneeze and a cough.

She stood up, although it wasn't very far in comparison to his height. Nevertheless, she wasn't going to let him intimidate her. She picked up the bag. "Let me see if this is—"

"It's yours, lady. Love Potions, right?"

"Yes." She found her label on the inside of the bag, then pulled the drawstring closed. "Love Potion Number Seventeen. Are you dissatisfied with the product? Do you want a refund?"

"No! I want to know who bought that and—"

"If you didn't buy it, then you aren't dissatisfied and you don't want a refund."

"You may be slow but you get there." His eyes narrowed. "Now what's your name and who bought that?"

"I'm Selene Morgan, proprietor of Love Potions, the best apothecary shop in New Orleans." She hesitated, trying to decide what would get rid of him quickest, and noticed he had chocolate brown eyes. "Are you in love?"

"No."

"Then I wouldn't worry. Obviously this love potion isn't strong enough for you. My customer should have tried the potion with the chicken foot." A dimple played in her left cheek as she teased him,

10

suddenly finding humor in the situation.

"Chicken foot!" He looked disgusted and ran a hand through his thick blond hair. Feeling more out of place all the time, he glanced around the room decorated in shades of rose. It was too damn feminine for him. He was used to the praires of Texas, to the smell of horses, tobacco, and leather. But he wasn't going to back down now.

"Of course, a chicken foot is not exactly the most pleasant scent to wake up to in the morning, but it's effective." She continued to smile, enjoying his discomfort.

"Are you serious?" He suddenly wished he'd never entered the shop, except for the woman behind the desk. She might have her auburn hair pulled back neatly in a chignon and she might be wearing a simple green dress, but he'd bet money if he undressed her that he'd find a heart-stopping body. And maybe a wanton to match.

"Yes, I'm serious." The smile left her face. "After all, it's my business."

He was having trouble concentrating on the conversation. "You mean you actually sell love potions for a living?"

She nodded, her large green eyes steady. "And I do a good business, especially with men like you around."

"Men like me? What the hell do you know about me?" He was beginning to get the idea she didn't like him, and he usually had the opposite effect on women.

"I know you're rude and arrogant. And that's before I get to know you. I hate to think how long the

11

list might be then." Her heart was beating fast and she couldn't seem to stop wanting to touch him in some way, mostly violently. And it was so unlike her.

"What the hell kind of a way is this to run a business? Do you insult every customer who walks through the door?" Now he was starting to get mad all over again.

"You aren't a customer."

"You're damn right I'm not. And you're nothing but a swindler, preying off defenseless women. Love potions!"

"My customers are so satisfied they recommend me to others and my recipes have been handed down in my family, proven effective by years of service." She grasped the love potion hard to keep her hand from shaking. He was making her furious, and that realization made her even angrier.

"So you say." Watching her, he had trouble for a moment remembering why he'd come into her shop. "Now tell me the name of the woman who bought a love potion for me."

"I never reveal the names of my clients. However, I will tell this particular woman her taste in men leaves something to be desired."

"That's because you don't know a damn thing about men. You're obviously nothing but a cold-hearted shrew." He realized his fists were clenched and slowly relaxed them. She sure as hell had a way of getting under his skin.

"And I don't need to repeat what I think of you."

"I ought to warm you up just to show you what a real man is like." And he'd start with her hair. He wanted to see it free, like wild dark fire.

"There's no point in exhausting yourself needlessly."

"You're right." He raked her body with a pointedly cold, disinterested glance.

For once she wished she were taller, but her petite frame, with its curves carefully confined by a rigid corset, was little match for his size and strength. Still, she had a wicked tongue and knew it. "Sir, if you'll leave, I can get on with my day."

"I'll leave all right, but I'm not done with you. You're swindling people and I'm going to put a stop to it."

She walked across the room and opened the front door. "Leave my business alone, Mr.—"

"Drake Dalton. Remember it 'cause you'll be hearing it again." He gave her a hard stare, slammed his hat on his head, then left the shop.

She shut the door behind him, and leaned against it, suddenly feeling weak. She had never met such a disturbing man before. Normally she kept her emotions under tight control, but there was something about him, in addition to his rude behavior, that set her pulses pounding. He was infuriating and she wanted to hurt him.

She smiled, then walked over to her desk and picked up the small velvet bag. So he hated love potions. So he thought she was a fraud. Well, she would show him. What if she made love potions especially for him and he fell in love with her? Then she could tell him exactly what she had done and he would know how well her products worked. Afterward, she could laugh in his face and walk away.

Tossing the love potion into the air, she spun

around and caught it.

"Selene!" Rosa Duboney called as she walked down the stairs against the west wall at the back of the shop. "What is going on down here?" She glanced around as she moved toward the front door. "Are you throwing customers out now?"

Selene laughed, but there was a sharp edge to it. "I just had an argument with the most terrible man."

"Really?" Rosa raised an eyebrow as she turned to look closely at her friend. "I've never known anybody to get you that upset. I could hear you upstairs."

"Well, he's *not* anybody. But I'm going to take care of him anyway."

"What do you mean?" Rosa put her hands on her hips, her dark brown eyes showing concern and amazement. She was wearing a bright, multicolored robe, caught at the waist with a wide belt. A tignon of matching fabric was wrapped around her thick, black hair.

"Imagine that *cowboy* strutting in here and trying to frighten me." Selene glanced at Rosa's tall, slim body, envious as she always was, especially since her friend could eat all she wanted and retain her lovely figure.

"Frighten? Selene, please tell me what happened."

"It's simple. Some man from out West got one of my love potions put under his pillow. Instead of being pleased someone thought that much of him, he was outraged. Can you imagine? So he comes busting in here calling me a fraud and threatening to ruin my business."

"Oh." Rosa looked worried. "Do you think he can?"

"I don't know. Maybe." Selene suddenly sat down, her bravado slipping away. "You know how those doctors who call themselves 'regulars' feel about midwives, lay practitioners, and about me in particular."

"As if their schools, just because they cost more, are better than the medical schools for poor men, mulattoes, and women."

"You don't have to remind me, Rosa. I know all about the Popular Health Movement."

Rosa frowned. "Those regulars don't want working folks to have a choice, but it's not a choice they're offering. A lot of people can't afford them and don't want them anyway. All they know how to do is bleed you, give you huge doses of laxatives, or give you that calomel. Most people'd be better off without them." Rosa sat down in a small rocker near Selene's desk. "If you lost the business, a lot more people than you and me would be hurt."

Selene nodded her head in agreement, glancing around the shop. "Granny Morgan built this business after the War. We had nothing left but each other and her knowledge and expertise with herbs and healing. She sold love potions to send me to school. I'm twenty-four. I grew up here. It's all I know. It's all I want."

"And there's a lot of people who need you. We both know the love potions you sell, as well as the fancy creams and perfumes, support the work you do for the poor."

"I know, but—"

"Besides, these so-called doctors don't know half of what your granny taught you." Rosa took a deep

15

breath. "You can't let that man do anything to hurt Love Potions. Those regulars have been trying to get you closed, get your practice stopped, and all because they think it'll mean more business for them. It won't, but if that man gives them anything they can use against us—"

"Don't say it!" Selene's green eyes flashed dangerously. "What I'm going to do is fix Drake Dalton and good. But don't worry about your job, Rosa. You're the best assistant possible. In fact, you should be out on your own."

"If my skin were white, maybe I could make it. But I'm mulatto and that's that."

"You're French and Cherokee as well as African."

"I'm still a generation away from slavery, Selene, and you know it."

"Yes, but I'm not the only one those regular doctors are after. They want to keep mulattoes from practicing medicine, too, and people depend on you as well as me."

"I'll never stop helping my people, even if rich white men do pass a law against midwives. I've got to do what's right and at twenty-six I have time left to do it."

"Men!"

Rosa shook her head. "And don't even start on Alfred. He's breaking my heart."

"If he goes up North to pass as white, he'll have to leave you no matter how much he loves you."

"I know, and he's right. He can't marry me and take a mulatto wife. It'd ruin all his plans." Rosa stood up and began to pace. "I can't even ask him to stay here with me. His family has been free for generations and marrying white or light, always. Finally, he can pass. He's the product of so much selection, so much sacrifice. I can't ask him to give that up."

Selene was silent. She'd heard the argument before, too many times. There was no good answer. The only thing she knew to do was keep Love Potions going so she and Rosa had jobs which provided them money to help others. But to do that she had to deal with Drake Dalton. She glanced at Rosa. "I'm going to make him feel what it's like on the other side."

"Alfred?"

"No. Drake Dalton. He's not going to shut us down, Rosa. I'm going to make love potions for him. From me. And when he falls in love with me, I'll tell him the truth and he'll have to believe us. Then he'll have nothing to hand those regulars."

Rosa looked skeptical. "But you've never used the potions for yourself."

"That's because I never wanted the trouble a man brings. And I won't get it now. Mr. Dalton means nothing to me, but he needs to be taught a lesson." She looked wicked. "And I'm just the woman to teach him."

"I don't know. It sounds dangerous. Rich white men have so much power."

"Maybe so. But we do, too, if we use it." Selene opened the love potion Drake had left and dumped the contents on her desk. "This potion is mild compared to what I'm going to make for Mr. Drake Dalton."

Rosa nodded. "Yes, it might work. If he fell in love with you and you used a love potion, then he'd have proof that what we do is real." She looked sharply at Selene. "But what if it affects you, too?"

"Me?" Selene shook her head in denial. "He's nothing but a big-headed cowboy. I could never be interested in someone like that. Besides, I'm too smart to fall in love."

Chuckling, Rosa looked doubtful. "It's got nothing to do with smarts. Otherwise, I'd run from Alfred. You never met the right man, Selene. When you do, you'll probably fall harder than I ever have just because you put it off so long."

"You may be right, but there's one thing I do know. Drake Dalton is not the man to turn my head."

Giving Rosa a brisk nod, she stood up, walked to the front door, and stepped outside. She wanted to remind herself that Love Potions was unharmed. Unable to see the front of her business well enough, she walked across the street and stopped in front of the Café du Monde. Looking back, she took in every detail.

Love Potions occupied the lower level of a two-story building in a row of three-stories, all connected by a portico. The lower level was painted white and was mostly windows showing rows of jars containing dried flowers and herbs. The second floor, where she lived, was red brick. In front, it had two windows and one center door, all with white shutters, opening onto the balcony enclosed by a black wrought iron fence. On the steep slate roof, in the very center of her attic, was a single window.

The apothecary shop and town house above it had been her home since the War. With Granny gone, she lived alone but she wasn't lonely. She had too many friends, too much to do for that. Yet sometimes she wondered what it would be like to share her life with a man, someone she loved and trusted. But that was far in the future, if ever.

Satisfied all was in order at the front of her store, she watched her painted, hand-carved sign for Love Potions move slightly in the breeze off the Mississippi River. Glancing upward at the blue sky, she noticed clouds moving in from the Gulf of Mexico. They'd probably get a shower that afternoon so she wouldn't need to water the herbs and plants, from standing to hanging, that occupied much of her balcony. Actually, with frequent rain and plenty of sunshine, they required little attention.

She walked back across Decatur, left the door to Love Potions open for a breeze, and joined Rosa at the long work table in the back of the shop. The table was piled with jars of dried herbs, flowers, stones, and shells. In among those were pieces of fabric, ranging from velvet, satin, and silk to simple cotton in various colors and prints. Ribbon snaked across the table top, from flat to round, small to large, short to long, and in a rainbow of colors.

It was a fragrant, colorful nook, taking up most of the back of the store where the second floor formed a lower ceiling and the stairs cut it into a smaller area. Selene loved to work there. She felt some of her tension ease as she picked up a piece of fabric and watched her friend.

Rosa was deftly making a love potion. "Have you heard anything about Françoise or John?"

"No." Selene decided to turn the piece of black silk into a love potion. "I spoke with the police again this

19

morning, but they have no news."

"How hard do you think they've tried to find a mulatto madame and an Irish stevedore."

"Not real hard. But they'd have trouble getting anybody to talk to them anyway."

"True. But money talks and they have sources." Rosa hesitated. "We've got to do something. I don't think we can wait any longer."

"But what?" Selene bit off a long strand of black thread with her teeth. "How many have disappeared now?"

"About two dozen, as far as we know. And they're street people, being poor, whores, former criminals, or jobless."

"And we've helped all of them at one time or another. Not bad people. Simply desperate to survive." Selene threaded her needle, tied a knot in the end, then stuck it into the fabric and hit her finger. "Ouch!" Grimacing, she put her fingertip to her lips and sucked.

Rosa winced in sympathy. "If we know of over two dozen, all simply disappearing in the last few weeks, how many more might be gone?" She selected herbs from several jars, a frown marring her face.

"Do you suppose somebody is killing them? Are they running away? Did they get jobs up North?"

"I don't know, but surely at least some of them would have told us their plans if they'd had good luck, or even bad."

"I agree, but I still don't know what else to do."

Rosa looked up. "You've tried the police, the underground network. I've talked with my friends.

Nobody knows anything and plenty of people are getting scared."

"I don't blame them." Selene made tiny stitches around the black silk square, wishing she had as much control of her life as she had of the small bag.

"What do you think we should do?"

Selene stopped sewing and thought, looking toward the front door. She wondered when they'd have another customer. Much of their work was done on commission so they didn't depend on walk-in clients, but she was always glad of new business. "Have you seen those posters advertising Gustave Dominique's hypnotism lectures and seances?"

"Yes, but what does that have to do with us?"

"Hypnotism is a new way of healing people by mind suggestion and it can be used in place of ether or chloroform. I went to one of his lectures. And now I'd like to attend his seance."

Rosa dropped her work. "Selene! What's getting into you? First, you want to use a love potion on that Dalton fellow and now a seance. It's all dangerous and you know it."

"Maybe hypnotism only seems dangerous because it's new."

"I don't care what it is. You could get hurt." Rosa picked up a piece of fabric, tossed it down, then selected another. "New isn't always better, and you know it."

"I must build on what Granny taught me. If that seance is real and if any of the disappeared have been killed, then maybe one of them will speak to me."

"That's it!" Rosa stood up. "You don't know what

you're messing with. Without the right training, without the right controls, the right beliefs, the knowledge to deal with powers of the mind and spirit, that man could cause untold trouble."

Selene looked up. "I don't doubt you, but I've got to try something else and I'm willing to put myself on the line."

Rosa sat back down and took Selene's hand. "All right. I know you're desperate. But be careful. And give me some time. I'll look into another area that might help. I'll let you know about it."

"You're suddenly very mysterious."

"Only cautious." Rosa smiled. "Now let's get back to work."

Chapter 2

Drake Dalton cussed as he made his way down Chartres Street. No matter what anybody said, he wasn't impressed with the Vieux Carré, New Orleans's fabled French Quarter. True, you could get almost anything you wanted there and he hadn't passed up much. But he hated the damp air, the constant perfume of flowers in the air, the narrow streets with buildings looming over him, and the fancy-aired people. In short, he missed Texas.

But he'd been in a black mood since he'd left the Lone Star State. Selene Morgan hadn't helped matters either. In fact, she'd made it worse since she'd flaunted her business. There was no way around it. The proprietor of Love Potions was a swindler, selling nothing but lies and dreams, and he planned to stop her.

As he glared at the narrow buildings with wrought iron balconies, looking for number 1109, he decided he could be overreacting to Selene Morgan. But lately he'd had a gut full of cheating women. In fact, that's what had brought him to New Orleans.

Joy Marie. Who the hell'd have thought his sister-in-law would clean out the ranch's bank account and run off with some stranger while he was on the cattle drive to Kansas?

He'd always been fond of Joy Marie, treating her like a sister. And she'd been dependable, which was why he'd left her in charge while he drove the cattle north. Besides, she was lonely after the death of his brother and she'd needed plenty to keep her mind busy.

But he still got mad every time he thought back to the day a couple of weeks ago when he'd gotten home. The place had looked deserted. But he'd found Carlota and Jorge, the Mexican couple who had taken care of the house since his parents had built the ranch after the War Between the States.

He'd heard the tale from them about Joy Marie. She had met some smooth-talking man in Sisterdale and fallen in love. In a matter of days, no less. Carlota had tried to talk her out of going with him, but Joy Marie wouldn't listen to her. She'd simply explained that she was taking the ranch money as her dowry. And that was that.

After his anger had cooled, he'd become worried about his sister-in-law. Did the stranger have some hold over her, or had he threatened her, or was she truly in love? He was determined to find out, and if she was in trouble, rescue her. If not, she could have the damn money if that was all the Dalton family had ever meant to her.

Carlota had told him she had overheard Joy Marie make plans to go to New Orleans. So Drake had followed, but once in the Crescent City, it had taken him a while to locate her. In fact, he still wasn't sure the Joy Marie listed as assistant to Gustave Dominique on the posters all over town was *his* Joy Marie, but he was about to find out.

He frowned as elegantly dressed ladies passed him, wondering what dark thoughts they hid behind their sweet faces. He had few illusions about it now.

But at least one designing woman was out of his life. Suzanne dealt faro at the Diamond Stud and she'd put herself on the line during a game of cards with him. He'd won and she'd been warming his bed till that afternoon. So he'd figured she'd put the love potion under his pillow and he'd wanted Selene Morgan to confirm that fact. She hadn't, so he'd gotten it out of Suzanne, then kicked her out of his life. He didn't like underhanded dealing, secrets, or swindling women, and that was a cold hard fact.

He reached 1109 Chartres Street and stopped in front of an elegant building in an expensive area of the Vieux Carré. Upstairs, behind a wrought iron balcony, soft yellow light glowed through white lace curtains. Although the windows looked inviting, the heavy wooden door he faced wasn't friendly at all. Nevertheless, he knocked.

As he waited, his mind continued to churn. What the hell was this Gustave Dominique doing conducting a seance in a home? Of course, since he'd never been to one before, he didn't know what was usual. In any case, he wished he was someplace else. And he

25

would be if not for Joy Marie.

All the way over, he'd kept thinking it must be another Joy Marie because nothing he knew about his sister-in-law fit the image of an hypnotist's assistant and certainly not somebody who was involved with seances. But again, he had no idea what experience was necessary for her current job. As if she needed one. Clenching his fists, he fought the anger down. Now was not the time to go busting heads.

Suddenly the door was pulled open, and Drake had to look up. A man close to seven feet tall towered over him. Even with one arm missing, the giant was intimidating with heavy muscles straining against expensive evening clothes. White-blond hair was pulled back and tied at the nape of his neck.

"I'm here for the seance." Drake decided the man must be the butler and bouncer all rolled into one.

The man held out a cut crystal bowl. It was filled with cash, all bills.

"How much?" Now Drake understood why Gustave Dominique gave seances and demonstrations. They made money.

Making no response, the tall man simply continued to hold out the bowl.

Drake put in more than he wanted, and the man stepped back, allowing him to enter. Walking into a courtyard filled with the sweet scent of magnolias, he was glad he'd tucked his .45 into the waist at the back of his trousers. His coat covered the pistol, so no one would know he had it unless he had to get Joy Marie out by force.

The giant started across the courtyard.

Drake followed, noticing that light from the moon filtered in through the vines growing overhead. Several ornate wrought iron tables with matching chairs, all painted white, were nestled among blooming plants and twining ivy. Doors opened onto the patio, and he glanced around for a quick exit should it be needed. Unfortunately, the only way out seemed to be through the front door. He didn't like the odds, especially with the giant lurking about.

The man stopped outside a door, then opened it, waiting for Drake to enter.

Stepping inside, Drake heard the door shut firmly behind him, but he didn't hear a lock click into place. Glad of that, he knew he was still in a dangerous position. So he lookd around the room, determined to quickly set in his mind the layout, furniture, and situation.

The room was lit by candlelight, although a gas lamp was on the wall. An ornate silver candelabrum stood in the center of a round wooden table. Six people sat around it. The windows were closed and covered by black drapes, making the room too warm. The rest of the area was shrouded in shadows, and dark shapes suggested furniture.

Drake hated the situation. The dim light and shadows could cover up a multitude of sins.

A man at the table stood up. "Welcome. I am Gustave Dominique."

From what Drake could see, Dominique was about thirty-five, slim, five feet seven, with black hair, a waxed mustache, and sharp black eyes. Wearing an expensive black suit with a ruffled white shirt, the hypnotist looked sensitive and authoritative at the same time.

Drake hated him on sight.

"And this is my lovely assistant, Joy Marie." Gustave motioned to a woman on his left.

She stood up, smiling. "Hello, Drake. What brings you to New Orleans?"

Cool. Sophisticated. Beautiful. Late twenties. On the street, Drake would never have recognized her. This creature with her blond hair in a riot of curls, her face touched with powder, rouge, and lipstick, her curvaceous body squeezed into a black glittery gown that clung to her like a second skin, exposing the deep cleavage between her breasts, was a far cry from the buckskin-clad woman who used to ride the Texas range with him. But it was Joy Marie all right.

When Drake didn't respond, only continued to stare, Joy Marie turned to Gustave. "This is Drake Dalton. Remember, I told you about him."

"The brother-in-law." Gustave's eyes narrowed.

Drake finally found his voice. "I've come to New Orleans to talk with you, Joy Marie."

"How nice. Are you here on business, too?"

How could she not think he'd be worried and come looking for her? But he didn't say that. "No. You left without saying good-bye."

She smiled. "Oh, yes."

"I want to talk with you."

"All right. But it must wait until after the seance. We're about to begin. Will you join us?"

"No, I—"

"You're not afraid, are you?" Selene Morgan interrupted, turning in her chair to catch Drake's attention as she challenged him.

Surprised, Drake cursed to himself. He should have noticed her right away, but she was sitting with her back to him and he'd been so intent on Joy Marie and Gustave that he hadn't looked closely at anybody else in the room. That was stupid and he knew it. He could blame the dim light, he could blame a lot of things, but he wouldn't let himself off the hook that easy. "When you've run a herd of cattle to Kansas, there's not much in a room like this to frighten a man."

"Good." Selene nodded at the empty chair next to her. "Then you'll stay."

Drake sat down, outmaneuvered. But he didn't mind, not now. He wanted to see what Joy Marie was doing and he wanted to know what part Selene Morgan played in this little drama. From the way Gustave Dominique was watching Selene, he figured they were a lot closer than they let on. And that couldn't be good for his sister-in-law. How the hell many schemes did Selene have going?

"I see you two have met, Mr. Dalton." Gustave gave Drake a cold look.

"It concerned a love potion." Selene laughed, a husky sound. "He's not fond of them."

Gustave stroked his crystal watch fob. "You have to be careful in New Orleans, Mr. Drake. It is not the Wild West."

"Thanks for the warning." Drake bared his teeth

in a semblance of a smile. Gustave was pushing him and he wondered why. Was he afraid Joy Marie would go back to Texas with a little encouragement? Or did it have to do with Selene Morgan? Either way he was going to find out.

Gustave bowed slightly, then glanced around the table. "Let me introduce the other members of our group tonight. To your right is Madame Georges. Her gallant husband was killed in your unfortunate Civil War and she is trying to reach him."

Drake nodded politely, thinking that whatever Madame Georges had to say to her husband, she should have said over twenty years ago because she sure as hell wasn't going to talk to him tonight.

"Next to her is Captain Wright. His daughter was swept away in the Mississippi River a few months ago. He wants to know if she is all right."

Again Drake nodded, thinking that Captain Wright's daughter was not all right. She was dead. He glanced at Selene, wondering who she wanted, and surprised himself by realizing that if it was a boyfriend, lover, or husband he'd be glad to know the man was dead.

"And the last of our group is Mam'selle Vicente. She lost her fiancé at sea." Gustave looked at Drake. "Mr. Dalton, I understand you have also lost a loved one."

Drake frowned.

"His brother Raymond." Joy Marie's voice was soft. "He was my husband."

"But I don't want to talk to him." Drake gritted his teeth. "We said all we needed to say before he died."

Besides, who were these people kidding? They weren't going to talk to anybody dead.

"Sometimes it is not our choice about which of the dead wishes to speak with us. Isn't that so, Joy Marie?" Gustave glanced at her.

"Yes. I am only a medium, a channel for those who would speak, and guided by Gustave." She clasped her hands between her breasts and looked upward. The soft lighting made her look angelic, as if she had already taken one step to the other side of life.

Drake clenched his fists, forcing himself to keep quiet. If he said what he thought, he'd anger his sister-in-law and that'd get him nowhere.

"Joy Marie, do you feel my husband near?" Madame Georges asked, fanning herself.

"It's too early. The mood hasn't been properly set." Joy Marie smiled gently and hopefully. "But perhaps tonight will be the night."

"Then, please, let's go on." Mademoiselle Vicente's large, dark eyes were near tears.

Drake looked at Selene, wondering how she fit into this swindling scheme. Their gazes locked, and he felt a jolt of heat hit him. Damn! No matter what she did, his body wanted her. But that didn't mean he had to be taken in by her. She was trouble and he knew it.

Glancing away from him, Selene realized it was suddenly hot in the room. Drake Dalton had an almost unnerving affect on her, no matter how indifferent she acted in his presence. She wanted to be far away from him, but she had to protect Love Potions and her friends, no matter what. And that meant getting closer to Drake.

And she'd been lucky he'd come to the seance. Now she wouldn't have to hunt him down to put a love potion on him. He was working into her plans perfectly, and she was going to keep it that way.

But she almost wished she hadn't come because now she'd learned Drake had traveled all the way from Texas to find his sister-in-law. A widow. Was Drake in love with her? He must be. So how could she ever hope to get his attention away from this lovely, ethereal creature called Joy Marie?

Yet somehow she must, if she were going to prove the validity of her love potions. But she had a new fear. If there was a great love between Drake and Joy Marie, nothing could touch a force like that. Still, why had Joy Marie run away? Something was not right and she had to find out what.

Selene glanced at Drake. His clean-shaven face showed a strong jaw line and smooth skin. His sensual lips were taut, as if he were holding back great emotion. Love? Even thinking he loved another woman, she couldn't help wondering how he kissed. Was he gentle or rough or both? Then she was amazed at her thoughts. Her interest in him was strictly business, nothing personal, and she must remember that.

"Like what you see?" Drake raised a brow.

Embarrassed, she realized she had let her gaze linger on his lips too long. She blushed lightly, but held his stare.

He let his gaze travel over her face. "Not bad."

Turning her head determinedly away, she caught Gustave watching her. He must have seen the exchange, and she wished he hadn't. She didn't want anyone to think she was running after Drake Dalton.

"Ladies and gentlemen." Gustave looked around the group. "Please put your hands on the table and grasp the person's hand to your right and left."

Selene swallowed hard, then placed her palms on the table top. She would have to hold Drake's hand, but the intimacy was not something she wanted. What if her hand perspired? What if it itched? What if he held on too hard? He grasped her right hand with his left, his long, slightly callused fingers curling around her much smaller hand. Without thought, she returned the clasp, suddenly relishing the warmth and strength of him.

"If I hold you too tightly, tell me."

She felt a sinking sensation in the pit of her stomach and had to clear her throat before she could reply. "That's fine. You tell me the same."

He grinned, revealing strong white teeth. "I'm not worried about that."

Mademoiselle Vicente took Selene's left hand, turning dark, sorrowful eyes on her. "I want so much to talk with my fiancé one more time. He was gone so abruptly that I had no chance to say farewell." Her eyes filled with tears.

Selene squeezed her hand. "It'll be all right." And wished she could believe it.

"Now we'll begin." Gustave sat down beside Joy Marie.

Suddenly the room grew silent. In the distance they heard the sound of a fog horn and the clip-clop of horses moving down the street.

Gustave pulled out his crystal watch fob and held it before Joy Marie. He swung it back and forth, the light of the candles glinting off it. She watched, her eyes totally focused on the moving crystal.

"You are getting sleepy, Joy Marie. Very, very sleepy. Your eyes are growing heavy. Very heavy. You cannot hold them open. You want only to sleep." He kept the rhythm of the crystal perfect, stayed totally attuned to his subject, and continued to murmur soft, soothing words.

Joy Marie's eyelids lowered, then she tilted her head back until it rested against her chair.

"That's right. You are so sleepy you must close your eyes. Sleep. Relax. All is well." Gustave's voice was hypnotic, reassuring, compelling. "Now you will sleep, a deep, undisturbed sleep."

Selene felt sleepy herself, but Drake squeezed her hand and she felt the sensation pass. Could Gustave have put Joy Marie under that quickly, or was this some well-staged hoax? She watched more closely.

Joy Marie breathed deeply, rhythmically.

Glancing around the room in triumph, Gustave replaced his crystal watch fob. "Now, we can begin. Joy Marie, there are those here who would like to speak to loved ones on the other side. Do you sense anyone who would like to talk?"

Joy Marie did not move or give any indication she heard his words.

Selene glanced at Drake.

He raised a brow skeptically.

Suddenly the room grew cool. The candle flames moved in one direction then another, as if a gust of

34

wind had stirred them. Glancing around, Selene tried to see if a door had been opened. But all seemed the same. The room got colder yet and Joy Marie began to toss her head. Drake gripped Selene's hand hard, his body tensed for action. Then there was the sound of a bell ringing and Joy Marie jerked as if the sound were right by her ear.

Selene squeezed Drake's hand. She looked around the room for some explanation, but saw no bell or anything to prove or disprove what had happened.

Joy Marie sat up straight. "Beloved." Her voice was low, almost masculine. "You must not worry."

"Claude!" Mademoiselle Vicente cried, gripping Selene's fingers hard. "I'll come to you."

"No. You have your life to live. You are too young to follow me." Joy Marie's eyes remained shut, but her lips moved.

"But I want to. I can't live without you."

"You must. Think of your mother. I will be waiting for you when it is your time. But not before. Promise me that, beloved."

Tears ran down Mademoiselle Vicente's cheeks. "Yes. I promise. But it will not be easy to wait."

"Remember, I will always love you."

"And I you."

"But for now it is good-bye."

"No, not good-bye, but till later." Mademoiselle Vicente sobbed and dabbed her eyes with a lace handkerchief.

Joy Marie slumped against the chair.

"Don't break hands," Gustave said. "The power is flowing smoothly. Are you all right, mam'selle?"

"Yes." She continued to cry. "Thank you so much. I will see you are greatly rewarded."

"We are glad to be of help." Gustave looked at Joy Marie. "Is there anyone else who wishes to speak with us tonight?"

Silence.

"Does someone have a message for me?" Selene was unable to decide what was going on, but knew she'd be glad of any help. "Many of my friends are disappearing and I want to know what has happened to them."

"Is there someone in particular you want to speak with?" Gustave's dark eyes were now intent on Selene.

"No. I hope they are all still alive."

"Joy Marie, is anyone here for Selene?"

Again silence.

"I am sorry." Gustave looked apologetic. "We cannot control who comes through Joy Marie."

Selene nodded and intentionally didn't look at Drake. She didn't have to ask to know what he thought of the whole situation. But it was a very good show if it were a hoax.

"Please." Madame Georges's voice broke. "I need desperately to speak to my husband. Is he here for me tonight?"

Joy Marie remained silent.

"Perhaps another night, madame." Gustave looked apologetic.

Madame Georges bowed her head. "I know he wants to speak with me, if only he can reach me. Maybe he is too wounded. But I'll try again."

"Very good, madame." Gustave gave her a look of

sympathy and hope.

Suddenly Joy Marie sat up straight. "Drake, I want you to take care of her. She's got nobody but you to look after her now. She's in danger. You know I love her and I'd be there if I could." Joy Marie's voice was low and rough. "Partner, remember what we did with that rattler back up in the hills when you were ten. Do what you have to do but keep her safe."

Joy Marie collapsed against her chair, silent.

Selene felt Drake crush her hand as the chill left the room.

"That's it." Drake stood up, letting go of Selene's hand. "If this is some kind of a joke, I don't like it. You're not going to use my dead brother in this game."

"This is not a game." Gustave smiled in triumph. "You just heard your brother. Obviously he still cares for his wife, but I assure you she is in no danger."

"Wake her up. I've had enough of this." Drake was about ready to draw his pistol. There was no way in hell anybody in the room could have known about the rattler his brother had killed to save his life. Not even Joy Marie had known about it. Whatever was going on, he was having no part of it.

Gustave glanced around the group. "I am afraid the mood has been broken. We will need to try another night." He leaned toward Joy Marie. "When you wake up, you will feel happy and refreshed. Now, on the count of ten you will awaken." He slowly counted upward. "Ten."

Joy Marie's eyes opened, and she smiled, looking

lovely and fresh. "Did I help."

"As always." Gustave patted her hand. "How do you feel?"

"Fine. In fact, wonderful."

"But I feel very tired," Mademoiselle Vicente said.

"So do I." Madame Georges fanned herself. "But then I always do after a seance."

Selene didn't admit it, but she felt exhausted and wanted something to eat. However, mainly she wanted to leave. Something had happened and she wasn't sure just what. But whatever the case, it hadn't helped solve her problem.

"Joy Marie, I want to talk with you." Drake's voice was flinty. "Right now."

Chapter 3

"You're worried about me, aren't you, Drake?" Joy Marie walked around the seance table and put a hand on her brother-in-law's arm.

Selene hated the sight. Inside her reticule, a small drawstring bag she'd made for herself, she carried a love potion put together especially for Drake Dalton. She'd carried it with her everywhere she went in case she saw him. Now was the time to put it in his pocket, but Joy Marie could ruin all her plans.

"Did you enjoy the seance?" Gustave stepped close to Selene.

"Yes. Thank you." Irritated because he'd kept her from hearing what Drake was saying to Joy Marie, Selene tried to look pleasant. Any other time she would have been interested in talking with Gustave Dominique, but right now she had more important things on her mind.

"I am sorry we were not of more help to you." He moved even closer to her. "Did you say friends of yours were disappearing?"

"Yes. Sometimes it's hard to keep in touch with them since many are homeless, but I usually see them regularly. That is, until lately." She strained to hear what Drake and Joy Marie were discussing, but found it impossible.

"I would like to help you. Perhaps we could do something privately for you." He glanced at her lips, then back into her eyes. "A seance. Hypnotism."

Surprised at his interest, Selene suddenly felt uneasy. "That's very kind, but—"

"I'm helping her." Drake gave Gustave a hard stare, then took Selene's hand and pulled her close to him.

She gave Gustave an apologetic smile, then turned her attention to Joy Marie and Drake.

"Another time, mam'selle." Gustave shrugged, turning to speak with his other guests.

"Joy Marie, this is Selene Morgan." Drake pulled Selene's hand into the crook of his arm.

"I'm glad to meet a friend of Drake's." Joy Marie smiled. "It's a shame he had to come so far for nothing, but as I was explaining to him, I'm very happy and with the money from the ranch I'm financially secure. He has nothing to worry about. Will you reassure him?"

"I'm not quite sure how." Selene felt confused. Perhaps she'd been wrong about Joy Marie's feelings for Drake, but that didn't mean Drake wasn't in love with his sister-in-law.

"Listen to another woman, Drake." Joy Marie nodded. "Selene can tell you about love."

Drake slanted a glance at Selene. "Can you?" Then he focused on Joy Marie again. "I'll be in town awhile if you need me."

"Thanks for caring, but I'm happy." Joy Marie placed a quick kiss on Drake's cheek. "I know how much it would mean to Ray that you were this concerned. But I love Gustave and I plan to marry him. There's no need for you to stay in New Orleans."

Drake glanced at Gustave. "I'll be around anyway. We can talk later, Joy Marie. Alone."

Selene didn't protest as Drake led her into the courtyard. The night air felt good, for it was clean and cool. She inhaled the scent of magnolias, relieved to get out of the oppressive room and away from the seething emotions.

Glancing around, she was surprised to see the tall butler, who looked to be about thirty years old, step out of the shadows. He walked to the front door and opened it for them. As they walked past him, she couldn't help wondering how he'd lost his left arm but knew she'd probably never find out.

Back on the street, she breathed a sigh of relief. "I'm glad to be out of there." She started to remove her hand from Drake's arm, but he placed his hand over hers and held it there.

"That damn Gustave thinks he can take any woman he wants, but I'm here to tell him different." Drake walked fast, pulling her with him.

"If you want to go back to Joy Marie right now, I can take care of myself." Again, she tried to free her hand so she could take the love potion out of her reticule and put it in his pocket.

But he didn't seem to notice. "Right now there's nothing I can do short of kidnapping Joy Marie and I think she'd run right back to Gustave. She's a widow,

41

a free woman." He looked down at Selene. "Besides, I wouldn't leave you out here alone at night."

"I'm used to being alone, Mr. Dalton."

"Call me Drake." He pulled her hand farther into the crook of his arm. "Let's go over to the Café du Monde. I could use some coffee."

"I should be going home." She didn't want to appear eager. "Anyway, surely you don't want to be seen in the company of a swindler."

"I figure to change that."

"I am *not* a swindler."

"The Café du Monde is near Love Potions. You live over your business, don't you?"

"Yes." He was sharper than she wanted, but she still needed to have coffee with him for it would be the perfect opportunity to put the love potion in his pocket.

"I want to talk with you about Joy Marie, then I'll walk you home."

"I don't think I could be of any help."

"You're a woman. I need a lady's advice." He smiled, and his brown gaze lingered on her.

"All right. I'll try." She was glad they were going to the open-air coffee stand, for she was known there and she wouldn't worry about getting too close to him.

Drake guided her to Decatur Street, feeling her hand lightly pressing his arm. Being with her was making him want her more, no matter what he thought of her. He was going to have to be tough with himself where she was concerned and it wasn't going to be easy.

Seeing Joy Marie hadn't eased his mind. He didn't trust Gustave Dominique's hypnotism business, and he didn't like the man. But for now there wasn't much he could do for his sister-in-law except watch and wait. Then he remembered Joy Marie's words from his brother. They were exactly what Ray would have said. How the hell had Gustave managed that and why?

But he didn't have time to follow that thought because they arrived at the Café du Monde. Several people were sitting and talking while drinking coffee, but he led Selene past them to a quiet corner. They sat down at a small round table. He ordered café au lait and hot beignets. He'd learned to like the French doughnuts since arriving in New Orleans and the coffee was as strong as that brewed on a cattle drive so it suited him fine.

While they waited, he moved his chair closer to Selene. "What do you think of Gustave Dominique?"

"I hardly know him." She started opening the reticule in her lap so she could get out the love potion. "He's gained some respect from local practitioners."

"I don't mean that. Do you think he's hurting Joy Marie?" Drake couldn't help wondering if Gustave were Selene's secret lover. He hoped he was wrong.

"She seems to be happy."

"What about this hypnotism business?"

"I don't know much yet, but I'm interested in it. I've learned it's being studied and tested in France, England, and back East." She suddenly realized how comfortable she was with Drake, and it was a surprise

43

after their first meeting. "Of course, everything Gustave and Joy Marie did could have been a hoax of some sort."

"That's exactly what I think it was. But it's not like Joy Marie to be involved in something like a seance." He realized Selene didn't sound as if she knew anything about Gustave and he hoped to hell he was right.

"Perhaps your sister-in-law is very much in love and that explains everything." Selene hesitated, twisting the strings of her reticule. "Does that idea bother you?"

"It damn sure does. How she could fall for a swindler like Gustave after loving my brother is beyond me. Ray was a straight-shooter."

"You do care for her then." Selene felt her heart sink, realizing her plan might not work after all.

"Sure I do." He glanced up as the waitress placed steaming mugs of coffee with cream and a plate of sugar-covered doughnuts on their table.

Selene took a sip of coffee, burned her mouth slightly, and set down the mug. "So what are you going to do?"

"Joy Marie's happiness comes first, no matter what I think about Gustave. After all, I could be wrong, but I don't think so. I'm going to hang around awhile, maybe talk with her, try to find out what's going on."

"That's a good idea. I'm sure she'll be glad."

"I don't know. She's sure hell-bent for leather on him. And she wasn't real anxious to talk with me." He bit into one of the beignets, then quickly finished it. Taking several gulps of coffee, he glanced at Selene, realizing he'd talked only about his personal problems. He was here to find out about her. "So what was that about missing people?"

She stirred her coffee, thinking. "On occasion I help out those who can't afford expensive doctors."

He raised a brow, surprised. "And you haven't seen these people lately?"

"No, at least not all of them. And neither has anybody else. In fact, over two dozen people have suddenly disappeared. Who knows, maybe even more. I've talked with the police, but they don't know anything and haven't found out anything." She toyed with a beignet. "However, my friends are not of the highest social set nor do they have much money, so nobody is overly concerned about them."

"Who are they?"

"Former Confederates, freed slaves, prostitutes, widows, orphans. They're all people who could disappear and only the other homeless would notice."

"Do you think they're dead?" He was beginning to get a very different impression of Selene, if what she said was true, and he couldn't place this Selene with the swindler he'd first met. Which was the real woman?

"I hope not."

"When did you first notice the disappearances?"

"A few weeks ago."

Drake ate another beignet, then washed it down with coffee. "Was that about the time you started seeing posters for Gustave's hypnotism demonstrations?"

Selene warmed her hands around her coffee mug, considering his question. "Yes, now that you mention it."

"I knew he was up to no good. It reminds me of how Joy Marie disappeared off the ranch. I think there's a connection."

"You mean, do I think Gustave is making my friends disappear? Is he somehow hypnotising them away?" She frowned. "That doesn't make sense. I don't even know if it's possible."

"I don't know how he does it or why, but he looks guilty to me."

"You just don't like him and you want Joy Marie back."

"I want my sister-in-law to be happy, and I don't think that man can do it."

"She seems happy enough." Selene was beginning to think Drake really did love Joy Marie and she hated that idea more than she would have thought possible.

"What if Joy Marie's hypnotized all the time?" Drake glared around the area, noticing the scent of honeysuckle combined with the sweet smell of beignets.

"I don't think that's ethical or possible."

"Ethics! This is Gustave Dominique we're talking about." Drake curbed his anger and frustration. "That man is sharp, smart, and I'd say ready to do whatever it takes to get what he wants, including swindling grieving widows, fiancés, and fathers."

"Doctors are impressed with him."

"I'm not. I'm going to watch him closely, and you, too. I still want your business closed."

Selene felt her face heat. "After all we've discussed? You know nothing about Love Potions."

He leaned closer, and took her chin in his hand. She held her breath. Was he going to kiss her? She must get him closer if she were to put the love potion on him, and after what he'd just said, there was no other choice. Fumbling in her reticule, she found the small silk bag and clutched it in her palm.

"You make a man hasty. You make a man want to forget about every damn thing except you. But I'm not going to do it." He leaned back, nodding. "You're not going to trick me."

Sighing in frustration, she slipped the love potion back into her reticule. How was she going to get nearer to him? "Perhaps it's time I went home, Mr. Dalton."

"Call me Drake."

"I don't think we're close enough acquaintances for that."

"Would you like to be closer?"

She lowered her lashes. How forward should she be?

Again he lightly grasped her chin with his fingers, raising her head so she would look at him. "I thought you didn't like me." His dark eyes searched hers.

"What I don't like is your trying to destroy my business." She slipped the love potion out of her reticule again.

He leaned nearer, looking at her lips then her eyes, giving her a chance to move away from him. When she didn't try to stop him, he lowered his head and lightly touched her lips. Heat coursed between them, and she felt a sigh catch in her throat. He lifted his head and looked into her eyes again, surprise in his own. This time he pressed his mouth to hers hard and his heat seemed to burn into her.

Taking advantage of the distraction, she quickly slipped the love potion into his pocket. He completely misinterpreted her action, and covered her small hand with his much larger one. She could feel his heart beating fast beneath her fingertips and suddenly wondered if her own were doing the same.

Abruptly he pulled away, his eyes narrowed. "You think that'll get me to let up on your business?"

So the kiss hadn't meant anything to him, but that only proved the love potion hadn't had time to work yet. She shook her head, trying to clear it, and reached for her coffee. He stopped her, a strong hand around her wrist.

"You can't use your womanly wiles on me, Selene Morgan, and get away with it. I'm not some country boy a city woman can take advantage of. If you're swindling people, I'm going to see you stop it, and if you're in league with Gustave to hurt my sister-in-law, you're both in trouble."

She jerked her hand away and stood up. "In league with Gustave Dominique? Ridiculous. I'm sorry I wanted to help you with Joy Marie. Now stay away from me." She turned to go.

"I'm not going to stay away from you and you'd better get used to that fact."

Whirling around, furious, she glared at him. "I don't know where you get your arrogance. You have no control over me or my life. Maybe that's why Joy Marie ran away. If she had to put up with you bossing her around all the time, it's no wonder."

He frowned, feeling his own anger boil upward.

"Joy Marie's her own woman and always has been. She didn't run away from me."

"I bet she did. Any sane woman would."

She turned and left, hurrying out of the Café du Monde. But she could hear him following. Fortunately Love Potions was just across the street and once in her own home she would be safe. She rushed across Decatur Street, but at the door to Love Potions, he caught her arm and whirled her around.

In the shadows of the overhanging balcony, he pulled her into his arms and crushed her close. She could feel the steely strength of him, smell his scent, and feel the hard beat of his heart. But he gave her no chance to get away as he pulled her head back, jerking out the pins that held her hair in a neat chignon until it cascaded in a wild fiery mass around her. Then he buried his hands in her tresses, binding her.

"You can't get away that easy." He covered her mouth with his.

This time the kiss was filled not only with desire but with anger, with a need to control, to dominate, to possess. For some reason his passion seemed to ignite her own emotions, but her rational mind wouldn't let her succumb. She kicked out at him, trying to hurt him in return. But her petticoats and skirt were heavy, blunting the blow. He gave no indication of feeling it. Next she tried stepping on his feet, but his boots protected him. In frustration, she finally beat on his chest.

He raised his head. "You might as well give in and admit you want me."

"No, I—"

He didn't allow her to finish her sentence. Instead he thrust into her open mouth with his tongue, shocking her into silence. She had never been kissed like this before. Her senses reeled and she clung to him for support as her body grew surprisingly languid. She knew she should get away from him, but her senses seemed no longer hers to command. Instead, she was drawn to his heat, his power, his passion.

Shivering, she clung to him, realizing that she wanted him to continue, to do more, to overcome her inhibitions. She wanted him to kiss her until there was nothing in the world except the two of them and all the time for loving they would ever need. She could even smell the sweet scent of magnolias in the air and it encouraged her wild fantasy.

Then she froze, horrified. Everything they were experiencing was the effect of the love potion. As soon as she had slipped it into his pocket, he had become more agressive, more determined, more passionate. She felt relief wash over her. She wasn't just suddenly consumed with desire for a strange man. She had set up the situation with a powerful love potion and she had been caught in her own spell. Well, she could deal with that knowledge, and win.

He rained kisses over her face, gently touching her eyelids, the tip of her nose, then her lips again, his hands tracing warm patterns over her back. "I want you, Selene Morgan. You don't know how bad. And you want me, too."

"I'm a lady." This was not a game she knew and she felt clumsy and inept in her response.

"I know. And it's a hell of a thing to think about."

"You must let me go." She was trembling and couldn't seem to stop. She'd had no idea her potions would be so strong, for she didn't want him to let her go. Not now or ever.

"Let me kiss you again."

"No. It'll only make the situation worse."

"Selene, I swear I won't hurt you."

"Please, remember where we are . . . who we are."

He closed his eyes, shuddered, and dropped his hands. "Okay. Get inside. Quick."

She didn't have to be told twice. Still, she couldn't resist placing a quick kiss against his lips. She heard him groan as she slipped into Love Potions and locked the door behind her.

Contemplating her victory, she smiled. Then she felt the heaviness in her heart and knew she would have to pay a high price for her success.

Chapter 4

"That will be all for the evening, Jon." Gustave Dominique dismissed the tall Dane he had hired to serve as his man, performing any job from butler to guard. Actually, he had not hired the former seaman, for he did not trust people who worked for money. Wages did not buy loyalty and he put no faith in them. Therefore, he had other ways of dealing with those who worked for him.

Jon nodded, then shut the bedroom door.

Satisfied all would be seen to in the house by his man, Gustave turned his attention to Joy Marie. He frowned.

She took a step backward. "I—I don't know why my brother-in-law came. Believe me, I left no message. I told no one where we were going. I did everything like you said. Please, Gustave—"

"Drake Dalton! The man is here, sniffing around you." Gustave stalked her as she backed away from him. "And me."

"I'm sorry." She held out her hands, palms upward.

"And you want me to believe you are completely innocent?"

"Yes. I don't know how he found us."

"There is only one way. You left a message."

"No. I swear I didn't." Her voice had taken on a high, strained edge.

"Someone knew and I told no one *my* destination." His eyes narrowed. "Were you lovers?"

"Lovers?" At his change of attack, she was caught off guard. "Drake and I?"

"Yes. Did he move you into his bed after his brother died?" Gustave followed her.

"No." Anger, fear, and pain all warred in her features. "How can you think that? I told you. Only my husband. Drake and I were . . . *are* like brother and sister. Friends."

"A beautiful woman like you? A stud like him? On that ranch. Alone." His eyes glinted with anger. "A cattle ranch where a man has a constant eye on breeding. Do you take me for a fool?"

"Please, believe me." Continuing to move away from him, she backed into the bed and could go no farther. "Gustave, it's the truth. I love you now. Only you."

He backhanded her, a quick slap across her cheek. Her head snapped to the side. When she looked back at him, the imprint of his hand slowly turned red across her left cheek.

She raised a hand, not in defense but in entreaty.

He slapped her again, across the other cheek. This time her entire body twisted with the blow. But she turned back to face him again, tears in her large blue eyes.

"You hurt me." Still there was no anger or defense in her voice. Only confusion.

"You forced me. I did not want to hurt you, but I will not tolerate lies. There can be no deception between us."

"I didn't lie. Please—"

He punched her in the stomach and she slowly, quietly collapsed toward the floor. He stepped back to make room for her body.

"Now, Joy Marie, was Drake Dalton your lover?"

She didn't respond. Instead, she breathed deeply, rhythmically as she struggled to control the pain. The sound was a low rasp in the room.

Gustave nudged her with the toe of his boot.

She shuddered. "Yes, if you say so."

"No. *You* say so."

"Yes."

"Now, was that so bad?" He lifted her to her feet, smoothed her hair back from her face, placed a soft kiss on each cheek, and smiled. "I do not mind your former amours, Joy Marie. I mind your deception. If Drake Dalton is going to be a problem, I need to know about it. And I need to know everything about him to deal with him quickly and efficiently. Do you understand?"

She moistened her lower lip, and nodded.

Gently placing a kiss against her full red lips, he smiled again. "I will need to know *everything* you did together. Was he a gentleman with you or was he an animal, venting his lust quick and hard with little thought to your pleasure?"

Biting her lower lip, pain filled Joy Marie's eyes a moment, then was gone.

"And what he likes best. Did he like your mouth on him, your hands? Did he take you in the dirt, on a bed? Did he plan it so other men would see?"

She shook her head in denial, her eyes brimming with tears. But she no longer looked shocked.

"No?" He ran his tongue over his lips, his eyes now glowing hot with hunger. "Yes, you tell me . . . or better show me what you did with this Drake Dalton, this crude stud from Texas."

"But Gustave, he'll go away. I'll see to it. There's no need for us to think about him anymore."

"So innocent. So lovely. But not pure, of course." Gustave looked thoughtful, then pushed her onto the bed. "I can take no chances. I have worked hard to get where I am today and no Texas rancher is going to stop me."

"I love you. He's nothing to me. The past. That's all. It's just us now." From the bed, she smiled to please him. "Come show me how much you love me, Gustave."

He frowned, and pulled out his crystal watch fob. "We are going to share something, yes, but it will be what you let that stud do to you. Then I will know how to deal with the man, for if you know a man's passions then you know the man. And this man I will know, inside and out."

Sliding her against the soft pillows, he began swinging the crystal back and forth in front of her face. Her blue eyes widened as he chanted the words that would make her do his will.

"Just think of sleep now. You are sleepy, so very sleepy. And tired. Your eyes are getting heavy, very heavy. Your body is growing limp. You want to

56

sleep. That's right. Think of sleep now. Only sleep."

She blinked, looked concerned, and tried to struggle upward.

He pushed her back against the pillows. "Relax, Joy Marie. Trust me. Trust your love."

And she relaxed.

He swung the crystal back and forth. "That is right. Sleep. Your eyelids are heavy. Relax. You feel peaceful. Sleepy. So sleepy." His voice droned on.

Her eyes slowly shut.

He checked her pupils. Good. She pleased him in many ways. But he could not allow her to be a danger to him. He had gone through too much to get where he was to let a little Texas slut get in his way. He tucked the crystal away, then focused on her again.

"Now, Joy Marie, think of passion, of those early days with your husband. Think of the joy of sharing bodies."

She moaned and tossed her head, her fingers digging into the bedclothes.

"Think of me, Joy Marie, the man who makes you happy now. The man who satisfies your every desire. Of Drake Dalton's desires. And your husband's passion. We are all one and the same."

Her eyes opened, the pupils dilated with desire, and she smiled, a slow, sensual movement of her lips. Then she languidly raised a hand and beckoned him closer.

Oh, yes, Joy Marie Dalton was exactly what he wanted. He gently stroked the soft, smooth skin of her face, then pulled the pins from her blond hair. He pushed long fingers into her curly tresses, then yanked, letting the pain remind her that he controlled her completely. Her passion. Her life. Her sorrows.

She was a pretty woman, perhaps even a beautiful woman. And he wanted her. But he knew from experience that he would tire of her. And when that happened, he would still use her body, but with less finesse and much less consideration. At the moment he found it hard to believe the way he would later treat her, but he knew himself and what would come.

But for now there was only the power and the passion. He picked up a long feather he kept next to the bed and teased the sensitive area of her neck to the cleft between her breasts. Objectively, he watched her body respond. She arched upward, a fine sheen beginning to make her skin glow. Tickling her bare flesh, he felt powerful, totally in control as he felt himself harden. Yes, he could make her want him and he could do it against her will or with it, no matter. She belonged to him for as long a he wanted her.

He returned to her full, heavy breasts, for the moment confined by her clothing. But he knew what lay underneath and he played a game with her, with himself as he lightly touched the tips and watched her nipples harden. Then he slowly began unbuttoning her bodice.

As he did that, making her wait and want him all the more, he thought back to meeting her. She had been an easy subject from the first, readily succumbing to his crystal. It was due partly to her loneliness, but also to his charm and abilities.

Of course, she was not necessary to the overall scheme of his life. Rather, she was a reward. He had been surprised to find such a lovely, sensual woman living in the wilds of Texas. He had been stuck in a desolate town called Sisterdale while the stagecoach transporting him to the coast stopped to repair an axle. She had caught his eye when she had arrived to buy supplies. He had introduced her to hypnotism and she'd been his. Between the ranch money and Joy Marie, he had left Texas a happy man.

Now he was enjoying the fruits of his long labor started back in France. Soon he would take Joy Marie to his sugar cane plantation on Martinique. He had retained his French citizenship, so the French-owned island in the beautiful string of Windward Islands south of the Bahamas was perfect for his needs.

Eventually the entire island would be under his control and he would live there as royalty. Once on Martinique, Joy Marie would do anything he wanted, for she would have no way of escaping him. And perhaps he would slowly let her come out from under his hypnotism so he could enjoy her reaction to the reality of her situation.

But that was for the future. Now he had nothing more important to do than toy with the hot flesh of Joy Marie. That and learn more about Drake Dalton. He whispered several words and she went deeper into the trance, moaning, reaching for him, her body growing even hotter. And if her lust were for a dead man, the husband she still mourned, or for her brother-in-law, it did not concern him. All that mattered was his desire and power, and that he learn all he needed to know to control his destiny.

He pulled open her gown and jerked down her chemise, exposing her breasts. The tips were hard and he rubbed them, gently then rougher until she

59

began to writhe under him. He smiled. Her response made him think of his power and how he had gained it. He had studied hypnotism, a product of mesmerism, in France at the school of Paris under Charcot. But Bordeaux, Nancy, and Toulon were also centers of hypnotic research and he had studied the results of their tests as well.

When he had gained enough knowledge, he knew he did not want to help others as was the intention of most' practitioners, nor did he want to continue studying, testing, writing papers, trying to prove the importance and validity of hypnotism to skeptics of the medical profession.

From an impoverished aristocratic family, he wanted money, power, and a life his family had not known since the revolution. He quickly realized hypnotism was the way to get them. But not in France or England. America was more open to new ways of thinking and he set sail for its shores. Soon he was gaining recognition and money through demonstrations as he traveled from city to city.

But New Orleans was his last stop. After holding public and private hypnotism demonstrations for several weeks, he had managed to impress the local medical establishment with the use of hypnotism in place of ether and chloroform. And his private seances, with Joy Marie as the medium, had worked out very well indeed.

All in all, he would soon have all he needed and leave for Martinique, taking Joy Marie with him. Smiling down at her, he focused on her body again. Whispering several words, he watched as she suddenly began struggling with his clothing, her passion blazing so fiercely there was nothing else in her thoughts.

He let her strip him, amused at her easily aroused need. He wondered if her husband or Drake Dalton had ever drawn such passion from her. He rather doubted it, for Joy Marie was bound to have been raised with a woman's inhibitions and only a man who could unlock her unconscious could hope to touch her deepest desires.

But for now she was stripped of everything except her need and in this state there was not a woman who could compare to her. She stroked his body, running her soft hands over the hard contours of his compact frame. Suddenly he wanted her, too, and he didn't have to wait, didn't have to ease her into desire. She was ready, always ready for him. Tossing up her skirt to expose the creamy white skin of her thighs, he spread her legs. Since he never allowed her to wear drawers, the heat of her passion was exposed to him.

And he thrust into her.

At the sound of Joy Marie's moans and pleas, Gustave's man Jon looked upward at the open window, his fists clenched. He couldn't help imagining the sight of Joy Marie under Gustave and the Frenchman's hot, sweaty body possessing her.

The thought made him sick. And mad. But he made no move to stop what went on in the upstairs bedroom. Joy Marie wasn't his and never would be. She belonged to Gustave, so Jon couldn't defend her, protect her, or help her in any way. And he sure as hell couldn't touch her, for he was Gustave Dominique's man. Body and soul.

Anyway, Joy Marie was happy. But only because she didn't know about her future with Gustave. Unfortunately, Jon had seen them before, the women Gustave enslaved with his crystal and his charm and his body. They fell hard, but the Frenchman never loved, never made a commitment, never gave any of himself. And he always left them in the end.

It was none of Jon's business, except to see that Gustave got what he wanted. And kept it till he was through with it.

Jon hadn't minded before. But the women weren't usually like Joy Marie. They weren't innocent, hurting from the loss of a beloved husband, and alone with strangers. Still, that wasn't enough to change Jon. He had a hard heart himself. It was Joy Marie. She had touched him in a way nobody had in . . . he couldn't remember when, maybe ever.

Love wasn't a part of his life so he didn't love her. But he felt protective of her and he worried about her. That was disloyal to Gustave. He was caught between the two. But for now he did nothing. Joy Marie was happy. Gustave was pleased. All he had to do was keep them safe. And that was a job he knew well.

He paced the courtyard as Joy Marie's cries increased, forcing his mind to think of other things. Drake Dalton could cause problems. Selene Morgan looked like trouble. And he couldn't allow that. It wouldn't be long before it was time to set sail for Martinique and nothing must stop the trip. On the island, all should be well. Maybe Gustave would even marry Joy Marie and make her the mistress of his mansion. Then Jon could watch over her forever.

That thought made him sick inside.

As Joy Marie's moans reached a peak, sweat beaded Jon's forehead and he couldn't stop himself from thinking of how it would feel to be buried deep within her body. Him. Not Gustave Dominique.

And he cursed himself for disloyalty.

Gustave had saved his life in England, back of a tavern near the docks of Liverpool. A seaman all his life, he'd been brawling when overwhelmed by too many. Gustave had happened by, put a bullet into one and the rest had scattered. He hadn't been born a fool, and when Gustave had offered him a job, he'd taken it.

He'd owed Gustave his life, yes. But it was more than that. His days shipboard were over. He'd lost his left arm last time out and he'd almost lost his life from the following fever. He'd had no business down on the docks. But he hadn't been able to stay away. He'd started the fight, trying to prove he was still a man. But knowing he wasn't, knowing he'd end his days taking handouts, begging, or odd jobs. But he couldn't go back to Denmark and face his family and friends a cripple, a burden, a thing to be pitied.

And he'd cursed his pride.

So he was Gustave Dominique's man, all right, and he ate regular, slept in clean rooms, had money to buy women and liquor when he wanted. All he had to do was see that nobody crossed the Frenchman. He did that job well and he'd been satisfied till Gustave had brought Joy Marie to New Orleans. Since then, nothing suited him.

All he could think about was getting his hands on

her. Hell, much more than his hands. And it was stupid, dangerous. But that didn't seem to matter. He wanted her with a fierceness he wouldn't have thought possible.

And all she could see was Gustave . . . the tamer, destroyer, devourer of women.

Still, Jon couldn't stop listening, knowing, imagining what went on in the upstairs bedroom. Even if it made him furious.

For there was no hope. Joy Marie would never want a cripple, a man who couldn't provide her with the kind of life she deserved, who couldn't even take her home to the bosom of family and kin.

No. The last thing the beautiful Joy Marie needed was a one-armed Dane.

Chapter 5

"So, it's strictly business?" Rosa crushed lavender into a small red velvet bag.

"Yes." Selene glanced over their work table, but kept her attention on the front door of Love Potions.

"You're having lunch with Drake Dalton's sister-in-law to help save our business?" Rosa's voice was skeptical as she added powdered orris root and periwinkle to the bag.

"Drake asked me to help out."

"Selene, you know nothing about them. I thought you were going to prove to him the potions work, then forget about him. It'll be a lot harder if you get involved."

"I'm not getting involved."

Rosa stopped and looked at Selene. "You don't call having lunch with this Joy Marie Dalton getting involved?"

Selene stood up, paced a few steps, then turned back. "Drake's worried about Joy Marie and he asked me to have lunch with her so—"

"Is he in love with her?"

"I don't know."

"That would make a difference."

"I know." Selene began rolling a length of green ribbon around a finger. "Either way, I figure the more I know about Drake and his past, the better. Joy Marie might tell me a lot more than Drake ever would. Besides, there's something strange going on."

"What do you mean?"

"First, Drake said Gustave won't let him near Joy Marie. Second, why is she Gustave Dominique's assistant anyway? And third, why is Drake so worried about her?"

"I get the point. Your crusading heart won't let it be, will it?"

"Do you think I'm meddling?"

Rosa shook her head, and smiled. "You've been helping people all your life, Selene. I doubt if you're going to stop anytime soon."

"I'm concerned about her, too." Selene dropped the ribbon. "You weren't at that seance."

"Do you think Dominique has psychic power?"

"No, if there is such a thing. But he may be a good hypnotist. I think the seance was fake. So does Drake."

"And it didn't put us any closer to finding our friends, did it?"

"No. But I'm not giving up."

"Neither am I. Alfred's asking around, too."

"He hasn't been by the store lately." Selene's voice was hesitant.

"I told him he needed to start getting used to being without me."

"Oh, Rosa—"

"There's no help for it. He's going back East. I'm staying here. And I might as well change the way I think about him."

"As if you could."

Rosa glanced up, pressed her full lips together, then reached for a bottle of thyme. "I'm not weak. I'll do what I have to do."

Selene started to reply, but the brass bell on the inside of the front door rang.

Joy Marie stepped inside the store. She was wearing a demure rose print cotton gown. Her face was freshly washed. And her blond hair was pulled back into a chignon.

Selene hesitated, for a moment not recognizing Drake's sister-in-law. Then she hurried forward. "I'm so glad you could make it, Joy Marie. Please come in. I'd like you to meet my friend and assistant."

Joy Marie walked into Love Potions and glanced around. "You have a nice shop."

"Thanks." Selene motioned her toward the back.

Rosa stood up, holding a red velvet love potion. "Hello. I'm Rosa Duboney."

Joy Marie smiled. "I'm glad to meet you." She looked down at the colorful table. "Is this where you make the love potions?"

"Yes." Rosa sat back down.

"If I've come at a busy time, we could lunch later." Joy Marie sounded unsure.

"No. This is simply our usual mess." Selene picked up a blue satin bag, then set it back down.

"I'm sure it requires a great deal of knowledge and

experience to run an apothecary shop." Joy Marie was obviously trying to win Rosa's friendship.

"It does." Rosa continued to work.

"Well, let's be on our way." Selene started toward the front of the store. She knew Rosa well enough to know she didn't give her trust easily, especially to strangers.

"Nice meeting you." Joy Marie smiled at Rosa, then followed Selene.

Outside, Selene turned left. "I thought we'd lunch at Tujague's."

"I haven't eaten there yet, but I've heard it's quite good."

As they walked past two stores, Joy Marie looked around in pleasure. "I don't get out much."

"What a shame. There's so much to see in New Orleans."

"I know, but Gustave is very jealous of my time."

"And other men, I suppose."

"Yes. He was furious about Drake."

"But you calmed him down?"

Joy Marie frowned. "Somewhat."

"That doesn't sound good." She crossed a side-street, and stopped. "Here's Tujague's. If you like, you can finish telling me when we're inside."

They stepped into a long, narrow room. Square tables covered with white linen lined both walls. Since they were early, only a few tables were being used.

A waiter, dressed in crisp black and white, walked out of a back room. *"Bonjour,* Mam'selle Selene." He gestured toward a table near the front window.

"Merci."

He seated them, then walked away.

Joy Marie looked puzzled.

Selene chuckled. "Don't worry. You never have to make a choice. They serve only one selection, but it changes every day."

Joy Marie hesitated. "What if we don't like it?"

"You will. Trust me. Besides, aren't you ready for adventure?"

Joy Marie laughed softly. "Adventure in food. Yes, that sounds good."

"Besides, they speak French here and I thought perhaps you might not understand the language."

"No, I don't. In Texas we use a lot of Spanish." She shrugged. "I'd be lost if they asked for my order in French."

"But many people in the Vieux Carré speak Spanish."

"I noticed, but it's not quite the Texas version I'm used to hearing."

"Surely it's not too different."

The waiter interrupted them when he poured water in the stemmed glasses on their table. Soon he returned and set steaming bowls of soup in front of them and a basket of hot bread between them.

"Now you'll know why I eat here so frequently." Selene dipped her spoon into the soup. She wasn't nearly as concerned with the meal as she was in learning more about Joy Marie, Gustave, and Drake.

"This is delicious." Joy Marie looked surprised and pleased. "But quite different. What is it?"

"Turtle."

Joy Marie smiled. "It's best I didn't order. I'd never have asked for turtle soup. And now I'm glad I tried it."

Selene nodded, ate more soup, then focused on Joy Marie. She might not have much longer to question her. "About Gustave Dominique."

"He's a fascinating man, isn't he?" Joy Marie's blue eyes shone with love.

"Yes. I'd like to learn more about hypnotism from him. In addition to the apothecary shop, I also use medical skills I learned from my grandmother."

"Really? I envy your abilities."

"Thank you. But you're also quite talented. Was it difficult learning to be Mr. Dominique's assistant?"

"No. For the most part he does everything. I did a lot more on the ranch." Her voice sounded wistful.

"Do you miss your former husband?"

"I did before Gustave came along. Drake was away a lot. I was lonely. But not anymore." She took a bite of bread. "This is good, too."

Selene picked up a piece of bread. "But Drake came after you."

"Oh, Drake. He has this thing about family. I can't imagine why. There's nobody left." She frowned. "Or maybe that's why."

"What do you mean, nobody's left?"

"Just that." Joy Marie hesitated, then rushed on. "Drake's parents died from a fever. My son, Drake's nephew, died from a fall. Then my husband died. I'm all that's left." She toyed with her spoon, then set it down and turned haunted eyes on Selene. "At Dalton Ranch, everywhere I looked I saw death, loss, and pain."

70

"I'm sorry."

"Drake hurt, too, but he had the ranch. And any woman he wanted in several counties."

"I thought maybe—"

"Drake and I?" Joy Marie shook her head. "No. When Gustave Dominique came along, I was ready to leave the past behind. And I didn't want to have to face Drake. He'd have talked family. He might even have killed Gustave to protect what was his."

"But—"

"You don't know Drake Dalton, Selene. And frankly, I warn you to stay away from him. I love him as a brother. He has always been good to me. But when it comes to Dalton Ranch, to what he considers his, the man is a bull. He'll fight to the death to keep his family, his land together." She took a deep breath. "And I need my own life. Away from Dalton Ranch. Away from the memories."

Selene nodded, feeling chilled. She'd wanted to know about Drake Dalton, but she hadn't wanted to know this. And she hadn't wanted to know about Joy Marie's pain. A child. A husband. No wonder she'd wanted to get away.

"Do you understand?"

"Yes."

"Will you help me with Drake?"

"I hardly know him."

"Yes, but if Drake has his way, that'll change. I know him."

Selene lost her appetite as she thought of the love potion she'd made for Drake Dalton. Was she getting into more than she could handle? No. She had to believe in herself. She must remember all those who depended on her. And she mustn't allow herself to feel sympathy. Drake Dalton was her enemy as long as he tried to destroy Love Potions.

"Selene?"

"Drake's an attractive man, but he's not my type."

Joy Marie smiled. "From what I've seen, my brother-in-law is every woman's type, especially if he sets his mind to it." She finished her soup. "Will you help me?"

"I don't know what I can do."

"Knowing Drake, I'm sure he's got it set in his mind that Gustave kidnapped me or something. It's not true. *Impossible*. I love my Frenchman—his work, his spirit, his life. And we're talking about marriage."

"I'm happy for you."

"Thanks." Joy Marie suddenly looked unhappy. "I don't want Drake ruining my plans."

"I see." Selene was uncomfortable. She didn't trust Gustave Dominique, but it was obvious Joy Marie would listen to nothing bad about the man who had taken her away from the pain of her past. She could understand, but she was more worried than ever. Most of all, she couldn't turn down someone who had asked for help, especially somebody who had nowhere else to turn. "I'll do what I can, Joy Marie, but Drake doesn't much approve of me or what I do."

"Drake always was slow to take to new ideas." Joy Marie leaned across the table and clasped Selene's hand. "Thanks."

"What do you want me to tell him?"

The front door opened and a shadow fell across them. "I want you to tell me what the hell you're doing in New Orleans, Joy Marie." Drake pulled out a chair and sat down at their table.

Joy Marie frowned, then threw an accusing glance at Selene.

"Don't blame Selene." Drake fixed his sister-in-law with a dark stare. "Dominique's bulldog won't let me see you. You don't go out much. But you can be damn sure I know most any move you make."

"I'm not part of your family anymore, Drake." Joy Marie's words were clipped.

"You'll always be a Dalton."

"Not if I change my name to Dominique."

Drake looked surprised. "You'd marry that man?"

"I love him. I told you that. I'm happy. Nothing would please me more than to become Madame Gustave Dominique."

"But the ranch—"

Joy Marie shook her head. "It's *your* ranch."

"You helped me run it."

"But no more." Joy Marie stood up. Tears filled her eyes. "Can't you understand? There's only sorrow for me in Texas. Dalton Ranch is one big graveyard for me. I never want to go back. I want to live with Gustave. Now leave me alone." Desperate to get away, she knocked her chair over as she rushed from the table and out of the restaurant.

Drake stood up and took a step after her.

Selene grabbed his arm. "No. She needs to be alone. You're upsetting her."

He hesitated, then sat down. "She hates me because I'm a Dalton, doesn't she?"

"I don't think she hates you. I'm not sure if she even knows what she feels. She simply wanted to get away from the pain, from the memories."

"What did she tell you?"

"Enough."

He glared, his eyes full of suspicion.

"She simply said that all the Daltons were dead except you."

"That's right."

"Mam'selle?" The waiter hovered nearby, obviously disliking the need to interrupt.

Selene glanced at him, then back at Drake. "She forgot her lunch."

"I'll eat it."

She nodded at the waiter. He righted the chair, picked up the empty bowls, and left.

"What are we having?" Drake moved around to take Joy Marie's place.

"I don't know."

"What?"

"Haven't you eaten here before?"

"No."

Selene sighed. She wanted to go after Joy Marie and find some way to comfort her. But Drake would never let her go alone. Besides, another confrontation was the last thing Joy Marie needed. And the last thing she felt like was food.

"I thought you'd ordered." Drake looked confused.

"They don't give you a choice here."

He thought about it. "If I don't like the food, I'm not paying."

Selene rolled her eyes. "The food's wonderful and I don't want to hear any more about it."

"You're sure in a good mood."

"I'm tired of having to explain Tujague's lack of menu. I eat here frequently and that's that."

"Okay. Don't get upset about it."

"I'm not." Selene bit her lower lip in frustration. "What else did you learn from Joy Marie?"

"Mam'selle Selene." Again the waiter interrupted as he placed steaming plates in front of them.

"*Merci.*" She was glad of the distraction. It seemed as if she and Drake could only be angry with each other.

"What's this?"

"I'm sorry you missed the turtle soup."

"I'm not." He looked disgusted. "I had in mind a hunk of rare beef."

"No doubt. This is stuffed crab with rice, I believe."

"I could starve."

"We'll order coffee for dessert."

"No. We'll go across the street for beignets."

"You can do that. I've got work to do."

Drake ignored her comment and started on the food. He nodded once in approval, then quickly cleaned his plate.

She regained her appetite as she enjoyed the delicious flavor of seasoned rice and crab. Watching Drake, she wondered if he was ever gentle or quiet. Did he know how to do anything except fight? Somehow she couldn't be too hard on Joy Marie for escaping, if that had been what had happened. But with Gustave Dominique and his hypnotism, who knew the truth.

"If you have any left over, I'll take it." Drake picked up a piece of bread.

"Stop watching my food. I want it all."

"I was afraid of that." He finished the bread, then leaned back in his chair, suddenly serious. "What do you think's going on with Joy Marie?"

"Drake, I honestly don't know. She seems to want Gustave Dominique. But he's a hypnotist. Is he any good? I don't know. Is he scrupulous? Again, I don't know. Does he love Joy Marie?"

"We don't know." Drake clenched a fist. "My gut feeling is that Dominique is a swindler. He's got Dalton money and Joy Marie. He can have them both if he loves her and takes care of her. But if he doesn't, I'm going to take them away from him."

"You've said that. But how can we know the truth? I did what you wanted. And I like Joy Marie. But there's not much else I can do."

"You can stay in touch with her, Selene." Drake leaned forward. "I can't do that. Dominique's turned her against me."

"Why should I help you when all you want to do is destroy my business?"

"It's for your own good. And a lot of other people's, too."

"You don't know what you're talking about." She stood up and dropped her napkin on the table. "In fact, I don't think you know a thing about women. Maybe that's why you're not married." She started for the door.

Drake threw down some money, not knowing the price any more than he'd known the menu. He hated the idea. He frowned at the waiter before hurrying after Selene.

Outside, he grabbed her arm and swung her

around. "I'm getting tired of women walking out on me. What the hell does this town do to its ladies?"

"It's not New Orleans, Drake. It's you. Don't you know how to be a gentleman?"

He frowned and pulled her toward the Café du Monde. "Don't turn this around on me. I'm trying to help people and I'm not letting any smooth-talkers change my mind."

As they neared Love Potions, she pressed her hand against his arm. "Listen, I did what I could with Joy Marie. I'll keep in touch with her. All right?"

"Thanks." He stopped and ran a hand through his thick hair. "Am I being too rough on her?"

"You're being too rough on everybody. This is civilization and I think we handle life a little differently than out on your ranch."

He smiled. "Maybe. But I still want what I want." He put a fingertip under her chin and tilted her face toward him. "Sure you don't want some beignets with me?"

Oddly, she felt a hot current invade her where his finger touched. And his smile changed him, making him seem almost boyish. She liked this Drake Dalton. Too much. And she figured she could blame the love potion. But was it working on him?

He leaned forward and placed a kiss, more proprietary than sensual, on her lips. Then he gave her a hard stare. Heat was in his brown eyes. And passion, too. "I'll see you tonight."

Then he turned and walked across the street.

Chapter 6

"Was that Drake Dalton I saw outside the window?" Rosa raised a brow as Selene entered Love Potions.

"If you're trying to make a point, there's no need. I knew Drake was joining us for lunch. He wanted to talk with Joy Marie, but Gustave Dominique won't let him near her." Selene sat down behind her desk and slumped. "I can't seem to do anything but argue with Drake. For once, I don't think my love potion is working."

"That bad?"

"Joy Marie was *not* glad to see him. In fact, they argued and she left."

"How was the food?"

"I enjoyed it."

Rosa chuckled.

"You think this is funny, don't you?"

"I warned you another restaurant might be more to Joy Marie's taste."

"She didn't get past turtle soup. Drake took over

and said he'd rather have a thick, rare steak. We're sitting in one of the best restaurants in New Orleans and he wants to eat ranch food." Selene grimaced. "I don't think there's any way to get through to that man. I tried to get him to back down about Love Potions, but he's obstinate."

"Sounds like somebody else I know."

"Who?"

Rosa simply looked at her.

"If you mean me, I'm . . . well, there are certain things one must fight for. That's all."

Rosa shook her head. "We had some business while you were gone."

"Good. I've got to concentrate on work. I simply will not let some bullheaded Texan interfere with my life."

"He already has."

"Thanks. You could leave me with a few illusions." Selene drummed her fingertips on the desk.

"Look in the cash box."

Selene glanced down. They'd selected a square wooden box to pad with cotton then cover in blue silk. Attractive, it looked nothing like a cash box. She flipped up the lid and saw a pile of bills lying on top of the change.

"What'd you do, rob a bank while I was gone?"

"No. Mr. Dominique was here."

Selene straightened her spine.

"He was very interested in the shop."

"What was he doing here? He knew Joy Marie was having lunch with me. Was he watching us? Did he see Drake join us?" Selene snapped the lid shut, then

80

stood up and paced. "I don't like this, Rosa."

"I don't either. Gustave Dominique is a dangerous man, Selene."

She stopped. "What'd he buy?"

"Nice things for Joy Marie. Face and body oils and creams. Perfumes. Bath salts. Shampoo. That type of thing."

"Love Potions? Herbs?"

"No. Nothing like that. But he asked about you and said he'd be back."

Selene sat down at the table. "I think this is going to be a lot more complicated than I originally thought."

"I hope this means you'll be more careful."

"Of course, Mr. Dominique could simply be a jealous man, trying to make sure Drake Dalton stayed away from his woman."

"Could be." Rosa sewed tiny stitches around a square of rose silk. "But I think he's deeper than that."

"So do I." Selene sighed. "Sorry. I'm not being much help, am I?"

"We're doing fine. I've about finished that special order for Madame Diana."

"Thanks. I'm so worried about Love Potions and our missing friends that I'm not thinking straight."

"I'll take care of business. You just make sure we still have it when this is all over."

"That's a deal." Selene stuck out her hand and they shook. Turning back to the table, she picked up a bottle of periwinkle. As she screwed off the lid, the bell rang on the front door. She glanced up. Gustave

Dominique stepped into the shop. Taking a deep breath to steady herself, she set down the bottle.

"*Bonjour,* lovely ladies." Gustave smiled as he walked toward them.

Rosa nudged Selene with her elbow.

Selene stood, but she could think of nothing to say. The Frenchman was dressed as impeccably as usual, with his mustache waxed and his wavy hair neatly combed. The crystal she knew he used in hypnotism dangled from the watch at his waist. He was a handsome man who was powerful, pleasant, and well spoken. Joy Marie loved him. Drake hated him. Rosa didn't trust him. And Selene didn't know what to think.

"You are surprised to see me?" Dominique stopped in front of Selene.

"No." She hesitated, wondering how much she should reveal. "Rosa told me you'd been in earlier."

"Yes. I am sorry I missed you."

"I had lunch plans."

He smiled, showing teeth slightly stained, then glanced around the store. "I admire what you have done here. And your products are of the finest quality. Joy Marie was delighted when I gave her what I had selected."

"I'm glad. We do our best."

"I understand you also do some work as a medical practitioner."

"Yes. Some. Herbs." She clasped her hands, then unclasped them.

"Have you had as much trouble with the regulars as I have?"

"They seem to think there is only one way to heal. *Their* way."

"And that is not always the best, is it?" He picked up a perfume, smelled it, then set down the bottle.

"Not from what I've seen of the patients who've come to me almost dead from heroic treatment."

"Heroic. An apt term for such rough medicine. It will either kill you or you will get well on your own."

"I've heard practitioners have been interested in your hypnotism lectures."

"Yes." He focused his dark eyes on her again. "I have talked with a wide variety of medical people. All are interested in my work, but hypnotism takes time and effort to learn. I fear chloroform, although more dangerous, will win the day simply because it is easier to use."

"But what about hypnotism in working with problems of the mind?" Selene began to relax, realizing they shared a common interest.

"Yes, that is where I believe hypnotism can make a big difference. I have conducted studies in this area, but there is much more to do before we completely understand the mind."

Selene nodded. "I'd like to hear more about this."

"I will be glad to discuss it with you. Perhaps over lunch."

"Yes. Thanks. And I'd like to learn more about the seances, too."

"Another interesting experiment. Of course, I am always ready to share my knowledge with another practitioner. In fact, after we discuss this more, I would be happy to allow you to be a subject. That way you could understand hypnotism more fully."

"I'll think about it."

"Good. Then I will call on you soon for lunch." He started toward the door.

Selene followed him.

In the doorway, he suddenly turned. They were very close. He smiled, letting his gaze wander over her features. "I would like to get to know you better. I believe we have much in common. Much to share."

Selene felt heat rise to her face. "I—"

"Selene!" Drake called as he hurried across Decatur. Stopping beside them, he glared down at Dominique. "I won't let you hurt Joy Marie."

Dominique shrugged, threw an amused glance at Selene, then focused on Drake. "I am sorry you think your sister-in-law is unhappy, but I assure you, again, she is satisfied to be with me." He bowed to Selene. "Until later, *ma chère*." He quickly walked away.

"What'd that fool call you?" Drake watched Dominique, his brows drawn together in a frown.

"Beloved."

"What!" Drake whirled around. "There had better not be any reason for it."

"Only an expression, I'm sure."

"I don't want you seeing him alone."

Disgusted, Selene walked into Love Potions and started to shut the door.

Drake stopped the door with his hand. "Not so fast."

"I have nothing more to say to you."

He followed her into the store. "I'll take you to dinner."

She turned back. "After such a pleasant lunch, you can imagine how much I'd like that." Her voice dripped with sarcasm.

Drake looked surprised. "Lunch was okay if there'd been more of it."

"Why don't you go back to Texas. Joy Marie is happy. My business is going well. And Gustave Dominique seems to be a man who cares about hypnotism and how it can help others."

"Now he's done it to you!" Drake grabbed Selene's arms and shook her. "That man's trouble and I'm not going to let him get you, too."

"Take your hands off me this instant." Selene's eyes sparked green fire.

"I can't let that Frenchman smooth-talk his way around all you women." He gently massaged her arms, as if to take back the earlier pain.

Selene jerked away from him, not wanting to admit to feeling the tingling his touch had sent through her body. But she was suddenly vitally aware of Drake as a man.

Rosa walked over to them. "He hasn't smooth-talked *me*. I don't think Gustave Dominique's entirely honest, but till be does something wrong, there's little we can do."

"You mean until we *catch* him doing something wrong." Drake frowned.

"Either way." Rosa smiled to take the sting from her words. "I think you're being hard on the women you know, Mr. Drake. Perhaps a little smooth-talking would get you farther, too."

Drake turned to Selene, then raked her body with a quick glance. "You may have a point there, Rosa. I have been known to do a little of it in my day."

"I bet." Selene stepped away from them, wondering if she should get the love potion back from Drake. It didn't seem to be working.

Suddenly a small towheaded boy, his clothes clean but worn and patched, rushed into the store. "Miss Selene, Joe's gone down bad."

"Jimmy, what happened?" Selene walked over to her desk, pulled her medicine bag out of a bottom drawer, then turned back.

"Joe worked docks today. Line busted. Winch hit his head."

"Oh, no." Selene looked at Rosa.

"Go on. I'll take care of the store."

Selene gave her a quick hug, walked around Drake, and headed out the door with Jimmy.

"Wait a minute." Drake started after them. "You might need help."

Selene glanced back at him. "We don't need your assistance or interference."

"The hell you don't." He stayed right behind them.

Selene decided to ignore Drake and hope he'd go away. She concentrated on keeping up with Jimmy as he crossed Decatur and headed for the Mississippi River docks not far away.

She didn't question Jimmy. A wharf rat, he'd lived on the docks all his life. He didn't know the names of his parents any more than anybody else did so he became everybody's child and, at the same time, everybody's guardian angel. He worked some, he snatched food here and there, and watched everything. He knew most of what went on down on the docks, and if there was trouble, he knew where to get help.

Thinking about Joe, she wished he'd been hit anywhere but his head. He was mulatto, with more brawn than brain, and usually got hard labor. But only that now and then. He was Jimmy's friend. Between Joe's size and Jimmy's smarts, they took care of each other. Nobody bothered them and they were satisfied.

But with Joe hurt, both of them were in trouble.

"You fix him, Miss Selene. You fix him." Jimmy gave her a hard stare.

"I'll do what I can. Where is he?"

"Had the boys carry him to Clay's."

"Good." She wanted to squeeze Jimmy's hand or hug him, but knew better. He considered himself a grown man, not needing any comfort. But she knew better. Nevertheless, she did nothing. She only hoped she'd be in time and that Joe's injury could be helped.

Turning down a side street then an alley, Jimmy led Selene to Clay's Corner. Built right on the alley, a gray wooden building attached to the back of a brick warehouse proclaimed neither its name nor its business. But it was always busy. And noisy.

As soon as Drake saw it, he started cussing, and grabbed Selene's arm. "You're not going in

87

a place like that."

Furious, she whirled on him. "Let me go. A man in there needs me."

"A lady shouldn't—"

Jimmy raised his fists. "Let her go, mister. That's Miss Selene. Nobody hurts her."

Surprised, Drake looked from one to the other. He hated to shatter Jimmy's illusion of strength. On the other hand, he didn't want Selene going into a sailors' dive where who knew what went on. But obviously, she was used to it. He shouldn't be surprised. He'd known she was a swindler. Was she a whore, too? He dropped his hand.

Selene turned away.

"But I'm not letting you out of my sight." Drake wasn't done with her yet.

Jimmy went to a side door, which he opened for Selene. She stepped into a storeroom and saw Joe on a pallet of quilts against one corner. A lantern spread soft yellow light over his dark face. As she knelt beside him, she glanced back. Jimmy hurried over to her and Drake shut the door behind him.

"Jimmy, tell Clay I'll need some boiling water." She knew there was no time to lose.

Jimmy put a small hand on Joe's chest. "Miss Selene's here. She'll fix you up." He touched Selene's shoulder, then went through a curtained doorway into the main room.

Selene heard Drake move closer. Soon he loomed over her. "Stay out of the way." Her voice was threaded with steel.

"I'll help if I can."

She didn't respond, for her thoughts were already back on Joe. Lifting the lantern, she examined his face. Blood matted the hair. The skin around his eye and the left side of his face was already mottled, rapidly turning blue and purple. It was also swollen. He was unconscious. She checked his heart beat, then his breathing. Slow but within the normal range.

Jimmy came back through the curtain, carefully balancing a bowl of water. He set it beside Selene. Then crouched nearby. "How's he?"

"Alive." She opened her medicine bag. "I can't tell you more yet." Taking out a clean white cloth, she dipped it in the water, withstood the heat as it touched her fingers, then began gently wiping away the blood from Joe's head. He didn't move and she was glad he couldn't feel the pain.

She kept working, and when the water in the bowl had turned red, she stopped. "More water, Jimmy."

Without saying a word, he picked up the bowl and left.

"Is he going to make it?" Drake looked over her shoulder. He'd seen men hurt on the ranch, on cattle drives. His mother had been fairly skilled and they'd missed her ministering touch when she'd died. Doctors were few and far between. If Selene was as skilled as she seemed, they could use a dozen like her in central Texas.

"I don't know yet. If you want to be helpful, please hold the lamp up so I can see better."

Drake lifted it and got his first good look at the

man. The sight wasn't pretty.

Selene felt around Joe's head and found a long gash. It wasn't too deep and it didn't worry her nearly as much as the blow. The skull felt slightly dented beneath the cut. That bothered her. Pressure on the brain. It wasn't a good sign at all.

Pushing the curtain aside, Jimmy hurried back. He set the bowl down again without spilling a drop.

"I'll be honest with you, Jimmy." Selene turned to look at him. "Joe may not make it."

Jimmy pressed his lips together, squeezed his eyes shut, then rushed out the side door.

"Don't do after him." Selene reached into her medicine bag again. "He knows how to be alone."

"Damn it! That boy needs a family."

"The dock's his family." She began threading a needle, reminding herself of making love potions. But this was for a life-or-death purpose. If only healing a man were as easy as coaxing him to fall in love, her work would bring no pain.

"The dock! That's no family."

"Drake, please be quiet. We can talk about Jimmy later. Right now, Joe needs all our attention." But she thought about Drake's loss of family and realized why he was so concerned about a boy alone.

Drake grew quiet and watched as she dampened a clean cloth with something from a bottle, wiped it over the wound, then began sewing.

"You're good at that."

"Experience." She concentrated, forcing herself not to worry about Jimmy. At least Joe was not in pain.

She worked quickly and quietly and finally had the gash stitched together. Again she cleaned it with an astringent she prepared herself, one she'd learned from her Granny Morgan. Then she washed Joe's face with warm water, noticing that he was starting to perspire. His skin was cold and clammy to the touch. Another bad sign.

Shutting her eyes, she thought of Joe as he had been, strong and whole, and as he could be again. As he *must* be again.

Suddenly the side door opened, and Jimmy stepped inside. His eyes were puffy. "Sorry, Miss Selene. But Joe and me—"

"It's all right. Come here."

Jimmy knelt beside her. "He looks better now."

"He shouldn't bleed anymore." She turned to watch him. "Joe may make it, but it's going to be close. You see, I can't tell what's been damaged inside his head. He may come out of it and be fine. But we can't count on that."

"What can I do?" Jimmy's voice was haunted.

"You need to stay with Joe all the time. Keep him warm. Keep a light in here. And I'm going to make a special herbal tea for him to drink."

"But—"

"We'll hold the cup to his lips, then let the liquid trickle into his mouth. He'll swallow some." She put an arm around Jimmy's shoulders and pulled him close. "But I'm not going to leave."

Jimmy hesitated, then put his small hands around Selene. She hugged him close.

"I can carry Joe some place more comfortable."

Drake watched them and thought of his dead nephew. He'd be about Jimmy's age now. And Selene. Maybe he'd misjudged her. This was no scheming woman. She really cared. He swallowed hard around a lump in his throat. Family. It seemed about everybody in New Orleans was Selene's family, while he had none. Not even Joy Marie. But hell, he didn't need anybody.

Selene glanced up and Jimmy backed away, looking slightly embarrassed.

"Thanks." She checked Joe again. "But we don't dare move him. I need some more quilts. I've got to keep Joe warm and Jimmy will need something to sleep on, too."

"Don't worry about me, Miss Selene. You watch Joe."

She smiled.

"I'll get you whatever you need." Drake knelt and set the lantern on the floor. "Just tell me." He pushed back a damp lock of hair on Selene's forehead. "I'll get you some food."

"I don't feel very hungry, but Jimmy should eat."

Jimmy squared his shoulders. "I can take care of myself."

"I know you can." Drake gave him a man-to-man look, and was once more reminded of his nephew. "But we must see to Selene and she needs food."

Jimmy nodded.

"Drake, please go to Rosa and tell her what happened. She'll know what I need. And some food would be good."

He squeezed her shoulder. "I'll get a carriage and

be back soon."

At the door, he looked back, hating to leave them alone.

"I'll take care of them, sir." Jimmy stood straight, as tall as he could make himself.

Drake nodded, then was gone.

Chapter 7

Three days later Selene watched Joe take his last breath. She had done all she could and yet felt guilty she hadn't been able to save his life. When she turned to tell Jimmy, she saw understanding on his face.

He ran outside.

"You want me to get him?" Drake started for the door.

"No. Let him be awhile. He won't want us to see him cry." Selene pulled the quilt over Joe's face, then stood up. She ached all over. She'd had no sleep, little food, and the worry and tension of constant watch had taken its toll. She'd tried. She always tried, but sometimes it wasn't enough.

Drake put an arm around her shoulders and pulled her into his strength and warmth. She leaned against him, relishing the comfort and knowing she shouldn't. He was her enemy but it felt so good to be held by him. She shivered and he tightened his grip.

"You did all you could." His voice was low. "My

mother lost them sometimes, too. You don't always win."

"I know, but it hurts. Now Jimmy's alone."

"If I've learned anything about you in the last few days, he's not alone."

She glanced up. Drake's eyes held admiration and something more. Desire. She looked away, but it didn't stop her heart from beating faster. Not only did she want his comfort but she wanted his respect, and she disliked wanting it. However, she didn't blame herself for she knew it was simply the effect of the love potion.

"You want me to take care of Joe's funeral?"

"He had a lot of friends. They'll want to do it."

"And Jimmy?"

"I'll take him home with me." She hesitated, remembering the small, determined face. "Or I'll try to."

"You can't leave him alone."

"I know." She sighed, then pushed away from Drake. For a moment he resisted, then let her go. Without his strength, she suddenly felt cold and exhausted. But if she relied on him too long, she knew she'd want to do it forever. "Thanks for your help. You didn't need to stay with me, or go after food and medicine. You must be tired, too. I'll handle everything from here."

"You're going after Jimmy?"

"Yes. He and Joe had a little place back of the warehouses. I think he'll be there."

"You're not going alone. It's the middle of the night."

"I'll be okay. And Jimmy trusts me."

"He trusts me, too. Besides, he reminds me of my nephew."

"It's over, Drake." She was too tired to argue. "Go on about your business."

He pulled her to him. "You *are* my business while I'm in New Orleans. If you go after Jimmy, I'm going with you."

She shook her head, so tired he was almost making sense. But he wasn't. She hardly knew him. And he was in town for Joy Marie. "Just go away, Drake. I'm *not* your business."

He held her against his chest, then gently stroked her back with strong hands. "Angel or devil, which are you? Do you heal people or trick them out of hard earned money?" The movement of his hands grew harsh. "Whoever you are, I've got to find out. One way or another."

Again, she pushed away. "It doesn't matter who I am. Right now we must think of Jimmy. Come on. You can go with me to find him." She was too tired to fight Drake or even worry about him trying to destroy Love Potions. She must think of the living and that meant keeping Jimmy safe. "But first will you tell Clay about Joe? He'll see to the funeral."

"Yes. I'll be right back."

When Drake slipped through the curtain separating the storeroom and the bar, Selene looked down at Joe's covered body. Tears gathered in her eyes. Wherever he was now, she hoped he was happy and at peace. "Don't worry, Joe, I'll look out for Jimmy as you always did."

But somehow the words weren't comforting. She turned away and walked to the door. Opening it, she stepped outside. The night was warm and humid. The sweet scent of magnolias and honeysuckle filled the air. The sound of men, happy, angry, drunk, came from Clay's Corner. She breathed deeply and thought about Jimmy. How she would care for the boy she didn't know, for he was used to being on his own. But she would make sure he had a good home.

Drake stepped outside. "I thought you'd gone."

"And would you have come after me?"

"Yes." He pulled her hand through the crook of his arm. "Clay'll take care of Joe from here."

Selene didn't respond as she led Drake into the darkness surrounding the warehouses. Instead, she thought of Joe when he was tall and strong, or Jimmy laughing and talking with his big friend, and of their loss. Everyone's loss. But life had to go on.

A short time later they stopped outside a little shack put together with bits and pieces of discarded wood, slate, paper, and fabric. Yellow light gleamed here and there through cracks and slats. It didn't look like much, but Selene knew it was home to Jimmy.

She knocked on the door.

Silence.

She knocked again.

"Go 'way," Jimmy called from inside.

"It's Selene and Drake. We want to talk with you."

"You didn't save Joe."

"I'm sorry." Selene felt worse than ever. "I did what I could."

"We want to help you, Jimmy." Drake put a hand on the door and it bowed inward.

"Go 'way."

Selene felt tears sting her eyes again. "Jimmy, we

98

all miss Joe. But we *need* you to be with us now."

Silence, then the door was pulled open. A tear-stained Jimmy looked out the doorway. "You need me?"

Nodding, Selene tried to smile but couldn't. "You and Joe always ran errands for me. I'll still need that. Plus, only you know what's really going on down at the wharf. We need your help finding those who've disappeared."

Jimmy looked at them suspiciously. "Joe'd seen something. 'Bout our friends. He was gonna tell me that night."

"You mean he knew something about the disappearances, but he died before he could tell you?" Selene felt her heart beat faster.

Jimmy nodded.

Drake and Selene exchanged surprised glances.

"I'd like you to stay with me, at least for a few days." Selene decided Jimmy could be in danger. For the first time she was worried that Joe's death might not have been an accident.

"Got my own place." Jimmy's chin jutted forward with determination.

"I know, but—"

"Selene needs a man with her right now." Drake gave Jimmy a knowing look. "And she needs somebody to help her find her friends. I think you're the man to do it."

Jimmy squared his shoulders. "I *can* do it." He glanced around. "But I've got to lock up my place."

As Jimmy went back into his house, Selene smiled at Drake. "Thanks. I was afraid I wasn't going to reach him."

"You better take good care of him."

Selene frowned. "Don't you know how to do anything but give orders?"

His gaze slid to her lips. "Yes. There're a few other things I can do . . . well."

She tossed her head. "I'm sure I could care less about them."

"I bet I could change your mind." He stepped closer.

Forcing herself to remain still, she sensed the magnetism of him, the almost overpowering maleness, and felt herself respond. Again, she wanted to lean into him, to savor his strength, his warmth, his power. Then she shook her head. It was nothing but the love potion. And she mustn't let it affect her.

"I'm ready." Jimmy stepped out of his darkened house, locked the door, then pulled something out of his pocket. It squirmed. "This is Joe Junior, my frog."

Drake chuckled and glanced at Selene.

"Wanna pet him for luck?" Jimmy thrust the frog toward Selene.

She hesitated only a moment before touching Joe Junior between the eyes. "Nice frog."

Laughing, Drake took Joe Junior, held him up, looked him over, then handed him back. "Good-sized frog. Where'd you find him?"

"Got in the house. Joe tamed him." Jimmy tucked Joe Junior back in his pocket. "I figure as long as I've got Joe Junior around, I'll—" His voice broke.

"Why don't we go back to my place now?" Selene knew there was no good way to grieve. Only time would heal Jimmy's wound.

As they walked back toward Love Potions, Selene realized how much her life had changed since Drake Dalton had entered her shop. Good, bad, or indifferent, she had to deal with it. But she hadn't been prepared for a man like Drake, or dealing with Jimmy and Joe Junior either. Suddenly she had to think of clothes, food, even education. And what did frogs eat anyway?

But she didn't voice any of her concerns. Instead she tried to think of something to make Jimmy feel better, but she quickly gave up on that idea. She knew he was a smart boy who couldn't be deceived into thinking he was happier than he really was.

They walked back in silence. When they arrived at Love Potions, Selene quickly unlocked the front door. Stepping inside, she lit a lamp on a low table, then beckoned Jimmy forward. As the young boy walked past her, she stepped into the open doorway, blocking Drake's path.

He frowned. "Jimmy needs a man right now."

"No. He needs a mother."

"Men are what he's used to."

"But a woman's what he needs." She tried to push the door shut.

He blocked it with his boot. "You're the most contrary woman I've ever met."

"I don't care what you think about me, I'm—"

He wrapped a strong hand around her arm and jerked her outside. Then he shut the door behind them. "Jimmy doesn't need us arguing over him."

"What's he to you? You're a stranger here." His hand was hot. Suddenly she couldn't stop noticing how tall he was, how strong, how sensual, and she felt a quick rush of passion sweep her. Startled, she took a step backward, but he didn't let her go.

"I've been with Jimmy the last few days, Selene. He reminds me of my nephew. I want to stay and help." He released her arm. "Why don't I go across the street and get some beignets and café au lait? We could all use it."

"How can I trust you? You've sworn to destroy my business."

Drake glanced up at the Love Potions sign. It creaked in the breeze. "We could take turns watching Jimmy. That way you'd get some sleep."

"Rosa—"

"She can help out in the morning." He moved closer. "Don't fight me, Selene." Clasping her chin, he raised her face so she'd look at him. "You've got to get some rest and I'm willing to help." As if reluctantly, he lowered his face and pressed hot lips to hers.

She jerked away, feeling burned. "I can't trust you."

"Trust me for tonight."

A shiver ran through her and she glanced back inside. Jimmy had curled into a ball on the floor just like a lost puppy. She couldn't afford to argue anymore. Drake was right. She could use his help. There was no choice but to think of Jimmy first. "All right."

"You won't regret it." He turned and strode across the street.

"I'm already regretting it." But she didn't say it loud enough for him to hear. She didn't want to be anywhere near Drake Dalton. The love potion was

102

too strong. She wanted it to work only on him, but she was afraid she was getting caught in her own trap.

She felt another chill sweep her, then pushed thoughts of Drake from her mind and went inside.

Jimmy was asleep, exhausted. She hated to wake him just yet, so she left him where he was. She lit several lamps as she made her way through Love Potions. At the work table in back, she picked up a pale blue shawl, knitted from thick cotton, then walked to the front of the store and laid it over Jimmy.

She smiled. Even with a dirt-smudged face, tattered clothes, and wild hair, he was a winsome child. And so alone. Like Drake. She paused. Now why had she thought that? Drake was certainly no helpless child. He owned a sprawling ranch in Texas. He was independent. He needed nobody. Just like Jimmy. But Jimmy was very vulnerable, whether he knew it or not. And he very much needed a family.

Suddenly Selene hugged her arms to her body. It would not do to think of Drake Dalton as needy. He obviously wasn't. A powerful man like Drake didn't need anybody. And certainly not her. He was trying to ruin her business and she must remember that. She must not be gentle with him. She must think only of herself and the people who depended on her business.

There was a bump at the front door.

Selene looked up in surprise, then recognized Drake's shadowy form. She opened the door.

"Thanks. I've got my hands full." Drake stepped inside, carrying two mugs in one hand and a mug with a sack dangling from his fingers in the other.

"I'd better take that." Selene took the sack from his hand, noticing the calluses from a life of rough work. She wondered how his fingers would feel against the smoothness of her own skin. And she was shocked at her thoughts. Pushing them away, she walked briskly back to her desk.

Drake glanced down at Jimmy, a smile curving his lips, then followed Selene. "Roping a calf is easier than carrying all this."

"Thanks." She took one of the mugs from him and set it on the table.

He set the other two down. "Think we ought to wake Jimmy?"

"Looks like the smell of beignets already did that." Drake glanced around.

Rubbing his eyes, Jimmy stretched, threw off the shawl, and hurried toward them. "Don't eat without me."

Selene tore open the sack, using it as a plate, and inhaled the delicious aroma of hot French donuts. Suddenly she felt starved.

Drake carried two chairs to the desk and they all sat down. As Jimmy reached for a mug of coffee, Drake handed him another mug.

"Milk for you, young man."

Rolling his eyes, Jimmy didn't complain. Instead, he picked up a donut and began eating, pausing only long enough for gulps of milk.

Drake watched him, a satisfied smile curling his lips.

"I'm glad you thought of the milk." Selene was beginning to think there was more depth to Drake, more kindness than she'd realized. He'd proved it over and over the last few days. And she was almost sorry. She didn't want to like him.

"Jimmy's a growing boy. At the ranch, we'd have him milking morning and evening. He'd grow tall and strong."

"What's a cow like?" Jimmy's eyes were intent.

"Well, a cow's . . . well, there're bulls and steers and yearlings and heifers and . . ."

"Are they mean?" Jimmy stopped eating.

"Some of them are. Mommas with babies will go for your gut with their horns. That's why you ride a horse and carry a lasso. If you want to catch a cow, you better plan on roping it."

Jimmy's eyes were shining. "You're a real cowboy?"

Drake nodded. "But it's tough."

"Sure." Jimmy looked affronted. "That's why cowboys are tough. Maybe I'll be a cowboy when I grow up."

"I thought you were going to be a sailor." Selene didn't know if hero worship of a man who would soon be gone was a good idea.

"That too." Jimmy's eyes were bright with admiration.

Drake chuckled. "Finish your milk, partner. You've got to be strong to rope a steer."

"Right." Jimmy quickly downed his milk.

Suddenly Selene felt as if something had been taken from her. Drake was after Love Potions. Jimmy adored him. She felt vulnerable to the Texan. And afraid. If she wasn't careful, he might take everything she valued.

105

She stood up. "I think we'd better get you to bed, Jimmy. You'll feel better in the morning."

"I'm better now." Jimmy pulled out Joe Junior and stroked him. "Joe wanted to be a cowboy."

"I bet he'd have made a good one." Drake got to his feet. "But cowboys have to get their rest, too."

Jimmy stood, gave Drake a hard stare, then nodded to himself. He put Joe Junior back in his pocket. "Right. And cowboys always help ladies, don't they?"

"Yes."

Selene watched them, and for a moment she thought she saw tears sparkle in Drake's eyes. But she must have been mistaken. He was nothing but a rough, tough cowboy.

"Miss Selene, I'll help you in the morning." Jimmy stood straight and proud.

"Thank you, Jimmy. In the meantime, there's a small room off our work area. Rosa sometimes uses its single bed. I think you'll like it."

Jimmy nodded, but his eyes stayed on Drake.

"Okay, *hombre*. Let's get you to bed." Drake looked around for a door.

"You gonna stay here?" Jimmy looked expectant. Drake glanced at Selene.

"No. Drake has his own place. There's not room here." She picked up a lamp.

"But you've got lots of space."

"I'll be back tomorrow." Drake's voice was rough, as if he'd been thinking of the possibility of spending the night with Selene.

She walked over to a low door cut into the wall. If you didn't know it was there, it was hardly noticeable. She pulled it open and walked inside. Setting the lamp down on a table near the single bed, she turned back a quilt her grandmother had made. The starburst pattern was one of her favorites and she was suddenly struck with longing for the steady strength and common sense of Granny Morgan.

She glanced around the small room, which she used to store supplies and hold completed special orders as well as an extra bedroom. It was simple but efficient.

Jimmy followed her inside, looked around, nodded his approval, and sat down on the bed. He dropped one boot to the floor, then started on the other.

"We'll get you a bath in the morning." She knew her grandmother would have had Jimmy bathed first thing, but she didn't have the heart to put him through any more.

Jimmy frowned and gave Drake, who had bent down to peer into the room, a disgusted look. "Women!"

Drake chuckled.

"I'll leave the lamp." Selene headed for the door.

"I'm no baby." Jimmy looked insulted.

Selene blew out the lamp, then stepped through the doorway. "Good night, Jimmy." She left the door ajar, then turned to Drake.

"I want to talk to you." Drake put a finger to his lips to indicate he didn't want Jimmy to hear, then pointed upstairs.

Chapter 8

Drake looked around Selene's bedroom and parlor combination. Near the door was a medallion-back sofa of mahogany and dark green silk. An oil painting of a sunset over the ocean in a massive gold frame hung above, and behind it were several peacock feathers. A book lay open on a small matching table in front of the sofa. And a bookcase filled with books was against the wall.

Selene stood near a poster bed with a green and mauve flowery print cover of damask. The single window at the back of the room was covered with matching print drapes. And a tall wardrobe and dresser of French influence dominated the other walls. A mauve silk scarf with fringe draped the top of the dresser and on that Selene had placed a comb, brush, and other feminine items.

"Nice." Drake hated to admit it, but the more he learned about Selene, the better he liked her. He'd wanted her from the first, but liking her was not something he'd expected. And didn't want.

"Thank you. It's not a lot of room but it's plenty for me. And behind that door is a small kitchen and bath." She glanced down at the floral carpet beneath her feet. Having Drake in her bedroom made her nervous and she wished she'd never brought him upstairs.

"Do you mind if I sit?"

She motioned toward the couch. When he sat down, she took the small rocker nearby. Sitting in her grandmother's chair, she was reminded of their many talks. She would sit or lie on the floor and listen to Granny Morgan as the rocker creaked. For a moment she felt overcome with longing for her grandmother, then pushed the feeling aside.

"What did you want to talk about?" She clasped her hands tightly together.

"I want to know what's going to happen to Jimmy, and I didn't want him to hear us talk about him."

"There's not going to be any argument. This doesn't concern you. I appreciate your help with Joe, but you'll be going home soon and I don't think Jimmy should get attached to you. He's been abandoned enough times already."

"Abandoned!" Drake stood up and paced. "I'd never do that to the boy."

Selene rocked. "You're not from New Orleans. You'll be going home. Jimmy will stay here. His friends will take care of him."

"Does that mean you?"

"I'll see that he's all right."

"What? Where? When?" Drake stopped in front of

110

her. "I told you he reminds me of my nephew. I couldn't save my own flesh and blood, but I can damn well make sure Jimmy's not left alone."

Selene stood. They were face to face. She could feel the heat of him. Suddenly distracted, she could only think of Drake's body, of his nearness, and of touching him. Furious with herself, she stepped away. "You're insulting. Do you think nobody can take care of themselves or the ones they care about without you?" She clenched her fists, glad of the anger, and glared at him. "For your information, everybody was doing just fine till you arrived in New Orleans."

He stalked her, but she stood her ground even when he stopped close, his eyes narrowed in anger.

"Do you call losing a couple dozen of your friends taking care of those you care about?"

She flinched and turned away.

"Look at me."

Walking toward the bed, she glanced back. "I don't have to look at you, I don't have to listen to you, and I sure don't need you. Now, get out."

Drake covered the distance between them in several long strides. He grabbed her arms and spun her to face him. "You've been asking for this since I first met you."

She tried to twist away, but he increased his grip.

"It's not that easy, Selene." He jerked her arms behind her back and anchored them there with one strong hand around her wrists. With the other hand, he shoved the pins from her hair until the auburn tresses fell in a wild mass down her back. He captured her head with his hand, tilted it back, and held

111

her steady for the slow descent of his face.

"Stop!" Furious, she struggled, but couldn't get away.

Dark brown eyes seared her. Hard, hot lips touched hers. She tried to toss her head, but he held her as he placed the painful kiss on her lips. Anger raced through her and she bit him, pleased to taste blood.

He raised his head to look into her eyes. "You want to play rough?"

"I want you to leave." She was breathing in short, shallow bursts and realized her breasts were touching him with each breath. She stopped breathing.

And he pulled her closer so that their bodies melded, their heat igniting. Her breasts pressed against his hard chest. She took a shaky breath and tried to clear her mind, tried to cool her emotions, and wished she'd never decided to make love potions for Drake Dalton. She, of all people, knew the strong emotions that could be released by love, whether out of frustrated passion or fear of being trapped in love. Dangerous.

"I'm not going to leave. Not yet." He lowered his head again. "Kiss me."

"Why?"

"You want to. Tell me you do."

Selene hesitated. She must not let herself be trapped, but she must remember her goal. Drake still wanted to close her business. If kissing would make him fall in love with her, then she must do it. But she wouldn't enjoy it.

She shut her eyes. But Drake didn't kiss her. Instead, he pulled her face gently against his chest and simply held her close for a long moment. She could feel the beat of his heart against her, the texture of his shirt beneath her cheek, and the scent of him filled her nostrils. Then he slowly began stroking her hair.

This was not what she'd bargained for. Anger. Pain. She could handle that. But gentleness, tenderness made her want to run and hide. Far, far away.

He freed her wrists, then lifted her hands to his neck. "Hold me."

Again, she felt a ripple of fear pulse through her. He wasn't playing fair. He was becoming more dangerous to her by the moment. But she did as he bid and stroked his thick hair before twining a hand around his neck while using the other to feel of a hard, broad shoulder. In that instant she felt desire stab her.

Shoving his fingers into her hair, he pulled back her head so he could once more look into her eyes. Obviously satisfied with what he saw there, he lowered his face until his lips touched hers. He kissed her lightly, then harder, finally nibbling her lower lip until she moved against him.

"So sweet." His words were a husky whisper against her mouth.

She didn't want to want him. She had to stay in control. But when he flicked his tongue against her lips, she moaned and clung to him harder.

"Let me really kiss you."

"I . . . you are."

It was all the space he needed to thrust his tongue into her mouth, binding them with a heat and sensuality that made her knees weak. Now she had no choice but to cling to his strength, for her own seemed to be seeping into him. Her body was on fire as his tongue plied deep into her mouth, teasing her, taunting her, testing her. And when it withdrew, she could only follow, tasting him, feeling him until she knew she would never be able to forget him.

And she realized she was succumbing to the love potion. In that moment, fear overcame passion, and she withdrew, physically and emotionally. As best she could.

"Selene?"

She buried her head against his shoulder and tried to retrieve her strength.

Stroking her back, he held her close. "I won't hurt you."

She shivered, and stepped back. But he only let her go to the length of his arms. "You *are* trying to hurt me and I can't let you." Her husky voice was not her own.

"I want you. You want me. Let's forget Love Potions."

"And in the morning?" She was having more and more trouble standing her ground.

"Don't think about that. Think about us."

"No." She jerked away and forced herself to walk across the room. "You'd better leave, Drake." She kept her back to him.

Silence followed her words. "Maybe you're right." His voice was rough. "I don't need any more hard-hearted women in my life."

She whirled around, furious, to see him walk from

the room. But she didn't go after him. Instead, she listened to him descend the stairs, walk across the store, then shut the door behind him. It would lock by itself so she had no need to leave her bedroom. But what she wanted to do was run after him and bring him back so she could bury herself in his warmth and passion.

But she wasn't going to be that stupid. She was going to get undressed and go to bed. In the morning it would all look better. And this would be a vague nightmare. That settled, she turned down her bed. And was surprised to see her hand tremble.

More upset than ever, she lay down and pulled the covers over herself fully clothed. Then she closed her eyes and willed sleep to wash away her problems.

Late the next morning, Selene stepped back from Jimmy and smiled in satisfaction. He was clean, his hair trimmed, and he was wearing a pair of new brown trousers and a blue and brown plaid shirt. Instead of looking pleased, however, he was frowning.

"Are you done fussin' over me?" Jimmy pulled Joe Junior out of his pocket and stroked him.

Selene smiled. "Yes."

"Then I'm goin' down and see 'bout Joe. And our missin' friends." He put Joe Junior back in his pocket.

"Be careful." She resisted the impulse to keep him safe with her, for he would never tolerate that type of control and she knew it.

115

The bell on the front door chimed as Joy Marie and Gustave entered the shop.

"Good morning." Joy Marie gave Selene a quick kiss on the cheek, then noticed Jimmy. "And who might this be?" She knelt down beside him.

Jimmy frowned.

"Jimmy, I'd like you to meet Joy Marie Dalton and Gustave Dominique." Selene stepped protectively closer to the young boy.

"Hello, Jimmy." Joy Marie's eyes filled with tears. "You remind me of my own son."

"Does he wanna go down on the docks with me?" Jimmy looked her over.

"No. He can't." Joy Marie took out a handkerchief, dabbed at her eyes, then smiled. "He had an accident and died."

"Same thing happened to my friend Joe."

"I'm sorry." Joy Marie looked at Selene in distress. "Is there anything I can do?"

Gustave stepped forward, gave Jimmy a long look, then focused on Selene. "We'd be happy to help out. His parents?"

Selene shook her head negatively. "Jimmy's going to stay with me awhile."

"You're so busy, Selene." Joy Marie beamed. "We have plenty of room for Jimmy. Don't we, Gustave?"

"If it'd make you happy, *ma chère*."

"Jimmy, would you like to stay with us awhile?" Joy Marie's voice was high and fast and sweet. "I'd buy you lots of toys. Special food. Whatever you wanted." She took Jimmy's hand.

He snatched it back. "I got business." He slipped

around them all, nodded to Selene at the front door, then shut the door behind him.

Joy Marie took several steps after Jimmy, then turned back to Selene. Her eyes were once more filled with tears. "My boy'd have been about his age."

"I understand. But Jimmy's lived all his life in New Orleans. He has friends here. He's happy."

"But Gustave and I—"

"You'll see Jimmy again." Gustave put an arm around Joy Marie. "He's staying here, isn't he, Selene?"

"Yes. You can come back and see him anytime." Selene tried to make Joy Marie's loss easier.

"I'll buy him a present." Joy Marie smiled. "What do you think he'd like?"

"Surprise him." Selene wished she could do more, but Joy Marie would have to deal with her loss on her own, just as Jimmy was doing.

"We came to invite you to lunch," Gustave said. "But perhaps we came at a bad time."

"I'm sorry, but we're getting ready for Joe's funeral and I need to be here for Jimmy."

"Of course." Joy Marie squeezed Selene's hand. "Another time then."

Selene smiled. "Make it soon." She walked them to the door.

"We still have not had our hypnotism discussion." Gustave let his gaze travel over Selene's face, then linger on her lips. "I will come for you soon about that."

Selene shut the door behind them, then leaned against it. If her life got any more complicated, she didn't know what she would do. And she didn't even want to think about Drake, his kisses, his body. No. She walked determinedly across the room and sat down at the worktable. It was time to make another love potion for Drake Dalton. She'd make it as strong as possible for she had to get this over with quickly or she'd never last. He was too potent for her to handle.

Just as she was finishing Drake's love potion, the bell on the front door chimed again. Rosa and Alfred walked in, arm and arm. Selene watched them, thinking how wonderful it must be to be in love like them. Then she remembered their heartache. No, love brought pain as well as pleasure. It was a dangerous emotion, best left alone.

"We saw Jimmy down on the docks." Rosa stopped by the worktable, watching Selene's quick hands.

"And we talked to Clay about Joe's funeral." Alfred checked his pocket watch. "We're going to give Joe a big send-off right through the streets of New Orleans."

"Thanks." Selene was struck as she always was by Alfred James's good looks. He was of medium height and build, and his curly black hair set off to perfection his dark blue eyes and finely chiseled features. Yes, he could pass as white, but if he married darker skin than his, it was doubtful his children would. And Rosa was darker than him.

"Has Drake Dalton been around?" Rosa looked at Selene.

"I haven't seen him today." Selene felt her face grow hot, then was furious with herself because nothing had really happened the night before.

"He was such a big help with Joe and Jimmy that I wondered if he'd decided to call off his attack on Love Potions." Rosa looked hopeful.

"I don't think he's changed his mind about our business." Selene finished Drake's love potion and put it in her pocket.

"Damn fool," Alfred said. "We're not going to stand by and let people be hurt."

"But what about those who've disappeared?" Selene stood up.

"You haven't heard anything?" Rosa picked a red ribbon and began twining it around her fingers.

"No." Selene leaned against the table.

"The police were no help about Joe's death." Alfred put his hands in his pockets and rocked back and forth on his heels. "But I can't blame them. Jimmy didn't know much himself."

"But I'm more worried than ever now." Selene felt frustrated.

"I know." Rosa squeezed her hand. "Look, you went to that seance and it didn't do any good. Have you thought of voodoo?"

"No." Selene hesitated, thinking. "But I guess it's another place to ask about Joe and the others."

"Everyone in our community is concerned about what's going on." Rosa glanced at Alfred. "Our religion is part African, part Catholic, part necessity, but it's here to help people. And particularly you because you're at the center of all this."

Selene nodded. "I'm willing to try anything."

"I'll ask about you attending a ceremony," Rosa said, smiling.

"I've got to be going." Alfred gave Rosa a look that

119

said he would rather be with her than anywhere else.

She took his hand and led him to the door. They exchanged a quick kiss, then Alfred left. Rosa walked back to Selene.

"Is he still going to New York?" Selene hated to say the words.

"He's found a job. He needs to leave by the end of the month."

"I suppose his family's happy."

"Yes. And no. They like me. And they'll miss him."

"I bet he'd stay if you asked him."

"He should go. It's right."

"You're talking with your head, not your heart."

"My parents were slaves. They never had the luxury of love and I'm not sure we do either."

"Rosa, no!" Selene took her hands and squeezed. "Your happiness should come first if you can possibly make it happen. That man loves you."

"I know. But he can never get paid what he's worth down here because of his background."

"He's got a good job. He's respected. He's trusted."

"But up North a clerk with his experience can get twice as much. If his color is right." Rosa shut her eyes. "And his children will be well educated."

"You could be his mistress, not his wife." Selene was shocked at her own words.

"I know. But it wouldn't be fair to any of us. No. Alfred's going North and that's that." Rosa turned abruptly away. "Let's talk about something else."

"Gustave and Joy Marie stopped by."

"What did they want?"

"Lunch. But he still wants to see me."

"I bet." Rosa frowned. "That man is hiding something."

"But it doesn't matter to us. We've got to concentrate on helping Jimmy and finding our friends."

Rosa smiled. "You're right, let's get some work done and we'll both feel better."

Chapter 9

Drake had a grip on Selene's arm that she thought might break it at any moment. But she'd given up trying to get free. He'd gotten the idea that as long as he had a hold on her, nothing could harm her. She'd also given up trying to convince him that just because he wasn't familiar with the customs of New Orleans everything around them was a danger.

Of course, there was danger. She felt a sudden lump in her throat. Jimmy had never come back that day he'd gone down to the docks. She'd looked. Drake had looked. All Jimmy's friends had searched. But Jimmy'd simply disappeared like the others. The police knew nothing. And Joe's funeral had been celebrated without his best friend.

But Selene would not believe Jimmy was dead.

So she had one more reason to attend the voodoo power ceremony. Outsiders were seldom invited. But the *gens de couleur*, people of color, were as concerned as she was about the disappearances. Something had to be done. And a special ceremony had been called. She'd been asked to attend and Drake had decided she wasn't going without him so he'd rented a horse and buggy and driven them north. And although she hated to admit it, she was glad he'd come along.

Still she gave him a dark look, then turned her attention back to Rosa and Alfred, who were leading them down a trail through the dense vegetation that surrounded Bayou St. John. She could hear the sound of drums growing louder as they neared the ceremony, and a sudden chill swept through her.

But she wasn't cold, for the night was warm and humid, making her skin damp and soft to the touch. Long filaments of moss hung from the trees and caught in her hair as she walked. As she pushed it aside, she inhaled night air filled with the sweet, heavy scent of flowers and trees in bloom. Crickets and frogs added their songs to the pounding of drums and she felt anticipation build in her. Maybe at last she would learn something.

Soon they reached a circular clearing where men and women of color danced to the beat of drums. Drake stopped and held her back as Rosa and Alfred walked forward to greet friends and acquaintances.

"You don't have to hold me so tight." Selene tried to shrug off his hand.

"I'm not letting you out of my sight." He eased his grip, sliding her hand through the crook of his arm.

She was uneasy. The seance had been one thing, but this was quite another. She felt as if she were being drawn farther and farther into unknown territory and she didn't like it. Still, she had to help her friends.

124

As she glanced around, she thought of voodoo's roots in New Orleans. *Gens de couleur* root doctors had been part of the slave communities since the beginning, drawing their knowledge from their native African religions even though they had been prohibited from practicing them. Eventually the Catholic religion had become part of the African religions through the work of such powerful priestesses as Marie LaVeau. Now Voodoo was an integral part of New Orleans and a power in its own right.

Watching the dancers, Selene realized the majority were women, mostly mulatto but a few white. They wore *tignons*, handkerchiefs tied around their heads in five- or seven-point forms which had once distinguished free women from slaves. Clothed in simple colorful dresses, they formed a moving mosaic as they whirled to the rhythm of the drums.

They swirled around a candle-lit *vever* made of red brick dust to the sound of hand-clapping, foot-stomping, humming, deep-throated male cries, and high-pitched female calls. Their language was Creole, a mixture of French and African.

Soon the rhythm invaded her and she swayed in time to the beat, but she noticed Drake stood rigidly beside her. Rosa and Alfred joined the dancers, looking beautiful and perfect together. Once more Selene hated the idea of their separation. But she put that from her mind as she watched the drummer. A tall, wiry man with grizzled hair, he played a special drum, cowhide stretched over a half-barrel. And he beat the rhythm with a jawbone.

Rosa motioned for Selene to join the dancers. Feeling the rhythm pounding through her, she turned to Drake. "Let's dance."

"No." He frowned. "We shouldn't be here in the first place."

"You went to the seance."

"I was looking for Joy Marie."

"But Drake, we've always danced in New Orleans. In the streets to celebrate, or at parties, or—"

"This isn't the same and you know it." He gripped her hand harder. "I'm not making a fool of myself and neither are you."

She looked back at Rosa and shook her head negatively. Rosa simply waved and continued to dance. Selene felt more left out than ever. She hadn't expected to learn much at the seance and she didn't expect to here, but there was always the chance she might.

As the drumming and dancing built to a crescendo, a tall mulatto woman walked out of the darkness of the trees into the moonlight and candlelight. A huge snake was coiled around her body and she stroked it as she moved. The dancers made way for her. She swayed to the sound of the drums, then her feet began to stamp out a rhythm of their own. The other dancers drew back, chanting, clapping their hands, swaying together as they watched her dance.

"She must be the high priestess." Selene's voice was low so only Drake would hear her.

"A what?"

"Voodoo Queen."

Drake nodded, then focused on the priestess.

As the Voodoo Queen danced with her snake, a mulatto man carried a mug, dripping with liquid, to her. Bowing, he handed it to her. She drank, returned the mug, and he backed away. Stroking the snake, she continued her dance, more wildly, more sensually, more powerfully than ever as the drums increased their pace. The other dancers picked up her rhythm as they caught the spirit, the energy of the priestess.

Suddenly the Voodoo Queen dropped to her knees, threw back her head, and cried out, a long, low keening sound. Then she turned toward Selene and pointed. "Quest woman." Her eyes rolled back in her head. "An island. To the south. Beautiful land, clear water. Seek there for your answers." She collapsed against the ground, her head on her knees. Silence followed. Finally she raised her face and once more looked at Selene. "Erzulie guide you."

The crowd cheered, then surrounded the priestess, lifting her high to carry her back into the woods.

Excited, Selene clutched Drake's arm. "An island! That's what I've been waiting for. Now I know where to look for the disappeared." Enthusiasm filled her voice.

"An island?" Drake sounded disgusted. "How many islands are off the coast? It's a ruse."

"How can you say that? You saw and heard her. The disappeared are on a beautiful island surrounded by clear water to the south."

"How far south? What island?" Drake turned to go. "This is a waste of time."

Selene stood her ground. "We've learned something. An island."

"It's a lot of mumbo jumbo like the seance." He hesitated. "You're going to have to get your answers the hard way and that's questioning every living soul down on the docks."

"That's what I've been doing." She tried to pull away from him. "This is the best news I've gotten and I'm not going to let you spoil it for me."

"Selene." Rosa walked up to them, carrying bowls and mugs. Alfred was right behind her.

"Have some congris." Rosa handed a steaming bowl of food with a spoon to each of them. "We have a lot to celebrate, don't we?"

Selene smiled. "Yes."

"What is this?" Drake looked suspiciously at his bowl.

"Hopping John." Rosa's voice warmed. "Black-eyed peas and rice cooked together with sugar. It's good. Try some."

"And here's tafia." Alfred handed them mugs. "It's alcohol made from molasses, white rum, and anisette." He drank from his own mug.

Drake looked skeptical, but took a drink of tafia. He nodded. "You're right. It's good."

Balancing the bowl on top of the mug, Selene took a bite of congris. She rolled her eyes at the delicious flavor. "Thanks, Rosa, this tastes wonderful."

Rosa moved closer. "The priestess spoke to you. What do you think?"

"It's a beginning." Selene felt excitement build in her again. "I hadn't thought about islands before. We can ask some of the captains what they've seen and heard."

"Yes. It's somewhere new to look." Rosa glanced around. "She may say more tonight, but don't feel you must stay. Enjoy the food, the dance, and maybe now we can find our friends." Rosa turned to go, then looked back. "With Erzulie, Our Mother of

128

Charity, to guide us, I know all will be well."

"I hope so," Selene said.

Rosa lifted her mug in a salute, took a drink, then she and Alfred walked back to join the other dancers.

Selene watched the dance thoughtfully, sipping tafia. "It's a strong drink."

"Think you can handle it?" Drake grinned.

Challenged, she took a large swallow, then coughed as the fiery liquid burned to her stomach.

Drake laughed, and drank more of his own.

"I haven't seen you try the congris."

Drake grimaced.

"It's good." She ate some more. "But it's not beef."

Finally, Drake took a bite. "Not bad. But I could sure use a hunk of steak."

As she ate and drank, watching the dancers, feeling the beat of the drums pulse through her body, she relaxed. Somehow everything would be all right. Drake had been given a message at the seance. She had received one here. Surely it would all add up to finding their friends.

When she realized she was feeling slightly tipsy, she handed her mug to Drake. He finished the drink, then set their bowls and mugs aside. There was a look in his eyes now that spoke of something as ancient as the dance before them, something that had begun the moment they had met, something that drew them together despite their differences. It was something Selene had fought and would continue to fight, but for now she simply wanted to relax and enjoy the night . . . and Drake.

He put an arm around her waist and led her away from the ceremony. As they walked back through the trees, his hand seemed to grow in heat and weight. At the carriage, he turned her toward him, his hand still possessively around her. When he lowered his head, she didn't resist, for the rhythm of the drums pounded in her veins, the tafia made her mellow, and the sensuality of the night wrapped them in splendor.

Selene moaned as his lips touched hers, the heat branding her, burning her, making her reach up and pull him toward her. She was begging for more, knew it, yet couldn't stop. When his tongue slid into her mouth, she welcomed it, tasting the sweetness of him, feeling the strength of him, wanting it all for her own. She felt his hands glid down her back to cup her hips, pulling her into him. With his hardness pressed against her, she wanted him all the more. And was no longer surprised. For she could still hear and feel the vibration of the drums, and in Drake's arms her passion was rising as all her reservations melted in the heat of the moment.

"Sweet Selene." Drake broke the kiss as he trailed kisses over her face, then returned to her lips as if starved. He toyed with her lower lip, nibbling, sucking, teasing, then thrust back inside.

She swayed against him, losing her strength to his power once more. Only this time she no longer cared that he was consuming her. When he pushed his fingers into her hair, releasing her fiery tresses, she shivered and wound her arms around him more tightly than ever.

Burning with need, she realized she couldn't get enough of him or feel him close enough, and deep in her center, heat ignited that burned and ached and demanded release.

"Drake, I'm on fire." Her voice was raspy and low.

But he heard and was encouraged to dare more. He clasped her breasts with his hands, feeling the tips harden against his palms. He groaned and sought to free them, but the tiny buttons of her bodice stopped him. Frustrated, he jerked and the dress parted, sending buttons flying. Once more he sought her breasts, but this time only the sheer fabric of her chemise stopped him.

He lifted her in his arms and set her on the carriage seat, then joined her. Pulling her against his chest, he pressed hot kisses to her face, then down her neck to her breasts. Finally, he pulled aside the fabric, saw the gleam of her pale flesh, tipped by rosy centers, then lowered his face to draw a nipple into his mouth while he warmed the other with his palm.

Selene writhed against him, moaned at the excitement he was creating inside her, and thrust her fingers into his thick hair to pull him closer. At the moment she cared nothing for rules or right or wrong. There was only the two of them drawn together by hunger and desire forever. And she wanted him deep within her, wanted him to ease the burning that was consuming her, and for a brief moment was surprised at the intensity of her own desires.

As Drake moved a hand up her leg under her skirt, she shivered but didn't consider stopping him. She wanted him to slake her desire at its core. When he placed his hot hand over the center of her passion, she shuddered with need and stroked his broad shoulders. Clothes might be between them, but clothing could be removed. When his hand sought the waist of her drawers, she was anxious to help him so she could feel his flesh against hers.

But suddenly she heard feminine laughter and a deep male voice nearby. Others were seeking solace in the darkness around the ceremony. And Selene turned cold.

They were not alone in the woods. The voodoo ceremony came rushing back to her mind. They were at Bayou St. John to help others and not to satisfy their own desires. There wasn't time for them. Besides, it was all the love potion anyway and she couldn't forget that.

Brought back to reality, she struggled against Drake, pushing at his shoulders.

"Stop, Selene." He groaned and wouldn't let her go. He tried to kiss her again, but she tossed her head. Frustrated, he pulled his hand from under her skirt and grasped her hair to hold her steady.

"No, Drake. Please stop." She shivered, knowing she really wanted him to go on forever.

But her words penetrated his passion. Cursing, he dropped his hands and took long breaths to steady himself. He looked everywhere but at her.

"I'm sorry." She knew how he felt, for her own heart still raced and her body felt cold and hot and foreign. Needing him, she still knew it was only the work of the love potions. Nothing they had felt was real.

"You're right. This isn't the time or place." Drake's voice was rough. Finally, he glanced at her.

His brown eyes were dark and haunted in the moonlight.

Selene knew what she had to do, but she didn't want to do it. She didn't know how much more she could take of their passion. But she pulled the new love potion from her pocket and concealed it in her hand. Then she leaned toward him. He was so distracted he didn't notice as she slipped it into his pocket. He thought she was simply looking for comfort.

He put an arm around her shoulders and held her against his chest. She could feel the hard thud of his heart and it matched her own. What would once have given her pleasure in knowing her love potions were working now only gave her pain. For she had been caught in her own trap. But she didn't love him. It was passion alone that bound her to him and that she could control . . . *would* control.

He placed a gentle kiss on top of her head and picked up the reins. "I'll take you home." He started them down the road. "I can't take much more of this, Selene."

She wanted to move away from him, but couldn't. It felt too good this one last time. "I understand."

"Do you?" He looked down at her face.

Smiling, she squeezed his hand. "I'm a lady."

"It's a hell of a thought." He paused and seemed to consider his words. "I hope your passion isn't a trick to get me to leave Love Potions alone because it won't work. I can buy what I need."

She froze, for a moment so furious she could hardly think straight. The insult cut deep. Then she realized he was right. The purpose of their passion was to get him to leave Love Potions alone. But it was his fault, not hers. He had started the game, and she would finish it. For he could not buy what the love potion promised. As long as the power of the potion persisted, he could only be satisfied with her. Selene Morgan.

But the game was not finished. It was her turn to make the next move. And she would not lose. Sliding away from him, she frowned. Suddenly cold and alone, she wrapped her arms around herself. "That's insulting. Take me straight home."

He gave her a long look, then his own armor went back into place. "That's where I'm headed."

Chapter 10

Selene read the invitation again, then crumpled and threw it on her desk. She didn't want to go. Gustave Dominique made her uneasy. But she still wanted to discuss hypnotism with him. Besides, she couldn't very well reject his luncheon invitation again, not if she were to continue her friendship with Joy Marie. She simply wished they weren't going alone and that the restaurant he had chosen wasn't so far away. Lake Pontchartrain formed the northern boundary of the city and she would have to endure a long, intimate ride with the Frenchman to get to the Blue Bayou Restaurant on its southern shore.

She glanced around Love Potions for reassurance. All seemed to be in order. Business was good. No regulars had come calling so perhaps Drake Dalton had stayed his hand for the moment. Unfortunately, inquiries from ship and boat captains had brought no new information, for the islands south of New Orleans hadn't had any sudden influx of people. Puzzled, she didn't know quite where to look next, but she had no intention of abandoning Jimmy and her other friends to whatever fate had befallen them.

"Selene, perhaps you shouldn't have accepted the invitation." Rosa looked concerned.

Glancing at the table in back where Rosa was working, Selene shrugged. "Too late now. He'll be here any moment."

"I wish you weren't going to Pontchartrain. We have several good restaurants nearby."

"He said in the note he wanted to do something special." Selene picked up a forest green shawl with pale green fringe and wrapped it around her shoulders. "Besides, I can take care of myself."

Rosa shook her head.

"Well, I can."

"Normally, but I don't think Dominique is normal."

Selene laughed. "Who is?"

"Nevertheless, I—"

The bell chimed on the front door as Gustave Dominique pushed it open and stepped inside. Seeing Selene, he smiled. "You look lovely, *chérie*." Walking over to her, he took her hands, held them out from her sides, and looked her over. "Stunning." Then he noticed Rosa. "And you are as lovely as usual, Mam'selle Rosa."

Rosa inclined her head, then went back to work.

Gustave focused on Selene again. "My carriage awaits you. It is a beautiful day. Shall we go?"

Selene picked up her reticule, a small green draw-string bag, which matched her dress of grenadine silk in forest green with turquoise faille for the apron effect that swept into the bustle. She was also wearing a small straw hat with green and turquoise plums and she'd tied it in a bow under her chin.

She was glad she'd taken so much care with her appearance, for Gustave was as dapper as usual in a light gray tweed suit with black braid edging the jacket. He also wore a black and white striped tie, a crisp white shirt, and a black bowler hat.

Giving Rosa a quick smile, she allowed the Frenchman to escort her outside. True to his word, a carriage awaited. Gustave had outdone himself by hiring one of the most opulent vehicles Selene had ever seen. The time and money he was spending on their simple lunch made her more concerned than ever. What did he want? For she had no doubt Gustave did little if anything unless it was for the good of himself.

But she voiced none of the thoughts that were swirling in her head. Instead, she allowed him to help her up into the carriage. When she was seated, he joined her in the back seat, and the driver snapped the whip over the horses. As they started down the street, Selene tried to relax against the tuffed leather seats, but with Gustave so close by, she couldn't.

"A beautiful day for a beautiful lady." Gustave slid closer to her.

"Thank you." She tensed and distracted herself by looking at the city, aware that under the gilt and glamour nestled the dark side of New Orleans. And it was the dark side that had consumed her thoughts of late.

"No thanks needed. If I can make you happy, then

I am a contented man."

She turned to him, surprised at his words. If she didn't know better, she'd have thought he was joking. But his dark eyes were serious. And she thought of Drake in comparison. He'd be making no glib comments. Instead, he'd be insulting her . . . or grabbing her. Her heart suddenly beat faster. Drake Dalton would not be able to resist her last love potion. But when he succumbed, how would she resist?

"Your thoughts seem far away, *ma chère*. I hope I have not offended you."

Rewarding his persistence with a smile, she decided to lie. "I'm simply enjoying the day. I rarely drive through New Orleans so I'm delighted with the view."

"I thought the ride would do you good since you worked so hard to save Joe and you have worried so about Jimmy. If I can lift your spirits, even slightly, I am pleased."

"Thank you." She knew before the afternoon was over she would be very tired of thanking him. But it was what he wanted to hear, for he grinned with pleasure. And once more she was surprised by his crooked and stained teeth. Not that it mattered so much to her, but that it was in such sharp contrast to the rest of him.

"Mr. Dominique, I will be quite happy with a quick lunch in the city if—"

"I will not hear of it. Besides, I am thinking of my own pleasure, too. And before we go any farther, I must insist you call me Gustave. Especially since we

138

are to be friends."

She hesitated, knowing she had little intention of ever being his friend. But he had put her in an awkward position. "Thank you, Gustave." And she grimaced inside at having to thank him again. "You must call me Selene."

"A lovely name."

"Tha—I was named after my grandmother."

"Delightful. And you have always lived in New Orleans?"

"Granny Morgan raised me where I live now. I do what I've always done. You'd probably think my life has been rather dull."

"You could never be described as dull."

She watched as they left the Vieux Carré and headed north on Bernard Avenue. "But you've lived the more interesting life. After all, you've come all the way from France. So why don't we talk about you."

"You are much too modest, Selene." However, he appeared pleased. "But you might be interested to know I am descended from a noble French family. Unfortunately, I have yet to inherit the title." He smiled. "But that is only a matter of time."

"So you must feel at home in New Orleans." She adjusted the bow under her chin to keep from fidgeting.

"Yes, indeed. But I will soon be leaving for a place also French."

Surprised, Selene turned to stare at him. "Where?"

"Martinique."

"An island?" Her heart beat fast.

"Yes. Martinique is part of the French West Indies. It is a beautiful land surrounded by the clear, turquoise waters of the Caribbean."

"What are you going to do there?" Her mind was racing as fast as her heart. If the Voodoo Queen had been right, then Gustave might have taken Jimmy and the others to Martinique. But why?

"I am developing a sugar cane plantation. My mansion is almost complete and there I will live the life of royalty." His dark eyes took on a fanatical expression.

"How nice." Selene's voice was faint. "And do you need a lot of workers?"

"*Beaucoup.*" He chuckled. "But there is not much other work on the island so I can obtain the help I need."

"That's good." Her mind raced. What if he weren't telling the truth? What if he needed workers? Then she scoffed at herself. What point could there be in kidnapping and transporting two dozen people to Martinique? So few hardly seemed worth the expense and trouble. And if he did need workers, why would Jimmy have disappeared? No, she wasn't any closer to the truth than before.

"Selene, Joy Marie is going with me." He turned to concentrate on her.

"What?" Again, she was surprised.

"She is devoted to me and I would not want to disappoint her by leaving her behind." He hesitated, then took Selene's hand. "But my affections are elsewhere."

Concentrating on slowing her racing heart, she didn't look into his eyes. She could see Lake Pont-

140

chartrain in the distance and wished desperately to be there. And more than anything she wanted her hand back. She tugged lightly.

He gripped her fingers. "Not so quickly, my shy one. I want you to visit me, as well as Joy Marie, on Martinique. She is quite fond of you and you could enjoy yourself. You will be surrounded by beauty. You will dine on the best of food. Your clothing will be the finest in the world." He leaned closer. "Say yes."

"You're hurting my hand."

Easing his grip, he did not release her fingers. "I am so sorry, but you must understand your power over me. I am helpless where you are concerned. And maddened by you."

This time, she did look at him. His eyes were haunted with the need to possess. She shivered and jerked her hand away. "Joy Marie is my friend. I will not hear another word of this."

"Do not think badly of me. You have captured my heart. But I will speak of it no more for now. Simply remember my request. I can make you very happy on Martinique."

"No more! If I did visit, it would only be to see Joy Marie." She wanted to jump out of the carriage and run from him, but she made herself sit still.

"Your presence in my home would be enough."

She looked down the road and felt relief at the sight of Pontchartrain. Soon she could get away from him. But first she had to reassure him so he wouldn't pressure her or try to get even closer. "We can be friends and colleagues, if you like. I'd enjoy learning more of hypnotism."

141

"We will discuss it over lunch, *ma chère*. You know I can deny you nothing."

Once seated at the Blue Bayou, Selene could easily believe Gustave's words, for nothing was denied either of them. They sat on a covered balcony overlooking an inlet of Lake Pontchartrain. Seagulls swooped overhead and sparrows sang in nearby trees. Boats plied the waters of the huge lake as clouds rolled in from the south.

At the table, Selene noted the crisp white tablecloth and fine silver, china, and crystal. In the center was an arrangement of fresh gardenias and their sweet scent filled the air. Behind them, a string quartet played music that Selene had decided could only have been composed in France, for it was little like the lively music she heard in the French Quarter.

Across from her, Gustave smiled pleasantly as he enjoyed the scene he had set. And perhaps she would have enjoyed it, too, if it had been less like a stage setting and more like real life. She wished she were back in the Vieux Carré despite her beautiful surroundings.

Gustave lifted his glass of champagne and saluted her. She raised her glass. He clinked them together. And she sipped, staying very much aware of the fact that she must not lost control.

As the next course was set in front of her, she realized the meal he had ordered could last all afternoon. They had already eaten escargots, roast pheasant, and caneton à l'orange.. The food was delicious. And she thought of Drake. He could do justice to all the food, but she never could. She suddenly realized that if he were there, she would be enjoying the meal, the setting, everything.

Immediately she squeezed him from her mind. It was the love potion talking, nothing more. Leaning forward, she smiled. "How did you become a hypnotist, Gustave?"

"My favorite subject. I am a man not constrained by the past or by society or by gossip. I believe humanity moves forward, sometimes slowly, sometimes by leaps. Hypnotism is a leap. But, of course, not everyone believes as I do."

"But don't you think we build on the past?"

"Yes. But we must not let it hold us back." He drank champagne. "We must never let ourselves be bound by the morals or beliefs of the masses. We are not sheep to be led by superstition but by scientific discovery."

"Yet—"

"Hear me out, *chérie*. Hypnotism is built on the work of Mesmer, but it discards his superstitious questions. Hypnotism is scientific, proved by years of research. I studied at the School of Paris under Charcot. He is the best. But I also studied reports from Bordeaux, Nancy, and Toulon."

"That's impressive."

"Thank you. I worked hard, but I did not want to spend my life doing research. I wanted to spread the word that hypnotism has many benefits."

"What about the seances?"

"Some of the studies show that clairvoyance can be induced in some people through hypnotism." He shrugged. "I have used it in seance work as an experiment, but I am still a skeptic."

"Then the seance was a hoax?"

Again he shrugged, and smiled. "It works by helping people. Beyond that I do not make promises."

Selene took a bite of the next dish and was pleasantly surprised by a sweet-tart sauce over flaky fish. Gustave's explanation convinced her that his seances had been staged just as much as their lunch, and now she doubted his hypnotism ability as well. He might simply be a very clever con man with nothing to teach her or anyone else.

Gustave was turning out to be the swindler, and he was the one Drake should be after. Not her. Suddenly she felt greater concern for Joy Marie. What hold did the Frenchman have over Drake's sister-in-law? Could love have affected her so quickly, so strongly? Selene's mind turned to how Drake made her behave. Yes, perhaps it was simply love for Joy Marie, but with the wrong person.

She didn't feel much more like eating, for she wanted to see Joy Marie and try to talk her out of going to Martinique. But what business was it of hers? No, she couldn't interfere with Joy Marie's life. Drake was doing well enough at that and she knew it was wrong.

Frustrated, she took a sip of champagne.

Gustave pulled out his crystal watch fob and swung it back and forth. Light played through the facets, drawing Selene's attention to the beautiful crystal.

"It's pretty, isn't it?" Gustave's voice was soft and low.

"Yes." She was fascinated.

"When we are alone, I will teach you all about hypnotism." He continued to swing the crystal.

"I'd like that." Perhaps he knew more than she'd realized. Had she discounted him too soon?

"Would you be my student as well as subject?" His dark eyes glittered. "On Martinique we could have plenty of time alone to study."

"Well, I—"

Suddenly there was a loud commotion behind them. The spell broken, Selene looked around and was shocked to see Drake barging past the string quartet like a rampaging bull. She was so glad to see him and so angry at the same time that she stood up.

Gustave jumped to his feet, his face red with anger.

"So this is where I find you." Drake grabbed Selene's arm and jerked her to his side. He shook her slightly, set her behind him, and turned on Gustave.

The Frenchman took a step backward. "You are interrupting our lunch."

"I'm interrupting more than that." Drake raised clenched fists. "I've had a gut full of you on my territory."

"Your territory?" Selene stepped forward, but Drake pushed her back.

"If you harm the lady, I will be forced to retaliate." Gustave stood his ground.

"Mister, it's not the lady I'm going to hurt. If you know what's good for you, you'll get out of town, out of the country, and stay there."

"You cannot scare me. Better men have tried."

Drake stepped forward, towering over Gustave.

"Maybe better men, but not madder men. Now, I'm warning you one last time. You leave Selene and Joy Marie alone."

Gustave flicked an imaginary piece of lint from his sleeve. "Contrary to your obviously crude upbringing, women are not toys, nor can they be bought and sold. And they certainly do not exist to live in *your* territory."

Drake raised a fist.

Selene grabbed his arm and held on. "Don't hit him, Drake. You'll kill him."

"If all you've got are words to back you up, Dominique, you're in trouble 'cause I can flatten you right now."

"I am unafraid. Power. That is what backs me up. And I am not talking about brute strength." Gustave shrugged, glancing over Drake's shoulder. "I think it is time for you to leave."

Selene looked behind her. Two massive men, obviously employed by the restaurant, were bearing down on them. She tugged at Drake's sleeve. "You'd better go."

Drake glanced around, walked over to the men, and talked to them quietly. They left. Then he turned back to Gustave.

The Frenchman was pale with shock.

"Like I said." Drake smiled, and there was no mirth in the movement of his lips. "Get off my territory." He turned and began dragging Selene with him.

"Let go of me." She was not going to be carted around like a sack of flour, nor was she going to be used as a pawn between two men.

"Be quiet."

She dug in her heels. "I'm going to scream for help."

"You're going to shut up." He picked her up, gave Gustave a warning look, and strode from the balcony with Selene struggling in his arms.

Chapter 11

"I can't believe you carried me out of that restaurant." Selene fumed, although she was beginning to see the funny side of it. Gustave's face had been livid and it was a treat to see. But she was still mad about Drake's high-handed actions.

"You went alone with him. Anything could have happened." Drake drove the carriage along Lakeshore Drive, following the curve of the lake eastward.

"I was being treated to a delicious lunch."

"It looked like seduction to me."

"You *would* think that."

"If I hadn't saved you, you'd probably be in his bed right now."

"No!" Anger rushed through her. "You didn't save me. You ruined my lunch. And made me look like a fool. Stop this carriage at once."

He ignored her.

"I mean it, Drake. I'm not riding another moment with you. First, I let you kidnap me, but I'm not going to let you insult me." She hit his shoulder.

"Now I want out."

"You didn't *let* me do anything."

"I'm going to jump."

He put a hand on her arm and squeezed. "You're going nowhere till we talk this out."

She hated to admit his strength was greater than hers, but it was. He'd taken her from the restaurant because he could and now he kept her in the carriage because he could. And she wasn't a weak woman. How did she deal with him? But more importantly, why had he come for her?

Suddenly she saw the situation in a different light. Drake was furious. Why? Why should he care if she dined with Gustave? And then she understood. He was jealous. Why? The answer to that was easy. Love potions. Jealousy and anger came with love and passion. The fury seeped out of her. She'd brought this on herself, especially by making that last potent potion. It was what she wanted and now she had to deal with it.

"We're going to stop down here by the lake, alone, and you can explain what the hell you were doing with him." Drake's voice was tense.

"I don't have to explain myself to you." Drake had forced her to use the love potions on him so she owed him nothing, and certainly not an explanation. She crossed her arms under her breasts. "We're nothing to each other."

Drake growled, pulled the horse off the road, and sat looking out over the dark waters of the lake. "We've been through too much for you to say that." He hesitated, but didn't look at her. "The fact is I want you."

She held her breath. Was he going to make a declaration? Could she catch him now? Inhaling sharply, she waited, not knowing what to expect.

"From the way you've been acting, I thought maybe you'd come to . . . care. For me."

Now she did look at him. His jaw was set. A frown pulled his brows together. And his fists were clenched. She inhaled sharply. "I can see how happy that idea makes you."

He glared at her, then back at the lake. "You can't be trusted. For all I know, you're in league with that swindler Dominique."

"Is everybody in the world a cheat except you, Drake?"

"No. But you've got to stop hurting innocent people."

"Have you seen me hurt anybody?"

He didn't answer.

"Tell me." She didn't touch him, but she wanted to pull him to face her. "No answer? That's because you have no proof and you're too stubborn to admit you're wrong."

Finally, he turned to her, his gaze searching her face. "I want to believe you." A look of pain crossed his features. "But now I find you out here with Gustave. What plots were you hatching? And what about Joy Marie?"

"I don't owe you anything, especially since you insult me at every turn." She bit her lower lip. "What I do is none of your business."

"I've made it my business."

Frustrated, she stood up. "You can't."

As she started to step down, he followed, jumping

151

down and putting his arms around her waist. As he lowered her to the ground, he let her body slide down the length of his. Heat leaped between them.

"I went crazy when I found out you'd gone off alone with Dominique." His breath was warm on her face.

"Does this mean *you* care?" She was playing a double game, knew it, but couldn't stop. She wanted a confession from him, an apology, everything. But more than that, she wanted his kisses. She was caught in her own trap, but she didn't love him. Never that.

He gently pushed fine hairs back from her forehead. He toyed with the bow under her chin. "You've never dressed this way for me."

Impatient, she stepped away and walked toward the lake. She heard him follow.

"Are you in love with Gustave Dominique? Like Joy Marie?"

She took off her hat and let it dangle from her hand by its ribbons. The wind off the lake felt cool against her face. She didn't want to hurt Drake. But she couldn't let him hurt her either.

"Answer me!" He swung her around to face him.

A tenderness invaded her at the frustrated passion carved into his face. She touched his lips, his nose, stroked his eyebrows. He tossed his head. And she smiled. "No."

He stilled. "You're sure?"

"Yes."

Then he lifted her and twirled her around before pulling her to him and wrapping his arms around her body to hold her close. "Tell me you care for me, Selene. Your kisses have told me so, but I need to hear

152

it from your lips."

"No. I won't tell you that."

He set her away from him, a frown marring his face. "Why not?"

"You've sworn to destroy my business. Until that's settled, we're enemies."

"What if I changed my mind?"

"You'll need proof for that."

"Yes, but what if *you* changed my mind?"

"Do you mean—"

"I want to take you back to Texas."

Shocked, she simply stared at him.

"If you're away from your business, then—"

"No." She turned toward the carriage. "Besides, I won't be any man's mistress."

"Selene, I didn't—"

"I don't want to hear it." She'd won enough. She couldn't take any more. "What you should be hearing right now is that Gustave is moving to Martinique and taking Joy Marie with him."

"What!" Drake spun her around. "Say that again."

"That's what he told me in the restaurant."

Drake paced down the beach, then turned back. "And Joy Marie's going with him?"

"That's what he said." She walked over to him. "And, Drake, Martinique's French. Joy Marie won't be on American soil anymore."

"Much less Texas." He faced the lake. "What do you think?"

"If Joy Marie's happy, then she should be all right." What Selene couldn't say was that Gustave had just made a declaration of love to her. That couldn't bode well for Joy Marie's future happiness and she felt to blame. "And if she isn't happy, she can always leave."

"But will she?"

"You need to make her feel comfortable about returning to Texas if she needs to."

Drake nodded. "I should see her. Can you set up another meeting?"

"Yes, but I don't know if she'll come."

"Don't tell her about me."

"I hate to do that again."

"Selene, I'm worried about her." Drake turned haunted eyes on her.

"All right."

"Did Dominique say why he's going to Martinique?"

"He's building a sugar cane plantation and a mansion."

Drake whistled. "Where'd he get the money?"

"I don't know. He says he's an aristocrat so—"

"The French nobility were killed or left penniless." Drake paced again. "If slavery hadn't been outlawed, I'd think he was stealing people and selling them."

"You're still determined he's involved with the disappearances."

"He's my best bet. But now I don't know." He took her hand. "Have you heard anything about Jimmy?"

"No. I thought maybe I'd learn something from Gustave, but—"

"Is that why you had lunch with him?"

She nodded. "But I wanted to talk with him about hypnotism. To tell you the truth, I think he may be a

154

fraud all the way around."

"And Joy Marie loves him."

"She thinks she does."

"It amounts to the same thing."

"I'm worried about her, Drake. And Jimmy. But there doesn't seem to be much I can do."

He raised her hand to his mouth and gently kissed the palm. Shivers ran through her. Then he kissed the tip of each finger.

"We'll find them somehow." He put an arm around her shoulders and led her back to the carriage.

Late that afternoon, Selene waited for Joy Marie in the Place d'Armes. The square had been established in the early 1700s as a drill field, but it had become a beautiful park of ancient trees, flowering shrubs, walkways, and benches. Enclosed with a wrought iron fence, the square offered solace from the busy life of the Vieux Carré. Since it was just down the street from Love Potions, Selene frequently visited it.

However, at the moment she was impatient. She had sent a message to Joy Marie, not knowing if Gustave had returned or if he had finished his lunch alone. She hoped he had stayed at the lake so Joy Marie would be free to join her.

As she waited, she glanced around and was once more impressed with the beauty of the Cathedral of St. Louis. Its three spires reached high into the sky, dominating the area around the square. Equally beautiful inside, magnificent paintings adorned its ceiling and nave.

But even thoughts of the church couldn't distract

her long. She looked around for Drake, knowing he would be along soon. She wanted to speak with Joy Marie before he arrived, but time was running out. She only hoped she was doing the right thing by bringing them together again, but she wanted Joy Marie to feel she had a home if Martinique didn't turn out right. And she didn't know how it could.

Selene nodded and smiled as people passed her, then she saw a carriage pull up and stop. Joy Marie waved to her as the driver stepped down to help her from the coach. Selene remembered the tall, blond giant with one arm from Gustave's home, and she was amazed to see how gently, actually tenderly, he helped Joy Marie down. Then her attention was caught by Joy Marie's beautiful and expensive gown of pale blue silk with a matching hat of lace, bows, and feathers.

Joy Marie lifted a hand toward the driver. "I won't be long, Jon."

He bowed. "I'll circle the area till you are ready."

Turning, Joy Marie rushed to Selene.

"I'm so glad to see you." Selene held out her hands.

Clasping them, Joy Marie gave her a quick kiss on the cheek, then stepped into the square. "Thanks for inviting me. I didn't know if I'd have time to come, but I wanted to say good-bye and this seemed the perfect moment."

"Good-bye?" Selene stood still, stunned.

"Yes." Joy Marie held out her arms, then twirled around. "How do you like my new dress?"

"It's beautiful. But—"

"Come, let's sit down and chat a moment."

While she collected her thoughts, Selene led them

to a stone bench nestled in front of flowering bushes and under a huge spreading oak tree. Checking to make sure she had a good view of the entrance, she turned her attention back to Joy Marie as they sat down. "You're saying good-bye?"

"I thought Gustave might have told you by now."

Selene flushed. She didn't know if Joy Marie knew about their lunch or not. Doubting it, she decided not to mention the event. "What do you mean?"

"I'm going with Gustave to Martinique."

"When?"

"Tomorrow."

"What!" Selene stood up in agitation, then sat back down, taking Joy Marie's hands in hers. "So soon? I don't know what to say."

"Be happy for me, Selene. Gustave has bought me a new wardrobe. I'm helping my maid to pack now. The ship sails at dawn."

"Weren't you going to say good-bye?"

"Yes. But I was waiting till the last moment. First, I've been so busy preparing for the trip, the new way of life, and all. Second, I didn't want Drake to know very far ahead of time. You know he would try to stop me."

"He only wants your happiness."

"I *am* happy. Gustave's taking me to his sugar cane plantation. I'm going to be mistress of his mansion. It will be a wonderful life, but mostly because I'll be with the man I love."

Selene remained quiet.

"Gustave thinks we must live like royalty to be happy, but it doesn't matter to me. I'd be happy anywhere with him, and if he wants me to be a grand lady, perhaps with a French title, then that is what I'll do. But mainly, I want to be with him." She squeezed Selene's hands. "Am I wrong?"

"No, of course you're not wrong to want to be happy, to be with the man you love. You've been through so much, lost so much, you deserve happiness. But—"

"I know what you're going to say. I'm not married. Maybe it is a sin. But Gustave doesn't want to marry until he receives his title. That way he would be a count, or whatever, when I married him."

Selene cleared her throat. "What about children?"

Joy Marie blushed. "Nothing would make me happier than to have another child. Gustave's son or daughter. And if that happens, then of course we will be married." She dropped Selene's hand and stood up to pace. Finally, she stopped. "Please don't think badly of me for being . . . well, I suppose I'm Gustave's mistress."

Selene stood up and hugged Joy Marie. "I don't think badly of you at all. I want you to be happy. That's what matters."

"Thank you. But I'm afraid Drake won't see it my way."

Selene glanced toward the entrance. Fortunately, there was no sign of Drake yet. "I think Drake will understand. In fact, he wants to talk to you."

"Oh no! You didn't invite him again."

Selene nodded.

Joy Marie rolled her eyes, then sat down. "Well, I suppose now is as good a time as any to tell him. Frankly, I'm glad you're here to protect me. He values your opinion."

"I don't know about that." Selene joined her friend on the bench again.

Joy Marie chuckled. "But not more than he values your body."

"That's blunt."

"It comes from living a wicked life, I suppose."

Selene laughed. "There's nothing wicked about you, Joy Marie. And as long as you're happy, it's all right."

"Yes." She turned intent blue eyes on Selene. "Drake is a good man. He's gentle and kind. Normally. He could use a woman like you. And I know he wants you."

Shaking her head, Selene frowned. "Drake and I are destined to part ways soon. But I'm glad he brought us together and I want you to write. I'll miss you. It seems like so many people are leaving lately."

"Jimmy. Have you learned anything?"

"No. But I won't stop trying to find him."

"Good. He reminded me so much of my son. But that's done with now." She leaned closer. "Selene, will you come visit me? There'll be plenty of room and I know Gustave would like to discuss hypnotism with you. We'd have fun. Please say yes."

"I don't know. There's the business."

"Rosa can handle it."

"And I've got to find Jimmy and the others."

"Perhaps you could learn something in the islands."

Selene smiled. "I'd like to visit you, but—"

"Wonderful. Come anytime. I'll be there."

"Thanks." She hesitated, glad Joy Marie wouldn't think she was completely abandoned by her friends.

"Are you going to continue conducting seances?"

"No. I guess not. Gustave did them mostly for money. And to help people, of course."

"But if you have a gift for—"

"I did it for Gustave. He controlled everything. I do hope I helped some people in trouble though."

"I'm sure you did." Selene was more convinced than ever of Gustave's duplicity. But maybe Joy Marie had helped ease the mind of a few troubled people along the way.

"I won't mind leaving the seances behind, Selene. They were fun, but I'll have plenty to do in Martinique."

"Yet—" A stone came tumbling down the path and hit Selene's boot. She glanced up.

"Good afternoon, ladies." Drake smiled.

Joy Marie stiffened.

"Don't leave." Drake stepped closer. "Joy Marie, I want you to know you'll always be welcome at Dalton Ranch."

Joy Marie's eyes misted. "Thank you. I'm sorry we've been at cross-purposes. But I'm very happy. I have a wonderful new life. Gustave and I set sail tomorrow at dawn for Martinique."

Drake's face paled, but he controlled his temper. "Tomorrow?" His voice was hollow.

"Yes. It's been rather sudden for me and I've been so busy shopping and packing that I didn't have time to tell you. Besides—"

"You were afraid I'd make trouble."

Joy Marie nodded.

"No," Drake said. "You're a grown woman. I want you to be happy. If Gustave makes you happy, then that's good. But there'll always be a place for you at the ranch. You're my sister, no matter what.''

Joy Marie stood up, tears misting her eyes. ''Thanks.'' She hugged Drake, then stepped away. ''Good-bye.'' Giving them each a fond look, she turned and hurried down the path.

Drake started after her, but Selene took his hand and pulled him down to the bench. Together, they watched Joy Marie leave the square.

''There's nothing you can do short of kidnapping her and taking her back to Texas.'' Selene felt more worried than ever.

''I'd like to do that.''

''But you can't.''

''No.'' He dug the toe of his boot in the dirt. ''I need to get back to the ranch. I've been gone too long already.'' He looked at her. ''Are you coming with me?''

''No.'' Surprisingly, it wasn't the answer she wanted to give.

He stood up. ''Then I'll have to stick around awhile longer.''

She glanced up at him in surprise.

''I'm not done yet, Selene Morgan. Not by a long shot.'' He turned and walked away.

Chapter 12

"And you'll see Drake Dalton gets this note tomorrow but not before noon?" Selene's voice was firm.

"Yes."

"Promise he won't get the message till the afternoon."

"I promise."

"All right." Selene pushed the note, carefully sealed in an envelope, and a hefty tip to the day clerk at the River Oaks Hotel.

"Room 202." The clerk pocketed the money and the letter.

"I don't need—"

"You've forgotten the key, my dear?" Drake said from behind Selene.

She gasped and whirled around.

Drake grinned, obviously well pleased with himself. He dangled his room key in front of her face, then glanced at the clerk. "I'll take care of my . . . cousin."

"Very good, sir."

Grasping Selene's hand, Drake slipped it through the crook of his arm and led her toward the stairs.

"But—"

"You couldn't stay away and decided to surprise me?" Drake's voice was low and intimate.

"No, I—"

"No need to explain, Selene. You know I want you. I'm glad you finally gave in to reason."

"I just happened by and had friends staying here and so—"

"Don't bother trying to lie. It won't work. We both know what we want, don't we?" He squeezed her elbow as he guided her up the stairs.

Selene's mind was racing wildly but not getting anywhere. She couldn't believe she'd been caught. Sure she could slip in and out without Drake seeing her, she was furious with herself for not having planned better. The last thing she wanted him to know was the truth, for she didn't think he'd react well.

"You've been avoiding me for a week. Were you trying to make up your mind about us?"

"I think I'd better leave."

"You just got here." He stopped in front of Room 202, inserted the key, and unlocked the door, all the while keeping a firm grip on Selene. "I'm not taking no for an answer. Not this time."

He pushed her into the room, shut the door, and locked it. Then he turned to her and grinned, a feral movement of his lips.

"Drake, there's been a misunderstanding."

"Cold feet already?"

"No. I just—"

"If you didn't come here to see me, why were you down in the lobby?" He frowned. "Another man?"

"No. That is, I . . . good question." She glanced around the room. It was comfortably furnished, but not palatial. Just the sort of place Drake would pick, but not Gustave Dominique. Damn the Frenchman! He'd gotten her into this mess, but she'd have to get herself out.

"That's not funny, Selene. You know I'm jealous." He walked to her side, but didn't touch her. "So, if you aren't here for me, why are you here?"

She walked to the window, pulled back the sheer white drape to look at the Mississippi. There was something reassuring about the wide, muddy river. But it didn't give her an answer for Drake. "Perhaps I'm nervous."

"I'll fix that." He started across the room.

She held up a hand. "Do you have something to drink?"

"Whiskey."

"That'll do."

"You don't have to get drunk to do this, do you?"

"No. I thought it might help calm my nerves."

He didn't reply, but headed for the whiskey and glasses.

Plucking at the white fabric of the drape, she tried to think of some rational reason for being in Drake's hotel other than the truth. Still nothing would come to mind.

She didn't want Drake to know she was going to Martinique. Not now. Tomorrow would be soon enough. The note would explain everything. How she had duped him into wanting, and loving, her with the love potions and exactly where he could find the potions in his clothing. How he now had nothing to hurt her business with anymore. How she was going to Martinique for a visit with Joy Marie and Gustave. Any one of those things was enough to drive him into a white hot rage, but all three could make him murderous.

She wanted to be far away when his anger hit. When he'd cooled down, he'd go home to Texas and that would be that. She'd won, but she didn't want him to know it yet. She had to keep his trust till tomorrow at dawn.

When he brought the whiskey to her, she turned around and smiled, a slow, seductive movement of her lips.

He tossed the bottle and glasses on the bed. "I don't think you're going to need that after all."

She shivered when he put a hand on her shoulder, but she remained still, knowing so many depended on her. There had been no new disappearances since Gustave had left and she very much feared she would find her friends, and Jimmy, on Martinique. If they were still alive, she had to find a way to rescue them and to do that she couldn't afford to have Drake go with her. Gustave would let her in his mansion, but if Drake were with her, she'd never get close. Or worse, Drake would join the other disappeared. No, for all their sakes, Drake had to think he'd been abandoned by Joy Marie and Selene, too. Then he'd go home safely to Texas.

When he thrust his hand into her hair, sending the pins flying, and turned her so he could look into her eyes, she bit her lower lip. If she'd known it was going to be so difficult to give him up, she'd never have started the game. Never. But with his mouth on hers and his body pressed close, she forgot everything except the madness of the moment.

"Selene." He left her lips to press soft kisses across her face. Stroking her hair, he thrust his fingers into it, then pulled her close.

She could feel the pounding of his heart, smell his scent, and as his mouth came down on hers again, she moaned low in her throat. When he thrust between her lips, she drew him closer, letting her hands glide over the strong muscles of his shoulders, then delve into his thick hair. Flooded with sensations, she began to lose herself in him. And didn't care.

"You don't know how badly I want you." He paused and looked at her, his eyes dark with need.

"I want you, too, but—"

"Shhhh." He began unbuttoning her bodice. "There's no need for words. We're alone now, together."

She shivered beneath his touch, noticing how gently, how deftly he dealt with her clothes. But then he had done it before with women, probably many women. A coldness invaded her, but she pushed it aside. Could she expect anything less from a virile man like Drake Dalton?

When he pulled open her bodice, he inhaled sharply. "Beautiful." He cupped her breasts, covered only by the sheer cotton of her chemise, and lowered his lips to them.

At the heat of his mouth, she moaned and clutched

167

him around his lean waist, wanting so much more of him. When he stripped the fabric aside and took a nipple in his mouth to suck, she trembled all over. Suddenly weak, she knew she would feel strong again only with him slaking the burning that was filling her.

Suddenly he lifted her in his arms and carried her to the bed. Placing her supine, he quickly unbuttoned his shirt and flung it aside. He was well muscled and tanned, obviously from working hard in the sun. And golden blond hair covered his chest.

When he joined her, she ran her hands through his exposed chest hair, excited by seeing so much of him. He was even more handosme than she could have imagined and now she wanted to see all of him. But more than that, she wanted to feel his hot, hard body naked against her. Surprised at her desire, she blamed her love potions, for she had never felt this way about any man before.

"Do you like what you see?"

She was so surprised at his words that she glanced upward and found a smile on his lips. "Yes." She was glad he wanted to please her, as she did him, and lowered her face to place a quick kiss on each of his nipples. When he groaned and moved restlessly, she became bolder. Running her hands over his chest, she felt his nipples harden. Excited, she wanted even more.

Pulling her on top of him, he let her breasts graze his chest and she moaned in response to the roughness of his hair against the sensitive tips. Then he pressed her against him, letting his hands massage down her back. Cupping her hips, he moved her against him so she could feel the heat and hardness of his passion.

When he pulled up her skirt and felt her derriere through her drawers, letting his fingers slip between her legs, she froze, shocked at this new intimacy. But excitement was building in her and she felt a warm wetness where she burned. She wanted his fingers inside her, touching her as intimately as possible, and was once more shocked at her reaction to him. But there seemed to be nothing she did not want from him. Groaning, she moved against him, pushing herself into his hardness.

Drake growled and rolled over with her so he could press himself into her. He kissed her again, sliding his tongue into her mouth as he pushed his hardness against her. She writhed under him, her clothes twining around her as she sought to get closer to him.

Finally, he raised his head. ''Let's make this easy.'' He sat up and began unbuttoning his trousers.

And Selene realized she was at the point of no return. She wanted Drake, wanted to see him, hold him, have him fill her. But if they shared their passion, she would never be able to forget. And how could she walk away from him? She couldn't, not if they completed what they had begun. Yet her blood boiled for him. She was caught in her own trap. Rosa had warned her. If only she had been able to slip out of the hotel without seeing him.

Love potions. What they felt wasn't real. She must remember that. When the power of the potions faded, they would no longer burn for each other. She must remember that. This was a fleeting emotion. And if she didn't go any farther with him, she would be able to walk away more easily. And forget him more easily. And go on with her life more easily.

Yet it was hard to be rational, to think of the future rather than the present. But she must. She must stop their desire, and now. But how?

She must change his emotions, and therefore hers. Abruptly, she sat up.

He smiled at her. "Sorry I'm slow."

She took a deep breath, hating herself for what she had to do. "How many other women have you had in this room?"

Shocked, he simply stared at her for a moment. "Other . . . women?"

She looked down at the bed, forcing a coldness into her. "I'm not the first in this bed, am I?"

He looked confused. "It doesn't matter."

"Yes it does. If you care about me—"

"Selene, damn it." He pushed her back against the bed. "Be quiet."

"I can't stop thinking about those other women. Were they fallen women? Or were they ladies like me whom you seduced?"

"Damn!" He hit his fist against the pillow and sat up.

"Tell me, I have to know."

"I didn't seduce you." He stood up and buttoned his trousers. "We both wanted this. I thought."

She began buttoning her bodice.

Reaching for the whiskey, he poured himself a drink then downed it in one swallow. "You're killing me."

Redressed, she sat up. "I suddenly realized I needed love for this, Drake, and I don't think you know much about love. I'm not sure I do either. At least this kind of love. Either way—"

"Selene, stop it." He threw his glass against the wall and it shattered.

She flinched. "I'm leaving." She walked to the door.

"Don't go!" He came after her, grabbed her arm, and tried to pull her against him.

"No. Please. Leave me some respect." Tears were in her eyes, and they were real. She hated to hurt him, and herself as well. But if they made love, the pain would be ten times as great.

"I respect you, Selene. Damn. Let me prove it." He dropped his hand. "All right. If you'll come to Texas, I won't touch you. I'll woo you however you want. Only don't walk away from me. Not like this."

She swallowed. If he made it any harder, she was going to sit down and cry. She had wanted him mad, not pleading for her to stay. She only wished she was heartless. "Drake, there are plenty of other women. You don't need me. Please go home. Leave me in peace."

"Selene, give me a chance."

"No." She opened the door, then glanced back. He wasn't looking mad anymore. Determined. It was the only word to describe him.

"You can't forget me, Selene. Or that bed." He gestured with his head toward the rumpled bedspread. "I'll give you some time to think about us, then I'll be after you."

"Stay away." She took a last, long look at him,

then stepped through the doorway and pulled the door shut behind her. Taking a deep breath, she walked away.

Only one thought kept her going: when he read the note, he'd be so mad he'd never want to see her again.

And that was what she wanted.

Part Two

Martinique,
Windward Islands
Summer 1886

Chapter 13

Drake Dalton stomped along the back streets of Saint Pierre. The city might be considered the pearl of the Caribbean and Martinique the Isle of Flowers, but he'd never wanted to know those facts. In fact, he could have lived a lifetime without knowing them. He was too far from Texas to be happy, although he had to admit Martinique was beautiful in a lush sort of way like overripe fruit or an easy woman.

Beyond all that, it was getting dark. He was tired, hungry, and he wanted a room, a bath, and a hot meal. Better yet, he'd take Selene Morgan, the present bane of his life. He couldn't decide if he should be pleased she wanted him to fall in love with her by making love potions for him or punish her for going alone to Martinique. And if he caught her in the arms of Gustave Dominique, he knew which it would be.

But first he had to find her, and Dominique. That was not proving as easy as he'd assumed when he'd left New Orleans. A ship had carried him through the Caribbean Sea to Fort de France. Once debarked, he had discovered most everybody on Martinique spoke French or Creole. Fortunately, some English and Spanish were understood so he'd been able to get along, but he was on Gustave Dominique's turf and knew it only too well.

He'd spent a few days in Fort de France asking questions and getting few answers, especially about Dominique. When he'd figured out most of the sugar cane plantations were in the northern part of the island, he'd gone to Saint Pierre up the western coast. From where he stood, he could see Mount Pelée, a volcano probably four thousand feet high towering over the city. To him, the mountain looked dangerous and unnatural, but nobody else seemed to think so. He wished for the wide open spaces of Texas, then cursed the Frenchman again.

After he'd walked through the best part of town, and been turned down at the best hotels, he had ended up in the outskirts of Saint Pierre. French colonial buildings of white stone and red tile roofs had given way to cracking plaster and rotting wood. But by now he didn't care. He wanted a room for the night. Any room.

In his mind, all this added up to power. Gustave Dominique's power. For all he knew, Dominique might own the whole damn island, for why else had people shut up whenever Drake had tried to question them and why else were all the hotels filled? The islanders were friendly people, but not to Drake. Other travelers found places to stay in good hotels, but not Drake. He'd finally decided Dominique had people all over the island reporting and carrying out his orders. And at the moment those commands were to make life miserable for Drake Dalton.

Or he could be overreacting to being away from Texas so long, mad because Dominique had Joy Marie and Selene, and feeling out of place on the Frenchman's turf. But he didn't think so. His gut instinct told him he was being watched and indirectly kicked off the island. But he wasn't so easy to discourage and Dominique would soon realize that.

Yet it wasn't his immediate problem.

He looked around. The evening air was filled with the scent of flowers. Mulatto men lounged against walls and drank tafia, and he knew they were drinking the rum because the strong, sweet drink was made for export on Martinique and was readily available. Women walked by, carrying baskets or bags or children. Drake couldn't help but look. Upon reaching the island, he'd been told of the legendary beauty of Martinique women and he believed it. If not for thoughts of Selene, he could have followed any of those swaying hips home.

Again, that wasn't his immediate concern. He was looking for a place to stay, and if Saint Pierre was anything like the other port city of Fort de France, there would be a seedy inn or two on the back streets.

Soon he found one. A gray wooden sign, hanging by one corner, announced a place to stay in three languages. Drake read the English and decided the Pink Flamingo Inn would suit him fine. Once inside, he wondered if there had ever been any pink in

177

the place at all, for it was mostly faded paint on warped wood, faded cushions on leaning furniture. And it smelled like sweet tafia, spicy food, and musty furniture.

But he got a room.

It was small, dirty, the single bed had gray sheets, the wash bowl was dark with grime, but a fragrant breeze blew in through the open window. He set down his battered leather travel bag, and looked outside. Night was settling over the city. He could see Mount Pelée to the north and he thought of Selene. Were they both standing under the shadow of the volcano? Was she thinking of him as he was of her? Was she all right, and Joy Marie, too?

But those thoughts would get him nowhere. He needed food and information. He also wanted a bath, but he knew that was out of the question in a place like the Pink Flamingo. He took off his shirt and jacket, then poured water into the wash bowl. After rinsing off his face, neck, and torso, he put on a clean shirt.

He was about as good as he was going to get, but he disliked leaving his bag in the room. The lock on the door wasn't much and he didn't figure it would keep out anybody who wanted inside. But he wasn't going to carry the bag around when he questioned people. He'd just have to take a chance.

Pulling open a pocket inside the bag, he took out a knife and slipped it into his boot. He unrolled a shirt that had been protecting his gun and holster, then buckled the belt of the holster and put it over his left shoulder so the .45 hung under his arm. Last he put on his jacket to conceal the pistol. Now he was ready to face the streets of Saint Pierre and get some answers.

He left the room, locked the door, and headed downstairs. The noise of laughter, conversation, and clinking utensils as people ate and drank filled the main room. He was surprised to see most of the tables and chairs were full. The Pink Flamingo was a more popular place than he'd have suspected. While he had the chance, he grabbed one of the chairs at a small table in the corner.

As he sat down the chair creaked, but he didn't let it stop him. Most of the furniture in the room looked moments away from collapse, but nobody else seemed to notice so he assumed it was sturdier than it looked. He glanced around at the motley assortment of people and was glad he'd worn his .45, even if he had rather it'd been on his hip.

Several mulatto waitresses moved about the room with grace and skill, never hurrying, never allowing anyone to harass them. Drake had to admire their ability, as well as their natural beauty.

Finally one stopped by his table. She flashed sparkling white teeth and spoke in Creole.

He shook his head, not figuring they had a menu. "I want something to eat and drink."

Nodding, she turned and walked away.

He hoped she got the message, but what else would he have wanted? And then he grinned. Well, he knew what a lot of men would want from her, but maybe he hadn't looked that kind of hungry.

Settling back in the chair to wait, he glanced

around. He ought to be questioning everybody in the room, and he wished he could understand the conversation that drifted to him from the other tables. But he was hungry and there was plenty of time to get information after he'd filled the hole in his middle.

Besides, he could rent a horse and ride the whole island to find Gustave Dominique's plantation if he had to do it. He'd learned Martinique was only about fifty miles long by twenty-one miles wide. Compared to riding the range in Texas or a cattle drive to Kansas, covering that amount of land was nothing. But he didn't think he'd have to do it. Dominique had to be someplace close.

Soon the waitress set a bottle of tafia and a small glass on the table. She smiled. "Tafia."

"Thanks. *Merci.*"

As she walked away, he watched her move and thought of Selene. And that made him hot. He poured himself a drink. He was getting used to the sweet, potent rum and liked it. If he got a chance, he'd take a case back to Texas. Along with Selene. And Joy Marie.

He smiled to himself. He wasn't quite sure what Selene had proved by making love potions for him, but he did know he'd gotten the wrong idea about her from the first. She helped people, not hurt them. And she was the most fascinating woman he'd ever met, as well as the most desirable.

But he wasn't sure she'd ever turn all that love and care and help on one man or one family. She was used to helping so many people, loving so many. And that thought brought a sadness to him. He didn't know how to share and didn't want to learn.

One thing he'd found out in New Orleans. He wanted a woman for Dalton Ranch. And he wanted that woman to be Selene Morgan. She was the right woman for the job, but he didn't know if he could persuade her. She was so independent, so self-assured, and so many loved her. Besides, she already had her own business.

But she wanted him and he'd use that to bind her to him if need be. His dark eyes blazed. He'd do whatever it took to get her. When it came to taking care of Dalton Ranch and his family, he'd expend any amount of money, time, and effort. But making love to Selene would be no price at all. He wanted her badly and he didn't care who knew it.

Love. Well, that was something different. He didn't need it. What he needed was the land nurtured, his family continued, and his passion slaked. Selene could do all of that if she would. The question was how to get her to come to Texas and stay. Love. If she needed to love him to do it, then he'd make sure she fell in love with him. And the first step to that was to get her in his bed.

Filled with determination, he glanced up to see the waitress place food on his table.

"Crabe farci." She pointed to the plate. "Crabs of the land. Fattened . . . on pepper leaves." Then she indicated a bowl of thick green soup. "Calau."

"Merci." The food didn't look like anything he'd eaten before, but since it didn't seem to be killing anybody else, he tackled it with gusto. And found it spicy and good.

When he'd finished it all, he leaned back in the chair. Satisfied, he poured another drink of tafia, and felt pleased with himself. It was simply a matter of time now before he rescued Selene and Joy Marie and took them back to Texas.

He left some money on the table, picked up the bottle of tafia, and headed outside. It was warm and humid, but a cool breeze blew off the Atlantic. He walked down the street, stopped, asked a few questions, got no response except a spattering of French, and continued. He didn't seem to be getting anywhere till a man walked up to him and eyed his bottle of tafia.

"You ever heard of Gustave Dominique?" Drake was willing to try anything.

"*Oui*. M'sieur Dominique is well known."

"Can you tell me how to get to his place? Some friends of mine are visiting there."

"Is that a bottle of tafia I see?"

"Sure is." Drake raised the bottle and shook it, showing it to be two-thirds full.

"Let's sit down and share it. We'll talk." The stranger headed into a dark alley.

Drake hesitated, not liking the situation. But this was the first person willing, or able, to talk and he couldn't pass up the chance. He stepped off the street.

The man held out his hand and Drake placed the bottle in it. "Let's sit."

"Okay." Drake turned to look for a comfortable place.

"Get off Martinique while you can." The stranger's

voice was full of menace.

Drake went for his pistol, but felt a sudden sharp pain at the base of his skull as liquid splashed over his face. He saw bright light, then nothing as he slumped to the ground.

Awakening to the sound of a low voice crooning in French, Drake listened. Where was he? What had happened?

Suddenly it all came back to him. The stranger. The hit on his head. The blackness. He cursed silently at his stupidity. He'd been as bad as some greenhorn. He'd known better than to go into the alley, but he'd been so desperate for information he'd put aside common sense. At least he wasn't dead. But was he out of danger?

Taking a chance, he opened his eyes. As he moved his head to look around, a sharp pain shot through his head. He instantly shut his eyes.

The voice stopped, and he felt a warm hand against his brow. He chanced a look. An older mulatto woman, her face filled with concern, bent over him. She wore a bright red tignon tied around her head. She smelled of flowers and herbs. A print apron covered her faded red dress. Her hand was soft and comforting. She smiled, then spoke to him in Creole.

"I can't . . . understand you."

She nodded, then got up and left the room.

Cautiously moving his head, he glanced around. He was lying on a pallet on a wooden floor in a small room. Late afternoon sunlight slanted in through open windows. The air was warm, humid, and filled with the scent of herbs and flowers. It reminded him of Selene's shop.

That thought brought him to a seated position. His head pounded and he winced with the pain, but he didn't lie back down. He had to find Selene. If Dominique was willing to kill him, what might he be doing to Selene and Joy Marie? Yet the Frenchman wanted the women so perhaps their danger wasn't as great as his own, but he still wanted them off Martinique as soon as possible. And now he wanted to pay back Gustave Dominique for ordering somebody to bash in his skull.

The woman returned, bringing with her a small mulatto girl who wore a faded print dress and no shoes. She gave him a beautiful smile, glanced up at the older woman, then sat down near Drake.

"Ancient Mam says I do the talking for her."

Relieved somebody spoke English, Drake leaned toward the child. "Where am I? What happened?"

"I am Josephine. I am named for the Empress. She was born not so far from here."

"Good." Napoleon. Drake's French history was not particularly great, but he did remember the famous couple. He hadn't known Josephine was from Martinique, or he'd forgotten, and he didn't particularly care. But if it was important to his interpreter, it was important to him. "Can you tell me where I am?" He spoke more slowly.

"Ancient Mam's house."

Drake forced himself to be patient, and glanced

around the room. Ancient Mam sat near a window and was sorting dried herbs. Again she reminded him of Selene. Could the herbs actually work? His mother had had ointments and methods of healing, but she had bought most of her medical supplies from a general store, or at least, he'd thought she did. Now he wasn't so sure.

Ancient Mam spoke in Creole, nodding at the girl, then went back to her task.

"You got hit." Josephine pointed at his head. "One of Ancient Mam's grandchildren found you. Brought you here. She healed you. Now she wants to know why you are here, why you ask questions about the Dominique man, and if you bring trouble."

"I am Drake Dalton from Texas . . . in the United States."

Josephine smiled. "We know Texas. Horses. Pistols. Cowboys. Right?"

Drake laughed. "I am a cowboy." He looked at Ancient Mam, then back at the girl. "Are you her granddaughter?"

"Great-granddaughter. She is very old. And wise."

"Ask her if those herbs, those roots and things she's handling, really work?"

Josephine laughed, then covered her mouth with her hand to stifle her outburst. She glanced at Ancient Mam and spoke rapidly in Creole.

Ancient Mam laughed, too, showing a mouthful of white teeth, then she spoke and nodded toward Drake.

"She says yes." Josephine smiled. "But the spirit and mind and body must help." She hesitated, as if searching for words. "The sick and injured must believe and be willing to change. But Ancient Mam is a powerful root woman. Nobody questions her."

Drake thought about Selene and what she did. He could understand her better now, for she healed not only the body but the mind and spirit as well. What she did must work, for she had many friends and people continued to ask for her help. It still seemed a mystery to him, but he began to accept her abilities, as well as those of this Ancient Mam.

"Soon you will be strong again." Josephine glanced back through the doorway, as if she'd rather be outside with friends.

"Please thank Ancient Mam for me and tell her I'm here to find two friends of mine. Women. Selene from New Orleans. And Joy Marie from Texas."

Josephine giggled, then spoke to her great-grandmother.

Ancient Mam gave Drake a sidelong glance, then responded.

"She says you are a strong man for two women."

"No. They aren't mine."

Josephine giggled again. "And this Dominique man has taken your women so you come to get them back?"

"No." Drake thought about it a minute. "Yes, that's right. *My* women."

Josephine spoke to Ancient Mam once more, then listened as the root woman spoke at length. Finally Josephine turned to Drake, her face serious. "She says you come for your women, true, but more important you come in answer to her summons.

Erzulie sends you."

Drake started to protest, for he didn't know any Erzulie, then he remembered at the voodoo ceremony in New Orleans the high priestess had mentioned Erzulie. "Who is Erzulie?"

Making a quick gesture with her hand, as if to ward off bad luck, Josephine shook her head. "A powerful goddess. She brought you here and protects you still." She glanced at Ancient Mam, listened for a moment, then looked back at Drake. "Dominique bad man. He has the evil eye. He turns good men into zombies, good women into slaves. To rescue your women, you must defeat him and end his power."

Drake rubbed his head. It hurt worse than ever. "What do you mean by zombies?"

"You will see."

He started to ask another question, then decided it probably wouldn't help. Zombies and slaves? He needed to talk to Selene and find out what was really going on because nothing made sense except that Dominique was evil and he already knew that. "Are Selene and Joy Marie living with Dominique? And where is the Frenchman's plantation?"

Josephine consulted her great-grandmother. "Two white women are living in his great house. His fields are not far from here."

"And where is here?"

"Near Saint Pierre."

"Will you take me to Dominique's house?"

Josephine turned to Ancient Mam. "Yes. But she asks you promise to help set our people free."

"I don't know how I can help. If Dominique owns

187

the land and Ancient Mam's friends are working for him, then it's all legal." He hesitated. "Unless he's got kidnapped people from New Orleans being forced to work. Now that'd be something for the law."

Josephine spoke to her great-grandmother, listened to her reply, then turned to him. "You will not be able to get your women without our help. Zombies with dogs patrol. But I am small and I know a way in and out. For your promise I will lead you there."

Drake didn't know what was going on or if anything he was hearing was true, but he owed Ancient Mam and he always paid his debts. "All right. I'll do what I can, but I don't know how much it'll help."

"Do you swear you will help our people on the heart of the good and just Erzulie?" Josephine's dark eyes were intense.

"Sure."

"And do you swear the same on the heart of Selene and Joy Marie?"

Drake hesitated, then nodded and immediately wished he hadn't moved his head. "Yes. I'll do what I can."

Josephine spoke with her great-grandmother, then turned back to him. "You must rest. We go tonight if you are well enough."

"I'm well—"

"But not till the birds are long at perch."

"I'll be ready."

"I will bring food, then you must sleep." Josephine stood up.

"Okay. And thanks."

She looked him over, then shook her head. "Save your thanks. Perhaps you will not like your bargain." She inclined her head to her great-grandmother, then walked from the room with all the dignity of her namesake, the Empress Josephine.

Chapter 14

Moonlight cast the sugar cane plantation house in silver and shadows. Drake couldn't help comparing Gustave Dominique's Victorian, French, and West Indian architectural style home with his own Mexican adobe house on the ranch. The structures couldn't have been more dissimilar and he worried about which Selene would like best.

At the moment it was the least of his worries and he knew it. Still, he couldn't help wanting to nail Dominique to the wall of his fancy house, and leave him to rot.

Josephine touched his arm, then put a fingertip to her lips.

She didn't need to remind him to be quiet. He knew he wasn't moving silently enough, but he hadn't been since they'd left Saint Pierre. The fact was he didn't know *how* to walk quietly through this type of land, although Josephine moved with the silence and speed of a nocturnal predator. And he was impressed.

Still, they'd gotten within sight of Dominique's house and nobody had stopped them. But they'd followed a narrow trail through rocky mountain terrain and sometimes thick jungle, skirting Dominique's land as long as possible. In a way he was glad it wasn't daytime because he was already sick of the color green. And he wasn't away from it yet.

Suddenly Drake caught sight of a man with a dog on a leash. Cursing silently to himself, he jerked Josephine down with him. Concealed by the profusion of island plants beneath huge mahogany trees, he held his breath. But his concern was for the dog because being out of sight wouldn't make a damn bit of difference to a canine nose. However, with so many flowers and plants in bloom, he hoped the dog wouldn't be able to catch their scent. He'd also had a bath and washed his clothes in a stream near Ancient Mam's place so he was as clean as he was going to get.

Josephine didn't move. Drake was impressed with her again, and thought of his dead nephew. They'd have been about the same age. Jimmy's age. Once more he wondered what had happened to Jimmy and if he was on Dominique's plantation. But why kidnap a boy too young to work hard in the fields? It made no sense. But nothing had made much sense since Joy Marie had run away with Dominique.

The guard looked toward their hiding place, the dog sniffed the ground, then they walked onward. But Drake and Josephine didn't move. They waited until silence enveloped them once more before standing up. All appeared safe.

Taking his hand, Josephine led him to another trail. She pointed from it to the house, made several symbols in the air in front of his face, then disappeared back into the dense foliage.

He was on his own. But protected by Erzulie. Unfortunately that idea gave him no comfort at all. As he'd first thought, he was on his own. And he felt a sense of relief. Now he didn't have anybody else to worry about. He could move free and easy. Glancing around, he memorized the lay of the land so he could return the way he'd come. Then he studied the house.

Two-storied, its base was concealed by a variety of bushes, flowers, and plants, and a huge mangrove grew along one side. From what he could tell, the house was made of wood with a tile roof. A verandah supported by narrow wooden columns and an ornate grillwork fence enclosed the first floor and a matching balcony surrounded the second. The house reminded him of a fancy Mississippi steamboat without the huge paddlewheel. The steep roof had a couple of windows which might indicate living quarters for the servants.

All in all, it wasn't his type of house. But the main thing was he figured he could get up the tree and over to the balcony. The bedrooms should be on the second floor and he could check them since in front there were two center doors with two windows the same height on each side. The shutters were open to let in night breezes and it would be easy to walk right in through the windows. Of course, it was important to find Selene first because he wasn't ready to confront Dominique.

He touched the .45 in the holster under his arm, glad he'd had it on him when he'd been hit. Not wanting anybody to know he was alive and well, he hadn't gone back to the Pink Flamingo Inn to get his travel bag. Anyway, he'd figured it was long gone. He had his money and his pistol so anything else could be replaced.

For once glad of the lush tropical plants, he started up the path knowing he was concealed. Moving as quietly as he could, he hurried. He didn't know what he'd find in the house, but he wouldn't have been too surprised to find Selene and Joy Marie chained in the attic and kept naked and weak for the Frenchman's pleasure.

That was one thought too many and he pushed it from his mind to concentrate on getting into the house without being seen. He wished there had been more noise in the countryside, as in the city, for even the night noises of predators or the wind in the trees wasn't enough to cover up any loud sound he might make.

As he reached the end of the trail, he dropped to his knees, then to his stomach. Inching along on his elbows, he left the protective vegetation to look at the house. It was quiet and peaceful in the moonlight. And still.

Until a man walked around the side of the house. Drake froze. A guard. Suddenly light flared in the man's hand as he lit a cigar, then it was dark again. Drake cursed silently to himself. Now how was he going to get up the tree to the balcony?

Backing up, he slid down the path until he could stand without being seen. He headed back along the trail until he came to a fallen branch. Picking it up, he tossed it as far as he could. When it fell, it crashed into thick plants and flowers away from the house.

Then he stepped off the path and hid.

Soon he heard the guard running down the trail in the direction of the sound. When the man was out of sight, Drake moved quickly up the path toward the house. He hesitated at the edge of the plants, didn't see anyone around, and ran to the mangrove. He stepped up on an exposed root, then grabbed a low branch. Swinging up into the tree, he was hidden. He listened while he waited for the pounding in his head to ease. The house was quiet but he could hear the guard in the distance. He wouldn't have long.

Quickly climbing the tree, he stopped on a wide branch that was close to the balcony. He took off his boots, wedged them between two branches, then climbed out onto the limb. Checking to make sure the guard was still away, he swung outward, grabbed a column, and twisted over the fence above the wooden floor. He landed with a slight thud. Kneeling, he listened for any noise and heard nothing unusual.

But his head was pounding, making it impossible to keep his balance. The pain made him grind his teeth, but he remained quiet as he tried to control the agony. Hunched down, he waited for the pain to recede. When it finally did, he began creeping along the balcony.

Staying low, he approached the first window. He looked inside. The bed was empty. He moved on, watching the yard for the guard, but so far he was safe. He passed the doors and came to the next window. Someone was sleeping there. He stepped through the window and walked into the room. Fortunately moonlight gave him enough light to see and he peered down at the sleeping person.

Joy Marie. She was all right. He felt a quick sense of relief, then walked back to the window. He hesitated when he saw the guard return. As he waited for the man to walk to the front of the house so he wouldn't be able to see him, he glanced back at Joy Marie. Were was Dominique?

Red hot anger flooded him. Only one answer came to mind: Selene's room. Heedless of the guard, he stepped out of the bedroom and ran around the house to the side. He passed the window that led into Joy Marie's room, but stopped at the next. The bed was occupied. He stepped through the window and hurried to the side of the bed. Drawing his .45, he jerked back the covers.

And exposed Selene. Alone.

She woke up, saw him, and opened her mouth to scream. He clamped a hand over her lips and pushed her back against the bed. Giving in to the impulse to kiss her, he laid his pistol on the pillow next to hers and replaced his hand with his mouth.

But she struggled, beating at him with her fists and trying to turn her face away. He thrust long fingers into her hair to hold her still. Her tresses felt like corn silk. She was soft and warm and smelled like gardenias. So sweet. He'd been too long without her . . . without any women. And she belonged to him.

Yet she refused him entry to her mouth and tried to twist away from him. Anger and lust combined to send energy pulsing through him. His head pounded. His heart beat fast. And he was so hard he thought he'd thrust right through his trousers. His woman.

How dare she reject him? He jerked her hands above her head and straddled her. With her between his legs, he almost lost control.

But if either of them made much noise the whole damn house would be down on them. Where was that devil Dominique anyway? Had Selene already succumbed to the Frenchman's lust in the hot tropical sweetness of Martinique? The idea of Dominique between Selene's legs, riding her like a stud bull, made him see red.

He growled low in his throat and tightened his hold. She was *his* woman. A Dalton. She would taste his blood, smell his scent, and feel him spasm hot inside her. After that, no other man would ever be able to satisfy her. Her desire would be for him alone. And love would cloud her eyes forever.

But she had to accept him first.

Raising his head, he kept her wrists imprisoned in one hand while he clamped a palm over her mouth. She moaned low in her throat, shook her head, and tried to buck him off. He rode her, feeling the heat of their bodies combine in the sultry island air. Her skin was flushed with heat, damp with sweat, and the fevered silkiness made him want her all the more.

"You're mine, Selene." His voice was a low rasp in the darkness.

She stilled.

Suddenly he realized she might not have recognized him before. Dalton blood. She must never mistake him again. He bit his lower lip till he tasted the saltiness of his own life force, then he raised his hand and lowered his face.

"Drake?"

"Yes."

He pressed his lips to hers. And she opened her mouth. He thrust deep inside her with his tongue. Turning savage in his need, he twined his hands in her hair and possessed her mouth till she was moaning and writhing beneath him. The fury of his desire was so strong his teeth raked her lips and he tasted saltiness. She bled for him. He kissed her again, this time with worship, and as their blood mingled he felt a powerful emotion fill him. And his body shuddered in response.

Raising his head, he pressed soft kisses to her eyes, the tip of her nose, her chin. He released her wrists and smoothed strands of hair back from her face. Then he stopped, willing his body to control. He must be gentle now. He must woe her. He must seduce her. Then she would be his when the night was done.

"Drake?" Her voice was soft with wonder. "What are you doing here?"

"You." He could hardly keep from ravishing her. "Did you think I'd let you get away so easy?"

"But the love potions. I thought—"

"I changed my mind. *You* changed it."

"But—"

"Love me, Selene." He kissed her lips again.

"You don't understand." She tossed her head in frustration. "This isn't real. It's the love potions making us feel this way."

"I don't care. I want you." He cupped her hands in his, willing her to believe him. "I *must* have you. Tonight."

She shivered, despite the warmness of the evening

and the heat of Drake's body. "I brought this on myself. I didn't understand the power of my love potions. I'm caught in my own web."

"Our web." He nuzzled her neck. "Love me, Selene."

"But I only made the love potions to force you to see what I did was real."

"I believe you. Isn't this real?"

"No." She hesitated. "I mean, yes. What we feel is real. But it won't last."

"We'll think about the future later. Right now we want each other. Isn't that enough?"

"It's more than enough. It's too much." She touched his face, tracing his features with her fingers. "I missed you."

"Good." He steeled himself to let her touch him, although he wanted nothing so much as to crush her to him and lose himself within her.

"Good? That's cruel."

"No. I followed you. If you hadn't missed me, do you know how I'd feel now?"

"Yes. No." She dropped her hand and looked away from him. "Don't you hate me for deceiving you?"

"I could never hate you." He pressed kisses to her face. "Don't you know that by now?"

She frowned. "I don't know. I just—"

He covered her lips with his and thrust into her mouth. There'd been enough talk.

As he kissed her, he rolled to the side, taking her with him. He ran rough palms down the softness of her shoulders and arms, exposed by the sheer nightgown, then he moved to her breasts and felt the tips harden. Further excited, he massaged her breasts, feeling their fullness, their softness, knowing he'd never let another man touch her this way. When she moaned low in her throat, he pulled her close so he could feel her heat the entire length of him.

But he couldn't wait much longer. He had to feel bare flesh against bare flesh. He had to know she was completely his woman. Parting their lips, he looked at her face. Her eyelids were heavy, her lips swollen from his kisses, and soft moonlight cast highlights in her dark hair. *His* woman.

He sat up, jerked open his shirt, pulled it out of his trousers, and threw it on the floor. Not hesitating, he unbuckled his gunbelt, then undid his trousers and pulled them off. He tossed everything to the floor. Naked, he turned back, wanting her to look at him, needing her to want him. He knew other women found him desirable, but would she?

"Drake." Her voice was low, hesitant. And she was looking at him, her gaze traveling up and down his length. "The love potions . . ."

He jerked her nightgown down, exposing her breasts. The rosy tips were hard. She took several deep breaths, but didn't cover herself.

"Take it off." He had to see all of her.

She hesitated, watching his face, then slipped the sheer fabric down her legs and tossed her nightgown to the end of the bed. Naked, she turned to him and smiled.

He knew he'd won. A fierce longing filled him. He hurt he wanted her so much. Then he forgot everything except the scent of her hair, the softness of her skin, the heat of her body as he enveloped her in his arms and held her close while his hands began to work magic on her, finding the most sensitive places from her throat to her breasts to the silken triangle of hair between her thighs. When he touched her heated depths, she groaned and thrust upward against his hand.

Breathing hard, he felt her, letting his fingers slide in and out as she reached out to him, caressing his shoulders, his back, then lower to his buttocks. Soon he could hardly control his wild desire, but he held on till he bent over her, kissed her lips once more, then fitted himself between her thighs, raised her hips, and touched the tip of his manhood to her moist entrance.

"Drake?" Her voice was part purr, part concern, part excitement.

He ignored her voice to concentrate on her body. He nudged slightly inside her, felt her quiver, and held her still. Moving in further he felt their heat fuse, and he trembled, not knowing if he would be able to wait long enough to bring her pleasure. Then he felt a barrier to their desire. He withdrew, then thrust inward again. No, he was not mistaken. The Frenchman hadn't touched her.

She was his alone and he drove in deep. She cried out, then was quiet as he moved in long, slow thrusts, feeling her silken flesh capture and hold him within her. As he moved faster and harder, she moaned and tossed her head back and forth. Soon she moved in rhythm with him as she whispered his name, clasping at him with her hands, trying to pull him in deeper and deeper.

As they spun toward ecstasy, he lowered his body and sought her mouth. Plunging in his tongue, he filled her completely and as they spiraled out of control together he spasmed deep inside her and felt her body quicken around him. In that instant, he knew he had made her a Dalton.

When they returned from their summit, he cradled her head against his shoulder and stroked her, soothing her, hoping she wouldn't be angry with him now.

He cleared his throat, not wanting to talk or think or reason. He only wanted to feel, to know that Selene was finally his woman. A few words and a paper meant nothing to him. What counted was what they had felt.

She was silent, her heart beating hard against his chest, her fingers playing lightly in the hair on his chest.

"I hope I didn't hurt you." He felt as if he was a boy with his first woman.

"No." Her voice was faint.

He sat up to look into her eyes. "You're not mad, are you?"

Her expression was faraway.

Cursing silently, he pulled her close and held her. "I didn't know you were a virgin. I mean, I suspected it. I wanted it. But—" He broke off. If he wasn't careful, he was going to make the situation worse.

"Do you think anybody heard us?"

He laid her gently against the pillows, got up, and walked across the room. Looking outside, he could see no movement, hear no sound. He went back to the bed and sat down. "We were quiet."

"It didn't seem quiet."

"Believe me, we were." He still didn't know if she

202

was mad. "I want you to go back to Texas with me."

She pushed the pillows up against the headboard and leaned against them to regard him. "It was good."

He smiled. "It'll get better."

"But I hurt, too."

"I know. I'm sorry. You were—"

"Yes, but you were gentle."

He hated talking about it. Standing up, he started to pace until he noticed she was watching his body. He sat back down. "I can't stay here."

"No."

"Where's Dominique?"

She frowned. "We've got to talk, Drake. And I don't mean about us."

"It's simple. I'm taking you back to Texas."

"I wish you'd stop saying that. I have a life in New Orleans. This was just . . . well, pleasant."

Furious, he clenched his fists, desperately controlling his temper. "All right. That can wait. Right now I want to know what the hell Gustave Dominique is doing on Martinique."

Chapter 15

Selene stood in front of an open window in her bedroom. She could see moonlight glinting off the Caribbean Sea. Beautiful. A soft breeze cooled her face, bringing with it the scent of tropical flowers. Peaceful. Behind her she could feel Drake's magnetic presence. Dangerous.

Pushing soft tendrils of hair back from her face, she tried to think. She'd given herself to him. Despite her best intentions, she'd welcomed him into her arms, into her body, into her life. And she knew better. It was simply the love potions at work. But now the ache between her legs made it something more. Much more.

She was no innocent girl who didn't know the consequences of what they'd done. She could become pregnant. But would that be so bad? Unmarried, she could still take care of her child. Her girl or boy would not be without love or a home. A stigma would be attached, but she could live with that and so could her child.

But did she want Drake Dalton's child? She shivered, feeling chilled despite the warmth of the night. If she did, she knew the baby would be beautiful, strong, intelligent. But her life would be changed forever. Did she want that right now and with Drake Dalton?

She nodded. Yes, a part of her wanted it very much, but it was a primitive instinct. Her mind told her to wait and watch, to learn more about Drake, to see if the affect of the love potions lasted. But her emotions didn't want to be cautious. She had missed him more than she would have thought possible and the pain of never seeing him again had been with her every day. Earlier, when she'd first awakened, she'd thought it was Gustave attacking her, then she'd realized it was Drake and for a moment she'd thought it must be a dream.

But what they'd shared was no dream. Afterward she had been careful, or as careful as she could be after what they'd done. Gustave's new house had the latest in plumbing and her room had its own bath. She had washed away Drake's touch within and without. And she'd known it was for the best. Too many depended on her right now for her to think of her own pleasure and happiness first. Besides, Drake had never mentioned love or marriage and she didn't know if it would make any difference if he did. She had her own life to live and she wasn't at all sure he would ever be a permanent part of it, even if she had his child.

Turning from the window, she watched as he walked out of the bathroom. He was dressed again. If Joy Marie or any of the servants heard noise from her bathroom, they would assume she couldn't sleep.

And Drake could hide if they were suddenly interrupted.

But for the moment she was simply thankful they were both dressed again, for it was the best possible defense against flinging herself into his arms.

Drake walked over to her, but didn't touch her. "I won't hurt you, Selene. You don't have to build a wall between us."

"It's not so easy for a woman."

"I know." He took a deep breath. "If there's a child, I'd never abandon it. I'd love it."

She glanced at him. "Thanks. But it'd be *my* child."

Darkness stained his face. "You'd better think again. It would be *our* child and we'd raise him or her in Texas."

Squaring her shoulders, she turned to him. "Are you talking marriage, Mr. Dalton?"

"Damn right." He grasped her shoulders. "Selene, I'm not joking. If you have my baby, it'll be a Dalton and I'll make sure it carries my name. Forget anything else."

"Then take your hands off me and don't touch me again because *my* child may or may not be a Dalton."

He dropped his hands as if stung, and turned away.

She almost pitied him, then hardened her heart. What they discussed was too serious to take lightly. And their emotions were too unstable to discuss the situation calmly. Yet she wanted his arms around her and she wanted him back in her bed. And she could almost see a small daughter with his blond hair and her green eyes.

She stopped her mind and wrapped her arms

207

around her waist. She must not be foolish. He was just some cowboy. He wasn't her type at all.

Drake turned back. "I can't keep my hands off you, Selene, and I'm not going to try. I want you and I want your babies, *our* babies, and I intend to have you all." He jerked her into his arms and pressed his lips to hers.

Shocked, she started to succumb, then she stopped her reaction. She mustn't let him overpower her. Others depended on her. People she had known before Drake. She bit his lip.

He raised his head and his dark eyes glittered with emotion. "I know you want me."

"It's those love potions." Tears misted her eyes. "Please, Drake, help me be strong."

"Damn!" He tucked her head against his chest and held her. "Hell, Selene, I can ride drag, eating cattle dust all the way from San Antonio to Ellsworth, I can sit up day and night for a week with sick cattle. I can shoot a sidewinder dead in the head at fifty paces. But I can't stay away from you. I'm not that strong."

Putting a hand under her chin, he raised her face. He looked into her eyes, then kissed the tip of her nose. "You'll have to be strong enough for both of us till you prove what you want to prove."

Tears slipped from her eyes and ran down her cheeks. He kissed them away, then led her to a chair in front of a window. "Sit down. Touching you and not having you is killing me."

She glanced out the window, then down at the rococo chair of dark wood with plush burgundy velvet upholstery. It and a matching chair were positioned on either side of a round table made of expensive Jacaranda wood. A Tiffany lamp dominated the center of the table and several books lay scattered over its top. She had sat there looking out over the Caribbean many times, but she had never expected to be sharing the experience with Drake.

She sat down, then watched him take the other chair. He looked so good, especially after their lovemaking, that if she hadn't known better, she'd have sworn she loved him. As it was, she couldn't think about it. When the love potions wore off and she could think rationally again, then she'd make some sort of decision. Till then, she simply had to endure.

"Tell me about Joy Marie." Drake looked anywhere but at her.

Selene took a deep breath, tried to smile, failed, and glanced out over the sea. "I'm not sure what to think, but I'm more worried than ever."

"What's wrong?"

"Everything and nothing. It's the nothing I don't know how to deal with."

Drake raised a brow. "I don't understand."

"Well, just like in New Orleans she seems perfectly happy, says she's perfectly happy, but I've seen her confused."

"What do you mean?"

"She'll be doing something, like arranging flowers and talking about future plans for the house when she'll suddenly get this strange look in her eye as if she has no idea where she is or what she is doing. Then she'll sort of shake her head and go on. It's spooky."

Drake nodded.

"But she does seem happy. She has become the perfect plantation mistress, or what I guess is supposed to be one. She plans elegant meals, directs the house servants, and is furnishing the rest of the house. She has entertained and visited with the other planters. And is learning French."

"That worries you?"

"It is a very sumptuous lifestyle, Drake. I'm not used to it and I'm not comfortable with it. But Joy Marie seems to be. Is this what she had in Texas?"

Drake glanced around the room as early dawn light began to brighten it. "No. I mean Dalton Ranch has a good, solid house. It's well furnished. Comfortable. But it's not sumptuous. We don't fix fancy food. It's a working ranch, Selene, that's what it is."

She nodded, although she had little idea of what a working ranch was supposed to be like. "Joy Marie is running this household as if she were born to it, whatever her background. And she seems happy most of the time." Selene crumpled the soft fabric of her silk robe. "But I don't know how long Gustave will keep her here. They're still not married." She hesitated. "And I've seen marks on her."

Drake tensed. "Marks!"

"Be quiet. Don't wake the household."

"What kind of marks?"

"I could be mistaken about how she got them. Yet even in this heat she usually wears dresses with long sleeves and high necks. I've accidentally surprised her a few times in her room when she was in her underclothes. I've seen bruises on her arms and even her chest once."

Drake growled. "Gustave!"

"But she said she'd fallen on the stairs." Selene twisted the fabric of her robe harder. "That could be true. She's not used to the house yet. I don't want you to get mad and go after Gustave."

"You're protecting that Frenchman?" Drake's eyes glittered dangerously.

"No. But if you hurt Gustave, you could hurt Joy Marie. And he's been talking to me."

Drake stood up and looked out the window, his fists clenched. "What does he want?"

"He says he wants to marry me."

Drake twisted and hit the wall with his fist, then he grimaced, breathing hard. "That lousy, two-timing bastard. We're getting Joy Marie out of here." He started for the door.

Selene ran after him, grabbed his arm, and held on. "No, Drake. Wait. There's more."

"More?"

"Please sit down and hear me out. Yes, we've got to do something, but we've got to be careful. Too much is at stake, too many could be hurt if we don't handle this right."

He stalked across the room and sat down. "I've got to get out of here soon or they'll see me."

"I know. Just a little longer." She paced in front of him, paused to look out a window, then continued. "I've found my missing friends, Drake. They're working Gustave's sugar cane fields. And he's brought in criminals from New Orleans. They're guards."

"How do you know?"

"I've recognized a few of them. Remember, I've always healed whoever needed me."

Drake took a deep breath. "How'd Gustave get them here and what's he holding over them? Or is he paying them? Were they kidnapped or did they come of their own free will?"

"I don't know." She sat down and turned troubled green eyes on him. "I haven't had a chance to speak with any of them. But I've seen that they all do what he says when he says it. Just like Joy Marie does. And he's got islanders working the same way."

Drake nodded. "Zombies."

Shivering, she pulled her robe more closely around her body. "Where did you hear that term?"

"I didn't get here easily, Selene. Gustave tried to have me put out of action in Saint Pierre. I ended up at the house of a woman called Ancient Mam. One of her grandchildren had found me unconscious. She helped fix me up and—"

"What happened?" Selene looked alarmed.

He touched the back of his head. "Got hit with my own bottle of tafia."

She hurried to his side. "Let me look at it."

He pulled her hands away. "Don't touch me, Selene. I'm all right."

Shutting her eyes, she took several deep breaths, then walked away. "I could help."

"You'd only make me feel worse." He frowned. "Ancient Mam's great-granddaughter showed me the way here. Her name's Josephine. From what they say, Gustave's turning local workers into zombies and making them till his fields."

"There's a work shortage here, I've learned, just as there has been since the slaves were freed. I figure that's why Gustave wanted people from New

Orleans. But I don't know for sure. I'm still trying to find out what's really going on."

"What about Jimmy?"

"He's here, too."

"Is he okay?"

"Yes. But he's not the old Jimmy. He's like Joy Marie. Happy and satisfied. When I asked, Gustave explained to me that Joy Marie needed a boy to replace her lost son and Jimmy needed a mother, so he did what he thought was best. He also explained that some people from New Orleans were now working for him and they might be some of the people who'd suddenly disappeared from my area. He said they were much better off here. I didn't argue because I didn't want to arouse his suspicions."

"Damn!" Drake ran a hand through his hair. "Dominique must think he's Napoleon of Martinique."

"Dominique of Martinique. He's power-hungry. I'm sure of that. I'm scared of him and I don't mind admitting it." She hesitated. "He wants to hypnotize me and show me how it works."

"Don't do it, Selene." Drake gave her a hard stare. "Stay away from him."

"I can't. I'm living in his house and I may be the only one who can get through to him."

"We've got to find out what he's doing to these people first."

"Well, they aren't zombies. I mean they aren't the dead come back to life. At least they aren't as far as I know."

"Selene!"

"Who knows what the truth is anymore? I think

Gustave's hypnotizing them. It's a new process and I don't know enough about it to tell for sure. I don't even know if what he seems to be doing is possible. I only know that Gustave Dominique is getting exactly what he wants from people and they are satisfied about giving it to him. If that is hypnotism, then that's what he's doing. If they're zombies, like this Ancient Mam suggested, then they're zombies. But either way, Drake, something is not right. And yet, what if we're wrong?"

"And Ancient Mam, too?"

"She could be mad at Gustave for taking the family land or anything. We don't know her. I'm confused. Gustave makes everything seem so plausible that I . . ."

Drake stood up and walked over to her. He looked at her for a long moment, then lifted her into his arms.

"Drake, please . . ."

"I need the comfort of holding you as much as you need it." He sat back down in his chair and held her close, stroking her long hair. "We'll handle this together, Selene. If something's wrong, we'll find out what and right it. If everything's fine, then we'll leave. Okay?"

She shivered against him, then stilled. "I'm sorry if I've been hard on you."

"You're under a lot of strain." He hesitated, gazing out at the Caribbean. "I'm a grown man. I can control myself. And I promised Ancient Mam I'd help free her people if I could."

"But first we have to figure out what's going on here."

214

"Yes."

"I may have to let Gustave hypnotize me, Drake, just to learn the truth."

Drake's arms tightened around her. "No. We'll find another way."

"What if there isn't one?"

"There must be. Give me time to look around."

"All right. That's been part of my problem. I've been trying to learn things, but Gustave keeps a close watch on me and he usually has somebody follow me . . . to protect me."

"A guard." Drake looked at the sky as it lightened. "The whole damn place is guarded, but I'll find a way around that. Now, Selene, is there any way you can help Joy Marie?"

"I'm trying. Don't you think I've been trying?" Her voice filled with frustration. "And Jimmy, too. We act like a family when we have evening meals in the dining room. Everyone talks as if it's perfectly normal, but it's not. It's scary." She buried her head against Drake's chest. "I'm so glad you're here. I needed help."

"You've got it." He stroked her arm. "Are you sure I shouldn't kidnap Joy Marie and Jimmy? I could have them on a boat and out of here tomorrow."

Selene shook her head negatively. "What if Gustave has hypnotized them? Just getting them away from him won't make it go away. And what if it could hurt them somehow? Besides, what about those left? I can't abandon them, too."

"I find it hard to believe in this hypnotism stuff. I don't see how he could be turning people into zom-

215

bies. It doesn't make any sense, Selene. What is he doing?"

"Leave that to me."

"Don't do anything foolish. The Frenchman's smart and clever. If he's doing something to these people, maybe he's using some sort of island drug. I've heard those can be potent."

"Yes. Maybe you're right."

Suddenly there was a knock on the door.

Selene froze in Drake's arms.

"Selene, it's Joy Marie. I thought I heard you up."

Drake stood, gently set Selene on her feet, then placed a soft kiss on her lips. "I'll be in touch." Then he stepped through a window and was gone.

"Selene! Are you all right?" Joy Marie rattled the doorknob.

"Yes. I'm coming. Just a minute." Selene glanced around the room, saw nothing of Drake's, then threw the covers back over the bed as she walked to the door. Taking a deep breath, she hoped Joy Marie wouldn't be able to tell what had happened during the night. She unlocked the door and opened it.

Joy Marie smiled, gave her a quick hug, then walked into the bedroom. She glanced around. "I thought I heard voices."

Selene followed her. "Want to sit down? I couldn't sleep and I've been . . . reading out loud to myself to try and feel sleepy."

Joy Marie cocked her head. "I thought I heard you take a bath."

"Yes. I thought a hot bath would help me sleep."

"Gustave's not back yet, is he?" Joy Marie looked around the room again.

Selene felt her heart beat fast. She hadn't thought Joy Marie was suspicious. "I haven't seen him."

"If you want to try and sleep, I'll go."

"It's too late now. Why don't we have breakfast up here? We can ask Jimmy, too."

Joy Marie smiled. "He's a wonderful boy, isn't he? I won't ever feel lonely again now that he's with me. And Gustave. We make a lovely family, don't we?"

"Yes." Selene glanced around, wondering if Drake were safely out of the house. If she could keep Joy Marie and Jimmy with her for a while, it should make it easier for him to escape. "Why don't I order breakfast?" She pulled the bell rope, knowing a servant would quickly be with them. It wasn't something she was used to yet.

"That's good." Joy Marie walked to Selene again and hugged her. "I'm so glad you came to visit. With Gustave gone making plans and setting up business in Fort de France and Saint Pierre, I'd be very lonely without you."

Selene hugged her back. "I'm glad I'm here, too, but I'll need to be returning to New Orleans fairly soon."

"I understand you have your own life. When everything is settled here, I'll be just fine." She smiled. "But you must always come to visit. After all, you're an old friend of Jimmy's."

"Yes." Selene turned away. Joy Marie wasn't quite as naive about Gustave's feelings as she'd seemed, but she still obviously had no intention of giving up the Frenchman. And worse, she saw nothing wrong with keeping Jimmy on the island. Pulling her robe more tightly around her, Selene turned to see a servant

217

standing in the doorway.

"We'd like breakfast served here." Joy Marie indicated the round table. "And instruct Jimmy he'll be dining with us." She waved the maid away and turned back to Selene. "Isn't our big, happy family wonderful?"

Chapter 16

Selene, Joy Marie, and Jimmy were finishing break-fast when Gustave stepped into Selene's bedroom and sitting room combination. He bowed slightly, smiled, and walked over to the group. He kissed Joy Marie's cheek, Selene's hand, and bowed to Jimmy. In response, Jimmy stood up and returned the bow.

Selene simply watched in amazement at the change in Jimmy, for not only was Joy Marie playing the perfect mistress of the mansion but Jimmy had taken on the role of a young gentleman. And Selene had been given the part of the lady guest or visiting relative. But none of it was real. She had to keep reminding herself of that, for the roles were so fully realized she kept slipping into the play herself.

In effect, Gustave Dominique had bought, bribed, or hypnotized his way into having a country gentle-man's estate with a ready-made family. And she had no doubt that soon he would have a French noble-man's title as well. He had turned his fantasy into reality and the whole idea chilled Selene. But she mustn't let Gustave know her true feelings, for he was sharp and she wasn't enough under control for him to fully trust her.

Beaming at the three of them, Gustave threw wide his arms. "My family. I have missed you."

"You've only been gone two days." Selene determinedly watched the Caribbean.

"But those days seemed like weeks."

"Did you bring me a gift, Uncle Gustave?" Jimmy carefully controlled his diction.

"Yes, indeed." Gustave smiled benevolently. "And presents for the ladies, too." He clapped his hands and looked expectantly toward the door.

Selene sipped tea, wondering how she could escape the little family scene and find Drake. He'd left in such a hurry he hadn't told her where he was staying or where they would next meet. Already she missed him. She knew what Gustave meant about days seeming like weeks, but she doubted if the Frenchman really understood the meaning of his words.

"There you are." Gustave beckoned at someone in the doorway.

Jon stepped into the room, his head narrowly missing the top of the doorway. He held several packages in his right arm and a mulatto woman followed with more bundles.

Joy Marie clapped her hands with delight. "What have you brought us?"

"Put the presents on the bed." Gustave appeared very pleased with himself.

But all Selene could think about was what she had shared with Drake under those covers the night before. She had intended to check the sheets and clean

220

them if necessary before a maid had a chance to see them. Now she didn't know what she was going to do. All she wanted was for everyone to leave her room. Besides, it was the height of indecency for Gustave to be in her bedroom while she and Joy Marie were still in their nightgowns, even if covered by robes. Of course, it wouldn't be considered quite the problem if they were, indeed, a family.

When the packages were piled on the bed, the mulatto woman left. Jon remained, standing near the doorway and positioned so only his right arm was in view by those at the table.

Selene had noticed him standing that way before so his loss of a left arm would be less noticeable. Realizing he was sensitive about it, she had tried to be kind and ignore his loss whenever she dealt with him. But it was all too evident that it was Joy Marie who could make the difference in his life. Yet Joy Marie treated him as any other servant, for the only man she could see was Gustave Dominique.

"Jon, please have the breakfast things removed, and fresh tea and scones brought." Gustave straightened his cuffs.

Jon inclined his head, then glanced at Joy Marie. "Anything for you, madame?"

Joy Marie smiled at him. "No thank you." Then her gaze was drawn back to Gustave.

Jon backed from the room and disappeared.

"Now for a small party." Gustave set a chair between Selene and Joy Marie.

Selene tried to move as far away from him as possible, but it wasn't far enough, and soon she felt a warm hand on her thigh. Shocked and infuriated, she

221

pushed away Gustave's hand, then set back her chair so her legs weren't under the table.

Gustave smiled knowingly at her, then let his gaze roam over her state of dishabille. "You aren't going to join our party, Selene?"

"Of course I am." She stared out the window. "I'm simply enjoying the beauty of the scenery." Gustave was making sure she knew he was well aware of her state of undress and that she could do nothing about it without causing a scene. She supposed he thought she would be pleased that he noticed her, but he was making her furious.

"Martinique is a beautiful place." Gustave continued to look at her. "I am glad you like it so well."

Selene was saved from having to talk with him anymore, for two servants appeared and quickly cleared off the table, then reset it with a crisp white linen tablecloth and a bowl of fresh island flowers. A moment later another servant carried in a large silver tray and set it on the table. Quickly and efficiently, silver, china, and crystal were set in front of them all. Then the servants withdrew.

Joy Marie chuckled. "We've already eaten, Gustave, and now we have scones, butter, and marmalade. Are you trying to fatten us up?"

Gustave laughed and clasped her hand. "No, *chérie*. I am quite hungry myself. Will you pour the tea?"

"Certainly, dearest." Joy Marie made a production of serving the tea as she showed herself to be the perfect plantation hostess.

"You do that beautifully." Gustave smiled as he bit into a scone.

The happy domestic scene made Selene lose her appetite. Gustave's duplicity made her furious. And the possible hurt and pain to Joy Marie and Jimmy when the Frenchman decided to stop playing whatever game he was about frightened her. But for the moment there was nothing she could do except watch, wait, and try to learn as much as she could about Gustave Dominique.

Jimmy joined Gustave in eating the scones, and Selene was glad to see her young friend eating so well. She knew he'd never had such good food or so much of it before in his life. He was filling out, wearing expensive new clothes, and learning to ride a horse, shoot, all the things she supposed planters' sons did. But what would happen when Gustave tired of his new toys? She shivered and sipped hot tea. But it didn't warm her.

"Uncle Gustave, when do we get to open our presents?" Jimmy finished a scone and walked over to the bed.

Gustave laughed. "So you cannot wait? Go ahead and bring the presents to me. I will hand them out since only I know which parcel belongs to whom."

Jimmy picked up a large box.

"No. Look in the hall first." Gustave winked at Joy Marie, then Selene.

Jimmy stepped outside, gave a shout, then ran back into the room, his face red with excitement. "A scooter. And bright red. Can—may I take it outside, sir?"

"Remember your manners, Jimmy. First let the ladies open their presents."

Jimmy's face fell, then brightened as he glanced at

the other packages. "You're right, sir. And thank you for the scooter." Jimmy picked up a parcel and brought it to Gustave.

"That is for Joy Marie. You may hand it to her."

Joy Marie laughed with excitement as she took the package, tore it open, and lifted out the contents. "Oh, Gustave, you are much too generous." She held up a cut velvet shawl with satin fringe in brilliant turquoise. Crushing the soft fabric in her hands, she gave Gustave a quick kiss on his cheek. "Thank you, darling."

"I am glad it pleases you."

Selene hated to see what Gustave had bought for her because it was inappropriate for him to be buying her gifts. But if she didn't accept anything, she would create a scene and that would upset Joy Marie. She didn't want to do that or at least not yet.

Jimmy carried over a wooden box.

"I think you will like this, Jimmy." Gustave looked very pleased with himself. "Open it."

Setting it on the rug, Jimmy opened the lid. "Wow! A set of soldiers."

"French and British. I will teach you the important battles and how with a slight change in tactics the other side could have won."

Jimmy turned shinning eyes on Gustave. "Thank you, sir."

Selene bit her lower lip. Maybe she was judging Gustave too harshly. Maybe he really enjoyed giving Jimmy a new life, and Joy Marie, too. Maybe they actually were happy and their future was with Gustave on Martinique. But could she be completely wrong?

4 FREE BOOKS

TO GET YOUR 4 FREE BOOKS WORTH $18.00 — MAIL IN THE FREE BOOK CERTIFICATE T O D A Y

Fill in the Free Book Certificate below, and we'll send your FREE BOOKS to you as soon as we receive it.

If the certificate is missing below, write to: Zebra Home Subscription Service, Inc., P.O. Box 5214, 120 Brighton Road, Clifton, New Jersey 07015-5214.

GET
FOUR
FREE
BOOKS
(AN $18.00 VALUE)

ZEBRA HOME SUBSCRIPTION
SERVICE, INC.
P.O. Box 5214
120 BRIGHTON ROAD
CLIFTON, NEW JERSEY 07015-5214

Jimmy hurried to retrieve another parcel.

"That one is for Selene." Gustave handed it to her.

She pulled off the paper to discover an exquisite black lacquered Oriental box. Opening it, she saw the box was lined with red silk. "Thank you. It's beautiful."

"Beauty for the beautiful." He glanced from Selene to Joy Marie.

Jimmy ran back to get three other smaller packages. After handing them to Gustave, he sat down but could hardly keep still.

Gustave handed each a parcel, then sat back and sipped his tea.

Joy Marie opened hers first. "Oh, Gustave, French perfume. But it's so expensive."

"You deserve the best."

Selene found her present to be perfume, too, but another fragrance. "Thank you."

"We could not have the island flowers more fragrant than the two of you, now could we?" Gustave looked quite pleased with himself.

"You're so thoughtful." Joy Marie sniffed her perfume, then dabbed it on her wrists.

Jimmy could wait no longer and opened his box. "Oh, thanks!" He held it open so everyone could see the wide assortment of candies.

"Gustave, he'll be sick if he eats those all at once." Joy Marie frowned.

"I won't eat them at once. I promise." Jimmy looked anxiously from Joy Marie to Gustave.

"I know you will be prudent." Gustave nodded. "Now take your presents and get Jon to show you how to use your new scooter."

Jimmy stood up. "Thank you, sir." He bowed slightly. "Good day, ladies." Then he hurried from the room, holding his gifts close to his chest.

"I believe we will make a gentleman of him yet." Gustave's voice held great satisfaction.

"But will that help him on the docks?" Selene couldn't stop herself from asking that question.

"No." Gustave frowned.

"He's not going back to the docks." Joy Marie's voice was gentle. "He has taken the place of my boy. We'll adopt him as our son."

"I want Joy Marie to be happy. And Jimmy, too." Gustave clasped Joy Marie's hand.

"We all do." Selene started to get up and leave, then remembered it was her room.

"I know you have watched over Jimmy many years." Joy Marie's blue eyes were troubled. "But can't you trust me and Gustave to look out for him now? We can give him love, a home, family, anything else he desires."

"You mean well, of course." Selene hated her position, but she was still worried about Jimmy. "It's just such a big change for Jimmy."

"But he is adapting well, as you see." Gustave stood up. "You worry about too many people, Selene. You should concentrate on those who love you." He held out his hand for Joy Marie and she stood up, too. "Now there is much for me to do today. I have been too long absent."

"Thank you for the presents." Selene walked toward the door and was glad when they followed her.

"My pleasure." Gustave gave her a slight bow. "I

will look forward to seeing you at dinner."

Joy Marie smiled as she walked from the room, her hand on Gustave's arm.

Selene shut the door, breathed a sigh of relief, and hurried back to the table. She poured a fresh cup of tea, drank it, then set the cup down. China jarred against china. But she didn't care. She paced across the room, picked up the gift wrappings, crushed them together, and dropped them on the table. The perfume and lacquered box she set on her dressing table, thinking that Gustave had been smart not to give her clothes for that would have been insultingly intimate.

She looked at the bed and thoughts of Drake came flooding back. Sitting down on the corner, she pulled bedclothes into her arms and hugged them to her, remembering the passion she had shared with Drake. So dangerous. But so wonderful. Yet to touch him again meant so much more than shared desire. Did she dare do it? Could she not?

But she knew she had no answer yet. And while she had the chance, she must take care of the bedclothes. If Gustave found out through the servants what she had done with Drake, she hated to think of his reaction. She quickly closed the shutters on all the windows so no one could see inside. Tossing back the covers, she found evidence of their lovemaking and the blood from her first time. She pulled off the bedspread, the top sheet, then jerked out the bottom.

Carrying the sheet into the bathroom, she ran water in the bathtub, then began cleaning the sheet. When she was satisfied nothing could be detected, she wrung out the portion of the sheet that was wet, dried it as well as she could on a towel, then carried it back into the bedroom. But how would she get the sheet dried and back on the bed so nobody would know?

Suddenly there was a knock on her door. Startled, she froze, glancing around for a place to hide the sheet. The bedclothes were in shambles, she held a partially wet sheet in her hands, and there was no time to put it all back together again. She felt unbelievably guilty.

The knock came again. "Selene." Gustave's voice was impatient. "I must talk with you now."

"I'm not dressed."

"Put on your robe." He jiggled the doorknob. "Hurry."

"Oh, all right." Giving up, she threw the sheet down in the tangle of bedclothes and stalked to the door. Unlocking it, she held the door open and looked at him.

Gustave stared at her suspiciously. "Step aside. We need to talk."

"You must wait till I dress, then I'll meet you in the parlor."

He pushed her back into the room, then shut and locked the door behind him. When he saw the tossled bedclothes, he whirled on her. "I hired maids for this type of work, Selene. I will not have you turning your hands to this sort of thing. Can you not forget your lowly beginnings?"

"I have no lowly beginnings, for your information." Furious, she walked across the room from him, her long hair wild and untamed around her shoulders. When she looked back at him, her eyes were filled with green fire.

He smiled. "I should anger you more often. You are perfectly beautiful."

"I am perfectly angry." She faced him. "How dare you push your way into my room. It's indecent and you know it." But at least she had distracted him from the sheets.

"This is my home."

"And I am your guest."

"You are much more than that and you know it."

She shrugged. "I will leave soon."

"No." He crossed the space between them and pulled her toward him, his hands hard on her shoulders.

Trying to twist away, she discovered he was much stronger than he looked. "Take your hands off me."

"Your wish is my desire." He dropped his hands. "But you cannot deny me forever."

"I'm concerned about Joy Marie and Jimmy."

"You have such a soft heart, *ma chère*. I will not abandon them. I brought Jimmy here to be with Joy Marie. They need each other."

"And you thought I would follow." Did he do nothing without a master plan?

He chuckled. "I *knew* you would. When you finally realize we are destined to be together, then I will send Joy Marie and Jimmy back to Dalton."

"Drake?" Her heart beat fast.

"Yes. What could be better?" He hesitated, then took her hands. He squeezed them hard. "That may be sooner than I expected."

"What do you mean?" She tried to sound casual but was afraid she didn't achieve it.

"Have you seen Drake Dalton?"

She shook her head negatively, not trusting her voice.

"Look at me." He raised her chin to look into her eyes.

Forcing her temper to flare, she glared, then jerked away from him. She opened the shutters and looked out over the sea.

Gustave snapped the shutters shut and turned her around to face him. "Mr. Dalton has come to the islands. He is a more persistent man than I expected. But perhaps the prize he seeks is great enough that it is worth leaving his ranch unattended."

"You seem to know a lot about him."

"Joy Marie has confided in me."

Selene frowned. "Joy Marie loves you. Jimmy is happy here. Why do you want to send them away?"

"You. When I met you, my plans changed. You can learn to love me, Selene. I will make you a countess. You will have anything you desire. We will travel to France. Our children will be nobility, island planters. And if you want to continue your ministrations to the poor and homeless, then as a plantation lady it is perfectly appropriate." He stepped closer, his dark eyes intense. "Could you hope for more?"

She wrapped her arms around her stomach. Yes, she could. But she didn't say that. She had to keep her wits about her. She mustn't let his smooth words and luxurious pictures cloud her mind. Besides, she didn't need or want to be nobility. She didn't need her children to be rich and spoiled. She had a life she liked. She didn't need to change it to suit a man . . . any man.

"You are right." He smiled. "There is no need to answer. I offer you the world, my name, my title, my children. You could hope for nothing more. You are stubborn so I will give you time, but remember, my patience is growing short."

She could wait no longer to get answers now that he knew Drake was on the island. She must play a better game than she'd been playing. "I'm confused, Gustave. You know how important my business is to me."

Again he took both her hands in his smooth ones. "I understand that. And as I said, you could continue your work on Martinique. In fact, we would work together to explore hypnotism. Don't you see how we belong together?"

"But you have yet to teach me anything about hypnotism."

"Say you will consider marrying me and sharing my life, and I will set aside some time to hypnotize you. It is the best way to learn."

She shivered.

"Do not be afraid. It will not hurt you. Trust me, I will make you happy."

Steeling herself, she looked deep into his dark eyes. "Yes, I'll consider your proposal, and yes, you may hypnotize me."

"*Chérie!*" He crushed her to him, pressing his hot lips to hers. But when he would have gained entry with his tongue, she pulled away.

"Gustave, remember—"

"I know you are a lady, sensitive, innocent. I

promise to be gentle." Stepping back, he looked at her in triumph. "Soon, you will be mine."

He turned and walked across the room. At the door he looked back, saluted her, then unlocked the door, stepped outside, and shut the door behind him.

Selene sat down, her legs trembling. What had she done?

Chapter 17

That afternoon Selene escaped the house to pick wildflowers along the road leading to Dominique Plantation. Orchids, frangipani, oleanders, hibiscus and bougainvillea made a riot of color in her basket. Nearby flame and tulip trees were filled with gorgeous blooms. The air was scented with the fragrance of flowers and the variety of color was wonderful. However, she stayed away from the mancineel tree for she had been warned that during a sudden shower if she were standing under it for shelter the sap, diluted with rainwater, could badly burn her skin.

But so far it was a warm, sunny day and she had few worries about the nature around her, for she had been told there were no dangerous species of animal on the island except the fer-de-lance, or pit viper. If she avoided the undergrowth, she shouldn't come into contact with that particular snake.

But she also watched for spiders. Although she had been told they weren't poisonous, she had seen huge spiders outside the house and she had a fear of waking up with one in her bed. Of course, she was well aware the main danger on Martinique was of the human variety, but she still exercised caution amid the haunting beauty of the island.

As she walked, she came to a banana tree. She pulled off a piece of ripe fruit, peeled it, then enjoyed the sweet, creamy taste. Finished, she tossed the peel into the jungle and continued walking. Martinique was breathtakingly beautiful, and if not for Gustave, she could have enjoyed it completely.

As the road twisted to the right, she walked out of sight of the house. Relief flooded her. Now no one could see her. Gustave was busy with his sugar cane fields. Joy Marie, Jon, and Jimmy were playing with the new scooter. And she had convinced her usual guard she would simply pick flowers nearby, knowing that in the early afternoon most everyone rested and he would not want to follow her. Pleased with herself, she glanced around.

Suddenly a young mulatto girl stepped out of the undergrowth.

Surprised, Selene stopped.

"You are Selene Morgan?"

"Yes."

"I am Josephine. I am named for the famous French Empress from Martinique."

Selene smiled, enjoying the girl's pretty accent. "Yes. I've heard of you."

"Good. I am to lead you to M'sieur Dalton. Are you pleased to come now?"

"Drake didn't say anything about it earlier." Selene decided to be cautious.

"You can trust me. I am the great-granddaughter of Ancient Mam. We are descended from the Carib who were here before the French. Then we called our island Madinina." She smiled. "For many years we frightened the French soldiers. We killed them. They called us Amazons. Now there are not so many of us left, but the power is still ours. And the French are still afraid. I am destined to inherit the rule of Ancient Mam of Madinina." She straightened her back. "As a woman, I give you my word I mean you no harm."

Selene was astonished at the speech. A girl of nine or ten years of age had just vowed not to harm her. Did she even know what Amazon meant? Had the Caribs been women warriors? Right now it didn't really matter, but she suddenly wondered, thinking of Jimmy, if there were any children left. "You are so serious for a young girl."

"I have no time to be young. My great-grandmother is older than old. She must pass on her knowledge to me or it will be lost forever. I am the first to carry the secret of the ancient blood in many years."

Selene could think of nothing to say. Josephine was wrapped in dignity, in strength, and carried herself as an empress. She was obviously being trained to take over an important role on the island. But none of that mattered either. Trust was the question here.

"Will you follow me now?" Josephine inclined her head.

Selene hesitated, looking hard at the young girl's dark brown eyes, smooth colored skin, high cheekbones, and pointed chin. She was already beautiful and intelligent, obviously the result of a combination of Carib, African, and French ancestry. But beauty and youth could not sway Selene's decision. It was the steadiness in Josephine's gaze that decided her. "Yes."

"Follow me. And do not step off the trail." Josephine moved back into the undergrowth and out of sight.

Selene hurried to catch up, wishing she was wearing something more practical to go trekking through the jungle and rocky mountainous terrain. She had chosen a cotton dress of pale green and with the corset, petticoats, and stockings, she was far from cool.

Josephine, on the other hand, wore a blouse and skirt of white cotton, embroidered around the neckline and hem. The short-sleeved blouse had a scoop neck that could be worn on or off the shoulders. A rose satin ribbon was threaded through the embroidery to match the overskirt of rose and green madras. On her head Josephine wore an elaborately folded madras handkerchief with one end left sticking up like a plume. Around her shoulders she had pinned a matching shawl. She also wore silver Creole hoop earrings and a silver chain around her neck.

Selene had learned this was the traditional dress of Martiniquaise and she envied them the freedom and coolness and beauty of their clothes. In fact, she was thinking of leaving off her corset and wearing the same, if Joy Marie and Gustave wouldn't be too shocked.

At that moment she felt a spider web skim her face and she stopped. Taking a step backward, she looked around for one of the huge spiders. She saw none, then quickly patted her hair but touched no spider. Then she noticed Josephine far ahead. Hoping it had been an empty web, she thrust the spider from her mind and hurried to catch up.

Walking north toward Mount Pelée, Selene was once more transfixed by the beauty of the island. She saw giant ferns and bamboo, palms of numerous shapes and sizes, mahogany and gum trees, fruit trees and trees she couldn't possibly name, along with flowers, shrubs, and creepers. When they passed a stone forest where fossilized trunks gave testimony to the age of the island, she picked up a piece of fossil and placed it in her basket.

But underlying her appreciation of the beauty all around was the drumming of her heart in anticipation of seeing Drake again with all that now lay between them. She could no longer consider him a stranger or a man simply passing through her life. Their lives had become entwined and for now she must consider him her best friend. Yet she was well aware of how dangerous he was to her.

Josephine stepped around a boulder near the path and disappeared. Selene hurried after her, then stopped in amazement, for the beauty of the island she had previously seen was as nothing compared to the scene that lay before her.

Water fell down the steep cliff of a rock face, white and foamy and steamy. At the base of the waterfall, water ran over a rock surface worn smooth by years of constant erosion. Trees grew on either side of the waterfall, their long trunks arching over the base of the falls. Vibrant green in the sunlight turned to deep green in the shade as it framed white water, sparkling brightly in the sunlight.

"He is there." Josephine pointed to a dark shape in the shadow of the trees.

Selene's mind jerked back to reality as Drake stepped into view. Her heart instantly beat faster.

Josephine's brown eyes, as ancient and knowledgable as a sparrow's, focused on Selene. "Go to your man." Then she disappeared into the jungle.

Go to your man. Selene wanted to deny those words, but they touched her heart with truth. Yet what did a child know? She forced the girl's idea from her mind and moved toward Drake and the waterfall.

"It's beautiful." She stared at the cascading water, feeling the spray sprinkle her face.

"Yes." But he looked only at Selene.

She glanced at him to share the moment, then realized he wasn't watching the fall. "The water, Drake." She gestured around them. "The lushness of the trees and flowers and fruit."

He drew her to him. "Nothing's more beautiful than you and Texas."

She chuckled. "I take it being compared to Texas is a compliment."

"It is." He didn't return her laugh.

"But does Texas have water like this?" Again she indicated the waterfall. "Or so many flowers? Or so much fruit on the trees just waiting to be picked? It's a paradise here."

Drake finally looked around. "Texas has enough

238

water and food for humans and animals to survive. Martinique is too easy."

"Easy?" She shook her head in amazement.

"Yes." He frowned. "A man could get soft living here. He'd forget life is a battle. He'd forget you've got to fight for what you want and take what you can get."

"Drake, that's so primitive."

"I'm not soft or easy." He raised her hands to his lips and kissed each fingertip. "But for you I can be gentle."

She bit her lower lip. Why did he always say the right thing? He made her weak when she needed to be strong. But maybe he was right, or partly right, about life. Her grandmother had struggled to survive the aftermath of the War, and Selene had always fought to help her friends. But now she felt tired, so tired.

Maybe she felt that way because of the ease of life Gustave had showed her. In the world Gustave had created, there was no work, no fight, no discord. She had a beautiful place to live, fine clothes, delicious food, wonderful friends. If she could shut her eyes to the lives of those who worked the fields or lived in shacks, then she could enjoy what the Frenchman promised her.

But she wasn't blind to the reality of life, although she almost wished she were, wished she could stop fighting, wished she could relax and let somebody else take over and make the decisions. Then she wouldn't be to blame and she could simply enjoy the luxury of another person's work, someone else's decisions. All she would have to do was give her body up to Gustave Dominique, and perhaps her soul as well.

"Are you all right?" Drake's gaze searched her face.

"Yes. Gustave came back this morning."

"I know."

"He brought gifts."

Drake smirked. "Does he think he can buy love and loyalty?"

"Apparently so. And the presents were beautiful. Jimmy has a new scooter and a set of soldiers."

"A scooter." Drake snorted. "He'd be better off learning to ride a horse and chase dogies."

Selene smiled. "Or unload a ship."

"If he gets too soft—"

"I know." She hesitated. "But Jimmy seems happy."

"There's a difference between being happy and being in control."

She arched a brow. "Can't they go together?"

"Yes. But you better make damn sure you're in control first."

Maybe that was her trouble. Drake made her feel out of control no matter how good he made her feel when she was with him. She looked away from him, and realized the waterfall didn't seem quite so beautiful anymore. "You can't control me, Drake."

"I don't want to control you. And I won't let you control me. But we're going to meet in the middle, someway, somehow."

She glanced up at him. His dark eyes were filled with determination, with passion. "And what if it's not possible?"

"Are you telling me your love potions don't work?"

Smiling, she touched his lips with a fingertip, then with her mouth. Before he could take her in his arms, she stepped back. "They work, but I don't know for how long or if they can help two people become one."

"I don't want one person, Selene. I want you and I want me. Together."

"In Texas."

"Right."

She smiled over her shoulder, then walked to the waterfall. "And I'm supposed to give up my life?"

"No." He followed her, slanted a harsh glance at the spray misting them, then took her hand. "I'm not asking you to give up a damn thing. I want us to build a life together."

She shook her head and sat down on a rock. "In New Orleans?" She set aside the basket.

"No, damn it." He kicked pebbles into the water. "Wait till you've seen Texas. If you hate it, then—"

"What?" She took off her shoes and rolled down a stocking.

Drake watched.

As she lowered the other stocking, she glanced up at him. "No answer?"

"When we get to Texas, we'll have all the answers we need. Right now I don't give a damn about anything except you." He knelt beside her and reached to pull her into his arms.

But she held up a hand to stop him. "No. I can't think straight in your arms."

"I stopped thinking a while ago."

She stood up and raised her skirts to her knees.

Drake groaned, but didn't stop watching her.

Water cascaded across a rock face that had been worn in the pattern of stairs. She decided to walk up it closer to the main fall. Stepping into the water, her foot slid on moss and she lost her balance. She fell, but caught herself with one hand. She lay stretched out across the rock, water flowing around her, soaking her clothes.

"Selene!" Drake ran toward her. "Are you okay?"

"Yes." She tried all her limbs and they still worked. "But be careful. It's slippery."

"Let me help you up." Keeping a foot on the bank, he leaned over and held out his hand.

She took it, but as she rose she overbalanced and slipped back, pulling him with her. He fell in the water with a loud splash.

"Drake, I'm sorry." But she couldn't help laughing at the two of them. They were both so wet.

He sat down beside her. "It's not funny. We could have broken something."

She laughed harder, then leaned back against the smooth, slippery stone. The water was cool as it flowed over her. "As long as I'm wet, I'm going to enjoy myself." She began undressing.

Drake watched her a moment. "This is getting less funny all the time." His dark eyes glinted. "If you think I'll watch you play naked in the water and . . . what if somebody comes along."

"You'll defend me, won't you?" She threw her dress on the bank, then followed it with her petticoats.

Finally, he grinned. "Maybe you're right." He started throwing his clothes after hers.

It wasn't easy with the strings wet, but she finally

got off her corset and threw it as far away as she could. But she left on her green silk chemise and drawers. She knew it wasn't safe to be around Drake completely nude and especially not if someone did happen by. But they were secreted deep in the jungle and she didn't expect to be disturbed.

As Drake pulled off his boots, she stood and began carefully making her way to the waterfall. Soon its spray stung her skin and she glanced down. Wet, her silk underclothes were almost transparent. But she tossed her head. She was going to enjoy herself and forget about everything except the beauty of the water and her pleasure in it.

The waterfall cascaded into a deep pool surrounded by rock. Sitting on the side, she immersed her feet and legs in the water. Water sprayed her body as she kicked her feet up and down, tossing more water into the mist. Laughing, she felt lighthearted as she cast her worries aside.

Suddenly strong, warm hands clasped her shoulders, drawing her backward against a hard chest. She leaned back her head and looked up into Drake's smoldering eyes. Desire swept through her and it must have shown in her own green gaze for he turned her toward him and pressed hot lips to hers. She moaned low in her throat, desiring him, needing him, and yet not wanting to make the commitment.

"Selene." His voice was hoarse as he toyed with her lips, letting his tongue tease her mouth until she writhed under his hands.

When she opened her mouth, he quickly plunged inside and turned her body into his so that her breasts, the tips hard, strained against his chest.

Again, she moaned and grasped his shoulders, reveling in the strength of him. He pushed her back against the rock, water cascaded over her, cool mist filled the air, and yet she was hot all over.

"Drake, please. I can't."

"Is it babies?"

She nodded. "And—"

He planted a quick, hard kiss on her lips. "Don't worry. You'll have your pleasure." He nibbled down her neck, then paused to excite her at the sensitive area between her neck and shoulder. She shivered, running her hands over his shoulders, down his arms, then back again.

Continuing downward, he licked at the moist fabric covering her taut nipples, then sucked. She arched upward and he clasped her full breasts in his warm hands. Then he moved even lower to pull down her drawers and cast them aside.

"Drake, no."

"Be still. I won't hurt you."

He spread her legs, knelt between them, then raised her hips slightly. When he pressed his mouth to her hot, moist core, she cried out in shock and tried to twist away.

"Trust me, Selene."

Passion overcoming her better sense, she lay still, but not for long as his fingers excited her then his tongue until she twisted her fingers in his long hair as she panted with building tension. Clasping his shoulders, she cried out as ecstasy took her and carried her to fulfillment.

Spent, she relaxed and he gathered her into his

arms. Pressing soft kisses to her face, he held her close. "Are you happy?"

"Yes." She blushed, trailing fingers through the water around them. "But, Drake, I'd never have thought—"

"Don't think."

She glanced at his face and was rewarded with a look of passionate possession. "This still doesn't mean we're going to Texas."

He chuckled. "You aren't an easy woman, Selene, but I figure when you finally give yourself to a man heart and soul, there'll be no turning back."

She splashed water at his face to distract him. The future wasn't something she wanted to discuss. Then she realized he was completely naked. And aroused. She looked at his hard shaft and felt a mingling of wonder, delight, and desire. Although what he'd done for her had been good, she suddenly wanted him deep inside her. But that couldn't be. Not now. Yet it didn't seem fair.

Reaching out to touch his manhood, she hesitated, but he quickly grasped her hand and pressed it around the hard, hot length.

"I want you to be happy, too." She threw him a questioning glance.

"I'll show you."

He began moving her hand up and down his shaft, teaching her the movement, the rhythm, the excitement. Seeing the way she affected him made her feel powerful. Yet she also felt humbled at the idea of giving, exploring, sharing so much pleasure with another person. She glanced upward to watch his eyes. Their gaze locked, then he lowered his face and kissed her as pleasure took him.

When his passion was spent, he kissed her hands. Giving her a satisfied grin, he pulled her close, then rolled them over the edge into the deep pool of water.

Sputtering, she came to the surface and felt his arms go around her, pulling her tight to his body. Surrounded by mist, he held them afloat with one hand on the bank. "You're right, it's beautiful here."

"But more beautiful in Texas?"

He laughed, then sealed her lips with a kiss.

Chapter 18

Selene eyed her pile of clothes distastefully and Drake wantonly. She wasn't even embarrassed about it which was a perfect example of her state of mind, or rather emotions, after succumbing to her passion once more.

While she sat on the bank letting her underclothes dry on her body, she watched Drake splash around in the pool under the waterfall. Unfortunately, she couldn't blame Drake Dalton of Texas for her feelings. She blamed, as she had so many times before, her love potions.

Rosa had warned her, but she hadn't listened. Thinking of her friend and assistant, she smiled. Just that morning before leaving for her walk, she had received a letter from Rosa. No more of their friends had disappeared in New Orleans, Love Potions had its usual amount of business, Rosa had found a part-time assistant, and Alfred was preparing to leave for a job in New York City.

Reading between the lines, she understood Rosa's

anguish over losing Alfred. She sent a small rock spinning into the water. How did one mend a broken heart? She was afraid if things kept going as they were in her own life, she might very well find out.

Drake levered himself out of the pool, then walked over to her and sat down. He grinned, taking her hand.

Aware of her dishabille, she still didn't care she was so caught in his spell. She couldn't stop looking at his bronzed, muscular body, or not notice the fact that he wanted her again . . . and was quite ready to act on it. Just the simple touch of his fingers sent waves of longing through her and she caught herself leaning toward him.

Snapping her eyes shut, she shook her head to clear it. "Drake, please put on some clothes."

Rubbing a thumb over her sensitive palm, he moved closer. "There's a lot more we can share, Selene." His breath was warm on her face.

She shivered, feeling tingles race from her hand to her heart. Fierce passion seized her. She bit her lower lip, hoping pain would make the desire recede. "I've got to get back, Drake. A guard, or Gustave, may come looking for me. Joy Marie will be worried."

He pushed a damp strand of hair back from her face. "They can't find us here." He traced her features with a fingertip. "I don't know how long it'll be before we'll get another chance to be together like this." He lightly kissed her lips.

"Drake, no!" She pushed him away and sprang up.

"That bad?"

"You know better." She hurried away from him to pick up her clothes.

He followed, turning her around to face him. "Be honest with me, Selene."

She looked into his brown eyes and felt her resolve fail. "I—I want you. All right?"

He smiled. "Very much all right."

"But I can't let you distract me. There's so much to do, so much to worry about. We must talk, but not about us. We must make plans." She stopped, very aware of the heat of his hands on her shoulders. "Help me."

"Damn, Selene, I'm no good at letting you go."

"Please."

He pushed fingers through his wet hair. "All right." He placed a soft kiss on her lips, then walked over to his clothes and jerked on his trousers. "Better?"

"Thanks. I'll get dressed, too."

"Want some help?"

She backed away. "No. I might not ever—"

"You're right." He pulled on his shirt, then sat down to put on his socks and boots. "So what are we going to do about Gustave Dominique?"

Selene thought as she dressed, watching Drake watch her. Suddenly she realized she was enjoying his pleasure in looking at her. Surprised, she blushed, then shook her head at herself. She might as well admit that with Drake in her life she had entered a world she had previously ignored. And she might as well admit, too, it was one she enjoyed.

For the first time she could really *feel*, not just understand, Rosa's commitment to Alfred and her willingness to give up her personal happiness to better the life of the man she loved. But would it be best for him to lose what he had with Rosa to improve himself financially? Selene knew she wasn't the one to answer that question.

Drake slipped the knife out of his boot and tested the edge with his thumb. "I think you should lure Dominique away from his guards. I can catch him by surprise, then beat him within an inch of his life and make him promise to let everybody go."

Selene stopped dressing to look at Drake in astonishment. "Beat him? Make him promise?" In underclothes, petticoat, and stockings, she walked over to him. "We're talking about Gustave Dominique!"

"So? He's a man like any other and less man than most Texans I know."

"But he's a hypnotist. No telling what might happen."

"I don't put much store in that mind stuff, Selene."

"Then you explain what's been going on."

"I told you. Drugs or something. He's French. It could be anything."

She whirled around and went back to dressing. "Anyway, you can't get him away from his guards. He's cautious."

"Not around you, I bet."

She blushed, and hated her reaction. It seemed as if being around Drake was continually embarrassing her and it was not a state to which she was accustomed. "You do have a point, though. Maybe I could make a trade with him—myself for all the others. I could stay with him, perhaps for a certain period of time, if he would let everyone else go."

Drake jumped up and rushed over to her. Dragging her against his chest, he crushed her to him. "No way in hell are you doing to do that. Get it out of your mind right now."

"But Drake." Her words were mumbled against his chest. She could hardly breathe he was holding her so tight. She pushed against him. He eased his grip only slightly.

"I don't want to hear any more about you sacrificing yourself to Dominique." He held her away from him so he could look into her eyes.

She nodded.

"Now let's get down to some serious thinking."

"Drake, I don't believe we have enough information yet. Gustave has agreed to talk with me about hypnotism and I plan to find out if it's really affecting these people. But right now I don't know which way to turn."

"Ancient Mam, Josephine, and their people will help us, or we'll assist them as it'll probably turn out."

"Josephine is impressive, isn't she?"

"Wait'll you meet Ancient Mam." Drake grinned.

Selene returned his smile, once more appreciating his strength and humor. "I'd like to meet her so we could talk about the changes Gustave has brought to Martinique."

"Can you get away?"

"I did today, but it's not easy." She finished dressing. "In fact, I should be getting back right now."

"Are you sure you don't want me to pound the information out of Dominique?"

She shook her head at him. "I'd like that very much, but we've got to think of Joy Marie, Jimmy, and the others."

"I'm going to do some more nosing around Dominique's plantation and the island. If I can find out about the workers—"

"And I find out about Gustave—"

"Then maybe we can come up with a plan." Drake stroked her cheekbone with his thumb. "But be damn careful. Don't take any chances with Dominique."

"I'll do what I have to do."

"I don't like the sound of that, Selene."

She smiled and took his hand. "Will you come see me tonight?"

"It'll take more than Dominique's zombies and dogs to keep me away."

She shuddered. "They aren't zombies."

"If for some reason I can't, I'll send Josephine."

"And I'd like to talk with Ancient Mam."

"I'll see what I can do." He glanced at the path leading back to Dominique's house. "I don't want you to go back." He hugged her, held her a long moment, then set her away from him. "But go on before I change my mind and forget everything else except you and me."

She gave him a quick kiss, picked up her basket of flowers, now sadly wilted, and hurried away. Once on the path, she glanced back, threw him a kiss, then stepped around a large rock and lost sight of him.

When Selene got near Gustave's mansion, she

decided not to come up the road in case someone was looking for her. She'd been gone a long time and she didn't know what she'd find back at the house. But after the interlude with Drake, she was more determined than ever to quickly put an end to the doubts and questions, then get on with her life.

Moving as quietly as possible, she replaced the wilted flowers with fresh ones and came upon the gazebo in back. She stopped near a tree to look at the pretty wooden structure that had been painted bright white. If somebody was looking for her, the gazebo might not be a bad place to be found. She could explain that she'd fallen asleep there.

She slipped from tree to tree, determined not to be seen before she got inside it. Finally reaching a large tree which spread its wide limbs protectively over the gazebo, she hesitated, ready to make the final dash. Suddenly she heard voices. Surprised, she hesitated, listening for the sound. Then she realized people were in the gazebo. Disgusted her plans were spoiled, she turned to go, but heard a voice lash out in anger.

"Get down on your knees, Joy Marie."

Surprised, Selene started forward to see what was going on, then remembered the need for caution. She put a hand on the tree near her, feeling rough bark against her soft skin. Moving slightly, she could see through the gazebo to the scene inside.

Gustave held Joy Marie by her shoulders. He shook her hard. Her hair came loose and tumbled down her back. He shook her harder. "You have been sniffing after those mulattoes, haven't you? Those dirty field workers. That is what you like, is it not?"

"No. Gustave, please. I love only you."

He stepped back and hit her in the stomach with his fist. She doubled over, and groaned.

Selene took several steps forward, then stopped herself. She mustn't give herself away, not yet. She could help Joy Marie now that she had proof Gustave was hurting her, but she had to do it in the right way and at the right time.

"Get up." Gustave's voice snapped with authority.

Selene had never heard him speak in that tone of voice before and it chilled her to her depths.

Joy Marie slowly stood up, holding her hands over her stomach. She gazed at Gustave and smiled. "You're all the man I want."

"And all you're going to have, you wanton woman." He toyed with her hair, then wrapped it around his fist and pulled.

Her features contorted with pain as he drew her face up toward his. When she was on her tiptoes, he jerked and she groaned. "Please don't hurt me, Gustave."

"You force me to hurt you. I am trying to make you a lady, but you want to rut with any crude male you see. It started with your brother-in-law and now it is my field hands."

"No, I never. I told you—"

He punched her again, and Joy Marie bent double.

Selene dropped the basket of flowers and collapsed against the tree. Has she been right in New Orleans? Was Drake really in love with Joy Marie? Had they had an affair before Joy Marie ran off with Gustave? She felt chilled.

Drake had said he wanted her to go back to Texas

with him, that he'd come to Martinique after her. But what if Drake was doing to her what Gustave was doing to Joy Marie? What if he was using one woman while he waited for another? Suddenly she felt sick at her stomach.

Joy Marie slowly stood, but stayed bent over as she protected her stomach with crossed arms. "I love you, Gustave."

"You stupid bitch. What do you know about love?"

Tears fell down Joy Marie's cheeks. "You don't mean that, Gustave. You love me, too. But you're afraid of loving me, afraid I'll leave. It's not true. We have our family. Little Jimmy."

Gustave grabbed her hair in a fist and jerked her head upward. He glared into her face. "Our happy little family, right?"

Joy Marie nodded. "I could give you children, Gustave, if you'd let me. We could have our own family. And Jimmy, too."

Selene pressed her back against the tree, feeling sick and scared. What was real? Could she believe no one, not even Drake? Or was it all a crazy game of Gustave's. But why? And why did Joy Marie let Gustave treat her the way he did? Surely love didn't mean total self-abasement? Hot tears burned her eyes, then splashed down her cheeks. She wanted desperately to leave, but couldn't. She had to learn all she could no matter how bad it got.

"Get down on your knees where you belong." Gustave spoke harshly.

Joy Marie knelt in front of him.

He pulled out the crystal he wore as a watch fob and swung it back and forth in front of Joy Marie's face.

"Yes." Joy Marie smiled. "Please, Gustave, take away the pain with your pretty bauble."

Selene blinked her eyes free of tears, and watched. She must set aside her feelings, she must concentrate on learning what she could to save Joy Marie.

Gustave swung the crystal back and forth. "You are feeling relaxed, Joy Marie. Sleepy."

Joy Marie nodded.

"You are going to show me what you do to hulking field hands, what you did with Drake Dalton, with your husband. You are going to show me as you did before. Remember?"

Joy Marie nodded.

He swung the crystal steadily and his voice continued to drone. "Sleepy. Soon your eyes will close. But you will be alert. You will feel good, sexy, ready to do my bidding. What you do will make you happy, will make you relive your love with your husband. And when you awake you will be pleased and satisfied."

Selene watched, more astonished by the moment.

"Your eyes are heavy, very heavy. You are sleepy." Gustave's voice was persuasive.

Joy Marie's eyes closed.

"But you are hot, very hot." Gustave put his crystal away.

Joy Marie tugged down her bodice, exposing her breasts, the tips rosy and hard.

Selene looked away, then forced herself to watch again. She dreaded what would come next.

"And you are in love, hungry for your man's body."

Joy Marie caught Gustave around his hips and pressed her breasts against him, sliding up and down on him.

"You know what your man likes. Baby."

Joy Marie quickly undid Gustave's trousers and pulled out his shaft. Taking him in her small hands, she massaged him to hardness. Then took him in her mouth.

Selene gasped and started to turn away. But she heard her name called. Shocked, she looked upward and encountered Gustave's eyes. He put a hand on Joy Marie's head, and smiled.

Selene didn't wait for more. She ran from the gazebo and didn't stop until she reached the house. Jimmy and Jon were on the verandah drinking lemonade.

"Selene, what's wrong?" Jimmy's voice held concern.

Eyes wide, she glanced from one to the other. She looked back over her shoulders, tried to speak, couldn't, and started up the stairs.

"Sit down, Miss Selene." Jon pulled a rocker near Jimmy's chair. "Folks've been looking for you."

She shook her head in denial, determined to get into the house and hide.

"Sit down." Jon got up and drew her to the chair. "You been by the gazebo?"

She glanced wildly around, then finally looked him in the eye. And saw understanding.

"It's not wise to go down to the gazebo late in the afternoon." He motioned toward the rocker. "You rest now. I'll get you some lemonade."

Selene collapsed into the chair.

"Want to see one of my soldiers?" Jimmy pushed a red-uniformed British soldier into her hand.

She took it automatically, unable to look away from the white top of the gazebo peeking up among tree branches.

"Uncle Gustave's teaching me about important battles."

Selene snapped her head around. "Uncle Gustave?"

Jimmy nodded, obviously quite pleased with the situation.

"What about your friends in New Orleans?"

Jimmy looked confused a moment, then his face cleared. "My friends are on Martinique. I'm happy here with Aunt Joy Marie and Uncle Gustave."

Selene felt further chilled. She handed back the toy soldier.

Jon stepped outside. "You got too hot out there in the jungle. You're not used to it." He handed Selene a cool glass of lemonade. "Drink that." He sat down. "You'll know not to go walking in the afternoons from now on, won't you?"

She took a long drink, hesitated, then finished the liquid. In a way it did make her feel better, but on the other hand it made her stomach even queasier. And she couldn't stop her mind from churning. Gustave didn't want Joy Marie's children because he planned to marry her. Perhaps Drake had taught her similar lessons for the same reason. For a moment she thought she'd throw up.

Were men all deceitful, hateful creatures? Or was

Gustave unique? She glanced at Jimmy. What would he do to women when he grew up? Could there really be any kind of love and trust? Maybe Rosa was right. Perhaps she understood much more than Selene had realized.

As her thoughts gathered force, she saw Joy Marie and Gustave walking up the path from the gazebo. Joy Marie was completely dressed again. Gustave plucked a blossom from a bush and tucked it behind her ear. Her laughter rang out, then she gave him a kiss on the cheek.

Selene's stomach turned. Had everyone lost all rational sense? She started to get up and go to her room.

"It'll be easier to face now than later." Jon rocked lazily in his chair.

Once more she saw understanding in his eyes and she remembered his attention to Joy Marie. Was he in love with Joy Marie Dalton, too?

But Jon was right and maybe he was one of the few sane people left on Dominique Plantation. She sat up straighter and smiled as Joy Marie walked up the stairs.

"Selene, we've been worried about you." Joy Marie gave her a quick kiss on the cheek. "Where did you go?"

Gustave's shadow fell across the two women. "Yes, where have you been, Selene?" He held up the basket of flowers. "Is this yours?"

She couldn't stop the blush that warmed her face, but she met Gustave's stare and kept the frozen smile on her face. "Yes. I'm afraid I must confess I saw a huge spider and dropped the basket. I couldn't make myself go back so I simply wandered the road, looking at all the beauty of Martinique."

Gustave handed her the basket. "If you want to go looking for flowers again, tell me. I know how to find the best ones."

"Thank you. I'll certainly be more careful in the future." She raised her chin. "By the way, where did you find my basket of flowers? In my headlong flight, I didn't know where I dropped it."

"Not far from here."

"Near the gazebo." Joy Marie smiled. "It's so pretty there, isn't it? But excuse me, I must run inside to make sure dinner is served promptly." She gave everyone a bright smile, then stepped into the house.

"Yes, it's been a long day and I believe I'll have a nap before dinner." Selene kept the smile on her face as she left the verandah.

Chapter 19

Selene sat on a rococo chair in her bedroom watching the sun set. Rays of red and orange and yellow sunlight played across the turquoise waters of the Caribbean. She felt confused, angry, embarrassed, and unsure what to do next. In her state of mind not even the beauty of her surroundings made her feel better.

Gustave hadn't been in the least concerned she'd seen him with Joy Marie. In fact, he'd seemed pleased about it. And that had certainly not been the reaction she'd expected. She studied her hands a moment, as if she could find an answer in them. Joy Marie had been quite happy when she and Gustave had come back . . . almost as if she'd just returned from an afternoon walk. But perhaps Gustave made Joy Marie as happy as she insisted. Selene shuddered at the idea.

Actually, nothing had changed. She still didn't have enough answers. In fact, she had more questions. She wanted desperately to discuss it all with

Drake, but did she dare trust him now? Had he been Joy Marie's lover or was that simply part of Gustave's fantasy world, too? It was getting more difficult to tell reality from fantasy all the time.

And the last thing she wanted was to endure another lengthy dinner with Gustave's little family. Perhaps she could plead a headache and have a tray sent up to her bedroom. On the other hand, she didn't want Gustave to think she couldn't face him after what she'd seen him do to Joy Marie. But she had already confronted him that afternoon so surely she wouldn't appear weak if she stayed in her room. When it came down to it, she simply wasn't up to anything else that day and especially not when she was expecting Drake later.

Getting up, she scribbled a note to Joy Marie asking to have a tray sent up, then pulled the bell rope. Pleased with her decision, she waited until the maid knocked, handed her the note, then went back to the windows. Night would soon be upon them and Drake would come to her. How could she face him after what she'd learned? What would she say?

She had no answer, no answer at all. Shivering, she decided to take a long, steamy, fragrant bath since she didn't expect to be bothered until late in the night.

Not long after, she ran fingers through the thick bubbles covering her bath water, dropped her silk robe to the floor, and sank down into the warm water. It felt wonderful and she was reminded of being with Drake under the waterfall, his hard body supporting hers. And the passion they'd shared. That thought made her tingle all over. She smiled to herself, wishing she could trust Drake and knowing she couldn't. Not yet.

With the door to the bathroom closed, the light from a single candle casting the room mostly in shadows, and the silence of the evening descending over the house, Selene felt her body relax. As the water cooled, she dozed, letting the aches and pains and frustrations dissolve into the scented bathwater. And she dreamed of Drake's mouth on hers, his hands caressing her body, touching her as no one had ever touched her before.

The door to the bathroom creaked open. Startled awake, she was disoriented and for a moment couldn't remember where she was. Then she noticed the person quietly entering the bathroom was carrying a tray. The maid. She relaxed again, then wondered why the servant was bringing her meal so early and to the bathroom.

"*Chérie*, I was distressed to learn you did not feel well."

"Gustave!" Shocked, Selene checked to make sure her body was still covered with bubbles. Fortunately, it was. "How dare you come in here?" Embarrassment was quickly replaced by anger. "I locked the door."

He chuckled. "I have a key. Are you not ready for your dinner?"

"I don't want it, or you, in here."

"Your wish is my command." He backed from the room, carrying the tray.

She sighed in relief and picked up a towel from the floor. But before she could get up, Gustave was back

263

in the doorway.

"Do you have any idea how beautiful you are in the candlelight, all rosy and scented and soft from your bath."

Selene blushed, and suddenly remembered what she'd seen Joy Marie do to him earlier. "I'm resting this evening, Gustave."

He crossed his legs. "What were you doing this afternoon, Selene? You know I do not like for you to wander around alone."

"A better question is what you were doing to Joy Marie?"

He chuckled again. "I thought it would come to that. I am keeping her happy, what else?"

"You were degrading her."

"No. She is a woman who needs to be needed, who needs to do for a man. To be happy she must make others happy. And she made me happy this afternoon." He nodded. "You were not shocked, for you are a physician and you must know a man's body as well as a woman's."

"That's not the point. You're hurting her."

"She has a certain place in my life and it suits both of us for me to keep her there."

"Would you leave so I can get dressed?" She was getting nowhere with him and now she was shriveling up in the bathwater. What had been warm and comforting had become cold and dangerous.

"I'll help you." He stepped into the bathroom, picked up her robe, and held it out to her.

Shocked, she frowned. "How dare you even think such a thing?"

"We are destined to be together, Selene. Why should we let the ways of those less noble affect us? I want to see you, touch you, hold you. Why should I wait?"

"Joy Marie. I won't have her hurt."

"What she does not know cannot hurt her."

"I don't want you here. Leave."

He regarded her a moment. "As you wish." He dropped her robe and shut the door behind him.

Grabbing the towel, she quickly rubbed her body dry, then slipped on the long robe. But it clung to her, revealing much more than she would have liked. She hoped Gustave had left her bedroom, but she doubted it. He wasn't done with her yet. Well, she wasn't done with him either. She had questions she wanted answered, and if she had to get them wearing nothing more than a silk robe, she would. Raising her chin, she left the bathroom.

Gustave turned from a window and the last rays of the sun bathed him in a golden glow. "You belong on Martinique, Selene. You are a rare flower among exotic flowers."

"Your pretty words won't work on me."

"I know. Your fragile beauty conceals a heart of iron. But I like that. You will have excellent children."

Selene walked over to him, deciding to get answers no matter the cost. "I came here to be with Joy Marie. I came here to learn more about hypnotism."

"And I have not obliged you, have I?" He lifted a tendril of her damp hair, then let it fall.

"No."

"And I promised to share my life with you, did I not?"

"Yes."

He gave her a considering stare. "I have not avoided speaking of hypnotism. I want to share that with you. But first I wanted you to know me better, to see my plantation, to enjoy the life I am creating here, to see your place within the scope of my world."

"You've done all that."

He slowly looked down the length of her, then back up to her face. "And I wanted to know you better. Much better."

"You know me well enough."

"You are a beautiful flower, but you have not opened yourself to me. Yet I know how to open you."

She clasped her arms across her stomach to stop the sudden shiver that swept her. "I think not."

"You do not understand the power or importance of hypnotism. But I will teach you."

"That's what I want." She fought down her anger, fear, and revulsion. Instead she thought of Jimmy, of Joy Marie, of her friends and how what she did now could help free them, if they needed it.

He touched the crystal watch fob at his waist, and smiled. "Sit here." He pulled a rococo chair near an open window, then he placed another across from it. Taking her hand, he led her to a chair and pushed her into it. He sat down across from her, their knees almost touching.

"Now listen." His voice was soft, low, cajoling. "A great deal of study on hypnotism has been done in France. After learning what I could there, I have traveled, adding to and perfecting my own theory of hypnosis."

Selene leaned forward, unaware that her robe parted to reveal the cleft of her breasts.

But Gustave was very aware. His gaze traveled from her face downward and he smiled as he leaned back in his chair. "My theory. Every person has an objective and subjective mind. The objective controls hearing, sight, taste, touch, and smell . . . the senses. The subjective controls memory."

"And so?"

"While the objective mind is capable of both inductive and deductive reasoning, the subjective mind is not capable of inductive reasoning."

"What is this inductive and deductive?" Selene wasn't sure if he was trying to confuse her or really explaining the theory of hypnosis.

"Inductive reasoning is arrived at by generalization. As a physician, you analyze the symptoms of a patient and arrive at a diagnosis, which is inductive reasoning. Deductive reasoning is the opposite. If you hear someone is sick with a cold, you will deduce the symptoms."

"Yes, but—"

He raised a hand. "Hear me out. Generalizations are decided through the inductive process and particulars through the deductive. The objective mind is capable of both while the subjective mind only the latter. In other words, the subjective mind reasons well when only the deductive process is involved, but not at all when the inductive process is necessary. As a result, the subjective mind accepts as reality any generalization which is given to it because it is incapable of the inductive process and has no way of disputing that generalization.''

Selene nodded, willing to let him ramble for he was beginning to make some sense.

"These two minds remain in a state of balance in all people. And it is the subjective mind, incapable of inductive reasoning, on which I work.''

"But how? I still don't understand.''

"You cannot expect to learn in a few moments what I have spent a lifetime perfecting.''

"No, of course not.''

"Suffice it to say, at this point, that through hypnosis, or waking sleep, I call the subjective mind into an active state. If it accepts what I say, then the objective mind will deal with my words as truth.''

Selene felt chilled. "Won't the person doubt when awake?''

He smiled. "I cannot make any person go against their basic desires and beliefs, but I can make suggestions that enhance or push their life experiences or their desires or their beliefs in the direction I want them to go.''

"Then hypnotism could be used to cure someone of a fear or—''

"To uncover and deal with a terrible memory, or in place of ether for surgery. Hypnotism has yet to reach its full potential, but I have made it work for me and many other people.''

"What about the seances?''

"That goes back to Mesmer and his animal magnetism research which is the basis of hypnotism.

268

With Joy Marie, we got some surprising results. The truth of seances? I honestly do not know, but it makes people happy to think they are talking with their lost loved ones so what is the harm?"

"It's not honest."

He waved a hand. "Honesty. Reality. That depends on the person."

"But truth is the truth."

"Not at all. Two men in the same battle will come away with a different tale. The truth, my dear Selene, is quite relative."

She frowned and bit her lower lip. She didn't believe him, but she didn't want to argue with him either. She needed him to keep talking. However, if he actually believed that truth was relative, then it explained his ease with a fantasy life on Martinique.

"Basically, I give people what they want and take what I want in return. Is that so bad?"

Selene clasped her hands, trying to think straight. Gustave's words confused her. When he put it like that, what he did to others didn't seem so bad. But she didn't think it was so simple. Or so nice.

"Is it?" He leaned forward and took her hands in his.

"I guess not."

He nodded, caressed her hands a moment, then pulled out his crystal watch fob. "The only way for you to fully understand hypnotism, Selene, is to experience it yourself."

"I don't know. I'd rather watch you do it to someone else."

He cocked his head to one side and considered her

request. "All right." He got up, crossed the room, and pulled the bell rope.

In a moment, the maid opened the bedroom door and looked inside. "M'sieur?"

"Come here, Jeanne. We are conducting a little experiment."

Jeanne walked into the room.

"Close the door and bring the candle from the bathroom." Gustave walked back to Selene. "Soon you will have few doubts as to my power."

Jeanne did as he bid and soon stood near them with the candle in her hands.

Gustave raised the crystal and began swinging it back and forth in front of Jeanne's eyes. "You are getting sleepy, very sleepy. You are tired, very tired." He continued talking in a monotone, repeating his words.

Suddenly Selene felt sleepy and quickly averted her eyes from the crystal. When she looked back, Jeanne stood still, breathing evenly, her eyes closed.

Gustave glanced at Selene. "Of course, she was not such an easy subject at first. After training, I can put a person into trance quickly and easily." He focused on the maid once more. "Now, Jeanne, pass your hand back and forth just above the flame of the candle. You will not feel the heat. In fact, you will think your hand is cold."

Jeanne passed her right hand back and forth, long enough to feel the heat, even for the flame to hurt, but soon she shivered as if chilled.

Selene stared in amazement.

"Now, Jeanne, drop your hand. You will awake

270

refreshed and happy. At my count." He counted down from ten. "One."

Jeanne opened her eyes, smiled, looked at the candle, then around the room in confusion. "Did you want something else, m'sieur?"

"No. That will be all." Gustave sat down across from Selene.

Setting the candle on the table, Jeanne clasped her right hand as if to warm it. "Is it too cold in here for you, m'sieur?" She looked confused.

Gustave smiled. "No. Everything is fine. That will be all, Jeanne."

"Thank you." Jeanne bobbed and left the room, shutting the door behind her.

"What do you think of that?" Gustave raised a brow as he looked at Selene.

"Amazing."

"It is so." He held the crystal before her eyes. "Now it is your turn, *ma chère*."

Selene clenched her hands. She had to learn more. And this was her only way. But she wouldn't let him hypnotize her. Instead, she would let him think he had, but she would be aware of what he was doing every moment. She smiled. "Yes, I want to learn."

He swung the crystal and its facets flashed with color from the last rays of the sun.

Selene focused on it and the sound of Gustave's voice, repeating, endlessly repeating his words of power. Her eyelids grew heavy, her breathing slowed. She felt sleepy. Leaning her head back against the chair, she closed her eyes.

"Selene, you can hear me quite clearly. I am your

271

friend. I have never hurt you. You can trust me. We are alike. We are both physicians, in our way. We will help others together. I provide jobs for workers on the plantation. That helps them. You can care for their injuries. That helps them. And you can help me."

Sunlight faded, the wind grew still, and Gustave watched Selene. He smiled and put away his crystal. "You are good at helping people, Selene, and I want you to help me. I need your love, your passion, your strength." He stroked her face, then leaned forward and placed a kiss on her lips.

She remained still and her eyes stayed closed.

"Loving me, slaking my passion, our desire, makes you happy and content. Your needs are fulfilled on Dominique Plantation and you have no need to go anywhere else." He stroked down the front of her robe, then paused at the cleft of her breasts.

Still she lay relaxed against the chair.

"Now, Selene, open your robe and show me your breasts." He withdrew his hand.

She hesitated, then slowly moved her hands upward, caught the edges of silk, and pulled apart her robe to bare her breasts.

He picked up the candle and held it close so he could examine her. "Very good, Selene. Very good indeed. Your body is as beautiful as I expected and I have only begun to explore it."

He set aside the candle, closed her robe, and sat back. "Selene, you want Gustave Dominique more than you ever wanted Drake Dalton or any other man. Your womanly desires will flood you and your heart will open whenever you see me. And when I call you baby, you will not be able to resist anything I ask of you."

He glanced out into the night, nodded thoughtfully, then looked back at her. "I am the embodiment of everything you want in a man. Everything." He raised her limp hand and kissed its palm. "When you awake at my count of ten, you will feel happy and refreshed." He began the count. "One."

She opened her eyes, yawned, and smiled. "When are you going to start the hypnosis session?"

"It is over."

"What?" She glanced around in concern. "I don't understand."

"You make an excellent pupil, Selene. I thought you would. We will do well together . . . baby."

She blinked, then smiled seductively and leaned forward. When her robe fell open to reveal her breasts, she didn't seem to notice, and when he reached forward and squeezed a nipple, she threw back her head, exposing the long line of her neck to him. With a fingertip he traced her smooth flesh from the tip of her chin to the cleft of her breasts.

Standing, he raised her to her feet, pulled her robe from her shoulders, then pressed her bare breasts against his shirt front. She shivered against him.

"Baby."

She wrapped long arms around his neck, and stood on her tiptoes, pressing herself full length against him. She pulled his head toward hers, opening her mouth for a kiss.

But he stopped her, grabbing her shoulders and

273

pushing her back. "You are a slut like the others, are you not, Selene Morgan? All it takes is a small suggestion and your high morals crumble, do they not?"

She looked confused, then wanton again.

He backhanded her. The hit made a pop in the quietness of the room and her head snapped to the side. She placed a hand to her bleeding mouth and looked at him in confusion. He pushed her down to her knees. She gazed at him with mingled frustration and desire.

"You are now in the correct position." He grinned, showing stained teeth. "We will do very well together. I will even marry you because I want you that much. But I will be master on Dominique Plantation and you and every other person will bow to my wishes. And when you do, you will be happy . . . baby."

She reached out a hand. "Gustave, please, you're everything I want." She grasped his trouser leg and tugged him toward her.

He jerked his foot away. "If I had time, I would give you the first lesson in how to please me. But dinner awaits. And you are going nowhere. Now stand."

She rose, her gaze never leaving his face.

"No baby."

At those words, she pulled her robe over her breasts and retied the sash tightly around her waist. Still watching him, she put a hand to her mouth.

He nodded, then walked to the door. "Eat your dinner. You will need your strength later." Giving her one last glance, he left.

She turned away, touching her tender mouth with a finger, and saw Josephine standing at one of the windows.

Josephine held up a hand for silence, shook her head, then disappeared along the balcony.

Selene started after her, then stopped. The message had been delivered. Drake would not be coming. She walked back into her bedroom. Glancing at the tray of food, she realized she was ravenous. She would eat and rest, for Gustave would be back to continue their studies.

And indeed, she needed her strength.

Chapter 20

Drake stood in the shadow of the balcony and looked in Selene's window. A candle burned on the table. She sat, as if mesmerized, on the bed with pillows piled up behind her head. Her thick auburn hair was loose and flowed down her shoulders to frame her full breasts straining against the bodice of a green silk nightgown.

He feared the worst. She had let Dominique influence her with hypnotism, drugs, or whatever he did to people. A zombie. He clenched his fists. Josephine's report about Dominique and Selene had been bad, but this looked worse. He'd warned Selene to be careful, not to let Dominique play his games with her. But she obviously hadn't listened. Now he didn't know what he was going to do.

Fortunately when Josephine had returned with the news, he'd still been at Ancient Mam's place and not on his way to Saint Pierre to gather information. With Ancient Mam's help, he'd learned Dominique was steadily gaining more power on Martinique by buying land cheap. Mulattoes were getting pushed off their small acreages just the same as French planters. Afterward, they had little choice but to work for Dominique.

And the Frenchman's people were loyal. Zombies, as Ancient Mam called them. Drake hadn't been able to get close to the workers during the day because of the guards and he didn't know if it would have done much good anyway. But Josephine could go anywhere and did. Plus, people would talk with her. So he'd learned a lot more a lot faster than he'd have done on his own.

He glanced around, making sure he was still concealed and that the guards were making their rounds as usual. He wanted to visit Joy Marie, but he couldn't trust her. About the only person who didn't seem to be under Dominique's complete control was his man Jon. And he was loyal to Gustave from what Josephine had been able to find out.

Frustrated, Drake knew he had to go in and talk with Selene. But he hated to do it because he was afraid to hear how happy she was with Dominique and how she was going to stay on Martinique forever, or some other such nonsense. If it came to that, he'd take her, Joy Marie, and Jimmy, get them on a boat and to Texas. He'd deal with the consequences then. But he wanted to stop the Frenchman and he owed Ancient Mam and Josephine for all their help.

He stepped through the open window.

Selene looked up, saw him, and gasped.

"Expecting somebody else?" His voice grated and he knew it.

"Yes."

He walked over to her bed with narrowed eyes and restrained fury. "Dominique?"

"Yes." She took his hand and tugged. "Sit down. I didn't think you'd come tonight. I'm glad to see you."

"Sure you are. That's why you're waiting for Dominique." He sat down, still holding her hand.

She smiled. "I've got exciting news. It's hard to believe but I've finally found out what Gustave's doing to everybody."

"And how'd you find out?"

"I let him think he hypnotized me."

Drake grabbed her shoulders and shook her. "I told you not to do that." He gazed into her eyes, trying to see if there were any difference, if Dominique had had his way. He couldn't tell.

"I had to." She tried to twist away, looking confused. "There was no other choice."

"You're sure he's not using some island plant and drugging everybody with it? You'd know all about that, wouldn't you?"

She frowned. "Yes, I know about plants and herbs. But that's not what he's using." She searched Drake's face as if for a clue to his behavior. "You're hurting me." She tried to get out of his grip, but couldn't. "Let me go, Drake."

He dropped his hands, suddenly afraid he'd lost her to the Frenchman. A wild fury took him. He grabbed her again, pulled her to him, and crushed her lips with his. When she responded, opening her mouth to him, running her hands through his hair, grasping his shoulders to pull him closer, he felt relieved. Then he thought of Dominique. The

279

damned Frenchman could have manipulated Selene into doing this very thing to throw Drake off his track. The elation left him. He hadn't won yet.

He pushed her away, then clenched his fists to keep from touching her.

"What's wrong?"

"What the hell do you think's wrong? Josephine told me what she saw so I rushed over here."

Selene nodded, twisting the bedclothes. "And you think that I . . . and Dominique? How dare you!" She slapped him, and the sound reverberated through the room.

Drake didn't move, although his face stung from the blow. Had he misjudged her? He hoped so, but she hadn't mentioned Dominique's hands on her or their kiss. Josephine wouldn't have made up something like that. But did Selene even remember what she'd done with the Frenchman?

"You're wrong, you know. Nothing happened. I simply found out about hypnotism. But you don't care about that, do you? All you care about is—"

"I was worried about you. I was afraid he might have hurt you." The blow hung between them as thick as a wall and he didn't know how to tear it down or if he wanted to try. "What did you find out?"

She inhaled sharply. "I saw him use hypnotism on Jeanne the maid. It works, Drake, and I don't know how to combat it except in one way."

"How?"

"It's what I told you earlier at the waterfall and I still think it's the best idea. Gustave wants me and I'll give myself to him in trade for the others."

Drake gave a short laugh. "You think you're worth

280

that much? Dominique is taking over this island and everybody on it. When he owns it all, he won't need the hypnotism or whatever he's using anymore. He'll own these people if they want to live here because he'll be in charge of the economy. With that kind of power, he can have any woman, or as many women as he wants." He knew he was hurting her, but she had to accept the truth: she could not always solve people's problems by martyring herself. "So why should he endanger his grand plans to have you?"

Selene blushed and glanced away from him. "Put like that, it makes me look foolish. I suppose you speak from experience. A man couldn't possibly want a woman like me that much. He'd want someone like Joy Marie." She rolled across the bed away from him and got up.

Surprised and confused at her reaction, he watched her pull on a green robe and belt it tightly around her. The movement further emphasized the curve of her breasts. Sudden hunger swept through him, but he fought it down. Now was not the time to give in to his body, no matter how much he wanted her or wanted to comfort her. He had to be practical.

She threw him a look of scorn. "Nothing to say? It's true, isn't it? You love Joy Marie."

Drake simply sat there, stunned. "Joy Marie?"

"It's she you've wanted all along. I've just been something to pass the time with until you could have her again. You want her back on your ranch and you'll take Jimmy to keep her happy. But what about me?" She pressed her lips together and looked away from him.

"Joy Marie?" Drake knew he was repeating himself and couldn't stop. But confusion was turning to anger. He stood up. "She's my sister. What the hell are you saying?"

"I'm saying . . . Gustave said . . . I overheard that you and Joy Marie, well, that the two of you were . . ."

"Lovers!" He strode across the room and stopped in front of her. Glaring down, he didn't touch her. He didn't dare. "I'll repeat it. She's my sister, and where I come from, a man doesn't touch his sister. At least, not like that."

"She's your sister-in-law."

"Same thing."

"No it's not and you know it."

He whirled around, walked to the window, looked out, then turned back. "None of that matters anyway. You're the woman I want, Selene. How the hell many times do I have to prove it to you?" He stayed away from her, afraid of his own anger.

"I want to believe you."

"If you don't believe me, there's not a damn thing I can do about it." He walked back to her. "And for your information, from what Josephine told me, you're only too ready to flip your skirts for Dominique. If you haven't already."

She slapped him again.

"That was one time too many." He grabbed her wrists and twisted her arms behind her back. She struggled, but her strength and size were no match for him. He knew it and so did she. But it didn't stop her from fighting him. He jerked her against him, forced her head back, and kissed her. She bit him. He cursed, then tried again. She struggled, writhing against him, but it only served to make him want her all the more.

As he tried to conquer her, his mind raced. How could she believe Dominique's words that he had touched his sister-in-law? Maybe Selene *was* hypnotized. Maybe the Frenchman had already buried himself deep inside her, coming back after Josephine had left. The idea made him see red and he lifted her off the floor. She struggled as he carried her to the bed and threw her in its center. He took off his gunbelt, laid it on the table, then began stripping off his clothes.

"Drake, no." She held up a hand, shaking her head in denial. "Not here, not now. Gustave could come back or—"

Drake shut the windows and locked them from inside. Then he turned back to her. "You're going to have to make a choice, Selene, and I don't give a damn what Gustave's been doing to your mind or body." He walked back to the bed and stood looking down at her. "Make your choice. Now. Dominique or me."

She shook her head, tears burned her eyes, but she opened her arms. "Come here, you fool."

He jerked off the rest of his clothes, sat down on the side of the bed, then slipped off her robe and gown. He pulled her into his arms and pressed hot lips to hers. This time she opened her mouth to him. He pushed into her warm, honeyed depths and felt her respond, her body molding to him, her tongue fencing with his, and her hands roaming his back, pulling him closer. His body ignited and he knew he couldn't wait long. He wanted her, needed her, and had to be deep inside her, for there was no other way to satisfy him or his belief in her.

"I mean it, Selene." He caught his breath. "Me or that damn Frenchman."

"You're the man I want, Drake. But it's not simple. You know that."

"It's simple as hell. You take me as your man, the only man in your life, and that's it. No going back." He pressed fevered kisses over her face, down her neck, then nibbled at the sensitive places along her shoulder.

Shivering, she swallowed hard. "But Drake . . ."

He pushed her back against the bed, covering her body with his. Night noises from the jungle intruded on them, along with the scent of flowers and trees in bloom. But he thought she smelled sweeter and her voice sounded more melodic than all of Martinique combined. "Let me make you mine, Selene."

Straddling her, he crushed her soft breasts with his hands, then moved lower to push his fingers into her hot, moist center. She arched upward, dragging her nails down his thighs. He welcomed the pain, anything that meant she was reacting to him. He followed his hands with his mouth, and when she made soft sighs and moans, he raised his head, gazed into her eyes, then lifted her legs to position himself at her entrance.

"I won't go any farther without your say-so." But he trembled with the force of his longing, hardly able to keep from plunging into her.

She hesitated, gave him a considering look, then impaled herself on him.

For a long moment he couldn't move. He was too

overcome with emotion. And desire. He wanted to make it good for her, but he didn't know how he could endure the tension. Yet as he began to stroke in and out, all he could think of was that she was giving herself to him without strings of any sort. He'd won her. Somehow she was finally his woman. And he'd never let her go.

He heard her moan with pleasure, then felt her match his movements with her own undulating body as the passion built and they struggled to become one. With each of his thrusts, they climbed higher and higher up the pinnacle of pleasure until finally he felt her spasm around him and cry his name. Joining them with a deep kiss, he burst inside her and knew they'd reached the heights of ecstasy together.

For a long moment he didn't move, simply held her, feeling their sweat cool and dry. Finally, he rolled to the side and pulled her close. Whatever happened next, this could never be taken from them. Never.

Although he didn't want to think any farther than the moment, he knew he must. He had to ensure Selene's safety, as well as the others. And to do that he had to deal with Gustave Dominique. He sat up, pushed the pillows up behind them, and leaned back.

Pulling Selene against his chest, he sighed. "We've got to talk about Dominique."

"Will you listen to me now?"

"Yes."

"He uses people's minds against them. Hypnotism could be a force of great good, but Gustave is using it for himself and I fear now, after what you said, the

285

only way to free everyone is to get him to agree."

Drake tensed. "Agree?"

"He has set up control words in their minds, twisted their ideas and beliefs so they believe what they're doing is right and what they want. He *must* change that." She hesitated, then pushed hair back from her face. "He must free them himself."

"Then I'll put my hands around his scrawny neck and force him. It'll be his life for theirs."

Selene shivered. "How can you get close to him? Jon or one of the other guards is always nearby."

"In your room?"

She blushed. "Yes. He will come here alone."

"When?"

"Tonight, I think."

"Then I'll wait."

"But Drake, you could be hurt. What if he calls out? What if Jon is in the hall? At his word, my room would be full of guards ready to kill you at his command."

"We've got to chance it, Selene. If this goes on much longer, he'll have control of the whole island and it'll be almost impossible to reach him. Right now, all that stands between these people and freedom is you." His voice grew harsh. "And that could change if he dominates you."

"You mean if he hypnotizes me, too?"

"Yes." He didn't say it because he couldn't stand the thought, but he believed she might already be under Dominique's spell. He could be walking into a trap with Selene as the bait. When he jumped the Frenchman, he might be fallen upon by a dozen guards. But it was a chance he had to take. Selene, Joy

Marie, and Jimmy were his family and he'd protect them to the death.

"He didn't, Drake. I was careful. I went along with him so he'd think I was in his power, but I'm fine. Trust me."

"You wouldn't know if he did, Selene."

"Yes, I would."

"All right." He hugged her close. "We'll talk about it later. Right now we've got to get ready for Dominique."

She nodded.

"If he comes too close to dawn, I won't have much of a chance of escaping if he calls the guards down on me."

"Then we'll make sure he doesn't." She straightened and looked him in the eye. "Gustave wants me. When he comes, it will be to possess me, I'm sure." She shivered. "When I take him into my arms, you can come out of hiding and capture him. Then we'll make the deal."

"I don't want his hands on you. Not again."

"It doesn't matter what we want. We'll end his evil rule and be done."

"Selene, there's something I better tell you. Dominique is a hell of a lot more dangerous than he appears."

"What do you mean?" Her breath caught in her throat.

"The more power he gets on Martinique, the meaner he gets. He's not as cool and controlled as he pretends. The other day he whipped a man to death for not jumping to his orders fast enough."

"Drake! How do you know?"

"Josephine saw it. She said he'd whipped men, and women, before, but never gone so far. It makes you wonder how many people he's killed or ruined in his drive for power and money."

Selene shivered. "And he acts so noble and pure."

"It's an act all right. And we're going to put a stop to it." He glanced around. "I'll wait in the bathroom."

"And I'll get cleaned up."

"You think he might notice another man had been here before him?" Drake picked up his gunbelt, checked the .45, then gathered his clothes.

"Yes. I think so." She got up. "You'd better hide now. No telling when he may be back."

"Right."

Chapter 21

Selene lay in bed, the dampness of the sheet she'd cleaned a reminder of what she'd just shared with Drake. She didn't berate herself for her passion and she didn't deny her need of Drake. In that moment when he had demanded his right as her lover, she had known he'd had that right. How long could the love potions affect them? She had no answer to that, nor did she have the answer to Joy Marie and Drake. But she wanted to believe him and she did.

However, right now, what counted was stopping Gustave. She knew the Frenchman would do anything to save his own skin and Drake Dalton could be most intimidating. Still, Gustave was a powerful man, used to getting what he wanted for he cast a fascinating spell over those he decided to make his. She had felt the force of his mesmerism earlier and it had taken all her strength to resist. Even so, there was a small part of her that was afraid, fueled by Drake's words, that she had become Gustave's pawn in that time alone with the Frenchman.

She shivered, and pushed the thought away. She *had* remained in charge of herself. That had to be the truth, just as Drake's words about Joy Marie *had* to be the truth. Nothing else would do.

But when would Gustave come to her? What if he didn't come that night? What if it was all a trap? No. She wouldn't, couldn't, believe that either. To distract herself, she felt of the silky smooth fabric of her nightgown. She wished it was thicker, more protection for when Gustave came later. But she had to appear docile, expectant, and as normal as possible.

Love potions. How had she ever gotten herself into this mess? Rosa would understand. Rosa had warned her. Suddenly she felt homesick for her apothecary shop on Decatur Street in New Orleans, for the scent of café au lait and hot beignets at the Café du Monde. Tears stung her eyes. How had she ended up on Martinique with strangers? Why had she roamed so far from everything she held near and dear?

And then her mind was filled with visions of faces: Joy Marie, Jimmy, Drake, her New Orleans friends. Maybe she wasn't with strangers after all. Maybe she had never made allowances for changes in her life, for something more or different than what she'd had as a child. Maybe she hadn't even allowed for the possibility of new people in her life. And maybe she had wanted the safety and security of what she'd always known.

Perhaps it was time for her to grow up. If she trusted herself, she couldn't be afraid of change, of meeting new people, traveling to new lands, or learning new techniques of healing. She smiled to herself as she thought of how much she'd have missed if she'd never met Drake or Joy Marie or even Gustave Dominique. Maybe she'd have preferred to miss some of it, but bad usually came with good. And she wouldn't have missed meeting Drake Dalton for the world.

She suppressed a laugh as she remembered the first time she'd ever seen him. He'd walked into Love Potions looking like a fish out of water. And so mad, so insulted. He'd flung her love potion number seventeen down on her desk and berated her. Soon she was as mad as he and determined on revenge. Well, she'd made him want her all right. She'd made him give up trying to hurt Love Potions. But had she made him fall in love with her? She wished she had the answer to that question.

Glancing toward the bathroom where Drake hid, she heard a soft tap on the door to her bedroom. Gustave. She froze, then knew she had to trust herself. And Drake.

Getting up, she walked to the door. On the third knock, she opened it.

Gustave gave her a lecherous wink, then scanned her scantily clad body. "You waited up for me?"

"Yes." Her voice sounded hollow as she stepped back, pulling wide the door.

"Dinner was boring. You missed nothing." He walked into the bedroom, then shut and locked the door. Leaning against it, he looked her up and down again. "Ready for me, I see."

She moved toward the bathroom and stopped, not wanting to be too obvious, but more thankful than she'd have thought possible for Drake's presence behind the bathroom door.

Gustave followed. "With that look in your eyes, you're more beautiful than ever."

She smiled, thinking that a murderous gleam must appeal to him.

He walked across the room, made sure the balcony windows and door were shut and locked, then turned back to her. "Come here."

Frozen, she hesitated. She wanted Gustave near the bathroom door, not across the room in front of the windows. She took a step forward and stopped, not wanting to go any closer to him. But how did she bring him to her instead of the other way around?

"Shy?" He laughed. "I can fix that, *ma chére*."

"No. I mean . . ."

He laughed again. "What you need is a man, a real man, in your life. Baby."

Selene blinked several times, then walked toward him.

"That's right." Gustave's voice was low and seductive. "Good baby. Come to Master Gustave."

She moved slowly, hesitantly, but inexorably toward him.

"That's right, baby."

She stopped in front of him.

"Kneel."

She did. And bowed her head.

He put a hand on the top of her head. "Now. Proclaim me your master. Forever."

The bathroom door slammed open.

"I'll be damned if she will." Drake held a .45 trained on Gustave's heart. "Don't move, Selene."

She remained on her knees, quiet.

"Drake Dalton." Gustave's voice was cold. "You made a big mistake coming here."

"I tracked the beast to his lair. No other way."

"One word from me and a dozen men will put bullets through you." Gustave looked contemptuous. "And don't expect help from Selene or anybody else in this house. You've played right into my hands."

"Wrong." Drake walked forward, his gaze never leaving Gustave's face. "Selene, get over here, but don't stand up."

She remained still.

Gustave smirked. "You waited too long." He looked down at Selene. "I'll continue and you can watch, Dalton." He ran his fingers through Selene's thick hair.

Drake growled.

"Baby, show me how much you want me." Gustave raised Selene's hand to the buttons on his trousers.

Drake flung himself forward just as Selene threw back her head and screamed aloud in fury. Standing, she drew back her right arm and punched Gustave in the nose. Then she stood in stunned amazement as the Frenchman staggered backward, holding his nose as blood dripped through his fingers.

Drake jerked Selene behind him and pushed

Gustave into a chair. Holding the pistol to Dominique's temple, he cocked the hammer. "Now, Gustave Dominique, I suggest you do as we say or it'll be my great pleasure to put a bullet through your head."

But Gustave didn't seem to notice Drake. His gaze was trained on Selene, who stood before him, hands on her hips. "You did not respond properly." Confusion filled his voice as he took out a handkerchief and held it to his nose. "I hypnotized you. I could not be mistaken, could I?"

Selene tossed back her hair and the fiery mane cascaded down her back. "You're mistaken about a lot of things, Gustave Dominique. Frankly, I'm the least of them."

Drake pushed the muzzle of the .45 against Dominique's temple. "You got a choice, Frenchman. You take your spell off the people of Martinique and you live. If you don't, you die."

Gustave focused on Selene. "I will make you a countess. You will rule with me on Martinique, in France. Power, Selene. Think of it. Power! Wealth! Nobility! What more could you ask of a man?"

Selene shook her head, noticing how Gustave seemed to shrink without his mantle of authority. "The only power I want is over myself. But I suppose that's something you couldn't understand."

"Those with power use it. Those who don't or can't succumb to the powerful." His voice was filled with scorn. He wiped his nose, tested it with his fingers, then put his handkerchief away. "There is no other way."

"Shut up." Drake looked disgusted. "You want to live or die, Frenchman? You better answer quick 'cause my finger's getting itchy."

"I can call for help." Gustave glanced around the room.

"Go ahead." Drake held his pistol ready. "You'd be dead before they got here."

"And you?" Gustave played his last card.

"Out the balcony, down the tree, and we're lost in the jungle. Think about it."

"Your word I will live?" Gustave sat very still.

"When you set these people free, I'll turn you over to the French authorities."

Gustave smiled.

"And Ancient Mam."

"That root doctor?" Gustave looked worried.

"Yes." Drake smiled coldly. "It's her people you're messing with on Martinique and Selene's in New Orleans. That's where you made your mistake, mister. Any damn fool knows you don't mess with a mama and her babies. I don't care if its a long-horn, a coyote, a bear, or a woman. You don't rile a mama. But I guess you got that one figured out by now."

"You give too much importance to the female, but I will accept your offer, M'sieur Dalton." Gustave glanced at Selene. "I will not forget this, *chérie.*"

"You better not." Drake kept his .45 at the French-man's temple. "Now you're going to call in the people of this house and one by one remove your spell. Later we'll take you out to the field workers. Then Ancient Mam'll get you."

"What about the French authorities?" Gustave frowned in concern.

Drake grinned. "You'll see them last."

The Frenchman cursed.

Drake glanced at Selene. "Will you get some of your stockings to tie his hands?"

"I'll be happy, too." She gave Drake a look of triumph, then crossed the room. Taking four cotton stockings from a drawer, she hurried back.

Drake kept the pistol against Gustave's head. "Okay, Dominique, put your hands behind the chair. You try to jump Selene or me and you're dead. No way 'round that fact so put escape out of your mind."

Sweat beaded Gustave's forehead as he slowly moved his hands backward until he clasped the chair with his arms, his hands touching.

Selene moved behind the chair and wrapped a length of stocking around Gustave's wrists. "Drake, tell me if I do this wrong."

"Do you know any seaman's knots?" Drake kept the .45 against Dominique's temple.

"Yes."

"One of those'll hold him."

She deftly tied one stocking, then looped another around Gustave's wrists."

"Tie his ankles to the chair, too."

Selene knelt in front of Gustave and tied one of his ankles then the other to the chair legs. Finally she stood, dusted off her hands, and placed them on her hips. "That should hold him."

Drake lowered the pistol, checked Gustave's

bonds, and pulled them tighter. "Good job, Selene. He's going nowhere fast." He sheathed his pistol in the holster on the gunbelt around his hips.

Selene opened the windows and early morning light filtered into the room. She put an arm around Drake's waist. "It's going to be a beautiful day."

"Yes. In more ways than one." He placed a soft, possessive kiss on her lips, then turned away from the windows. "You ready to wake the others?"

"More than ready." Walking over to the bellrope, she pulled it hard.

Soon, Jeanne answered the call, but her bright smile faded as she caught sight of Gustave tied to the chair and Drake with the .45 slung low on his hip. She turned to Selene. "Mam'selle?"

"It's all right, Jeanne. This is Drake Dalton. He's Joy Marie's brother-in-law from Texas. Would you tell Joy Marie I'd like to see her in my room."

"Yes, mam'selle. But M'sieur Dominique . . . should I call Jon?"

"In a moment. First I'd like to speak to Joy Marie. Everything is fine so go on with your usual duties."

Jeanne bobbed her head and backed from the room.

"Can you trust her?" Drake strode over to the door. "Will she call the guards?"

"I don't think so. Anyway, what can they do? We've got Gustave." She glanced at the Frenchman and noticed blood had begun to trickle from his nose again. She smiled, hoping it was broken.

Gustave snickered. "Do you two really think you

will get away with this?"

Ignoring him, Drake stood near the door and pulled out his pistol. "Selene, be ready to bash Dominique over the head if we're attacked."

She looked around the room till she found a heavy brass figurine she thought would knock Gustave senseless. Walking over, she set it on the table near him.

"Selene." Gustave's voice was low and urgent. "Use that on Dalton. It is not too late. Remember what I told you. Think of our plans. Once we get rid of Dalton, we can keep Joy Marie here if you like, or send her back to his ranch. Whatever you want, *ma chère*. You know how much I admire you."

Giving him a steady look, she shook her head. "You still don't understand, do you?"

"What is there to understand? Nothing is more important than power and position. Money makes both possible. And I have it."

"What about friends, love, loyalty?"

"Those can be bought if you must have them."

Selene turned away in disgust and heard a knock at the door. Hurrying over, she motioned Drake to step back out of sight, then she took a deep breath and pulled open the door.

Joy Marie stood in the doorway and Selene's relief turned to horror at the sight of Joy Marie's bruised, swollen, and rapidly discoloring face. Her friend hadn't bothered to dress, but had thrown on a beautiful rose satin robe which was in heartbreaking contrast to her face.

Pulling Joy Marie into the room, Selene shut the

door and hugged her close. "Darling, what happened?"

Joy Marie put a hand to her face and blushed in embarrassment. "I'm sorry to worry you, but I fell this morning."

"Joy Marie!" Selene couldn't stand the idea of Joy Marie still protecting Gustave.

"It's true, really. If I could just have a cold cloth, perhaps I could lie down. Would you mind if I stayed with you awhile? We could talk or have tea or—" She gasped when she saw Gustave. As she started to run to his side, Drake grabbed her arm and jerked her back. Confused, she looked up, saw her brother-in-law, opened her mouth to scream, then looked faint.

"Drake, let her go. Can't you see she's going into shock? It's too much too fast." Selene set Joy Marie on the bed and gently slapped her wrists.

"I'm going to beat that Frenchman within an inch of his life." Drake started for Dominique.

Selene grabbed Drake's arm and held on tight. "Please not now. We don't have time. Besides, he's got to be able to speak and if you beat him . . ."

Drake growled, threw Dominique a murderous look, then went into the bathroom. He came out with a wet washcloth and carried it to Joy Marie. He sat down beside her and tenderly washed her face.

She flinched at first, then sat very still. After a moment, tears began rolling down her cheeks. "You won't hurt him, will you, Drake? He's not as strong as you. And I love him."

"You don't love him." Drake threw down the

washcloth and got up in disgust. But he carefully raised Joy Marie to her feet. "Now we're going to let you talk to him."

Joy Marie's expression brightened, but the contrast with the swelling and discoloring of her face made her look even worse.

Selene took Joy Marie's hand and led her to Gustave while Drake set a chair in front of the Frenchman.

"Thank you." Joy Marie sat down, moving stiffly and as if in pain.

Drake put his hand on the .45 at his hip. "Okay, Dominique, do what you promised."

Joy Marie glanced from Drake to Selene in confusion. "You haven't hurt Gustave, have you? He's a very sensitive, smart man. Delicate, even."

Selene turned away, unable to stand the sight or hear the words as Joy Marie defended the delicate sensibilities of the man who beat her.

But Drake kept his eyes on Dominique. "Well? You need some prodding, Frenchman?"

"I need my hands free to use my crystal."

"Forget it." Drake's voice was rough.

Gustave sighed. "I'll try. But remember our bargain." He began to speak in a low, soothing tone. "Joy Marie, watch my eyes. Concentrate. You are feeling drowsy. Your eyelids are heavy. You want to sleep. You need to sleep. Rest."

Joy Marie's eyes closed and she tilted her head back against the chair.

"That's right, *chérie*, sleep." He glanced at Drake, then back at Joy Marie. "You are well, strong, and happy. Although your beloved husband is dead, as well as your son, you have found new friends and realize someday you may love again."

Drake's fingers tightened on the butt of his pistol and his eyes narrowed in warning to Dominique.

"When you awake, you will remember all that has happened to you since leaving Texas." He glanced up and smirked at Drake. "But the word 'baby' will have no more meaning or power for you than it did before you left Texas."

Drake nodded.

"You will never forget Gustave Dominique or what you shared with him. Good and bad."

Drake drew his .45.

"When you awake, no one will control you, Joy Marie Dalton, and you will feel refreshed and happy. At the count of ten, you will awaken." He counted down. "One."

Drake slid his pistol back into its holster.

Joy Marie opened her eyes, yawned, smiled, then glanced around the group. "My, have I been asleep? I—" Her happy look changed as her eyes widened in horror. "You!" She pointed at Gustave. She touched her face, then stood up, knocking over the chair as she ran to look in the mirror over the dresser. She groaned, then whirled around and ran back across the room. She slapped Gustave back and forth across his face.

"Remember the good times we had, baby." Gustave grinned, showing his crooked, stained teeth.

Joy Marie blushed, then slapped him again as tears

301

rolled down her cheeks.

Selene pulled Joy Marie into her arms and held her close. "It's all right. You aren't alone. You'll be fine now. He'll never hurt you again. Come over to the bed and sit down."

Joy Marie turned and looked at Drake. "I took the ranch money. I'm so sorry. And ashamed."

"It's all right. No harm done."

She burst into fresh tears, sobbing loudly.

Selene led Joy Marie to the bed and helped her sit down, but the crying didn't ease. She pumped up the pillows behind her friend and pulled the covers up over her legs. "Don't worry. Please."

Selene felt helpless. She simply didn't know what else to do for Joy Marie. She had been so concentrated on freeing her friend from Gustave's control that she hadn't thought of the consequences. Now she realized how painful and disorienting it was for Joy Marie to experience the memories as they flooded back all at once.

She pushed the damp washcloth into Joy Marie's hands and turned to Drake. "I'm going to make a tea to soothe everyone's nerves. I'll ask Jeanne to bring up the tea service and hot water."

Drake nodded, watching Joy Marie with a worried expression.

Selene walked over to the dresser and pulled out a large, green reticule she had made especially for the trip. Inside were her favorite herbs and other medical supplies. She hadn't needed them before, but now was the time to use them.

A grim expression on his face, Drake watched

Gustave. "We'd better get on with this, Selene. Maybe it won't get any worse. Joy Marie had been with him the longest."

"I'll ring for Jeanne." She selected several packets of herbs. "And I want to reassure Jimmy next."

"Call him quick." Drake turned back to Gustave.

Chapter 22

Several hours later, Selene sat at the round table in her bedroom. A breeze off the sea cooled the rapidly warming day. She tended a pot of herbal tea and spoke soothingly to one person after another as they left Gustave. Joy Marie sat in a chair near her and had been silent for so long she seemed lost in a trance. But Selene didn't disturb her for fear of making matters worse.

Glancing down at her green robe, Selene smiled to herself. At one time she would have considered herself in a shocking state of dishabille with so many people around, but under the circumstances it was of no importance. In fact, no one coming through her room was in their normal state of dress, and it was an indication of the changes sweeping Dominique Plantation.

She glanced upward and a slow warmth ran through her at the sight of Drake. He kept watch over Gustave and instructed the house staff as they entered the bedroom, although word had spread like wildfire and it was obvious everyone in the mansion had an idea of what was going on.

Her attention turned to Gustave where he sat bound in a chair. Jeanne sat before him, and when he finished with her, she stood up. Selene beckoned her over.

Jeanne stopped beside her, a dazed expression on her face. "Mam'selle, what am I to do now?"

Selene poured a cup of tea, set it on a saucer, and handed it to her. "This will make you feel better."

Jeanne took a sip of tea. "Are we sick? Did M'sieur Dominique hurt us?" She glanced back over her shoulder at Gustave.

"No. You're just fine. Gustave Dominique used some new medical techniques on all of you that he is now reversing, but you aren't hurt. Go on about your life as usual." Selene smiled. "The tea will help you relax. You might want to take a nap."

"But there is work to do."

"Then perhaps it's best if you do your usual duties."

"Thank you, mam'selle. I will." Jeanne finished her tea.

"But now you'll get a wage or some other payment for your work."

Jeanne smiled. "That would be good. My family can use it." She handed Selene the cup and saucer. "If you don't need me right now, I will attend to my work."

"Go ahead. We certainly need everything to keep running smoothly."

As Jeanne walked away, Selene glanced at Joy Marie but saw no change in her condition. It was all too evident she'd been affected the most by Gustave's manipulations. She shook her head, wishing she could do more for these people. The herbal tea she had brewed helped, but it did little to deal with the sudden change in their lives. Many of them wanted their jobs and were afraid of going hungry. She wouldn't let that happen, but something had to be done.

Looking upward, she caught Jon's gaze. He hadn't left Joy Marie's side since the household had been awakened. But he kept glancing at Gustave. He'd been with the Frenchman a long time. She hoped they didn't have any trouble with Jon, for he was a big, strong man.

She was distracted from her worries when she saw Josephine walk through the door, escorting an older mulatto woman. She beckoned them over to the table.

Josephine led the woman to Selene. "Please meet my great-grandmother, Ancient Mam."

Selene smiled as she stood. "I'm pleased to meet you after hearing so much good about you. And this is my friend, Joy Marie Dalton, Drake's sister-in-law."

Josephine inclined her head, gave Joy Marie a concerned look, then translated for her great-grandmother. "Ancient Mam speaks little English but she understands all."

Ancient Mam nodded.

"Why don't the two of you sit down at the table?" Selene indicated two rococo chairs. "Would you like tea?"

"Thank you, yes." Josephine made sure Ancient

Mam was comfortable, then sat down.

Selene sat, poured more tea, handed it around, then leaned back, suddenly feeling quite tired.

When Ancient Mam had tasted the brew, she smiled, nodded at Selene, then spoke to her great-granddaughter.

Josephine translated. "Ancient Mam says your tea shows you are a wise root woman. She also thanks you for helping her people. She calls on Erzulie to give you blessings, as well as to your man, Drake Dalton."

Blushing, Selene shook her head. "He isn't my man. But thank Ancient Man for her kind words."

Josephine translated again.

Ancient Mam laughed, spoke in Creole, then shook a finger at Selene.

"What did she say?" Selene leaned toward Josephine to better hear the translation, for she couldn't completely understand this Creole dialect.

"She said you were naughty to tease your man so."

Selene blushed again. "But really, he's not my man."

"Erzulie speaks through Ancient Mam." Josephine's voice held awe. "Erzulie is goddess of love, among other things, and she is never mistaken."

"I'm sorry. I didn't mean to insult Ancient Mam. It's just that I'm going back to New Orleans and Drake to Texas."

Again Josephine spoke to Ancient Mam and received a reply. She turned to Selene. "Ancient Mam says your long journey is not yet over."

Selene raised her brows in surprise and started to answer her, but a low voice interrupted.

"Thanks to y'all and Drake for keeping Joy Marie safe."

Surprised, Selene whirled around to look at Joy Marie, for the voice had come from her although it was much too low and raspy for her normal voice. Joy Marie's eyes were shut and her head rested against the back of her chair. She looked exactly as she had for some time. Selene reached out to touch her friend to see if she were awake, but Ancient Mam held up a hand to stop her.

Joy Marie's lips moved. "I asked Drake to keep her safe. He did. But Joy Marie needs to go home now. She's hurt. You'll heal her, won't you, Selene Morgan?"

Selene shivered, for the voice was the voice Joy Marie had used when her husband had spoken through her at the seance. Why was she using it now? What had prompted this reversal? And what did it mean? Suddenly she was angry. What had Gustave done to Joy Marie and how could she stop it?

"Help her. Promise." Joy Marie's voice grew faint as she tossed her head back and forth.

Ancient Mam spoke quickly in Creole.

"She says to agree so the spirit may depart." Josephine translated in a hushed voice. "If the spirit stays beyond its time, it might be trapped in this woman's body."

"Don't . . . leave her . . . alone." Joy Marie's neck muscles stood out with strain.

"I won't." Selene leaned close to Joy Marie. "I'll help Joy Marie. Don't worry. I won't leave her alone till she is well."

Joy Marie's breath hissed out in a long sigh. She

relaxed and her head slumped to one side.

Selene jumped up. "What happened? What should I do?" She poured a cup of tea and held it to Joy Marie's lips. But she got no response.

Suddenly Jon knelt and took Joy Marie's head in his large hands. He held her face steady. "Let her drink now."

Surprised, Selene glanced up at Jon and saw him struggling to suppress fury. But his hands were gentle and steady. She wanted to ask him how he felt about Joy Marie, but knew it wasn't the time or place. "Thanks."

She pressed the cup to Joy Marie's mouth and dripped tea between her lips. Josephine held a napkin under the cup to catch the dribble. After a moment, Joy Marie swallowed once, then twice, and finally swallowed more normally. Relieved, Selene set the cup aside.

Jon stepped back, but stayed close, his gaze never leaving Joy Marie's face.

"Joy Marie?" Selene stroked Joy Marie's cold hands. "Wake up. You're safe. No one can hurt you or force you. Joy Marie, please wake up. I won't leave you. I promise."

Joy Marie's eyelids fluttered, then she slowly opened her eyes and focused on Selene's face. She smiled. "I was dreaming. It was so sweet. I was back at the ranch. My—my husband was with me. And my son. It was before . . ." Tears filled her eyes.

Selene took her in her arms and patted her back. "It's all right. You're going home, Joy Marie. To Texas." Her eyes locked with Jon's and she saw his face tighten. "You'll be safe on the ranch."

310

"But Drake's mad at me."

"No he's not. He wants you back there."

"But Jimmy?" She looked wildly about the room.

"Jon, would you get Jimmy?" Selene motioned toward the boy.

Jon nodded, then walked over to where Jimmy sat playing listlessly with toy soldiers. He brought the boy back to Selene.

Selene smiled. "Jimmy, would you like to go to Texas with Joy Marie?"

Jimmy's eyes grew wide. "But Uncle Gustave said . . ."

Joy Marie shook her head. "I'm from Texas and I'm going home." Pain clouded her eyes, then she smiled wistfully. "It could be your home, too, unless you want to go back to New Orleans."

Jimmy looked at Selene. "What do you think?"

"It could be for a visit." Selene smiled encouragingly. "Drake'll teach you to be a cowboy."

Jimmy suddenly grinned, glanced at Drake, then focused on them again. "Do I get my own horse and rope and pistol?"

"Yes." Joy Marie took his hand and clung to it. "But not the .45. And there's plenty of room for a boy to play and lots of horses and cattle."

"When I'm older, do I get the gun?"

Selene chuckled. "You always did hold out for all you could get and I'm glad to see you doing it again."

Jimmy looked miffed. "Listen, Joe said I got the brains. I got a reputation to live up to. Joe Junior's watchin'." He pulled the frog out of his pocket. "Wanna touch him for luck?"

Tears stung her eyes as Selene stroked the frog

between its two bright eyes. And soon Jon, Ancient Mam, Josephine, and Joy Marie had all touched Joe Junior, too.

Selene glanced around the group. "Well, that ought to be enough luck to keep us happy for a long, long time."

Seeing what they were doing, Drake walked over and stroked the frog, too. "How's Joe Junior?"

"Right as rain." Jimmy smiled proudly. "Think he'll like Texas?"

Drake exchanged a knowing glance with Joy Marie, then grinned. "Anything living's going to love Texas."

"Hear that, Joe Junior?" Jimmy put the frog back in his pocket.

Drake glanced around the group. "That's the last of the people living in the house. I hope they're okay now." He glanced at the older mulatto woman. "Gustave Dominique's all yours, Ancient Mam. You can take him out to the fields and put him to work any way you want."

Ancient Mam gave Gustave a bright-eyed glance, then spoke rapidly in Creole.

Josephine translated. "First we take the zombie out of everybody, then we give Dominique to the French officials. But we will keep watch on him to make sure he is punished. If he is not or tries to escape, then he will be ours."

Ancient Mam stood and held out her hand to Drake.

He took her hand, looked at it a moment, then leaned over and kissed it.

She laughed and spoke in Creole.

Josephine glanced around the group. "I am to interpret. We request your help for a time . . . of transition. Dominique will sign our land back to us. We will sell this house and a small amount of land. As a group we will work the plantation, make tafia, grow food, and sell what we do not need. Dominique's power will be the power of our people now and we will flourish."

Selene felt tears sting her eyes again. They would all be well. "What about the people from New Orleans?"

Josephine consulted her great-grandmother, then interpreted once more. "They may stay and be part of our family or return. We will find money or work so their passage back will be paid. The criminals must go back, but after their sentence is over and if they are not troublemakers, they may return if they so desire."

"Thank you." Selene smiled at Ancient Mam, then glanced up at Drake. He put a hand around her waist and drew her against him. She was glad of his strength.

"We want you to know you will always have a home here on Martinique. You are one of our family now . . . forever." Josephine hugged each of them before turning to her great-grandmother.

Ancient Mam bowed to them all, then added a few more words for Selene alone.

Josephine translated. "Ancient Mam wants the two of you to share root secrets before you leave." She hesitated. "It is a great honor."

Selene inclined her head. "I am, indeed, honored."

Suddenly Gustave called out. "Go ahead. Make your plans. Divide my property between you. But I swear on the nobility of my family line that I will have revenge. I will get what I want. And nobody will stop me."

"I'll take care of him." Jon stepped away from the group.

"Can we trust you?" Drake put his hand on the butt of his .45.

"I'm M'sieur Dominique's man till the French put him in jail. He saved my life. I owe him. But I won't see any others hurt."

"What are you going to do afterward?" Drake glanced at Jon's one arm.

Jon shrugged. "I have had more years than I expected. It is enough."

Joy Marie squeezed Selene's hand. "He helped us."

"Look, if you want a job, come to Texas," Drake said. "I've always got a place for a wrangler on Dalton Ranch."

"A one-armed wrangler?" Jon looked skeptical.

Drake shook his head. "You got your right arm. That means you can shoot, you can cook, you can ride, you can rope. What the hell do you think you can't do?"

Jon looked confused, glanced down at the empty sleeve where his left arm should have been, and frowned. "As a sailor I needed both arms."

Clapping him on the back, Drake laughed. "Everything's big in Texas but ships and water. You come to Dalton Ranch and I'll work you till you'll wish you'd never heard my name."

Jon glanced around in pleasure, saw Gustave watching them, and froze.

"That is right." Gustave struggled against the

stockings that bound him to the chair. "Go ahead and abandon me, you Danish bastard. I saved your life. You owe me. Forever."

As Jon started toward Gustave, Drake grabbed his shoulder. "Whatever you owe him, it's paid. A man can't own another man, not forever."

"But if he hadn't saved my life and given me a job on the Liverpool wharves, I'd have starved."

Drake shook his head. "You're not a man to starve or let losing an arm stop you."

Jon stood still, considering Drake's words.

"Go ahead, listen to their lies." Gustave continued to struggle. "You owe me."

Straightening to his full height, Jon towered over everyone else in the room. He walked over to Gustave and leaned down so he was face to face with the Frenchman. "I *owed* you. I've saved your life several times over. When this is all said and done, I am a free man."

Gustave spit in his face.

Jon stood, wiped the spittle from his face, and walked back to Joy Marie. "I will take you to your room so you can rest." He held out his arm, then looked at Jimmy. "She could use your company."

Jimmy stood up and took Joy Marie's hand.

Joy Marie left her chair, put her hand on Jon's right arm, and smiled at Selene. "Will you come to see us in a little while?"

Selene hugged her, then Jimmy. "You two rest and I'll be there soon."

As they walked from the room, Ancient Mam signaled to someone standing outside the door. Six mulatto men and women walked inside. She pointed to Gustave. They untied the Frenchman and pushed him to Ancient Mam and Josephine.

"If you think a bunch of mulattoes can best a Frenchman of pure blood, you are sadly mistaken." Gustave glared at them. "You have won for the moment because of that Texan. But soon he will be gone and I will rule again. Then I will have vengeance."

Ancient Mam spoke in Creole.

Josephine translated. "The future lies in the heart of Erzulie."

"Nonsense!" Gustave looked around wildly, then tried to get free but was no match for the men and women holding him. "Selene Morgan, you have not seen the last of me."

Ancient Mam spoke to the mulattoes, and they carried Gustave, kicking and screaming, from the room.

She inclined her head to Selene and Drake, then followed her people.

Josephine turned to them. "Thank you for your help. We will talk more later." Then she left, too.

Alone, Selene turned to Drake. He took her in his arms and held her close. She reveled in his warmth and strength, knowing she needed his support.

Finally, he set her back so he could look into her eyes. "Are you all right?" His voice held concern.

"Yes. But I'm worried about Joy Marie."

"So am I." He gazed deep into her green eyes. "Would you come back to the ranch and take care of her?"

Selene searched his dark eyes for answers. "What about Love Potions?"

316

"Rosa can handle it awhile longer, can't she?"
She nodded.

"I want you at Dalton Ranch same as always, but
Joy Marie and Jimmy need you. Bad. You heal
people, Selene. All I know about is cattle." He hesitated. "Say you'll come to Texas with me . . . at least
for a while."

"Are you sure you want a root woman under your
roof?"

"Hell, I won't even kick if you put love potion
number whatever—the one with the smelly chicken
foot—under my pillow."

"It isn't smelly! It's the scent of herbs." She
laughed, then sobered. "Is it a long way to Texas?"

This time Drake chuckled. "It's a long way once
you get to Texas. It's the biggest state in the Union.
We've got the biggest, meanest longhorns ever been
driven to Kansas. And jackrabbits! They don't come
any bigger than in Texas. Wait till you see the sun-
sets. They're the most beautiful anywhere. And did I
tell you about . . ."

She kissed him. And for the moment he forgot
about Texas.

Part Three

Hill Country, Texas
Autumn 1886

Chapter 23

If Drake had been a fish out of water in New Orleans, Selene knew she was swimming upstream in Texas.

She was torn between being fascinated with central Texas, homesick for New Orleans, and concerned about her friends left on Martinique. Glancing upward, she wasn't surprised to see another beautiful sunshiny day. That's all there seemed to be in Texas. After growing up with frequent rains in New Orleans and experiencing afternoon showers on Martinique, the sudden lack of moisture seemed unnatural. And dangerous.

But Drake assured her there was plenty of water in the Hill Country of Texas, but it came mostly from rivers and underground streams. Truth to tell, there seemed to be plenty of water for drinking and cleaning at the ranch, but the dryness of the air was something she hadn't adjusted to yet. And didn't know if she ever would.

However, she had quickly seen the possibilities of expanding her apothecary business into the area, for in such a dry climate everybody needed more oils and lotions for their skin, or at least she certainly did.

Joy Marie had told her she didn't think cowboys would be buying much skin cream, scented or otherwise. But Selene had other ideas. If presented correctly, everyone could benefit from the formula she had in mind for the dry country of Texas. And that gave her a great sense of satisfaction, as well as making her feel useful. It was something she could do amid an avalanche of things she found strange at the least and daunting at best.

Drake was so preoccupied with the ranch she felt as if she belonged there a little less each day. She knew he hadn't planned it that way, but the work had piled up. People needed him, animals needed him, and he was exhausted by day's end. On the other hand, she'd never felt so little needed in her life and it rankled. If it hadn't been for Joy Marie and Jimmy, she'd have gone home to New Orleans and waited for Drake to come after her when he had time, if he ever did.

Thoughts of New Orleans brought her to the letter from Rosa that had arrived the day before. She'd been pleased to learn Love Potions was still doing fine. Rosa and her assistant were getting along well and taking care of the sick who came to them. But that didn't surprise her. Rosa had always been an excellent nurse in addition to her other skills.

However, Selene felt a little left out, especially since Granny Morgan had started the business. But she knew it was in capable hands, continuing to flourish, and that was what mattered.

Yet Rosa's emotional life concerned her. Rosa had written that Alfred had moved to New York City. He had a good job, was well paid, and no longer had mulatto friends. His life was everything his family had dreamed of and worked for through so many generations. What Rosa didn't say was whether or not Alfred was happy. She knew Rosa couldn't be completely happy without the man she loved. But Selene knew there was nothing she could do about the situation no matter how much she worried.

Finally she stood up, knowing she'd been using her thoughts to hold back the anger that had been building for an hour or more. But it was too late now. Childish or not, work or business, Drake had stood her up one last time too many. The picnic lunch had been packed, her horse saddled for over an hour, and she'd waited in the courtyard too long. Drake wasn't coming, or he'd get away too late to make any difference. In the meantime she starved and fumed and felt useless. Enough. She'd never been treated like this in her life and she was through with it.

She glanced around the courtyard, inhaling the fragrance of cedar. Walking over to the fountain in the center, she let cool water play over her hand. From an underground stream, the water was the life of the house and she never tired of enjoying it. She looked around at the stone benches that matched the fountain and at the stone walkways that cut through the transplanted cedar, chaparral, and other native plants. She was very much aware of the lack of flowers, although she supposed there would have been some in the spring and summer.

Picking up her hat, a wide Mexican sombrero which protected her from the sun, she walked into the sprawling living, family, parlor room. Again she was amazed at the starkness which was so similar to the land around her. The room, like the rest of the house, had white-plastered walls over a foot thick to keep out the heat. The walls were bare except for a few mounted animal heads and Indian blankets or baskets. The furniture was of heavy wood, stained dark, and covered with animal hides or Indian blankets. A huge fireplace occupied one wall with Indian pottery arranged in a corner.

As she walked through the room, trailing her hat, she marveled that in central Texas they had obviously not heard of Victorian, French, or any other style from the continent. And, without doubt, felt no need for it. Yes, in Texas they set their own style, and while she could appreciate its simplicity and local color, she had yet to become accustomed to it.

Walking into the kitchen, she again marveled at the quaintness of the large, bright, cheerful room that was always filled with wonderful scents and large amounts of food. However, she now approached her meals with caution. The first bite in Drake's home had practically burned out her mouth, throat, and stomach, so from then on she'd tested everything carefully.

A large, rectangular table of dark wood with matching chairs dominated one end of the kitchen. On it were clumps of dried red and green peppers, pieces of hand-thrown pottery, and a tablecloth and napkins of hand-loomed cotton. On one edge lay the saddlebags containing her picnic lunch. She reached for those.

"Señorita Selene, he has not come?" Carlota came in the side door, carrying an empty bowl.

"No." Selene smiled at the older woman to take the sting from her single word. She liked Carlota, as well as her husband Jorge. They had been with the Dalton family since Drake was a boy and they ran the house, keeping it clean and repaired, and food on the table. It was a big job, but they made it seem easy.

Carlota shook her head. *"Estupido*, that one."

Selene picked up the saddlebags. "I'm going alone. He promised to show me Seven Hundred Springs and I'll not wait any longer."

Setting down the bowl, Carlota turned around. "It is too dangerous, too far. You do not know the way."

"Drake told me how to get there. I've already been part of the way. I'll just follow the Guadalupe River."

"Rattlesnakes. Rock slides. Mud slides. Buzzards. Sunstroke." Carlota rolled her eyes as she thought of other calamaties. "Stampede. Lame horse. Renegades. No, it is too dangerous. Wait for Drake."

Selene smiled, already used to Carlota's dire predictions for anybody setting foot outside the house or, at best, the yard. But Carlota was like a mother hen to everybody and her short, plump body had nurtured any number of people for years, or so Drake had told her. In contrast, her husband, with bronzed skin from working in the sun and a wiry body from constant activity, hardly spoke to anyone. But signs of his industriousness were everywhere.

"Joy Marie needs you." Carlota began chopping peppers. "Jimmy, too."

"Joy Marie is in her room resting. Jimmy is helping Jorge. Besides, everything's set. I'm going."

"What about the horse?"

"I ride better than I did and Fancy's a gentle mare."

Carlota put her hands on her hips. "I see you will go." She shrugged. "If you do not return, it is not on my head."

Selene gave Carlota a quick kiss on the cheek, then hurried out of the kitchen before she started to doubt her own abilities to get to the Springs and back.

Outside, she noticed chickens scratched around the hen house, a calico cat slept in the shade of the house, and Jorge and Jimmy hammered on the door of the barn. She knew the cowboy's bunk house was empty this time of day, but her mare stood patiently in the shade in the small corral next to the barn.

Glancing in all directions, she saw not a sign of Drake or dust of an approaching horse. Anger flooded her again. She wouldn't wait, not any longer. She was going on with her life, with or without Drake Dalton. Stepping into the corral, she patted Fancy, a buckskin quarterhorse, on the nose, threw the saddlebags behind the saddle, then led the mare past the open gate.

Shutting the gate, she glanced around again, saw no sign of Drake, and mounted. She was proud of the way she'd taken to riding and had no doubts about handling the gentle Fancy. The sun was at the midway point in the sky so she would have a long afternoon to find the Springs, eat her lunch, and start back. Making the ride on her own would give her new confidence in living on the ranch without depending on somebody else all the time.

As she rode through the valley toward the Guadalupe, she looked up at the panorama of rolling hills, dotted with trees of varying shades of green. She could see far and it was in sharp contrast to Martinique, as well as New Orleans. But she understood why Drake loved the land. It had its own beauty. Yet it was lonely. And she didn't know if she could ever get used to that.

When she reached the Guadalupe, she admired the trees fed by the spring water of the river. Pecan trees, sycamores, and cypresses grew in abundance along the riverbank, as well as grass and shrubs. She was in no hurry and let Fancy set the pace along the narrow trail that wound along the embankment overlooking the stream.

The sun was warm on her shoulders and she glanced down at her green and rose cotton long-sleeved blouse, dark green cotton divided skirt, and brown leather cowboy boots. She wore brown leather gloves to protect her hands from the sun and reins. All were new, the clothes made by Joy Marie and Carlota, for she had quickly discovered that clothing suited to New Orleans and Martinique were simply not very serviceable on the ranch. Jorge had presented her with the hat. It had seemed too large and ungainly at first, but after a short time in the sun she prized it above all else.

As she rode, admiring the scenery and the beautiful Guadalupe River, she saw jackrabbits dart through the tall grass to disappear into the thickets, birds sang in the trees, and a deer leaped across the path to vanish behind a hill. She smelled dust and water and cedar on a breeze that cooled her face.

Martinique had been beautiful, but so bright, intense, and compact compared to Texas. New Orleans was a wonderful, busy, decadent city of untold pleasures. But pain and betrayal were the dark undersides of both Martinique and New Orleans. She looked around. Would she find that darkness in Texas as well?

When she came to a low place in the Guadalupe, she decided to water Fancy, have a drink herself, and eat lunch. She didn't know how long it would be till she reached Seven Hundred Springs or if she could even locate them, so she would have her lunch at the base of a cypress tree and admire the river as it flowed past.

She reined in Fancy, got down, then led the mare down to the river. Waiting while Fancy drank, she glanced around, enjoying the peace and majesty of the river valley. Perhaps she didn't need the sophistication of New Orleans or the intensity of Martinique to be happy. She bent down and picked up a plant. She didn't recognize it, but wondered if it had medicinal properties.

Suddenly excited, she decided to gather a number of herbs and take them back to the ranch. Carlota might know about the plants or others in the area. If she found new herbal cures or soothing plant properties, she could send them to Rosa to sell in the shop. She might even find new fragrances in the local flowers and fauna.

Pleased with her idea, she splashed cool water on her face, then took a long drink of the delicious spring fed water. She left Fancy to nibble grass while she sat down under a large, shady tree and opened the saddlebags. Carlota had packed tamales and tortillas. Although Selene had grown to like the Mexican food, she was still careful of the peppers.

Taking a small bite, she smiled with pleasure. Carlota had sent corn tamales made with sweet filling. Eating one, she leaned back and watched the river roll downstream. As she savored the moment, her mind roamed. Drake said the Guadalupe would eventually reach the Rio Grande, or Rio Bravo as it was called in Mexico. He had promised to take her there. But he'd been too busy.

Actually, she couldn't blame him for taking care of business. She'd have done no less, but she couldn't keep waiting around for him. Joy Marie felt better, although she would have sudden crying spells and couldn't stand to be alone. Selene made her a special soothing, strengthening herbal tea, but mainly Joy Marie seemed to need her presence. At this point, she could only hope that time would heal her friend's wounds.

On the other hand, Jimmy had taken to ranch life like an old hand and that fact made Selene happy. Jimmy followed Jorge around or trotted after Drake, asking questions, offering help, and learning everything he could. He insisted he'd be experienced and old enough to go on the trail drive come next spring.

She sighed. Even though she was happy for Jimmy, she still felt a small pain in her heart at losing him. He was growing up, learning from men, and he didn't need her anymore except to tell her about his exploits. With the nourishing food and hard work, he was growing taller, filling out already. Before she knew it, he'd be a man and off on his own.

When she went back to New Orleans, she'd probably never see him again. But she could never ask him to go back to his former life for she simply couldn't offer him what he had on Dalton Ranch.

Changes. She had felt them in New Orleans. She had begun to understand them on Martinique. But she would have to accept them in Texas, if she could. Shivering, she suddenly lost her appetite. She packed up the food, put it back in the saddlebags, and stood up. She had better be moving along. Unfortunately, being alone made her think too much and it wasn't something she was ready to do.

Mounting Fancy, she started back down the trail along the Guadalupe, but nothing seemed quite as pretty as before. Maybe it was because she no longer seemed to fit in anywhere. Joy Marie was at home and getting better. Jimmy was happily into a new life. Her friends from New Orleans had found a new home and family on Martinique. Rosa was handling Love Potions with ease. Was there no place for her anymore?

She felt tears sting her eyes. She was being silly. She felt alone because she was far away from home with people who had been strangers not long ago. While Drake had seemed to need and want her on Martinique, now he kept his distance and she never saw him alone. But why should that upset her so? It was what she wanted, wasn't it? Perhaps the love potions were finally wearing off. If so, then she would be free of Drake Dalton and she could return to her former life. Wasn't that what was best?

Blinking away her tears, she forced herself to concentrate on the land around her. She should enjoy what she was seeing and learn as much as she could before she returned to New Orleans. She wouldn't pity herself. Granny Morgan had taught her better.

Straightening her back, she suddenly noticed Fancy flatten her ears.

She'd learned that action by a horse meant they sensed danger or trouble or change. For the first time she wished she hadn't come out alone. Carlota's warnings came back to her. Rattlesnake. Renegades. Wild animals. She looked around for a place in which to hide and saw a curve in the trail up ahead. Maybe that would give her some cover.

Just as she reached the bend, she heard the thunder of hooves as a horse raced down the trail behind her. Startled, she urged Fancy forward, then looked back. A cowboy with his hat pulled low galloped a black stallion toward her. Dust flew around him, obscuring his identity. She decided the man must be drunk, for there was no room for two horses and riders on the narrow trail.

Rounding the bend, she reined Fancy off, then jumped down and led the mare to a nearby tree. There she waited, hoping the underbrush hid her location. For the first time she wished she'd asked Drake to teach her to use a pistol.

As the rider came around the bend, he slowed the stallion, searched the trail, then the land around it. Finally he looked in her direction and pulled his horse to a stop. As the dust settled around him, he leaped down and led his horse off the trail toward her.

"Drake!" Astonished, she simply stood there.

He threw off his hat, walked over to her, and put his hands on her shoulders. "What the hell do you think you're doing?"

For a moment she couldn't speak. All she could do

331

was take in the sight of him, for a beard stubble covered his lower face, he was dusty, and his brown eyes were furious. But none of that kept him from looking good. Still she was angry. "I'm on my way to Seven Hundred Springs, and if you'll get out of my way, I'll continue on the trail."

"What?" He clenched his jaws.

"I believe you heard me. Now, will you get out of my way?" She raised her chin, determined not to be intimidated.

"Like hell I will. I get back and Carlota tells me you've left to be eaten by wolves, bitten by rattlesnakes, ravaged by renegades, or—"

"I heard the same thing, but you know Carlota . . ."

"Carlota's right, but you're too stubborn to admit it."

"Right, is she? I believe I'm standing here without a mark on me. I *was* enjoying the day."

"Selene!" He shook her. "Couldn't you have waited?"

"I did wait, just like all the other times. While I'm here, I want to see some of Texas. You don't have time so I'm going on my own." She sounded childish even to herself but couldn't stop it.

He knocked her hat back from her head so it hung from a thong around her neck down her back, then he hugged her close and held her tight.

She couldn't help but notice he smelled like dust, cattle, and leather. Tears burned her eyes. She didn't care what he smelled like or how dirty he was because being held by him was still better than anything. And she damned her love potions.

332

Setting her back from him, he looked into her green eyes. "I'm sorry. I wanted you on Dalton Ranch. I still do. But it's been one thing after another. Rustlers now. And I haven't had that kind of trouble in a long time."

"I'm sorry, too. I know you have to work, but I mean it, Drake, I can't wait around anymore. I'm not used to it."

"Joy Marie still needs you."

"I know, but not all the time."

He ran a hand through his hair. "Tell you what. Let's go on to the Springs. I need a break anyway. We'll spend the night."

Her heart beat faster. It'd been so long since they'd been alone she had begun to think he didn't want her anymore. Maybe he still didn't. Maybe he was simply too tired to ride back to the ranch. "Won't everyone worry?"

"Carlota'll tell them where we are."

"But Joy Marie?"

"She'll understand."

"I don't know if I should leave her alone at night."

Drake frowned. "Are you telling me you want to go back?" He moved away from her. "Don't you want me to touch you anymore?"

She walked over and touched his back. "I'm not thinking of us. It's Joy Marie I'm worried about."

Putting an arm around her shoulders, he pulled her close. "She's better. It might do her good to be on her own one night. Besides, we need it, Selene. Hell, if I get any grumpier around the men, they'll all quit."

She raised a brow.

"If you have to know, not touching you is driving me crazy. Between keeping your reputation safe by staying away from you at the house and catching up on work around the ranch, I'm about ready to run away with you and say to hell with it all."

"Really?" Her breath caught in her throat. "And what about tonight?"

"I'll make an excuse to protect you." Putting a finger under her chin, he raised her head, then gently kissed her lips. Fire leaped between them. He shook his head. "Come on, otherwise we'll never leave this spot."

Chapter 24

As they reached South Llano River, Selene noticed the sun lowering in the western sky. On her own, she doubted if she'd have found Seven Hundred Springs. If she had, there wouldn't have been time for her to get back to the ranch by dark.

They'd ridden a lot farther than she'd have liked. Unused to so many hours in the saddle, her body protested at the unusual strain. Yet she wouldn't have missed the time alone with Drake or missed seeing the beautiful land. She realized that the longer she stayed in Texas, the more she liked it. Still her home remained New Orleans.

As she guided Fancy across the stream, she noticed again how easily Drake sat his horse, how tall in the saddle, and how naturally he moved with the animal. Yes, this was his home. The land, the life, the people were all a part of him. She knew he'd never be completely happy or comfortable anywhere else. And it gave her an idea of how much he had worried about Joy Marie to have left his ranch and followed her to

New Orleans then on to Martinique.

She glanced at him. He wore a white hat turned beige with use and weather, denims, a blue plaid shirt, a brown leather vest, well-worn brown boots, and brown leather gloves with fringe. His gunbelt was strapped around his hips and the handle of the .45 gleamed in the sunlight. On his saddle, he carried a coiled lasso and a Winchester, plus a rolled blanket and saddlebags behind. She'd learned that with what he carried on his horse he could stay out for days, even if he didn't carry food or water, for there was plenty of game and fresh water in the hills.

But her situation wouldn't be the same. She could find water, but food? Her saddlebags held plenty of Carlota's cooking and she was glad of that. In New Orleans she knew the best places to eat, she could order anything she needed or buy it in a store. But how did she go about dealing with a place where you did most everything for yourself? It was daunting. Yet the challenge was exciting, too.

"We'll be there soon." Drake pointed ahead. "Seven Hundred Springs feeds into the South Llano."

"Good." She laughed. "I may not be able to sit down again for a week."

He joined her laughter. "Wait till tomorrow and the ride back. I may have to carry you across my lap."

"That might not be so bad, stranger." She cast him a sultry look.

Shaking his head, he groaned. "Trust me, you don't want to ride that way. But *sitting* on my lap has its possibilities." He guided his horse near hers and clasped her hand. "Seven Hundred Springs isn't New

Orleans or Martinique. I hope you won't be disappointed. It's been a long ride."

She squeezed his fingers. "Long ride or not, it's been worth it to spend some time with you."

Leaning across their horses, he kissed her. "I feel the same." He cleared his throat and let go of her hand. "I know the ranch is a big change from New Orleans, but give it a chance. I promise you'll come to like it here."

"It's beautiful, but so lonely."

"Lonely?" He glanced around. "You're surrounded by life." He gestured wide. "Not counting the rivers, the trees, the plants, there're coyotes, deer, jackrabbits, racoons, and rattlers. Fact is, I could go on all day talking about the life here, but you get the idea."

"What about people?"

"There're folks who think that's the best part of all."

She frowned. "You mean, being away from people?"

"Right. People like Dominique."

A cloud seemed to pass over their heads. She glanced upward, but the sun still shone. "I know evil people are out there, but there are plenty of good ones, too."

Drake nodded. "But a bad one can cause enough trouble for a whole damn army."

She couldn't argue with that when she thought of Gustave Dominique.

"Men've been coming West for as long as this country's existed. They've come for a lot of reasons. Money. Bad luck. The law. But a lot of them, mainly the trappers, didn't want to see humans but once or twice a year. And that's the way they lived."

"I can't imagine it."

"Well, I can't either. But we've still got men, and a few women, around here like that. They'll come into one of the towns once or twice a year to trade skins for supplies. And they're happy people."

"Okay, you've convinced me."

He laughed. "I wasn't trying to convince you. I wanted you to know that if you feel isolated on Dalton Ranch, there're some people who'd think it was too damn crowded."

Chuckling, she smiled at him. "It's going to take me a while to understand the ways of Texas."

"Just make sure you give yourself plenty of time, 'cause I'm still learning about it myself." He snapped the reins against his horse's neck. "Come on, let's see the Springs."

Selene followed him up the other side of the bank, past trees, rocks, and bushes, then around a giant moss-covered boulder. She stopped beside him and caught her breath, for from a hillside, water poured out of hundreds of holes, flowing downward to form a stream of gurgling, white water that rushed toward the South Llano.

She was overcome with the beauty of the sight, with the amazing amount of water rushing naturally from the hillside. Perhaps Drake had been right about everything being bigger and better in Texas. She caught his hand. "It's magnificent. Is it always like this?"

"Yes. It's an underground reservoir. And that water makes some of the best beer you've ever tasted."

"I'd like to try some."

"Okay. We'll go into Sisterdale one day soon."

"Is that a town?"

"Yes. It's not too far from us on the Guadalupe. But in the meantime, you can have a drink of some of the best water in the Hill Country." He led his horse to the stream, got down, then helped her dismount.

She pulled the saddlebags off Fancy and handed them to him. "Here's our lunch."

Grinning, he snatched the bags from her. "I'm starved. I forgot to eat at the house."

Leaving the horses to graze, he found them sunny rocks at the base of Seven Hundred Springs and they sat on them with the water running around them.

Drake pulled out the tamales, took several for himself, then passed the others to her.

She smiled as she watched him eat, then she tried another tamale. Suddenly the food tasted delicious where before it had had little flavor. After eating one, she scooped up water with her hands and drank. It was cold and delicious. Splashing water on her face, she glanced at Drake.

He'd stopped eating to watch her. "You ever think about marriage, Selene?"

His question caught her off guard. She took another drink before answering. "Yes. But I'd never thought it was for me."

"Maybe not in New Orleans, but around here a lady's good name precedes her."

"Are you saying if I make many outings like this, total strangers in the Texas Hill Country will think I'm a loose woman?"

"They aren't strangers to me and they won't always be to you. I don't want you hurt."

"Is this a pro—"

"I just want you to think about it." He picked up a small rock and skimmed it across the water. "It would affect the children, too."

"I know." She didn't know whether to be insulted, pleased, or angry. Instead, she concentrated on the beauty of the Springs. Willows grew along the bank, reminding her of a woman's long hair unbound. Free. She wouldn't let herself be caught and shackled by other people's opinions, but she would protect herself. And her children when they came to her.

Drake turned to her. "Thanks for letting everybody think Joy Marie married Dominique and that he died on Martinique."

"To us he *did* die. I just hope it isn't something that comes back to haunt her."

"It'll be fine except everybody'll expect her to use Dominique's name now."

"That's horrible. And I imagine bad for her."

"I'm thinking about telling folks when the time comes that she's going to use Dalton since she'll be living here. What do you think?"

"A good idea." She trailed her fingers in the water. "People'll talk anyway."

"Let them. It'll settle down. Besides, where are all these people?"

"There aren't so many by New Orleans's standards, but there's plenty of ranches around, as well as towns. And San Antonio isn't too far away." He tossed another pebble. "Dalton Ranch is well known."

She smiled at him. "I suppose your family must be

like one of the old planter families in Louisiana."

"Something like that, but not so rich or old."

Laughing, she finished eating and handed him back the food. "Don't eat it all. I'm not up to cooking out here."

"Not even striped bass? Around here some of them grow to more than thirty pounds."

"No doubt they do. And do these bass ride horses, too?"

Drake chuckled. "Looks like I'm going to have to prove every one of my tall tales, aren't I?"

"Maybe. But you've gone a long way by showing me Seven Hundred Springs." She watched the water as it cascaded downward and was reminded of the waterfall on Martinique where they had shared passion. She wanted him again, but perhaps, from what he'd said, they should head back.

"I've got plenty more to show you, Selene."

"Should we go back? I suppose we ought to save my reputation, if possible."

"It's better not to travel at night." He gave her a thoughtful look. "Besides, I've stayed away from you as long as I can."

"And my reputation?"

"One night. We'll tell them you were so sore from riding by the time you reached the Springs we had to let you soak till daybreak." He laughed.

"That's not funny."

"But everybody'll believe the last thing you had on your mind was a roving cowboy."

She joined his laughter. "I suppose you're right."

"Come on, let's tether the horses and find a soft spot for our bedrolls."

"And we can listen to the Springs all night?"

"Sure. 'Cause I don't plan on letting you sleep much." He paused, then pushed a strand of hair back from her face. "You aren't sorry you came to Texas, are you?"

She shook her head, suddenly overcome with tenderness for him. He could be tough, brash, and rude, but underneath he had a gentleness that must have been born on the range, in the wide open spaces, given so much room to grow that he didn't need to be mean or petty or power-hungry. She also realized he was satisfied with himself so he didn't have to take life out of somebody else.

Giving her a quick kiss, he put an arm around her shoulders. "Come on. It'll be dark soon and we want to make sure we don't bed down on a rattler."

She dug in her heels. "If there's a chance—"

He laughed. "Nothing's going to harm you with me around." He looked about the area and chose a site under a willow tree. Bunching up fallen leaves, he spread their blankets over the mulch, then checked the makeshift bed with his hand. "Not as good as a feather mattress, but it'll do."

Eyeing the bed cautiously, she glanced around the area and realized that even if there were a lot of danger she'd probably never know it.

"Why don't you pick up some dry wood? I'll get some stones and we can build a fire."

"Good idea." She turned away to look for wood.

"But don't bring me a snake by mistake." His laughter joined the sound of the Springs.

She stuck out her tongue.

Drake laughed even harder.

Turning away, she went in search of wood. Privately she was surprised at herself. She hadn't stuck out her tongue at someone since childhood. But Drake made her feel lighthearted and young. And it felt good.

She brought back fallen twigs and branches. Sitting down beside him, she watched as he carefully broke and positioned wood over dry leaves. Finally, he struck a match and had a small, cozy fire burning.

She held out her hands to warm them over the blaze. "That's nice."

"Still mad at me?"

"No."

"Want to prove it."

She glanced at him. He was serious. Her breath caught in her throat at the look in his eyes. He hadn't been exaggerating earlier about wanting her. The fire in him ignited her own. "Yes."

He hesitated a moment, searching her green eyes, then pressed his lips to hers. She moaned as he opened his mouth and thrust his tongue deep into hers.

She knew it had been too long. How had she stood it without his touch? Shivering, she pushed fingers into his hair, feeling its texture, its length, its sensuality as he caressed her back. When he pulled her full length against him, she was only too ready to do whatever he wanted because she knew it would be what she wanted, too.

He sought her mouth again, tasting, teasing, testing, and when she responded heatedly, he groaned and nibbled down her throat to her neck. Stopped by her high-neck blouse, he began on the small buttons.

But he was impatient. He growled and sat up.

"Damn it, Selene. Let's get out of our clothes."

Smiling mischievously, she leisurely stroked the front of his shirt, then slowly began unbuttoning it. "Like this?"

"No." Frustration filled his voice. He pushed her hand away and quickly had his shirt unbuttoned. He pulled it off and tossed it away. "Like this." Then he grinned and reached for her.

She held up a hand. "Not so fast, cowboy. 'Don't you think you'd better do something about that six-shooter?"

"Sorry." He quickly unbuckled the gunbelt, checked his .45, then set it within easy reach of the makeshift bed. "That suit you better?"

She nodded, and began unbuttoning her blouse.

Watching, his dark gaze never left the growing view of her cleavage.

Finally, she opened her blouse to reveal a white cotton chemise trimmed with lace and green ribbon.

"You're not wearing much underwear anymore, are you?"

"I'm dressing for the ranch. And you."

He grinned, showing strong white teeth. Reaching for her, he pulled her close, then lowered his head. With his teeth he pulled loose the green bow that held the chemise together. He gazed at her bared breasts till he took one nipple in his mouth then the other as he teased them to taut peaks.

She trembled beneath his touch.

Next he slipped off her skirt and single petticoat, then pulled off her boots and stockings. Left in her chemise and matching drawers, she appeared provocative. Running a hand up her drawers, he squeezed her buttock, making her moan and reach for him. As he plied her soft, smooth flesh, she felt the hard muscles of his arms and back until she tossed back her head and pulled him closer.

Still unable to get enough of her, he raised himself on an elbow. "I've waited about as long as I can, Selene."

She traced his lips with a fingertip, then lowered her hand and unbuttoned his Levis. Taking out his hard length, she stroked him till he groaned and trembled. "I want you, Drake."

Without saying a word, he got up. Still watching her, he pulled off his boots, socks, and denims. When he came back to her, he was naked and ready. She reached up and drew him down. When their lips met, she felt his hands push up her drawers and find her moist core. As he massaged her, his fingers delving deeper and deeper, she felt her desire grow until she was writhing against him, aching, burning, twisting with need that only he could fulfill.

Rolling to his side, he pulled her against him so her full breasts were pressed tightly against his chest. Then he moved between her legs, positioned himself, and drove deep inside her. She responded, undulating around him, over him, pressing ever closer in a desperate need to join them completely. He controlled their rhythm as he buried himself deep inside her, thrusting, stroking, stoking the fire that scorched them.

And finally she cried out, moaning his name as the pleasure took her. And him. They burned brightly for a long moment, then plummeted back to reality, still wrapped in each other's arms.

Tears stung Selene's eyes and she hid her face against his throat. How could it be so good? She could almost believe she loved him. Almost. Maybe she would believe it if not for the love potions.

"It'll be difficult going back to separate bedrooms." Drake's voice was low and rough.

"Maybe I can enter your room through your window."

"Anytime you want, lady." He took a long breath. "I mean it, Selene. I can't take much more of being separated from you."

"What about my good name?"

He cleared his throat. "Would you consider marriage?"

She shivered, suddenly cold. "It's such a big step. And Dalton Ranch is so far from New Orleans."

"What about a trial engagement?"

"And tell people?"

"Yes."

She shivered again.

"That way you'd be more than Joy Marie's friend come to visit her."

"I don't know, Drake." She stroked his chest, feeling the fine hair under her fingertips.

"Hell!" He sat up. "You don't know? After what we've been doing, sharing? What does it take to convince you we're good for each other?"

"I don't doubt that, but it may not last. You know, the love potions."

Drake stood up. "I'm tired of running after you, Selene. Damn tired."

"But—"

"Go to sleep. I'm taking a swim."

"But—"

"Don't worry about me." He took several steps away, then stopped and looked back. "As if you would." Then he continued down to the stream and dove into the cold, deep water.

She sat up, feeling chilled. Pulling the blanket up to her chin, she looked upward. The stars in the night sky were bright, brilliant, and beautiful. Could the stars be bigger and brighter in Texas? They certainly appeared that way. And could the men be the same? Was she being a fool? Or was she simply being cautious?

Marriage. A wedding. Mrs. Drake Dalton of Texas. She shivered again. But what about Selene Morgan of Love Potions in New Orleans? Could they be the same person? She didn't know, but she did know she couldn't give up what her Granny had taught her or all she'd worked so hard to build during her lifetime. She put a hand to her stomach. What if she already carried his child? And what if she no longer wanted to live without him?

Tears burned her eyes. She had too many questions and too few answers.

But she still had time. Standing, she walked to the stream and looked for Drake. He swam downstream, his dark head just above the water. She sat down at the water's edge and put in her feet. It was cold and refreshing. She smiled. He'd be surprised to know she was a good swimmer. As well as a good learner.

Maybe it was time to give Texas—and Drake—a chance. A real chance.

Chapter 25

Selene wore a secret smile understood only by Drake as she glanced around the breakfast table the day after they'd returned from Seven Hundred Springs.

Engagement. Unspoken, unofficial and unannounced, it still bound them in a way as yet explored. Somehow their fragile commitment to each other seemed to extend to Joy Marie and Jimmy, as well as Carlota and Jorge, making them a real family rather than the fantasy one Gustave had tried to force.

Selene watched early morning light turn the darkness outside to gray as Carlota set eggs, steak, and tortillas, along with hot sauce, peppers, honey, and plenty of steaming coffee on the table. Jimmy drank milk as he greedily piled food on his plate. Joy Marie sipped her special herbal tea, a faraway look in her eyes. And Drake tackled his food as if he were going to eat everything on the table and ask for more.

Relishing the cozy scene, Selene thought of the cowboys in the bunkhouse eating the breakfast Carlota had sent over with Jorge. Soon they'd be ready to start the day, just as dawn broke over the ranch. She'd offer to help Carlota with the dishes and food preparation and keep a close eye on Joy Marie.

But that wasn't till later. For the moment she could enjoy the warmth of the moment, the family, the peaceful time. And she took great pleasure in it, for she was reminded of her childhood with Granny Morgan.

"I'm going down to the south forty today." Drake broke the silence at the table.

"Will you be gone all day?" Selene noticed a sudden tension in the air.

"Yes. I might stay the night." He drank coffee. "Rustlers hit there again. Stripped the beef and left the hide, hooves, horn, and bones. Buzzards were picking at the leftovers. That's how the cowboys found the remains."

Joy Marie set her teacup down with a clatter, leaned her head back against her chair, and shut her eyes.

"Is there danger?" Selene glanced at Joy Marie in concern.

"No." Drake frowned. "Those rustlers are long gone. They don't want to be caught. But it's a funny thing about them slaughtering cattle on my land instead of herding them away."

"Why is that strange?" Selene didn't understand the situation.

"More danger of being caught."

"Aren't your cows branded?" Selene toyed with her cup of coffee, not wanting Drake to go anywhere near danger.

"Yes. But they're yearlings, not full grown, and the brand could probably be altered and the cattle driven miles from here where I'd probably never find them."

"Yet if they kill them here, they leave the brand behind."

"Drake nodded. "But that's a lot of beef that'll spoil fast. It'll have to be sold in the area."

"And will that arouse suspicions?" Selene wanted to help him.

"Yes. But it won't matter if it's sold cheap enough."

"I see." Selene began to understand the dangers and frustrations of ranching.

"Fact is, it's strange all the way around and that's what bothers me." Drake drank more coffee. "Anyway, I'm riding out there with a couple of boys to see what I can learn."

"Be careful." Selene sent a silent message with her eyes.

"I will." He met her gaze and nodded.

"Drake, Joy Marie's in danger. Help her."

Selene looked at Joy Marie.

"You're all in danger." Joy Marie's voice was low and rough, just like the other times she'd spoken for her dead husband. "Don't go out to the south forty."

Drake half rose from his chair, then sat back down.

"What is the danger?" Selene was determind to keep a cool head and respond positively to Joy Marie, no matter what her friend was experiencing.

"Old danger. It is from—"

Carlota dropped a bowl full of beans. It crashed on the tile floor. She crossed herself, staring at Joy Marie in shock and horror.

Joy Marie's head slumped forward.

Selene hurried over and tilted her friend's head back. Joy Marie's eyes had rolled back in her head. "Drake, she's not breathing!"

He pushed back his chair and rushed to Joy Marie's side.

Jimmy dropped his fork and simply sat in stunned silence as he watched Joy Marie.

Carlota began praying.

Selene grabbed Joy Marie's shoulders and shook. "Wake up. You're all right. We need you. Drake needs you." She shook harder. "Joy Marie, come back. Jimmy needs you. I need you." Tears streamed down her cheeks as she continued to shake her friend.

Suddenly Joy Marie inhaled a long, wheezy rasp of breath.

Falling to her knees, Selene stroked Joy Marie's face. "It's all right. You're fine. Everything's all right. You're at home on Dalton Ranch."

Joy Marie opened her eyes, and smiled. "Don't cry, Selene. Please. But I wish you hadn't called me back. I was walking down this dark path, but at the end of it was a white light. Really bright. And standing in it was Ray. He was waiting for me, Selene. He still loves me." Tears brimmed over Joy Marie's eyes and ran down her cheeks. "I didn't want to come back, but you hurt me. I couldn't concentrate. Why did you do it?"

Selene gathered Joy Marie in her arms and rocked back and forth. "It wasn't your time, Joy Marie. We still need you. What about Jimmy, Drake?" Tears filled her eyes. "It's Gustave's doing and we can't let him win. Can we?" She looked into her friend's confused blue eyes. "Can we?"

Joy Marie shook her head. "No. But it was so peaceful, so beautiful. And Ray was there. I didn't want to come back, Selene."

"Did she die?" Jimmy's voice quavered. "If you brought her back, Selene, why didn't you do it for Joe? You're mean!" He knocked over his glass of milk and ran outdoors, slamming the door behind him.

"Oh, no." Selene stood up, took a step after Jimmy, then looked back at Joy Marie in confusion.

"I'll go after him." Drake placed a kiss on Joy Marie's cheek. "Take care of her." He squeezed Selene's hand, then followed Jimmy outside.

"Carlota, does Drake have any brandy?" Selene sat down beside Joy Marie.

Carlota wore a grim expression. "I will get it."

As Carlota left the room, Selene turned back to Joy Marie. "How do you feel?"

"Empty. I think something died in me, Selene, or something was born. I'm not sure which, but I don't think I'll be the same again."

Selene took Joy Marie's hands. They were cold. She tried to rub warmness into them with her own, but it didn't seem to help.

Carlota came back and set a whiskey bottle with two glasses on the table. "That is what Drake drinks."

"Thank you." Selene poured a small amount in each glass, handed one to Joy Marie, and took the other herself. The liquor felt like fire as it burned from her mouth to her stomach, but she welcomed the sensation.

Joy Marie tossed back her drink and held out her glass for more.

As Selene poured it, she realized her friend must have been drinking a lot with Gustave. But at least more color was now back in Joy Marie's cheeks.

Sipping the whiskey, Selene tried to keep her emotions under control, but she couldn't help worrying about Jimmy as well as Joy Marie. She glanced at Carlota, caught her gaze, and tried to smile in encouragement. But it didn't quite work. "I think she'll be all right. It's happened before, but not this bad."

Carlota walked over, gave Joy Marie a measuring look, then nodded. "What happened to her in that faraway land awoke her special eye."

"I don't understand." Selene glanced back at Joy Marie, but she seemed the same.

"She has the mother's gift of prophecy." Carlota crossed herself. "From my Mayan grandmothers the tale is told." Her voice softened to a singsong and she shut her eyes. "Astride the Great Tortoise, Mayual rides, Goddess of Four Hundred Breasts, Mother of Four Hundred Stars, seen by all who drink Her sacred brew and intoxicated by Her spirit, they tell of a time when Mayual was a woman living upon the Earth." Carlota opened her eyes. "It is passed down that Mayual knows all, understands all, and sometimes tells all. No longer on the Earth, she speaks through mortal women."

"And you think Joy Marie—"

"She is touched by Mayual. Has she been drinking the sacred, intoxicating liquid from the maguey plant? Mescal?"

"I don't know. But she's been drinking, probably whiskey."

Carlota nodded. "Her eye has been opened and she will forever speak the tongue of wisdom."

"You mean she can tell the future?"

"Yes. She has no choice. A gift from God. And Mayual."

"But—"

"Drake must not go to the south forty." Carlota crossed herself, gave Joy Marie a look of pity, then began cleaning up the spilled beans and broken bowl.

Selene was at a loss for words. She didn't know which way to turn so she leaned back in her chair, feeling so tired she didn't know if she could ever move again. Then she noticed Joy Marie was steadily emptying the bottle. Shocked, she stood up. "Come on, Joy Marie. You're going to bed. I think sleep is the best thing for you now till we figure out how to deal with the situation."

"You won't leave me alone, will you?"

"No." She helped Joy Marie to her feet, then began leading her from the kitchen. "Carlota, I'm sorry I can't help you, but—"

"Stay with her. I will tell Drake where you are when he returns. For now all is in the hands of God." She went back to work.

With an arm around Joy Marie's shoulders, Selene

led her down the hall to her friend's bedroom. Inside the room of light walls, heavy dark furniture, and handwoven blankets of neutral colors, Selene opened the drapes to let in sunlight.

Joy Marie sat down on the bed, holding her head in her hands.

Stacking pillows behind her back, Selene made Joy Marie as comfortable as possible, then she pulled a rocker next to the bed and sat down.

"Thanks, Selene. I don't know what I'd have done without you."

"Rest. You'll be fine."

"I don't know how much more I can take."

"You're strong. Much stronger than you realize."

"I don't feel strong."

"That's Gustave talking in your head and you mustn't listen to him."

Joy Marie gripped Selene's hand. "Sometimes at night I feel like he's watching me, like he's come for me, for you, for the ranch. I'm frightened, Selene."

"You've got to be strong. Jimmy needs you. We all do."

Joy Marie looked out the window. "I don't know anymore. If only Ray were here, and little Joey."

"But they aren't."

"Sometimes it seems like Ray's so close, still watching over me. Do you think that's possible?"

"I—I don't know." Selene remembered Ray's voice speaking through Joy Marie at the seance. But that had been Gustave's doing. Still, Drake had said Joy Marie had mentioned things at the seance only he and Ray had known. Chills ran up her spine.

"I think maybe Ray's still protecting me."

Drake walked into the room, with Jimmy behind him. He frowned. "You've got to realize Ray's dead, Joy Marie. He's gone forever. You must accept it."

"But Drake . . ." Joy Marie's voice held pain.

"No. I'm not going to listen to any more of it. Now, Jimmy's got something to say."

Jimmy stepped from behind Drake. "I'm sorry, Selene. I know you'd have saved Joe if you could've." He took Joe Junior from his pocket. "Here you can have him. He's the best I've got."

Tears stung Selene's eyes. She stroked the frog between its eyes. "Thanks, but you keep him. I'd have done almost anything to save Joe, but I couldn't."

"Is Joy Marie well now?" Jimmy took a cautious step toward the bed. "Does she need to touch Joe Junior?"

Joy Marie smiled and stroked Joe Junior.

Drake cleared his throat. "Joy Marie is confused. But we're going to fix that right now. Come on, all of you. There's something I want you to see outside." Drake left the room and Jimmy followed.

Selene exchanged a confused look with Joy Marie, then shrugged. "Do you feel like walking?"

Joy Marie smiled. "Maybe it'll do me good to get out in the sunlight.

Putting an arm around Joy Marie's waist, Selene helped her up, then walked with her back to the kitchen. Carlota had finished cleaning up the floor and was busy preparing the next meal. They stepped outside. Drake and Jimmy waited for them.

"Let's go." Drake headed for an ancient live oak tree set at a distance from any of the other buildings around the ranch house.

Jimmy hurried to match Drake's long strides.

Selene kept a firm grip on Joy Marie's hand, but didn't hurry. Whatever Drake had to show them could wait. Joy Marie's health and state of mind came first.

But soon Joy Marie began to pull back. Surprised, Selene glanced at her. Joy Marie's gaze was fixed just beyond Drake. Selene looked back and suddenly saw why. Near the oak tree was a small wrought iron fence enclosing several stone markers. The Dalton Cemetery.

Fury swept Selene. How could Drake be so unkind? But now it was too late to turn back, for Joy Marie knew exactly where they were headed. Selene increased her grip on Joy Marie's hand as they stopped beside Drake and Jimmy.

Staring at the small cemetery, Drake took off his hat and held it against his chest. After a time, he pointed toward a grave, then looked at Joy Marie. "That's my brother's grave, Joy Marie. Look at it good and hard. He's dead and buried. Read the marker."

Tears rolled down Joy Marie's cheeks. *"Raymond Dalton. Beloved Husband."* Her voice broke and she couldn't continue.

"Read the gravestone beside Ray's." Drake was unrelenting.

Joy Marie sobbed, choked, then continued. *"Joey Ray Dalton. Beloved Son."* She turned to Selene and buried her face against her shoulder.

Selene patted Joy Marie's back as tears burned her eyes. "Drake, this is cruel."

"No. It's got to be done. Joy Marie's run away from these deaths long enough. And they aren't the only ones." He pointed toward other graves. "My parents lie buried here, too. I lost my family, but I kept on going. Joy Marie's got to do the same."

Joy Marie raised her face. "But Drake, I can feel Ray near me and I never did before Gustave. It's like Ray's watching over me. And you. You shouldn't go to the south forty, Drake. I feel it strongly. Please." She held out her small hand to him.

Drake slammed his hat on his head. "This is damned nonsense. My brother's dead and that's that." He strode several paces away, then turned back. "I'm going to the south forty and nothing's going to happen except I'm going to find out who's rustling Dalton cows." He headed for the corral.

Joy Marie turned to Selene. "Can't you do anything?"

Selene watched Drake saddle his horse. "No. He's made up his mind."

"I better go with him." Jimmy looked concerned.

Selene shook her head. "Thanks, but Jorge'll need your help here."

Jimmy glanced at Joy Marie. "I'm sorry 'bout your son and husband. I lost Joe and it hurts."

Joy Marie knelt and hugged Jimmy. "Thanks. We'll comfort each other, all right?"

"You bet. Anytime you need to pet Joe Junior, let me know."

"I will." Joy Marie's voice quivered.

"Guess I best find Jorge." Jimmy threw back his shoulders. "There's work needs done 'round this place."

Joy Marie smiled.

As Jimmy walked toward the barn, Drake and two cowboys headed south.

Selene watched them go, a tightness in her chest.

Joy Marie squeezed her hand. "I could be wrong, Selene."

"Let's go to the house." Selene started walking back.

Joy Marie joined her. "I don't think I can sleep."

"I know what you mean."

"Maybe we can help Carlota." Joy Marie opened the back door and stepped inside.

Selene shut the door behind her.

Carlota looked around. "Did he go?"

"Yes." Joy Marie sat down at the table and clasped her hands.

"Grown men act like small boys sometimes." Carlota went back to chopping onions. "Rustlers. Rattlesnakes. Bears. Rivers. Wild bulls."

"I know Ray's buried in the cemetery. Maybe he's not near me now, but it feels like it. Besides, I know he'd be here helping me and his brother if he could. Isn't that right, Carlota?"

"Sí, pobrecito." Carlota sniffed and wiped at her eyes. "You both stay here and we cook. When Drake returns, we feast."

"Good idea." Selene desperately wanted something to take her mind off Drake. He had gone out with cowboys or alone many times so there was no reason to believe he'd be hurt this time. But she was almost beginning to believe Joy Marie had unexplained powers unleashed by Gustave's tampering with her mind. And it made her edgy.

But time dragged by even though they stayed busy in the kitchen, and after several hours Selene sat down. "When do you think he'll be back?"

"Not till sundown, if then." Joy Marie joined her at the table.

"If he doesn't come back until tomorrow I won't get any sleep."

"We shouldn't worry. He's a grown man. Right?"

"Yes." Selene wiped her hands on a rag.

"Whatever I said was brought on by Gustave and those seances." Joy Marie smiled. "You know what we think of Gustave so why don't we forget what happened at the table this morning and go on like nothing unusual happened."

"I like that idea." Selene smiled, wanting to do as Joy Marie suggested but knowing she couldn't. There was too much tension in the air.

Suddenly there were shouts outside and the pounding of hooves as a horse was ridden in fast.

Selene and Joy Marie locked glances, then both raced for the back door.

Out first, Selene stopped abruptly as a cowboy rode up. He jerked his lathered mount to a stop, caught his breath, and took off his hat. "Drake's bushwacked, ma'am. He's coming in on his own, but—"

"What's wrong with him?" Selene's voice broke.

"Shot in the head."

Selene felt faint, but Joy Marie supported her.

"You've got to be strong." Joy Marie's voice was steady. "You may be all that's standing between life and death for Drake."

"You're right." Selene became the efficient doctor she'd always been. "Joy Marie, get Carlota boiling water. Clean off the kitchen table. Cover it with a sheet. I'll have to work there. I'll need rags, bandages, and my reticule with the herbs."

Joy Marie hugged her close. "Selene, I want you to know whatever happens, I trust you. You're my sister."

Once more Selene's eyes filled with tears. "Sister, I won't let you down. I promise."

Joy Marie whirled around and hurried into the house.

Selene concentrated on the cowboy again. "How far behind is he?"

"Not far. I don't know how he's staying on his horse, but he's too tough to kill."

"Listen, I want you to round up some of the men and get back out there where he was bushwacked. Find anything you can and report back. In the meantime, I'll take care of Drake."

"Ma'am, fix him up."

"I will."

As the cowboy turned his horse away and headed for the barn, Selene looked to the south, shading her eyes, and saw dust from a rider. Drake. Soon she could make out two horses and riders. He still lived or he was tied to his horse. She paced back and forth, wanting to run to him but knowing it wouldn't help.

Finally, Drake rode up to the back yard, the other cowboy right behind him. A bloody bandana was tied around Drake's head. Blood had run down the side of his face, staining his shirt. But he still sat his horse. Pulling his stallion to a stop beside Selene, he attempted to smile, then toppled to the ground at her feet, unconscious.

Chapter 26

"Put Drake on the table." Selene forced herself to be calm.

The cowboys gently laid Drake on the sheet covering the long kitchen table.

Selene hadn't realized how big Drake was till he was a dead weight lying flat on his back. No, not dead. Limp. Unconscious. "Thank you. Would you two keep anybody else out of the house? Tell them what's going on and we'll let them know something as soon as we can."

The cowboys nodded their agreement, then left by the back door.

Selene looked at Drake, not wanting to believe what she saw but having to accept the reality. Around her the kitchen was unnaturally quiet, broken only by the rasping sound of Drake drawing breath. She didn't want to touch him, for she was afraid of what she would find.

"Selene?" Joy Marie's voice was soft, hesitant.

"How does he look?"

"Not good. It reminds me of Joe. Another head wound."

Carlota stepped forward and crossed her arms under her ample breasts. "We have water. We have clean cloths. I know where to get fresh moss and cobwebs to draw the poison from the wound."

"Thank you." Selene took her reticule from Joy Marie and set it on the table near Drake's head.

"I hope you don't think it's my fault." Joy Marie twisted a rag in her hands. "I tried to stop him, but—"

Selene put a hand over Joy Marie's. "Stop blaming yourself. It's not your fault. Somebody shot him. We'll find out who did it. All right?"

Joy Marie looked relieved.

Taking a deep breath, Selene washed her hands with soap, then rinsed them. Turning back to Drake, she touched the bandanna tied around his head. It was hard with dried blood. She was glad to see no fresh bleeding, but he'd lost a lot of blood and that wasn't good. She tried to untie the bandanna, but the knot was hard and the fabric stuck to his skin.

She glancd up. "I need a cloth soaked with hot water."

Carlota hurried to get it.

Selene turned back and picked up Granny Morgan's special knife. It was slim, sharp, and made for surgery. First, she'd use it to cut through the bandanna.

Carlota handed her two wet cloths.

366

Selene covered the bandanna with one, giving the blood a chance to soften. While she waited, she gently wiped Drake's face clean of dirt and blood and debris. He was pale but he breathed evenly. She was grateful for that.

She checked his hands and arms, legs and feet for any other damage. She listened to his heart, to his lungs, unbuttoned his shirt, searching for any injuries. Relieved to find nothing more than the head wound, she closed his shirt. She would concentrate on one area.

If the bullet had lodged in his skull or brain or even gone through, she didn't think he would still be alive or have been able to ride back on his horse. Encouraged, she still didn't know how his mind or memory would be affected. She hated head injuries for so little could be done.

She removed the wet cloth, now discolored with blood. Joy Marie held out a pan to catch the bloody rag. Carlota brought more hot, moist cloths as Selene cut loose the bandanna and dropped it in the pan. That done, she began cleaning around the wound, moving in closer and closer as she examined the damaged area.

"Carlota, would you bring the bottle of whiskey over here? I want to cleanse the wound."

Carlota gave Selene the bottle as Joy Marie looked on, her face pale and drawn.

Selene wet a cloth with whiskey, then slowly cleaned the wound. A gash the size of a .45 bullet creased the left side of his skull. The cut looked nasty. He had lost a lot of blood, but the wound was clean and the bullet hadn't gone deep enough to chip the bone or lodge in the skull. He'd been lucky.

Relieved, she smiled at Carlota and Joy Marie. "He should be fine if we keep him off his feet till he has a chance to heal. I'm going to sew this up, then get him to bed."

"Praise God and Mayual." Carlota wiped her eyes with her apron and turned away.

"I promise we'll find that bushwacker." Joy Marie's blue eyes glinted with fury.

"Will you get me Drake's razor? I need to shave his hair around the wound.

Joy Marie hurried out of the room, then quickly returned. "It's sharp. I checked."

"Thank you." Selene took more supplies out of her reticule and threaded a needle. She splashed whiskey over the wound and all the instruments. She gently clipped and shaved a narrow section of his hair. Finally, she began stitching the flesh back together. "I'm glad he's unconscious. This would hurt and he's already had too much pain." She realized she was mumbling from tension and bit her lower lip to stop herself.

"You're right." Joy Marie didn't watch, but busied herself cleaning up. "Do you need more cloths?"

"In a moment." Selene worked on in silence until she was done. "All right. A fresh cloth. Carlota, would you get moss for the bandage?"

"Sí." Carlota hurried out the back door.

Selene poured whiskey on a clean cloth, wiped the wound, then tied a bandage around his head. Done, she leaned back against the table, feeling weak.

Joy Marie poured her a whiskey and handed it to her. "Drink this and don't argue."

Selene didn't consider arguing as she gratefully accepted the whiskey. As the fiery liquid hit her stomach, she felt stronger. But she wasn't finished yet. She washed her hands, then began putting together herbs to make a medicinal tea. When she was satisfied, she put it on to brew for she wanted it to be strong no matter how bitter it tasted. She was still afraid of infection or shock, and she wouldn't leave Drake's side until he was out of danger.

"Selene, sit down now and rest." Joy Marie appeared worried.

"I want to get him to his own bed."

"Wait till Carlota gets back." Joy Marie sat down at the table near Drake's head.

Selene packed up her supplies, then joined Joy Marie.

"I'm impressed with your abilities." Joy Marie squeezed Selene's hand. "You're very good."

"I'll be good when I can save every single patient."

"You can't do that and you know it. You do a lot more than I ever could. I can't stand the sight of blood." Joy Marie watched Drake. "Carlota has experience, too, and she was impressed with what you did. In fact, a lot of folks around here could use a good doctor like you."

Selene checked Drake, then looked at Joy Marie. "Don't they have a doctor?"

"Doctors come and go. We've had some worse than none at all. But you're good and experienced, Selene, plus you know about herbs and medicine. I wish

369

you'd think about staying here at Dalton Ranch or, at least, moving into one of the towns. We need you out here."

"But my home is New Orleans and—"

"Who the hell left the barn door open?" Drake's voice was weak but angry. "I feel like every damn cow in the place is running through my head."

Selene and Joy Marie jumped up.

"How do you feel?" Selene put a hand to his face. He had more color now.

He coughed, then winced with pain. "I just told you. What the hell did you do to me, Selene?"

She shut her eyes and inhaled deeply, feeling relief flood her. "I sewed you up after you got yourself shot up."

He rolled his eyes toward her, then snapped them shut. "Damn! Where'd that bright light come from?"

Selene placed a cloth over his eyes. "Never mind about that, Drake. Is anything else broken or injured?"

"I fell off my horse, didn't I?"

"Yes. Right at my feet."

"I sure know where to land, don't I?"

"Yes, you do." Joy Marie put a hand on Drake's arm. "But you've got to rest now. And don't give Selene a hard time."

"Me?" He started to sit up, groaned, then laid his head back. Taking short, shallow breaths, he grimaced. "I'm the one she's cutting patterns on and sewing up."

"You've proved you can still think and talk, now I

want you to be quiet." Selene's voice was firm. "You must rest. I'm going to have two of the cowboys come in and carry you to your bed."

"I'll be damned if they will." This time he struggled to a sitting position.

"Drake!" Selene clutched his arm.

"If you want to be helpful, get me to my bed."

"Hurry, Selene." Joy Marie took Drake's other arm. "He'll never let his men see him weak. Why do you think he rode his own horse back here?"

"Men!" Selene took a firm grip on Drake's arm and let him lean on her when he stood up.

Together, they helped him from the kitchen, through the house, and to his bedroom.

He collapsed on the bed, shut his eyes, and lay still.

"Will he be all right?" Joy Marie stood over the bed.

"Yes, if he doesn't kill himself first." Selene's voice was full of disgust but her face held worry. "Would you wait in the kitchen and tell Carlota what happened when she returns. I don't want her to worry."

"Yes. If you need me, call."

After Joy Marie left, Selene shut the drapes, then the door. Finally she sat down on the edge of the bed and took Drake's hand in hers. "You were lucky, you know."

"Yes." His voice was weak. "And wrong."

"Wrong?"

"About Joy Marie."

"I don't understand it, but we're going to heed her warnings from now on."

"Selene?" He curled his fingers around her hand. "You'll watch out for things till I get back on my feet, won't you?"

"Yes. Don't worry. I'll keep Jimmy and Joy Marie in sight. I've already sent men back to check the ambush spot. I'll let you know what they find out."

"Good. Post guards around the house and the barn day and night. Keep the men in close. This is more than rustlers."

"I will, but right now I want you to rest. It's the only way you'll heal."

"I'm okay, aren't I?"

"Yes. But give your body a chance."

"Yes, ma'am. You're the doctor."

"That's right. And I'm going to be feeding you a nasty-tasting brew and I don't want any complaints." She stroked the bandage across his forehead.

"Do I get a kiss?"

She placed a gentle kiss against his lips, then sat up. "Now, go to sleep. I'll wake you when it's time for your medicine."

Late that night, Selene changed Drake's bandage, noting the seepage was clear and normal. He grumbled, but didn't cause her any other trouble. She checked the teapot, decided the brew was still hot enough, and poured him another mug. When she held it up to him, he gave her a dirty look.

"You're trying to kill me with that stuff. Give me

some whiskey. That'll make me feel better fast."

Selene shook a finger at him. "Now drink, Drake. You promised to be a good patient."

"That was before I tasted that evil brew. What's in it anyway? Something out of the Louisiana bayous?" Although he complained, he took the mug anyway. He gave the liquid a dark stare, then turned it up and drank it down in one long swallow. He squinted as he handed back the mug. "I hope that's it for a while."

"I think it's doing you good."

"Self-defense is what's causing me to improve. And what are you doing sitting in that rocker anyway?" He threw back the covers and beckoned her over.

"No. You're sick, Drake. If I come over there, who knows what might happen."

"I know what *would* happen."

She smiled again. "You need to save your strength."

"You could do all the work."

Finally, she chuckled. "I'm glad you're feeling so much better."

"I feel awful. My head hurts. My mouth tastes like a barnyard. And my whole body aches." His gaze raked her body. "But you could make me feel a whole lot better fast."

She laughed. "You're really bad when you're sick, aren't you?"

"I hate being helpless."

"You're far from helpless. But a few days in bed won't hurt you."

"Days!" He sat up, groaned, then lay back against the pillows.

"If I have to tie you to this bed, I will." She used her sternest voice. "You must keep your head down, Drake. I don't want any complications from this."

"Don't talk so loud. My head's pounding."

"I'm not talking loud and your head is hurting because you sat up."

"So it's all my fault."

She reached over and took his hand. Stroking the rough palm, she looked up at him thoughtfully. "I wish the cowboys had found more than a Winchester casing at the site where you were ambushed."

"Not much help, is it?"

"No. Nor were the few scuff marks where somebody had waited. Drake, I'm worried. Do you have enemies?"

"A man's bound to make some enemies. But this is a planned, calculated attack. I don't understand why."

"I don't either. But everybody's got to be careful till we find out who did it."

"It's connected to the butchering of my cows. But why?"

Selene got up and paced across the room. Pulling back a drape, she saw several cowboys talking near the barn. She saw another near the house. If she didn't miss her guess, the cowboys were already guarding the place. Later, she'd give them Drake's orders about posting guards. But would it be enough? She had felt so safe here after all they'd been

374

through, but now she was afraid there might not be a safe haven for any of them.

She glanced around Drake's room, noticing his personal touches. A worn bridle he was repairing had been tossed across his dresser. Torn denims in need of mending lay over the back of a chair. A faded photograph of a couple in a white painted cast-iron frame set on the dresser near the bridle. She picked it up and carried it to the lamp to see better.

"My parents. It's their wedding picture. You can't tell much about it now, but they had on fancy dress." He hesitated, obviously recalling memories. "They always loved each other, good times and bad."

"I'm glad for them. I know it must have been a great loss to you when they died." She set the frame back in place and returned to the rocker.

"Yes. But Ray was around to keep me in line. Then he married Joy Marie and they had Joey. We were a real family again till—"

"It's a nice cemetery."

"Mom planned it. She did that kind of thing." Drake crumpled the bedclothes in his fist. "Sometimes the living's short and fast out here, Selene. Maybe I was wrong to bring you."

Selene's breath caught in her throat. "My life hasn't been easy either. I barely remember my parents. The War killed them both. When it was all said and done, my family lost everything. Granny Morgan took me to New Orleans and we survived together. Sometimes it was rough, but we always had each other. Love and friends make the difference, Drake. We can't ever forget that."

He held out his hand.

She took it, feeling tears sting her eyes.

"Will you go over to my dresser? Open the top drawer and look in the right front corner. There's a chamois bag I want you to get."

Surprised, she gave him a puzzled look, then went to the dresser. She glanced at the wedding portrait again, and opened the drawer. It was a jumble of clothes. She ignored that and found the small leather bag. Bringing it back, she held it out to him.

"No. Open it."

She sat down, pulled open the drawstring, and emptied the contents into her palm. A ruby ring glinted in the lamplight. She inhaled sharply, then touched it with her fingertip. The stone was large, round, and clear. The setting was ornate and rose gold. She looked up at him in surprise.

"That belonged to my grandmother, to my mother, and I want you to have it."

She closed her fist over the ring to hide it. "I can't, Drake. It's a family heirloom."

"It's an engagement ring."

"But nobody knows and we haven't discussed—"

"You could wear it on a thong around your neck." He glanced around the room. "There's one in here somewhere."

"I might lose it."

"Selene, we're talking about friends and we're talking about love and we're talking about family." His dark eyes glinted dangerously. "I almost died today. What would have happened to Dalton

Ranch, to Joy Marie, Jimmy, Carlota, and Jorge then?"

"What does that have to do with the ring or with me?"

"You're strong enough to take over."

She stood up, walked away from him, then turned back. "We're talking about a Texas cattle ranch. I can't believe my ears. You are leaping from a ring to a ranch. And scaring me."

"Sorry. But that bullet scared me." He motioned her back.

She sat down in the rocker and watched him warily. "You should be resting."

"I can't sleep. There's too much on my mind. You wouldn't know about it, but these are rough times for cattlemen. Up north, the blizzard of '86 killed tens of thousands of cattle. The OS Ranch in Kansas lost nearly eleven thousand head, The Circle M's losses were over five thousand."

Selene looked horrified.

"It was the greatest blizzard ranchers have ever seen. It started on the last day of December 1885, coming out of the north and moving south. Cattle drifted from the Dakotas to Texas, halted only by drift fences or cuts and coulees. The cowboys knew better than the cows what was going to happen. And a lot of them followed their herds, trying to save them and knowing they couldn't. Most of those men were found frozen, alone, near their dead horses in the shelter of some gulch."

"That's horrible."

"And this is just the telling of it. The news traveled

south, along with the cows and cowboys. I drove my herd north early because they were crying for cattle at market. The price was good but I knew why. I saw what was left on the way north, Selene. I saw death. A lot of death. And I'll never forget."

"I understand."

"No you don't, but you can try." He took a deep breath. "After that blizzard we're left with a simple fact: if it's another hard winter, if those ranches lose many more cattle, they won't make it. And I figure a lot of them are looking south to Texas and our herds to make up their losses or save their ranches."

"Can they do it?"

"They've already bought cows from us, but we can't make up tens of thousands."

"Do you think one of them might try to force you out and take over Dalton Ranch?"

"Not one of the big outfits like the Swan Land and Cattle Company or the Worsham Cattle Company, but rustlers who've lived on the edge, feeding off the big outfits, are hurting now. Somebody just might have moved south ahead of the winter."

"What do you want me to do?" She twisted the ring in her hand.

"Joy Marie's not stable enough to handle the ranch now. Jimmy's too young. Carlota snd Jorge keep the house and buildings going. The cowboys take orders."

"But they all have more experience than I do."

"They haven't got as much heart, Selene. And they're not used to taking care of people. You are."

"But you'll be fine. I don't see any need for this conversation." She stared at the ruby and it gleamed like fresh blood.

He reached over and gripped her hand. "Wear the ring. If something happens to me, promise to keep Dalton Ranch going till Joy Marie or Jimmy or somebody can take over. As my fiancée, you'd have the power."

Tears stung her eyes. "Drake, you're asking so much of me. I don't know if I could do it even if I promised. I run an apothecary shop. I doctor people. What I do *not* do is run a ranch. How can you ask this of me?"

"You can do whatever you set your mind to do, Selene Morgan, and that's a fact. Besides, sick cows, sick people, what's the difference? They all need you."

"Well, there is a difference, but I doubt if I'd ever convince you of it." She hesitated, suddenly feeling cold. "You'd have been one of those cowboys who followed his herd from the Dakotas to Texas or died with them, wouldn't you?"

He nodded. "I'd never have let them die alone." Looking past her, he seemed to see beyond the bedroom. "You ever hear a cowboy song?"

"No."

"When you're on a drive, you're looking at three months from Texas to Kansas. Those dogies are nervous. At night most anything can stampede them. But the sound of a cowboy singing soothes them. You're so tired by the end of the day you don't see how you can ride watch but you do because you know how much worse it'd be if they stampede."

She nodded, fascinated.

"So we ride our ponies and sing songs. Sad, lonely, little songs like this:

Oh, say little dogies, when will you lie down
And give up this shifting and roving around?
My horse is leg weary, and I'm awfully tired
But if you get away, I'm sure to get fired.
Lie down, little dogies, lie down
Hi-yo, hi-yo, hi-yo!"

"Oh, Drake, you have a fine voice."

"Believe me, the cows don't care about that. They like to know you're there and maybe they'll like your song well enough to lie down and sleep."

"I don't know what to say."

"Remember, the reason we drive them north is for the slaughterhouses. We feed and clothe the folks back East. But it's the cattle we're bound to, by blood and bone and sweat. And we never forget a drive. Every push north is different, made so by the cows. We all end up dead, Selene. Man and cow. It's getting there that shows our worth—not the price per head or the cost of silver spurs."

Touched, Selene nodded. "You're right. And how can I turn you down?"

"Then you'll take the ring?"

She opened her palm and looked at the glittering ruby. They'd all seen so much blood. "I'll wear the ring on a thong around my neck, but not for its worth but for what it represents."

"And what's that?"

Smiling, she squeezed his hand. "I didn't have to follow those in my care through a blizzard, but I followed my people to Martinique. Now that I'm here, I can do no less."

Drake raised a brow. "I'd hoped I might hear a vow of eternal love."

She leaned forward and placed a soft kiss on his lips. "Keep listening."

Chapter 27

Three days later Selene sat beside Drake on the buck-board seat of a ranch wagon as he drove them toward Sisterdale. Jimmy had wanted to come with them, but they'd decided he'd be safer at the ranch under Jorge's watchful eye. Joy Marie insisted she wanted to stay with Jimmy, but Selene knew her friend simply wasn't ready to handle questions or gossip about her time with Gustave Dominique. And she couldn't blame her.

Glancing at Drake, she hoped he would be all right. She'd have kept him in bed longer if she could have, but that was impossible. He'd made jokes about the shaved strip through his thick hair, threat-ening to shave his whole head to match it or wear his hat all the time. He was wearing his hat and she planned to keep it that way, for she enjoyed his hair too much to let him shave it.

Although she'd wanted to visit a small Texas town, she was in no hurry after Drake had been bush-wacked. She didn't want him in any more danger.

Putting her hand on his shoulder, she drew his attention to her. "Are you sure going to Sisterdale is right? We could still turn around."

"I already told you folks in town need to see I'm alive and kicking. Word'll spread to the bush-whacker."

"And he'll know to come after you again."

"I'll be ready."

She shivered, glancing around at the dry, rocky grasslands and tree-covered hills. She could imagine streams gurgling merrily on their way where she couldn't see them and she wished she could feel as happy as the brooks must sound. On the other hand, a bushwhacker could be back in the brush aiming a Winchester at them. Her cozy vision vanished.

Drake put a warm hand over hers. "Don't worry. We'll come out of this all right. Besides, don't you want to try some of that Four Hundred Springs beer?"

"Yes. I just don't want to pay too high a price."

Drake chuckled. "I'm okay. You fixed me up fine."

"This time."

"Be alert, Selene, but don't worry 'cause it'll eat you up inside."

"You're right." But she couldn't stop worrying.

She tried to relax by taking her mind off Sister-dale. She'd worn a simple dress of dark green silk, with a matching hat and a reticule to hold a variety of medical supplies just in case they needed them. She also wore black boots and black kid leather gloves. Joy Marie had told her she looked very professional and like a competent doctor. Mainly, she had wanted

384

to look serious and able to hold her own should that necessity arise.

Raising her hand, she touched Drake's ruby ring through her dress. It lay nestled between her breasts and seemed to carry a warmth all its own. She was letting him draw her in deep, too deep, but she couldn't seem to stop.

She looked at him again and felt a warmness tug at her heart. He wore denims, a black and blue plaid shirt, a black leather vest, black boots, a black belt with a large silver buckle engraved with the head of a longhorn, and his .45. He'd tugged a black hat down over his eyes. To her, he looked tough, rugged, and sexy. And she wanted to go someplace alone with him, but knew it was out of the question.

Not long after, Drake drove them into Sisterdale. Selene glanced around with interest. One- and two-story buildings with a connecting boardwalk in front had been built along each side of a dusty main street. Signs on windows and hanging from the roof over the boardwalk announced businesses such as mercantile, barber shop, saloon, café, boardinghouse, and feed store. Homes had been built on the outskirts of town and on the streets back behind main.

Selene could see that Sisterdale was a thriving community, but in comparison to New Orleans or Saint Pierre on Martinique, it seemed quite small and countrified. Yet she was prepared to like it.

Drake stopped the wagon before Hatfield's Mercantile Store, then glanced around. Several people walked by. He nodded at them, then turned back to Selene. "You've got the list of supplies. Just give it to

Mrs. Hatfield. Hattie. Tell her it's for Dalton Ranch. She'll do the rest."

"But why would she accept the word of a total stranger?"

"She won't expect you to lie."

Surprised at his reply, Selene nodded, then jumped down from the wagon. She adjusted her skirts, pushed her reticule back on her arm, and raised her chin.

"It's not a battle, but I'll be at the feed store if you need me."

"I can handle this just fine." She squared her shoulders and turned her back to him.

As she stepped up to the boardwalk, she heard Drake drive away. A few people passed her, giving her inquiring glances. She smiled politely, then opened the door to Hatfield's Mercantile and stepped inside. It was dim and dusty and merchandise filled shelves and cabinets on the walls and long counters on the floor.

"You need something, ma'am?" A tall, big-boned woman in a dark blue cotton dress with her gray hair pulled back in a tight chignon walked forward. She looked Selene up and down. "You going to be here long?"

"I don't know."

"I'd pay to take a pattern off your dress."

Selene glanced down at her clothes in surprise, then back up at the woman.

She walked all the way around Selene, examining her dress more closely. "Look at that bustle effect, the apron in front, and the fringe. I don't know when I've seen something so pretty. The women around here'd fancy that design for Sunday best. Is your dress from France?"

Selene nodded. "By way of Martinique . . . in the French West Indies."

The woman paused, then finally looked at Selene's face. Her eyes grew round and she covered her mouth with a hand. "You must be Joy Marie Dalton's friend."

"Yes. I'm Selene Morgan." Selene held out her hand.

"I'm Mrs. Hatfield, but nobody's called me that since my husband died years ago. Hattie to you." She stuck out her own hand to shake Selene's, then flushed with embarrassment. "Sorry, but I've been washing and cleaning and my hands are the worse for wear."

"Let me see." Selene took one of Hattie's hands in hers and examined it front and back, noticing the splits in the skin and the rough redness. "That must be quite painful."

Hattie snatched her hand back, then hid both hands behind her back. "Nothing to stop me working."

"No, but I have a little something with me that should stop the pain and heal your skin."

"It's nothing, ma'am."

Selene walked over to one of the counters, set down her reticule, and pulled out a small bottle of white lotion. Turning, she smiled at Hattie, who had followed her. "Now, hold out your hands."

Hattie glanced around as if someone might be watching, then tentatively held out her right hand.

Selene unscrewed the lid on the bottle and poured a

generous amount into Hattie's hand. "Rub that into both hands."

Hattie held her hands far away from her body and vigorously began rubbing.

"Not so hard."

As the lotion soothed her skin, Hattie smiled, held her hands up for inspection, noticed the redness was fading, and looked back at Selene. "Where'd you get this stuff?"

"I made it."

Hattie frowned and examined her hands again. "What'd you mean?"

"I'm from New Orleans. I have an apothecary shop there. This recipe was handed down to me from my grandmother. She trained me to make soothing lotions, medicinal teas, and poultices."

Hattie's eyebrows rose. "Do say."

"I'm also a . . . a doctor."

Stepping back, Hattie examined her all over again. "Are you good?"

"I like to think so, but I readily admit I can't always save a patient."

"That's in the hands of God anyway." Hattie rubbed her hands together. "What'd you want for this hand lotion?"

"Keep it, use it." Selene glanced around the store, an idea forming in her mind. "And if you like it, perhaps you'd sell it here."

"Can't charge much. Women around these parts don't have much money and they sure don't have money for fancy creams and perfumes and such."

"But this is a medicinal lotion. Surely they could work better if their hands were healed."

"That's the truth of it." Hattie glanced around her store, considering. "You ever seen what milking day in and day out does to a person's hands?"

"No."

"It's right bad in the winter." She looked at her own hands again. "I bet I could sell it. Small bottles at first." Hattie picked up a chewed pencil and began writing on a piece of paper. "What'd you call the stuff?"

Selene smiled, thrilled to have found a business partner so quickly. "What'd you think would sell?"

Hattie scratched her head with the pencil tip. "Red Out Hand Lotion." She grinned. "What'd you think?"

"It's to the point. I like it."

"How soon can you get me the stuff?"

"It would have to be shipped from New Orleans."

"That'd cost."

"Yes, but we're building a market here so it'll cost more to get started. Also, I want men to buy this lotion as well as women."

Hattie stuck the pencil in her gray bun and stepped back. "That'll be a tall order."

"Maybe so, but we can do it, I'm sure." Selene was excited. "What about other towns around here?"

"Well, there's some."

"And you know their owners?"

Hattie looked suspicious. "Yes."

"What if I paid you a fee to introduce me to them."

Eyes wide, Hattie shook her head. "Are you a drummer or what?"

"No, I'm a businesswoman like you. And I think we can help each other. Fact is, if we do well with this lotion, I could start making it here in Texas, along with some other products. And medicines." Perhaps she'd found a place for herself after all. "You could sell them here."

Hattie walked away, turned back. "I do a lot of mail-order business. I can get lotions and tonics."

"Yes, but not fresh and as good."

Hattie looked at her hands again. "Well, okay, as long as it won't cost me money. I've got none to spare. Since Mr. Hatfield died, it's been hard going. My daughter usually helps me in here, but she just had her first baby and she's not doing so good."

Selene looked concerned. "What's wrong?"

"She came through fine, she got her milk, but she's staying weak and sickly. Her husband's getting mad 'cause things around the house aren't being done. I'm trying to help—that's how my hands got so bad—and keep the store running, too."

"Would you like me to have a look at her?"

Hattie's eyes brightened. "That's right, you said you're a doctor. I forgot 'cause of the lotion." She looked away. "No. That's okay. She's just slow recovering."

"But I might get her back on her feet faster."

Walking behind the counter, Hattie shook her head. "Just bring in that lotion when you've got it. Besides, I've no money for a doctor."

"I won't charge anything. I've got some medicine in my reticule. You're going to handle my lotions so I'll see after your daughter. Deal?"

Hattie gave her a long, slow, steady gaze. "You're looking after Miss Joy Marie, aren't you?"

Selene nodded.

"You're no Texan. You may take some getting used to. But I think you're going to be okay." Hattie pulled the pencil from her hair, tossed it on the counter, then hurried to the front door. Putting out a GONE TO LUNCH sign, she motioned Selene to follow.

Leading the way out the back door, Hattie crossed the alley and walked up on the porch of a small gray wooden house in need of repair.

Opening the front door, Hattie ushered Selene inside. "Mary Lou, I've brought you a doctor."

Glancing around, Selene noticed the house had two rooms and she stood in the one that served as a parlor and kitchen. The furniture was sparse and old. She followed Hattie into a small bedroom made up of shades of gray, from the walls to the furniture to the sheets on the bed where a woman and child lay together. The baby began to cry.

Hattie picked up the child and crooned. Soon the baby grew quiet. "This is my daughter, Mary Lou."

Selene knelt beside her. "I'm Selene."

"I can't pay no doctor. My husband's too proud to take charity . . . even from my mother."

"We'll work something out later when you're stronger. I'm living at Dalton Ranch, but I'm going to be needing some help."

"Trade doctoring for my work?"

"Yes, if that'd be all right with you."

Mary Lou nodded.

Relieved, Selene smiled. "Now, what's wrong with you?"

"Weak. Not enough milk for my baby."

Selene examined the dark circles under Mary Lou's

eyes, the pale skin, the dry hair. "Are you bleeding?"

Mary Lou's eyes widened, she glanced at her mother, then nodded.

Hattie looked shocked. "You didn't tell me."

"Not much." Mary Lou sounded defensive.

"It's all right." Selene kept her voice low and reassuring. "Are you in pain?"

Mary Lou nodded again. "My baby was so big."

"It'll take time to heal." Selene hesitated, then gathered her courage. "Hattie, if you'll take your grandbaby into the other room, I'm going to examine your daughter. I won't be long."

Hattie hesitated, gave Selene a sharp look, then walked out.

"You won't hurt me, will you?" Mary Lou's eyes were big.

"No." Selene pulled down the sheet, raised Mary Lou's gown, which appeared freshly washed, and quickly examined her. When the gown and sheet were back in place, she listened to Mary Lou's heart and lungs. Finally, she gently stroked her patient's head. "I believe you have a slight infection."

"I knew it. I'm going to die. My baby'll grow up motherless. He'll become a famous gunslinger and die a bloody death at seventeen. Shot in the back. By a bushwhacker. Or the law." Tears sprang into Mary Lou's eyes and she sobbed.

"No. Now, relax. You're going to be fine. I'm going to tell your mother what needs to be done and give her some medicine for you. If you have any trouble with your husband about this, you send him to me."

"You mean it? I'm okay?"

"Yes. Or you will be if you take care of yourself and do what I say."

For the first time Mary Lou smiled and the worry lines left her forehead. "Thanks, ma'am. I'll work hard for you later. I promise."

Selene squeezed her hand. "I'll stop by and see you soon." She walked into the parlor. "Let me see the baby, Hattie."

"And my daughter?"

"I'll tell you more outside, but she should be fine."

Hattie let out a sigh of relief and leaned against the door. "You don't know how worried I've been and not knowing a thing more to do."

Selene examined the baby, then smiled at Hattie. "He's a strong, healthy boy."

Hattie looked relieved, took him in her arms, then walked back to Mary Lou.

Selene stepped outside to wait, enjoying the fresh clean air.

Soon Hattie joined her. "You weren't just saying that to make her feel better?"

"No. When your daughter gave birth, she tore a lot and now has an infection. I'm going to give you a poultice to draw out the poison and herbs to make a medicinal tea for her to drink. She must be kept very clean and she must rest. Can you do all this or will you need help?"

"I'll take care of her and the baby."

"With the medicine I'm going to give you, she should heal soon. But she needs to eat well, too."

"I'll see to it. Her husband's a proud man, a good man, but he doesn't earn much."

"Food is part of the medicine. She has to be strong

to feed the baby. Why don't you have your son-in-law talk to Drake about working at Dalton Ranch . . . at least till your daughter's back on her feet."

"He won't take charity."

"It'd be work." Selene chuckled. "Real work."

Hattie smiled. "That's good news. I'll tell him. And he won't go against the word of a doctor. He loves her, you know."

"Good."

They entered the mercantile shop through the back door and were surprised to find Drake pacing inside. Seeing them, he stopped, planted his hands on his hips, and frowned.

"Where've you been, Selene?"

Hattie marched up to him and held out her hands. "See those? Best they've been in I don't know when so don't you go messing with that girl."

Drake shook his head. "Did you get Dalton Ranch's order filled?"

Selene looked guiltily and pulled the supply list from her reticule. "Hattie, here's the list for Dalton Ranch."

"I'll get right on it." Hattie picked up her pencil and began making notes on the piece of paper.

"We'll eat lunch while we wait." Drake scowled at them both.

"Just a minute." Selene set her reticule on the counter, pulled out a number of bags, selected two, and handed them to Hattie. "This one will make several poultices and the other makes medicinal tea. See she gets them both three times a day. The amounts and instructions are written on them. And I'll be back into town to check on her."

"Thanks." Hattie grinned. "Tell Joy Marie we miss her and bring her into town next time you come."

"I will." Selene grasped Drake's arm and led him from the store.

"What was that all about? I can't leave you alone for a moment, can I?"

"I just saw my first patient."

"Who?"

"Hattie's daughter. And Hattie is going to sell my 'Red Out Hand Lotion' right here in Sisterdale."

Drake chuckled. "You can't leave Texas now you've got a business going." He walked with her across the street. "Let's celebrate with a thick Dalton steak and Four Hundred Springs beer."

"Dalton steak? Did you find out something?"

"Damn right. Some stranger, cowboy by the look of him, came into town selling beef cheap. Most everybody bought some to smoke, cure, and cook."

"When?"

"I'd say right after killing my cows."

"But why kill your cattle and sell your beef right here in your own county?"

"I guess somebody wants to make me mad or look like a fool or both." He opened the door to the Sisterdale Café.

Selene stepped inside. "They killed your cows, then tried to kill you."

"And it's the last damn time." He looked around for an empty table. "But all's not lost. We're going to eat stolen Dalton beef right now. And enjoy it."

He led her to a table.

Chapter 28

As Drake drove them back to the ranch that evening, Selene thought of New Orleans. They'd picked up the mail before leaving Sisterdale and it had contained a much welcome letter from Rosa. In fact, it was a letter Selene would never forget.

Alfred had returned from New York. Disillusioned with living a lie, missing the woman he loved, and furious with himself for turning his back on his own people, no matter the beliefs of his family, he had quit his job.

In her letter, Rosa had thanked Selene in advance for allowing Alfred to live at Love Potions while they looked for a home of their own in the French Quarter. Happiness radiated from Rosa's letter as she described Alfred's confrontation with his family and their subsequent understanding.

Rosa had gone on to say that, reunited with his friends, relatives, and people, Alfred was a new man. He'd lost weight and become sick in New York. But he was healing, with Rosa's care, and looking for work while helping mulattoes struggle for better working and living conditions in New Orleans.

Now, Rosa had also written, she and Alfred would soon be married and she hoped Selene would attend the ceremony. Rosa planned to continue managing Love Potions as long as Selene wanted. And if Selene did decide to stay in Texas, perhaps Rosa could eventually buy into the business so they could be partners.

Tears filled Selene's eyes as she thought of the happiness of her friend. Time seemed to heal all wounds. She glanced at Drake. If she stayed in Texas, Rosa would be the perfect person to run Love Potions. But she didn't plan to abandon the business her grandmother had founded no matter what happened, for now she knew she could expand her apothecary business into Texas. But whether she stayed or not, she'd be happy to have Rosa as a partner.

"You asleep?" Drake's voice was soft and husky.

"No, but after all that beer and steak, I should be."

Drake chuckled. "I'm glad it went well for you in Sisterdale."

"I liked the town and the people. Especially Hattie. Of course, it's not New Orleans."

"But what is?" Drake laughed again.

She poked him in the ribs. "You'd be more likely to say, "It's not Texas, but what is?'"

"I've got to agree." He glanced at her. "Are you beginning to like Texas better?"

"Yes. I can even see a place for myself here. But Drake, I still have a life, a good life, back in New Orleans."

"I'm not in New Orleans. And neither is Dalton Ranch."

She sighed. "I know."

"I haven't heard you mention love potions lately."

"Do you think the affect has worn off by now?"

"You made them. I don't think anything you do comes undone."

Thinking about his words, she didn't reply. Could he be right?

"Fact is, you can make as many love potions for me as you want, Selene Morgan."

"You were supposed to hate that idea."

"I'm a changed man."

She slanted a glance at him. He looked serious. Well, maybe he was. Maybe they both were. She touched the ruby ring through her dress. Maybe she just didn't want to admit it because she'd have to make drastic changes in her life. But Drake could be worth it . . . worth a lot.

"Who the hell's at the house?"

Selene glanced up as Drake drove into the yard and stopped in front of the hacienda. Light spilled from the living room windows. A horse was tethered at the hitching post. And laughter drifted outward on the night breeze.

"I hope this isn't trouble." Drake got down, walked around the wagon, and helped Selene down.

"It doesn't sound like trouble."

"I don't like surprises." Drake glanced around the area.

Jorge hailed them from the barn, then hurried over.

"What's going on?" Drake tossed Jorge the reins of the team. "We can unload in the morning."

"You have a guest." Jorge smiled, nodding at Selene as he stepped up to the wagon and drove it away toward the barn.

"What guest?" Drake frowned as he escorted Selene to the front door.

As he pushed the door open, it was pulled inward. "Drake! Selene! Look who's here!" Joy Marie's eyes shone brightly.

Instantly concerned, Selene stepped into the living room. Drake was right behind her.

Jon stood in the middle of the room, a whiskey in his hand, a smile on his face. He shook Drake's hand, then Selene's.

Drake clasped him on the shoulder. "So you decided to take me up on that job."

Jon's smile fell, then he grinned broadly. "Yes. It's a job I want."

"I've got plenty of work for you."

"Do you want a drink, Drake?" Joy Marie looked charming in a pale blue cotton dress trimmed with ecru lace. "I've been playing hostess till you and Selene returned."

"A drink'd be great." Drake headed for the sofa and sat down. "Come on over, Jon, and tell me what's been going on back in Martinique."

Joy Marie handed Drake his drink, then squeezed Selene's hand. "Do you want anything?"

"No thanks. I'm already floating on Four Hundred Springs beer and grounded on the biggest hunk of steak I ever saw."

Laughing, Joy Marie watched Jon. "I'd forgotten

400

how handsome he is." Her voice was soft and confidential.

"You're right. And big." Selene noticed Jon was wearing a dark blue suit that strained against his muscles whenever he moved.

"Oh, yes." Joy Marie's voice was breathy.

"You two come here and sit down." Drake motioned them over. "If Jon's going to tell tales, he should only have to tell them once."

Selene sat down beside Drake and Joy Marie took a chair near Jon's.

"It's good to have us all together again, isn't it?" Joy Marie smiled at Jon.

"Jimmy's grown since I saw him." Jon clasped his hand over a crossed knee. "But he wasn't too happy about going to bed so early."

"It wasn't early for him. He'll be up at the crack of dawn helping Jorge. The two of you can talk more then." Joy Marie's voice brooked no argument.

Jon nodded, then glanced around the group. "First off, I've got to tell you the bad news."

They all tensed.

"After you left, everything went fine just like we planned. Everybody was working good, eating good, living good." Jon cleared his throat. "Then one day Dominique was gone." He snapped his fingers. "Just like that. Bribed enough French officials to get loose and he left Martinique before anything could be done."

Stunned silence was the only reply.

"Ancient Mam had that island turned upside down but Dominique was gone for good. Take my word for it. You don't want to ever see that woman mad. Anyway, she did big root magic and sent me to Texas." He looked at Joy Marie. "I was coming anyway soon as everything settled down."

"Why did Ancient Mam send you to Texas?" Joy Marie's voice was scarcely above a whisper.

"She said Erzulie told her Dominique had gone to Texas."

Joy Marie bit her lower lip and looked at Selene.

"That news might explain a few things." Drake clenched his fists.

"What do you mean?" Jon leaned back in his chair.

"Dalton cattle have been rustled and Drake was bushwhacked a few days ago." Selene shuddered. "If that bullet had been placed slightly differently, he'd be dead right now."

"Sounds like Dominique's out for revenge, doesn't it?" Jon took a drink of whiskey. "That Frenchman's got a long arm and a longer memory."

"But if he's in Texas, he's on my turf now." Drake's voice was a growl.

"I'm frightened." Joy Marie's blue eyes were big.

"We'll take care of you." Jon leaned over and squeezed her hand, then looked embarrassed and pulled back.

Joy Marie gave him a warm smile. "You're right. With all of you around, and Jimmy, too, I won't be alone and Gustave can't get close."

Selene remained quiet, thinking of the Frenchman and his clever ways. She was scared, too, and she didn't mind admitting it. "I'm glad you're here, Jon. Ancient Mam was right to send you to us. You know

Gustave better than anybody and I'm glad to have you on our side."

"I'll do what I can, but we've got to find him first." Jon finished his whiskey and set the glass aside.

"We will." Drake held his whiskey glass out to Selene. "Drink on it."

She took a sip of the fiery brew, then handed it back.

He nodded and finished it off.

"Tell us the happy news, Jon." Joy Marie smiled at him.

"Ancient Mam and Josephine send their love. Selene, Ancient Mam said to tell you she sent her package of island herbs to your store in New Orleans and she's waiting to get the one you promised."

"That's wonderful. Rosa'll be so excited. I wrote her all about it. And she should already have sent Ancient Mam the native herbs I promised to share with her. But now I have Texas herbs to share with them both. I've been talking with Carlota about the properties of some plants I found and I'm quite excited." She stopped and glanced around at the group. "Well, anyway, it *is* exciting news."

Joy Marie laughed. "Maybe for you root women, but how about the rest of us?"

"Just you wait—"

"Oh, no! I won't say another word." Joy Marie chuckled, then caught Jon's gaze. Suddenly she stopped laughing and grew quiet.

Selene noticed their distraction. Smiling to herself, she looked at Drake, who was staring at his empty glass. "Drake, it's been a long day and I'm

403

putting you to bed so you can get some rest."

He glanced up in surprise.

"I know you're tired. We can all talk more in the morning when Jimmy is up." Selene turned to Joy Marie. "You'll take care of Jon, won't you?"

"He's going to sleep in Jimmy's room. Jimmy offered his bed and is sleeping on a pallet."

Selene smiled, proud of the young boy from the New Orleans wharf. He knew a friend when he met one. "Come on, Drake." She stood up and held out a hand.

Drake got up and pulled her hand through the crook of his arm. "Glad you're here, Jon. And sleep easy. We've got guards posted all night."

Jon stood. "I'll be ready to work in the morning."

Drake shook his head. "Don't worry about it yet. There's plenty of time for that later."

As they walked out of the room, Selene heard Joy Marie and Jon speak to each other in low voices. Pleased, Selene remembered the way Jon had treated Joy Marie in New Orleans and on Martinique. She realized Jon must have been watching out for Joy Marie all along. And she was glad.

When they reached the door to Drake's room, he turned to her. "Are you going to tuck me in?"

"You're a big boy, aren't you?"

"Shouldn't you check my head?"

She smiled. "I'd like to check more than your head, but there're too many people around."

"You could do it quietly, couldn't you?" His hand traced a warm pattern up and down her back.

"You're a bad boy is what you are." She shivered and leaned into him.

He opened the door and pulled her inside. Shutting the door, he locked it, then lit a lamp. Soft light illuminated the bed with its cover turned back to reveal white sheets.

"Looks inviting, doesn't it?" His breath was warm on her face.

"Yes. But I've got a bed of my own."

"Only till I can make your staying in my room legal."

"Drake, I—"

He put a fingertip to her lips. "Not now. I want to hold you." He drew her into his arms. "Touch you." He stroked up and down her back with hands rough and gentle. "And smell you." He pulled the pins from her hair and let her auburn tresses fall loose to her waist. Burying his face in her hair, he inhaled. "You smell sweet and you'll taste even better." He chuckled. "I know."

Feeling suddenly weak, she put her hands around his neck and pulled his face down to hers. "You're a brute."

"Not gentleman?"

"No. You know how your words and touch affect me. Now how can I go to my cold, lonely bed? I'd lie awake all night thinking of you. And if I slept, I'd dream of you. Brute."

Drake grinned. "Maybe I ought to show you how much of a brute I can be."

"Only if you do it quietly."

He pressed soft, warm kisses over her face and the fire grew until he reached her lips. When she opened her mouth, he plunged inside, trading heat for heat until she shuddered against him.

Moaning under the onslaught of his kiss, she slid her hands down his back, jerked out the tail of his shirt, and clawed her way up the bare skin of his back.

He growled, broke off the kiss, and stared into her eyes. Emerald and ebony. Light and dark. Soft and hard. No words were needed as they spoke their need, their love, their passion through their senses. Still bound by her gaze, he wrapped her long hair round and round his hand as he forged a chain of emotion, the strongest bond of all.

"Your bed or mine?"

She took his hand and led him to the bed.

Reluctantly, he released her hair, then began undressing her. Excited as always by the sight of her body, he forced himself to move slowly, to savor the moment, to find one more way to tempt her. When she stood nude before him, he looked at her for a long time, then smiled.

"If I don't please you now, I never will." Her words were soft.

"You please me way beyond anything I could ever have imagined." He kissed her forehead reverently.

She unbuttoned his shirt, spread it wide, then thrust her long fingers into the hair on his chest, pausing to tease his nipples into taut peaks.

Grabbing her hands, he held them still. "I can't stand much, Selene."

"You don't need to." She sat down on the bed and spread her legs. "Come here."

He followed her to the bed and she undid his trousers. Taking his hard length into her hands, she pulled him to her, arching her body toward him.

Needing no more encouragement, he pushed his hands under her hips and raised her to his level. She wrapped her legs around his waist as he thrust inside her.

She moaned, winding herself around him. "Drake, please. I need you so."

Unable to speak, he simply plunged deeper into her and began to stroke. As she matched his rhythm, he increased the tempo till she was writhing against him, softly moaning, clutching at him until all was driven from his mind except the intoxicating power of the moment.

Finally, he silenced her with his mouth, then his tongue, binding them as completely as he could while he plumbed her inner depths in his desire to merge them forever. When they reached the heights together, he growled and held them there as long as he could, savoring the passion, the oneness, the glory.

And when they returned, he knew he could do no more to bind her to him. She must commit to him on her own or it would never be. He sat down on the bed, still holding her tightly against him. While waiting for his breath to ease, his sweat to dry, he knew in his mind, his soul, he waited for her answer. Would she belong to him?

After a time, she looked up at him. "Drake, do you think Jon came after Joy Marie?"

He didn't move. It wasn't what he'd expected her to say and it wasn't what he'd wanted to hear. But, even though he was disappointed, he didn't let it show. The decision about them was hers. "Maybe."

"Jon was very attentive to Joy Marie on Martinique, perhaps even in New Orleans. Now he's come here."

"I offered him a job."

"I know that's part of it. But you saw them together."

"You ought to be careful about pushing her off onto any other man right now. Dominique . . ."

She moved away from him. "I'm not. It's just that they seem so right together. Both of them are wounded. They can help each other heal."

He pulled her back to his chest. "I'm not disagreeing. I just don't want her to rush."

"I agree, but I want them to have plenty of time to be together."

"They'll get it." He toyed with the strands of her hair, wishing she'd talk about them, about her future on Dalton Ranch.

She shivered. "But none of us can really make plans as long as Gustave is around. Do you think he's in Texas?"

Drake kissed the top of her head, feeling better. She wasn't going to make plans till Dominique was dead or behind bars. He couldn't blame her. "I trust Ancient Mam, but it wouldn't take much thought to figure Dominique'd come after us. We ruined his plans, his dreams, his life."

"He's mad, right?"

Drake chuckled. "Right."

"How are we going to find him?"

"He's found us. The problem is to draw him into the open. A bushwhacker's got too much on his side."

"How can we do that?"

"He either had a lot of money stashed somewhere or he's back at making it the old way."

"Hypnotism demonstrations."

"Right. And the biggest city around here is San Antonio."

She leaned back. "So when do we go to San Antonio?"

He pushed pillows behind his back, then pulled her against his chest. "It so happens I've got some shorthorns being delivered there in a few days. When I pick them up, I'll nose around about Dominique."

"*We* can look for him."

Drake frowned. "If you think I'm letting you anywhere near that man again, you've—"

"If you think I'm letting *you* near him—"

Putting a fingertip to her lips, he shook his head. "In a minute they're going to hear us all over the house."

She kissed his finger, then pulled it away. "You don't go alone."

"I could take Jon."

She shook her head. "Jon knows Gustave. He needs to stay here at the ranch to take care of Joy Marie, Jimmy, and everything."

"But if Dominique has us watched, he could come here when we go to San Antonio. Or follow us. He might figure once he had us out of the way, he'd come back here." Drake ran a hand through his hair. "On second thought, I'd rather have you with me than leave you here."

"That's just what I thought. Besides, I trust Jon to take care of things while we're gone." Smiling, she cuddled against his chest, then looked up at him again. "By the way, what's a shorthorn?"

"We've been driving wild longhorns up to Kansas for years. They're tough, ornery, and can go days without water, but they don't carry as much weight as these shorthorns being imported from England. I figure we're soon going to get paid by the pound not the head so I'm looking to the future. I bought three bulls I'm going to breed with my cows. And that's just the start."

"Shorthorns." Selene thought of the future, realizing she was beginning to catch the excitement of Texas, as well as Drake Dalton.

"You'll be there to help me bring back the new breeding stock for Dalton Ranch."

"A new beginning."

"And I want you to be part of it."

Chapter 29

Drake called a war council around the kitchen table early the next morning. Jon sat at one end of the table. Drake sat at the other. Jimmy occupied the seat next to Jon's right hand, while Joy Marie took the other side. Selene sat near Drake and a place was left for Carlota, who was busy setting food on the table.

"I don't think there's any question that it's time to get Gustave Dominique and get him for good." Drake gave Carlota a quick nod of thanks as she filled his mug with hot coffee.

"But how?" Joy Marie poured a glass of milk and handed it to Jimmy.

"I've got business in San Antonio. I think that's where he'll be." Drake sipped his coffee.

"What makes you think so?" Jon asked.

"If he needs money, he'll give hypnotism demonstrations again, won't he?" Selene glanced around the group.

"Yes." Joy Marie drank coffee.

411

Jon nodded. "But what about the attacks on the ranch and Drake?"

"That's the trick." Drake gave everyone a serious look. "He could be watching the place and attack here when we leave."

"But Jon, if you're here with Joy Marie and Jimmy, then everything'd be safe." Selene silently pleaded with him to agree.

"How can you trust me? I was Gustave's man for a lot of years."

"We do." Selene looked at Joy Marie.

"He duped you, too." Joy Marie's words were soft. "Maybe not like the rest of us, but—"

"If Dominique comes riding in here with an army of hired gunmen, there's nothing I can do to save the place or anybody else." Jon looked disgusted. "I may be big, but I'm not that big. And I'm one-armed."

"Señor Dalton built this house to withstand an army." Carlota stopped beside Jon and crossed her arms. "It is well stocked, well armed, and we have guards posted. This Dominique would do well to avoid Dalton Ranch."

Jon shook his head. "I'm sorry. I didn't mean disrespect. But Gustave's a tough man."

Carlota tossed her head. "We have fought the Comanche. What is this man? *French?*" Her voice was full of derision. "I am not afraid of this foreigner with the evil eye. We are protected by God, and Mayual." She sat down and took Joy Marie's hand. "I trust this blessed child to warn us."

Jon looked around the group in confusion.

Joy Marie blushed. "I . . . well, I—"

"She warned us Drake was in danger before he was ambushed." Selene leaned back in her chair.

"So it's not over?" Jon picked up his cup of coffee and looked into its dark depths. "I'm sorry."

Joy Marie stiffened. "If that makes a difference to you, then . . . well, I can't help it."

"No." Jon glanced at her with concern. "I don't care personally, but I don't want you hurt anymore."

"It is a gift." Carlota patted Joy Marie's hand.

"Like Joe Junior's a gift." Jimmy held up his frog. "As long as I got him, I got part of Joe. As long as Joy Marie's Ray talks through her, she's got part of him." He glared defensively around the room. "What's wrong with that?"

Tears stung Selene's eyes. "You're right, Jimmy. There's not a thing wrong with it."

"Fact is, it's good." Jon looked determined. "If Joy Marie warned you once, she'll warn you again."

Joy Marie held up a hand. "Thanks for your support, but you can't depend on me to warn you. This is so new to me, so unexpected, and it could go away at any time."

Jon cleared his throat. "Ancient Mam told me to tell you that if you were still experiencing the voice when I got here, that you're a natural medium. She says it's a rare gift that should be treasured."

"But I don't understand it." Joy Marie's eyes filled with tears. "And I don't want it."

"You're upsetting her." Carlota put an arm around Joy Marie's shoulders.

"I'm going to have my say." Jon glared at Carlota. "I promised Ancient Mam. She said to tell you that you'd probably never have used this gift if Dominique hadn't developed it during those seances. Now that it's awakened, it won't go away. She also offered to help you with it or Josephine when she's fully trained."

"Thank you." Joy Marie wiped her eyes. "Look, I'm not going to feel sorry for myself. Selene heals people's bodies. Maybe, if it turns out that way, I can help them with their minds and emotions."

Selene beamed at her friend. "I think it's a good idea. Gustave taught me a little about hypnotism. I bet you know more, and you have your special gift. We could work together. Besides, even Ancient Mam has offered to help. What do you say?"

Joy Marie shook her head. "I say I can never set foot back on Martinique."

"That's all right." Selene grinned. "We'll bring Martinique to us."

"I don't understand." Joy Marie cocked her head.

"Rosa and I are exchanging herbs and recipes and doctor skills with Ancient Mam. I don't think Ancient Mam would object to sending Josephine, or coming herself, to New Orleans and Texas to study with us." Selene leaned forward. "Just think of all we could learn and share over the years. We could even open a mail-order business, or an office in San Antonio besides keeping up the one in New Orleans."

"Do you really think I could be part of it?" Joy Marie clasped her hands. "You know I can't stand the sight of blood."

"You won't be dealing with blood. Your expertise will be the mind and emotions and how they interact with the body. Of course we need you, Joy Marie."

Selene glanced around the room in triumph.

Drake shook his head. "All I can say is I hope my cattle have enough mental, emotional, and physical problems to keep you two at home."

Jon laughed. "I think it's too late for that. But maybe we can get them to run their empire from the barn."

Carlota stood up. "Don't laugh. Mayual does not speak through a mortal woman often, but when she does, Heaven and Earth move. Already word of Joy Marie's gift has spread. Soon others will come here to sit at her feet. She will need to travel nowhere. All will come to her." Squaring her shoulders, she turned and went back to cooking.

"I never argue with Carlota once she's set her mind on something." Drake shook his head. "Besides, for some damn reason she's been right as long as I've known her. And that's been all my life."

"As a Dane and a seaman, I never mock anything or anyone because I've seen enough on land and sea to realize we don't, *can't,* know all. I want no forces, seen or unseen, against me. And when I fight, I want to know my enemy."

"Gustave Dominique." Selene's words were soft but clear.

Jon nodded. "As I am in Texas, a land foreign to me, I accept Drake Dalton as my leader in this matter of Dominique. If you leave me in charge of defending the ranch, I will protect it with my life and the lives of my unborn children."

"Thank you." Drake looked touched. "But I don't plan for it to come to that. Selene and I will go into San Antonio and catch Dominique if he's there. If

415

'not, we'll still catch him, one way or another."

Suddenly Joy Marie sat up straight, but her eyes were closed. "Drake, danger awaits you in San Antonio, but you can win with Selene's help."

Everyone at the table turned to look at Joy Marie.

With her eyes still closed, she turned toward Jon. A smile played about her lips. "Jon, you're a good man. Joy Marie needs a good man. Take care of her." Joy Marie's voice softened but still remained low as she leaned back in her chair. "And tell Joy Marie I love her. I always will." Joy Marie's head slumped forward.

Selene jumped up and ran to Joy Marie's side. She slapped her friend's wrists until Joy Marie's eyes fluttered open.

Joy Marie smiled, looking happy, then she frowned as tears filled her eyes. She glanced around the group. "Ray. I was dreaming and he told me he loved me and he held me and then he . . . he began to fade . . . until he was gone." She stood up abruptly and looked wildly around the room. "I don't think he's ever coming back." Tears splashed down her cheeks and she ran out the back door.

Selene started after her, but Carlota stopped her. "Let Joy Marie mourn in private."

"Are you sure she'll be okay?"

Carlota nodded. "She has been through much and she is only now letting go of her past."

"Do you think she'll still be able to—"

"Mayual does not let go of her chosen so easily." Carlota crossed herself. "Joy Marie walks in two worlds now, carrying messages between them. It will not be an easy life."

"But we'll help her, right?"

Carlota squeezed Selene's hand, then went back to her work.

Selene sat down at the table. "Carlota thinks it best if we let Joy Marie mourn alone."

Drake finished his coffee and set his mug down with a thud. "I suppose it is, but—"

"I'll check on her in a little while." Jon's voice was steady. "I was with her and Gustave a long time. I think I understand her somewhat."

"When she comes back, I'll let her borrow Joe Junior for a while. He always makes me feel better." Jimmy set Joe Junior on the table and stroked his head.

"Good idea." Selene wished she could ease Joy Marie's pain but knew she couldn't. But what she could do was catch Gustave so he didn't ever scare or harm Joy Marie again. She glanced at Drake.

He nodded. "Selene and I want to get on our way as soon as we can. No point in waiting around here for any more of Dominique's tricks."

Jon stood up. "From what Joy Marie said, the Frenchman's in San Antonio. Be careful."

Drake took Selene's hand. "You can be damn sure of that."

When Drake and Selene arrived in San Antonio late that evening, the cow town was living up its name. Saloons, bawdy houses, gambling casinos, and cafés all spilled light and noise out into the dusty street of the busiest part of town. Cowboys rode their horses up and down the street, yelling, singing, drinking, arguing. Just as many cowboys sat on the boardwalk, drinking from bottles of whiskey and calling out to passersby.

Shocked, Selene simply watched the drama in amazement.

Drake chuckled. "I told you the ranch might be more to your taste."

"I wouldn't have missed this for the world."

"And I can guarantee these cowboys wouldn't have missed seeing you."

For the first time, she noticed they were attracting attention as they rode among the revelers. Soon, the cowboys began to whistle and call to her. She looked at Drake in astonishment.

He rode close to her, put a hand on the .45 at his hip, and looked all around. The whistles and calls stopped, but the looks didn't, nor did the cowboys who rode close, taking a good look at Selene.

"Drake, should I be afraid? I mean, are they serious or are they playing harmless pranks on unwary women?"

Drake chuckled.

"Perhaps 'unwary' wasn't the right word. Would 'innocent' be better?"

"Can you imagine a woman being innocent long around here?"

"Frankly, no. Then, again, unless these men took a mass bath, can you imagine anybody wanting them close? I can smell the liquor and cattle from here."

Drake laughed again. "If they knew what you'd said, they'd get their feelings hurt."

"They should have thought of that before they decided not to take a bath."

"I doubt if they decided not to take a bath. They either rode in from a long trail drive and hit the saloons or they came in off the ranches and did the same. A bath is way down their list of priorities. Wetting their whistle is first."

Selene turned her horse away from a particularly dusty, smelly cowboy who had ridden close to get a look.

Drake gave the cowboy a hard stare and started to draw his pistol.

The other cowboy saw his look, lifted a hand to his hat, and rode off fast.

"Thanks. All these cowboys make me uneasy." Selene glanced around. "I'll be glad to get to the hotel. I'm dusty, hungry, and thirsty, too."

"Was it too long a ride for you?"

"I now understand how cowboys get to be bowlegged. If you stay on horseback very long, it's bound to alter your anatomy."

Throwing back his head, Drake laughed. "Is that your decision after a long ride? How about three months up to Kansas?"

She glared at him. "I only hope I can walk when I get off poor Fancy."

"If you can't, I'll carry you." He leered.

Starting to laugh, she stopped herself. "We should be serious. Gustave could be lurking around any corner."

"It's late. First let's get us a room, then we'll look for Dominique." He continued on down the street, avoiding drunken cowboys who staggered into the street.

Selene paced him, still amazed at the boyish

enthusiam, if she could call it that, of the Texas cowboys.

After a moment, Drake glanced over at her. "You're not seeing San Antonio at its best. I think the city'll stand up to New Orleans. It has some beautiful homes, old Spanish missions, a fine market, and good businesses. But I'll show you all that another day. If Dominique's in town, this is where we'll find him."

He stopped in front of the Bluebonnet Hotel, got off his horse, threw the reins around the hitching post, then reached up for Selene. She slid into his arms, grateful for his support when her feet hit the street.

"Come on." He took her hand and led her up the steps. "Maybe they'll have a couple of rooms left."

She gratefully went with him inside. As he walked up to speak to the clerk, she glanced around at the furnishings that reminded her so much of Drake's home. It looked like a clean, comfortable hotel with few frills, and it was nothing like what she would have expected in New Orleans. As she glanced around, she saw several posters tacked to a wall.

She walked over to take a closer look. One poster announced the coming of stage entertainment by Lottie Lewis and the Cowtown Girls. The next caught her attention. Hypnotism demonstrations were being given in town every evening by a master hypnotist. A name was not mentioned, but Selene didn't have to think far to come up with Gustave Dominique. Naturally he hadn't given his name on the poster since that would have been making things too easy on them.

Motioning toward Drake, she saw him put two keys in a pocket as he walked over to her. She said nothing, but pointed at the poster.

"Joy Marie was right." Drake's voice was tense. Glancing up, he checked the clock on the wall. "If we hurry over to Cactus Pete's Saloon, we might catch the end of Dominique's demonstration."

"Let's go. I can't wait till tomorrow night to find out for sure it's him."

"Okay. Let me get the clerk to toss our saddlebags in our rooms and send our horses down to the stables." He walked over to the clerk.

She went to the front doors and looked outside, hardly able to wait a moment longer. Gustave Dominique. He couldn't be allowed to hurt anybody else ever again.

In a moment, Drake joined her. "Ready?" He held out his arm.

Taking it, she looked up at him. "Let's get him now, Drake."

He nodded, touched the .45 on his hip, and they stepped out to the boardwalk. Guiding them, he set a brisk pace among drunken cowboys, fancy women, and a few lawmen.

Soon they reached Cactus Pete's Saloon. Laughter filled the inside of the establishment and Selene glanced over the double swinging doors to see a cowboy on a small stage walking up and down, bobbing his head like a chicken and clucking. Gustave Dominique stood to one side, a smile on his face.

Selene stepped back and put a hand to her heart as if to still its racing.

421

Taking her hand, Drake smiled. "He's there. You want to go inside? I ought to warn you ladies don't usually go into places like that."

She looked down at herself. Besides being dusty, she was wearing her split skirt and blouse, a vest, boots, and a hat. "I guess I forgot my satin."

Drake laughed.

"However, I'm a cowgirl. I'm not dressed much different from the men in there. If cowboys can go inside, so can cowgirls. Right?"

Raising a brow, he shook his head. "No, but I'll be right beside you."

"Wait! He's finished. He's heading this way."

"Back to the side. We'll surprise him when he steps through those doors."

Selene did as Drake said, not even realizing she was holding her breath till Gustave Dominique pushed open the swinging doors and walked outside. Two men in black suits with .45s prominently displayed on their hips followed close behind him.

Drake stepped out.

Gustave stopped, glanced around, saw Selene, and smiled. The two men flanked him, tossing back their jackets and dropping their hands to their pistols.

"Neighborly of you to come calling, Miss Selene." He drawled the words in a Texas imitation.

"It's not a neighborly visit." Drake's voice was like steel and his hand hovered over his pistol.

"No?" Gustave chuckled. "And here I thought we were friends."

"I don't care how you got off Martinique, Dominique." Drake looked the Frenchman up and down.

"But you're in Texas now and that's my land. I want you off it."

Gustave laughed, chuckled. "If you have not noticed, I hired the best to guard me in this rough, dusty, uncouth town. The gentlemen at my side will see I stay in Texas as long as I like."

"You lose your hearing in jail?" Drake taunted him.

Gustave frowned. "That was a mistake instigated by you."

"I stayed my hand in Martinique." Drake's fingers twitched. "I promised Ancient Mam. Here nothing stops me."

"There are laws against shooting down unarmed men, Dalton."

"There're laws against bushwhacking men, too." Selene could stand it no longer.

Gustave glanced at her. "Did you just arrive, *ma chère?* You look a trifle dusty."

"How I look has nothing to do with this." Selene took a step forward, her fists clenched, then stopped herself. She couldn't let him make her mad.

"But it has everything to do with this. When Dalton gives up to the better man, then I shall enjoy the fruits of my labor. And I believe that will be the big feather mattress in your bedroom on Dalton Ranch."

Drake growled and stepped forward.

The gunmen moved in front of Gustave.

"Gentlemen, please." Gustave pushed the gunmen aside. "We are all old friends here. If you care to know, Dalton, I have already looked into buying your ranch. I have made a few well-placed friends since arriving in Texas. It might surprise you to know that I have already been out and ridden over your ranch. Good land. Good cattle." He cast a lazy glance over Selene. "Good women. It seems we have the same taste. May the best man win." He chuckled. "Me, of course." He started to turn away.

"Dominique."

The Frenchman stopped.

"If you aren't out of town by sundown tomorrow and on your way to the coast, I'll come looking for you."

Chapter 30

Selene watched Drake strap on his gunbelt then check his pistol. When he snapped the .45 back in its holster, there was a finality about the action.

She shivered as she glanced at herself in the mirror in her room at the Bluebonnet Hotel. She had dressed simply in her one change of clothes, a cotton dress the color of her eyes. Drake was clothed like a cowboy, but with the .45 on his hip and the look in his eyes, he might as well have been a gunslinger. And she was worried.

"Drake, I think a showdown on the streets of San Antonio with Gustave Dominique is dangerous."

He gave her a long stare.

"All day I've said I think the law should handle this."

"The authorities handled Gustave on Martinique. He's worked outside the law all his life. What makes you think he's suddenly going to respect it?"

"I'm afraid he'll hurt you."

"Thanks." Drake looked disgusted. "I can take care of myself."

She hugged him, but knew she hadn't reached him. "It's not that. I don't want you in danger."

"I feel the same way about you. That's why you're staying in this hotel room while I go down and face Dominique."

"Maybe he's left."

"We checked when we got back from your tour of San Antonio . . . for all the good it did."

"I couldn't concentrate. I'm so tense all I can think about is Gustave."

"And I'm damn tired of thinking about him."

Selene walked to the window of their room and looked down at the street below. During the day it was relatively quiet, but she knew how much it would change come sunset. Would Gustave be gone by then? She doubted it. She couldn't imagine him running, not with two gunmen backing him up. "What about Gustave's men?"

"They're not stupid. And I'm not without my own reputation in the area."

"He'll fight."

"Dominique's not a fighter. He's a manipulator. He hires others to do his dirty work."

"If you go down on that street, he'll have you bushwhacked again." Tears blurred her vision. "Drake, I can't stand the thought."

His face softened and he took her in his arms. "We've got no choice. Dominique's driven us to this. We must protect our own. Don't you see?"

"Yes, but surely the law—"

"We tried it before."

"Still, Drake, I'm so afraid of your being hurt again. Please, let the sheriff handle Gustave."

Drake hesitated, frowned, then stroked her back. "All right. I'll try it first."

She smiled, relieved. "Thanks."

"But I think it's a mistake. The law isn't something Dominique understands."

"But we're civilized people. We *must* try to get the law to do its job first."

He shook his head. "This is Texas. We've dealt out our own justice for a long time. And it works."

"The authorities can send Gustave back to Martinique."

Drake started to respond, then stopped. He looked deep into her eyes. "You're never going to understand violence. It's not in your nature. But I'm going to tell you straight out and you'd better believe me even if you can't understand it that some men *enjoy* hurting others and having control over others and building empires or even simple lives on the pain and suffering of others. Gustave Dominique is one of those men. And nothing you can do or say or think will ever change that fact." He shook her slightly. "And he'll keep doing it or trying to do it till he's dead."

Biting her lower lip, Selene glanced away. "I hear you, but I don't understand it. *Can't.* Yet I've seen the result of Gustave's work and I know you're correct."

"He's killed people, Selene, and—"

"He tried to kill you."

"Right. He won't stop trying to get what he wants

any way he can." Drake held her close. "The problem is you're too good to see bad. That's a dangerous condition."

"Fortunately, I've got you around to protect me." She attempted a smile.

"That's what I'm trying to do." He touched the pistol on his hip. "But we'll play this your way first time through. Then it's my way. I just hope we're not making a damn big mistake."

"Nothing's more precious than life."

"I agree. And that starts with you and me, Joy Marie, Jon and Jimmy, Carlota and Jorge, as well as the Dalton cowboys. Sometimes we have to make choices and now's the time. It's us or him."

She shivered and clung to Drake. "It's about sundown."

"You stay here. I'm going over to his hotel. If he's gone—"

"We celebrate."

"No. We follow him."

"But Drake—"

"It's a poker game, Selene. I called him and put my cards on the table. He either folds and runs or beats me. Either way the game's not over till he's in the ground or back in jail. Last night we played the first round. Today is the second."

"You'll be careful."

He placed a soft kiss on her lips. "I've got a lot to live for and Dominique's got a lot to pay for." Walking over to the door, he glanced back. "Keep yourself safe." Then he opened the door, walked out, and shut it behind him.

Selene hurried to the window and in a moment saw

Drake walk across the street toward Gustave's hotel. There wasn't much time to waste if she followed him. She didn't know what good she could do, but she wouldn't let him go into danger alone. She had to be close by and help if needed. Later, when he was safe, he could be as angry at her as he wanted.

She walked over to the dresser and picked up her reticule. It was big and fairly heavy from all the herbs and medical supplies inside, but if anything happened to Drake, she was ready to heal him again. Sliding the drawstring of the bag down her left arm to the crook of her elbow, she picked up her room key and stepped outside. She locked the door behind her, then hurried down the stairs.

Outside, she stayed in the shadows of the roof overhanging the boardwalk, then crossed the street with a group of people. As far as she could tell, Drake hadn't seen her and she planned to get as close as she could to where he was standing outside Gustave's hotel.

Concealing herself behind people and chairs along the boardwalk, she made her way closer to Drake. He went inside the hotel and she stopped, glanced around in alarm, then hurried to an alley formed by Gustave's hotel and a restaurant. Out of sight, she peered around the side. Drake walked back out and glanced up at the sky.

She shivered. Gustave must be inside his hotel and it was almost sunset.

Suddenly the door to the hotel opened and Gustave Dominique stepped outside. He saw Drake, nodded, and walked over to him.

Selene watched and listened, ready to run to Drake's aid.

Drake dropped his hand to his .45. "I told you to be out of town by sundown, Dominique."

Gustave smiled, raised his jacket to reveal he carried no gun. "You cannot shoot an unarmed man and get away with it in Texas, Dalton."

"Where're your gunmen?"

"Where they are needed."

Drake let the insult pass. "I'm taking you to jail."

Dominique shrugged, glanced idly around the street, then back at Drake. He pulled his crystal watch fob from his pocket. He held it up so the facets caught the dying light of the sun. Colored light from the crystal moved back and forth across Drake's face. "You might as well give in and stop fighting your fate, Dalton."

Drake didn't look at the crystal. He kept his concentration on Dominique. "Your parlor game doesn't interest me. And it's your fate we're going to seal." He grabbed the crystal and threw it against the brick wall of the hotel. It shattered and crystal shards fell to the boardwalk.

For a moment Gustave stood completely still, then he threw himself at Drake.

Drake stepped back, drew his .45, and caught Dominique by the shoulder, shoving the muzzle of his pistol into the Frenchman's ribs. "We're going to do this quiet-like and nobody gets hurt."

"You will regret you ever heard my name, Dalton." Gustave's face was red with anger.

"I already regret it. Now get moving."

"That crystal was priceless."

"I bet. It got the plantation on Martinique, didn't it?"

"But it was not my only one."

"Shut up and walk." Drake pushed Gustave toward the jail, keeping the pistol in the Frenchman's side.

Selene stayed at the edge of the alley and watched, thrilled her plan had worked so well. There was no need for violence and Drake had just proved it. Glancing around, she noticed everything looked the same. Nobody else realized what menace had been taken from the streets of San Antonio. And they were lucky.

She should get back to the hotel room, but she wanted to see Drake walk out of the jail triumphant. Then she'd hurry back and no one would be the wiser.

After a short time, the door to the jail opened and Gustave Dominique walked out.

Selene couldn't believe her eyes. She snapped them shut, counted to ten, then opened them again, thinking she'd see Drake. But it was Gustave who walked away from the jail and Drake who was still inside.

She hit her hand against the rough stone of the building. The Frenchman had tricked them. He'd set a trap and she'd sent Drake right into it. It was all her fault. Drake had warned her, but now Gustave was free. And she didn't know what had happened to Drake. But she was going to find out.

Stepping to the boardwalk, she started across the street. Suddenly hands caught her arms, lifted her off her feet, and jerked her back into the alley.

Shocked, she looked around. Gustave's gunmen had her. One grabbed her hand and held it while the other stuffed a bandanna into her mouth. Gagged, she groaned and tried to spit it out. But couldn't. She struggled, trying to twist out of their grip. Again, she couldn't. Frustrated, she kicked out, but was hampered by her long skirts. Finally, she stopped fighting, knowing she had to conserve her strength and think clearly. Drake and everybody at the ranch depended on her now.

Looking up, she saw Gustave walking quickly toward them. When he entered the alley, a cruel smile twisted his lips and his eyes narrowed.

She shuddered and tried to pull back. But his men held her still.

"*Ma chère,* you look much better than last night. I trust you rested well or at least were amused by the Texan."

Fury and hatred rushed through Selene. She wanted to hurt him and she would have if she'd been free. But she knew better, knew she needed to play along with Gustave's game in hope of freeing herself and getting to Drake. But it hurt to be so helpless. And she hated Gustave all the more for it.

"If you promise not to scream, I will take the gag out of your lovely mouth. Although, in truth, a few screams would make little difference around here."

She nodded, holding his gaze.

He removed the bandanna and put it in a pocket. "You wonder what has happened to Dalton?"

"Yes." She didn't trust herself to say anything more.

"So you are still interested in him?"

"I'd like to know just how clever you are."

"Very clever." He frowned. "However, Dalton destroyed my crystal. That angered me. He will get

432

no help from me now."

"Why would he need help? What's he doing in the jail?"

Gustave grinned. "Dalton is going to stand trial and hang for the murder of a loose woman who was killed near the Bluebonnet Hotel last night."

Selene's eyes widened. "But that's impossible."

"His words, and yours, will do no good against the word of three men who saw him do it but were too late to stop it."

"You killed a woman to frame Drake?"

Gustave nodded. "It was easy. But that is no longer my concern. Dalton is taken care of and now I will have his ranch and both his women."

Selene felt sick at her stomach. She was only grateful Gustave didn't seem to know Jon was at the ranch. But she couldn't let Gustave near Joy Marie again, or Jimmy, or the ranch. Or anybody. She took a deep breath. "Are you sure they'll hang Drake?"

"It was a particularly brutal, bloody death, Selene. I imagine Drake will be swinging in a matter of days. Now, are you ready to return to the ranch?" He held out his hand and one of the gunmen placed a .45 in it. He tucked the pistol in the front of his trousers. "You can make life at Dalton Ranch, or should I say Dominique Ranch, easy or hard for yourself . . . and for Joy Marie. I believe you know what I mean."

She took several deep breaths. She must not show any emotion. She must not give Gustave any satisfaction. And somehow she must get Drake out of jail. Acting to the best of her ability, she looked Gustave up and down. "Maybe you aren't so bad after all, Gustave Dominique."

"I thought you would see it that way. You are not stupid and you will not get what you would have had as my wife. But you might find you like being my whore. With my crystal I can make it good for you."

"It's something to consider." She licked her dry lips. "But I'd like to say good-bye to Drake."

Gustave raised a brow, considering, then he smiled. "Unbutton your bodice down to about here." He pointed at her cleavage. "And muss your hair." He laughed. "Then we will go tell Dalton good-bye."

She squared her shoulders and nodded in agreement. She couldn't let Gustave know how much he repulsed her. He wanted to gloat in front of Drake, wanted his rival to think his woman had so easily changed sides. Well, it was a small price to pay to get inside the jail and have a chance at freeing Drake.

Gustave watched her. "But wait. Is it safe for my men to let you free? Will you try to run or get away or call for help?"

"No. I promise to go quietly with you."

"If you go back on your word, you will be punished and I do not think you will like the touch of my whip." He flicked a glance at both gunmen. "Release her."

Free, at least of the gunmen's grips, she quickly unbuttoned her bodice and touched the ruby ring on the thong around her neck. She stopped a button short of revealing it. Drake. She'd do anything to save him. She thrust fingers into her hair, wet her lips again, then looked at the Frenchman for approval.

Gustave nodded, his breath quickening, and held out his arm to her. "Good. Gentlemen, you will be so

434

kind as to escort us to the jail, will you not?"

Selene put her hand on Gustave's arm, restraining a shudder of revulsion at touching him. She actually forced herself to smile. But her mind kept racing over and over one thought: she would never doubt Drake's judgment about men again if only they came out of this alive . . . with Gustave Dominique in jail. Or dead.

Chapter 31

Selene entered the jail, with Gustave and the two gunmen right behind her. She glanced around, all her senses straining to find Drake and a way to free him.

The front room of the jail held several chairs, a large desk, a gun rack, and a door that led to the cells. No one was in the room and she wondered if she could rush into the back, release Drake, and flee. But, of course, the cells were locked and the sheriff or one of his deputies had the key.

She focused on the door to the cells, and as if she had willed it, the door opened and the sheriff walked out.

He closed the door behind him and walked over to Gustave. "Sorry to keep you waiting, but I've got a couple of deputies out sick. The others are on patrol."

Gustave inclined his head, then gestured to Selene. "This is Selene Morgan. She wants to see Drake

Dalton. And Selene, I would like you to meet Sheriff Thompson."

"Good evening, sheriff. I do hope this isn't too much of a bother." She put on her best Southern charm. "You see I'm from New Orleans and that's where I met Mr. Dalton. I would appreciate a chance to tell him what I think of his actions."

Sheriff Thompson raised his brows, glanced from Gustave to Selene, then back again. He took off his hat and scratched his head, looking at her all the while.

She retained her poise under his scrutiny, knowing he was considering the disheveled state of her appearance and drawing his own conclusions. Even if he thought what Gustave wanted everyone to think, she didn't care. She planned to do anything she could to free Drake, so she used the time to size up the sheriff. He was a big man with graying dark hair. He wore his .45 as if it were an extension of his body. He was dressed in a dark plaid shirt, a vest, denims, a bandanna around his neck, and cowboy boots. A large key on a ring dangled from his belt.

She smiled at him, thinking she must somehow trick or overpower him to get the key to the cells. But he was an intimidating man and she didn't know how she was going to do it.

Gustave put a possessive hand on Selene's shoulder. "Sheriff Thompson, I would take it as a personal favor if you let Mam'selle Morgan see Dalton. She has something to settle with him."

Sheriff Thompson put his hat back on his head and nodded. "Okay. What have you got in that bag, Miss Morgan?"

438

"Herbs, medical supplies, that sort of thing. I'm a doctor."

"Let me see it." The sheriff held out a hand.

She didn't want him to touch her supplies, but she handed her reticule to him anyway.

He pulled open the drawstring top, fumbled around inside, sneezed, then handed it back. He rubbed his nose. "If smells could kill a man, that bag'd do it. But I don't think you've got anything in there powerful enough to do the job." He laughed and adjusted his gunbelt.

Gustave laughed, too.

But Selene didn't. She was well aware that any kind of medicine could be used for good or bad and therefore could be dangerous. "No, I don't have a pistol, if that's what you mean."

Sheriff Thompson nodded. "You look harmless enough. I'll take you back. But Dalton may not want to see you."

She smiled sweetly. "A moment is all I need."

The sheriff walked over and opened the door to the cells. He looked back at her.

Gustave stepped forward. "I will go with her in there." He smiled and reached to take Selene's arm.

"No. Only one visitor at a time." Sheriff Thompson hooked his thumbs in his belt.

"But Selene would feel more comfortable if I accompanied her. Besides, what difference can one person make?" Gustave no longer smiled.

"Sorry." Sheriff Thompson frowned. "If you want, you can go in after her, but not together. It's my rule."

"It's all right." Selene smiled and hurried past

439

the sheriff before Gustvave could stop her. Now the Frenchman would never get a chance to gloat and she was glad of that at least.

Her heart pounded as she glanced around the darkened interior of the jail. A narrow aisle ran between small, barred cells. Loud snores punctuated the silence as several men slept off their whiskey behind bars. She looked in every cell as she walked down the hall, hearing the sheriff's steps behind her.

In the last cell, sitting on the floor with his head leaned back against the wall, was Drake. She felt sudden panic rush through her. She'd done this to him and it was up to her to undo the damage. But how?

"Hey, Dalton." Sheriff Thompson's voice was loud. "You got a lady to visit you."

Drake looked up, surprise transformed his features, and color drained from his face. He stood up. "What are you doing here?"

She slowed her steps. Somehow she had to get the sheriff closer. She glanced back, thinking furiously. "Sheriff, you won't leave me alone with him, will you? He frightens me."

Sheriff Thompson grinned, shook his head, and walked to her side. "He's making no more trouble."

Smiling her appreciation, she pulled the ruby ring from around her neck. Glaring at Drake, she flung it at him. "You don't really think I'd marry a murderer, do you?"

Drake caught the ring. Stuffing it in his pocket, he looked at her in confusion.

"Don't try to appear innocent." Her voice was

440

harsh, for she knew she had to be convincing. "Gustave told me what you did. And to think I listened to your pretty words in New Orleans. It's obvious now Gustave Dominique is by far the better man and we're going back to his new ranch together."

"Selene!" Drake threw himself at the bars and reached through them for her.

She cried out in feigned fear and stumbled back from his outstretched hands, catching the sheriff by surprise as she fell against him. In the process she maneuvered Sheriff Thompson against the bars.

Drake took advantage of the moment, pulled the sheriff's pistol from its holster, and stuck it in his back. "Sorry, Sheriff Thompson, but you've got the wrong man." He jerked the key ring off the sheriff's belt and tossed it to Selene. "Sheriff, at this point I've got nothing to lose, so don't move or shout and you'll be fine."

"Don't be a fool, Dalton. You can't get away with this." Sheriff Thompson glared at Selene. "It won't go easy with you either, miss, but if you'll—"

"Dominique's your murderer." Drake's voice was harsh.

"Dominique!" Sheriff Thompson looked stunned. "You can't expect me to believe a gentleman like that'd do something so horrible."

"But you believe I would?" Drake sounded disgusted.

Selene opened the cell. "Get inside, sheriff. We'll explain this all later. Now there's no time."

"If you've got evidence . . ."

"No time." Drake motioned with his head. "Get in

441

the cell and don't give me any trouble."

Sheriff Thompson stepped into the cell. Selene followed him. Drake handed her the pistol. She held the .45 steady as Drake gagged the sheriff with his bandanna and tied his hands behind his back with his belt.

Taking back the pistol, Drake glanced around the space. "Sit tight. Don't make any noise. And you'll be free soon. Then you'll get all the explanations you need."

The sheriff glared at them and sat down.

Selene stepped outside the cell and waited for Drake to shut and lock the door.

Pocketing the key, he hugged her.

"Are you all right?" Tears stung her eyes.

"I will be as soon as you put my ring back around your neck." He handed it to her.

Smiling, she slipped the leather thong around her neck and felt the ruby ring settle between her breasts.

"What's it like out there?" Drake checked the ammunition in the .45.

"No other guards. But Gustave and his two gunmen are waiting for me."

Drake looked at the pistol in his hand, then at the door leading out. "There's only one way. Go back out there, make some excuse that the sheriff is right behind you, and when you step into the room, move away from the door and make sure you're not in my line of fire when I come out."

"Drake, what are you planning to do?"

"Whatever I have to. Now go on and stay out of the way."

"I'm sorry I didn't believe you before." She gave him a quick kiss, then hurried down the hall. Taking a deep breath, she opened the door and stepped out.

Gustave stood beside his two gunmen near the desk. "Where's the sheriff?"

"Right behind me." She left the door open and moved to one side.

Drake appeared. His pistol already drawn, he aimed it at the three men. "Drop your gunbelts."

Selene was shocked at the sudden noise that exploded in the room as the gunmen drew and fired. Drake returned fire, dropping to a knee. A gunman went down, clutching his chest as red covered his shirt.

She knelt on the floor, afraid of being hit by the bullets ricocheting around the room. Gunsmoke filled the area and its acrid scent burned her nostrils. She wasn't surprised to see Gustave scurry around behind the desk, but she was horrified to see Drake had been hit. She didn't know how bad the wound was, but blood dripped down his left arm.

Glancing up, she noticed the other gunman was edging toward the front door. Suddenly he fired at Drake as he made a dash for the door. One of his bullets caught Drake in the side, but Drake fired back and the gunman dropped to the floor.

Selene started toward Drake, wanting to bind his wounds, but he moved toward the desk. She realized Drake and Gustave were about to confront each other. Both had guns, but Drake was wounded and she didn't know how many bullets he had left. Gustave had the advantage.

She had to do something. Drake had to be weakening fast. If only she had a weapon. Then she thought of her reticule. Jerking it off her arm, she dumped the contents on the floor. Gunsmoke clouded her vision and burned her eyes, but she found what she was looking for. She emptied the contents of a small bag into her right hand. Looking up, she saw Gustave rise from behind the desk and shoot at Drake. He missed.

Before Dominique could hide again, Drake aimed his pistol at the Frenchman and pulled the trigger. Nothing happened.

Gustave stood up and slowly aimed his .45 at Drake's chest. He grinned. "You are out of bullets and out of time."

Furious, Selene took several steps toward Gustave and flung the herbal mixture into his face.

He cried out in agony, clawing at his face with one hand as he shot at Drake with the other.

Drake rolled away from Gustave, grabbed the pistol of one of the fallen gunmen, and fired at Dominique.

The Frenchman clutched his stomach as he sank to the floor.

Selene stood frozen, watching Gustave. Could he be dead?

Drake staggered to his feet, a hand over the wound in his side as blood seeped from his shoulder and his chest. He checked each man, then turned to Selene. "They're dead. All dead."

She took Drake in her arms and held him close, hardly able to believe they were both alive. Then common sense took over. "Let's get out of here and I'll bandage you." She turned from him to pick up her reticule, pushing its contents back inside.

Before leaving the jail, she walked over to Gustave and looked down at him. The Frenchman looked small in death. But she felt no pity for him.

She went back to Drake and put an arm around his waist. He leaned on her as they walked outside.

Drake glanced around. "People already running this way. Let's get out of sight." He led her to the alley beside the jail and sat down. "Fix me up here. They'll find us soon enough and we'll give them the facts then."

"Sheriff Thompson can send a telegram to the officials of Martinique, then Ancient Mam won't worry anymore."

Drake nodded, and held up his right hand.

She put her hand in his and sat down beside him. Then she looked at his wounds. After a moment, she breathed a sigh of relief. "You'll be okay. But you're going to have to take it easy for a while." She emptied the contents of her reticule again and selected what she needed as she listened to the sound of people running into the jail.

"What'd you do to Gustave?" Drake watched her tend his wounds. "He had me, then you—"

"Love Potion Number Eleven." She tore his shirt away from his shoulder.

"I don't understand."

"Love Potion Number Eleven is a hot love spell. I use cayenne, herbs soaked in hot sauce, other fiery type properties, and grind it all together. When it hit

Gustave's eyes, the pain had to be severe."

Silent a moment, Drake suddenly began to chuckle, then he laughed outloud.

"Stop that. It's making you bleed more." She quickly wrapped bandages around his side, stopping the flow of blood. "What's so funny about Love Potion Number Eleven anyway?"

"Who'd ever have thought a love potion would save my life. And end Dominique's." He glanced down at the contents of her reticule, then picked up a small green velvet bag. He handed it to her.

"What's this? It's not mine. I mean it doesn't belong in my reticule." She looked at him suspiciously.

He smiled. "I had Rosa make it for you before I left for Martinique."

She gasped. "You had a love potion made for me?"

"Yes. Rosa said she'd do it because she knew you really loved me but wouldn't admit it." He hesitated. "I never threw away those love potions you made for me."

"Then you really do believe in them." Dropping the love potion, she threw her arms around him and hugged him tight. Then remembered his wounds. Sitting back, she grinned. "Drake Dalton, any man who'd have a love potion made for me is my kind of man."

"Does that mean you'll marry me?"

She kissed him tenderly. "Yes. Frankly, I don't care anymore how we came together or what our love is all about. It exists and I can't live without you."

He lifted the thong from around her neck, took the

ring off it, and placed the ruby on the third finger of her left hand. "It fits."

"Did you ever doubt it?"

"No."

"But Drake, this doesn't mean I'm going to give up Love Potions or any of my new ideas. In fact, looking at our happiness, I don't think there can ever be enough love potions in the world."

"I agree." He bound her with a kiss, and tucked the small green velvet bag into her pocket.

HEART STOPPING ROMANCE BY ZEBRA BOOKS

MIDNIGHT BRIDE (3265, $4.50)
by Kathleen Drymon

With her youth, beauty, and sizable dowry, Kellie McBride had her share of ardent suitors, but the headstrong miss was bewitched by the mysterious man called The Falcon, a dashing highwayman who risked life and limb for the American Colonies. Twice the Falcon had saved her from the hands of the British, then set her blood afire with a moonlit kiss.

No one knew the dangerous life The Falcon led—or of his secret identity as a British lord with a vengeful score to settle with the Crown. There was no way Kellie would discover his deception, so he would woo her by day as the foppish Lord Blakely Savage . . . and ravish her by night as The Falcon! But each kiss made him want more, until he vowed to make her his *Midnight Bride*.

SOUTHERN SEDUCTION (3266, $4.50)
by Thea Devine

Cassandra knew her husband's will required her to hire a man to run her Georgia plantation, but the beautiful redhead was determined to handle her own affairs. To satisfy her lawyers, she invented Trane Taggart, her imaginary step-son. But her plans go awry when a handsome adventurer shows up and claims to *be* Trane Taggart!

After twenty years of roaming free, Trane was ready to come home and face the father who always treated him with such contempt. Instead he found a black wreath and a bewitching, sharp-tongued temptress trying to cheat him out of his inheritance. But he had no qualms about kissing that silken body into languid submission to get what he wanted. But he never dreamed that *he* would be the one to succumb to *her* charms.

SWEET OBSESSION (3233, $4.50)
by Kathy Jones

From the moment rancher Jack Corbett kept her from capturing the wild white stallion, Kayley Ryan detested the man. That animal had almost killed her father, and since the accident Kayley had been in charge of the ranch. But with the tall, lean Corbett, it seemed she was *never* the boss. He made her blood run cold with rage one minute, and hot with desire the next.

Jack Corbett had only one thing on his mind: revenge against the man who had stolen his freedom, his ranch, and almost his very life. And what better way to get revenge than to ruin his mortal enemy's fiery red-haired daughter. He never expected to be captured by her charms, to long for her silken caresses and to thirst for her never-ending kisses.

Available wherever paperbacks are sold, or order direct from the Publisher. Send cover price plus 50¢ per copy for mailing and handling to Zebra Books, Dept. 3469, 475 Park Avenue South, New York, N.Y. 10016. Residents of New York, New Jersey and Pennsylvania must include sales tax. DO NOT SEND CASH.